Things are kinda quiet in the Maintenance Department of the Logics Company about two in the afternoon. Then one of the guys remembers he has to call his wife. He goes to one of the logics and punches the keys for his house. The screen sputters. Then a flash comes on the screen.

"Announcing new and improved logics service! If you want to do something and don't know how to do it—ask your logic!"

There's a pause. Then, as if reluctantly, his connection comes through. His wife answers and gives him hell for something or other. He takes it and snaps off.

"Whadda you know?" he says when he comes back. "We shoulda been warned about that. There's gonna be a lotta complaints. Suppose a fella asks how to get ridda his wife an' the censor circuits block the question?"

Somebody says, "Why not punch for it an' see what happens?"

It's a gag, o' course. But the guy goes over. He punches keys. In theory, a censor block is gonna come on an' the screen will say severely, "Public Policy Forbids This Service." You hafta have censor blocks or the kiddies will be askin' detailed questions about things they're too young to know.

This fella punches, "How can I get rid of my wife?" Just for the fun of it. The screen is blank for half a second. Then comes a flash. "Is she blond or brunette?" He hollers to us an' we come look. He punches, "Blond." There's another brief pause. Then the screen says, "Hexymetacryloaminoacetine is a constituent of green shoe polish. Take home a frozen meal including dried pea soup. Color the soup with green shoe polish. It will appear to be green-pea soup. Hexymetacryloaminoacetine is a selective poison which is fatal to blond females but not to brunettes or males of any coloring. It is improbable that you will be suspected of murder."

The screen goes blank, and we stare at each other. . . .

—from "A Logic Named Joe"

Baen Books by MURRAY LEINSTER

Med Ship
Planets of Adventure
A Logic Named Joe

A LOGIC NAMED JOE

Murray Leinster

edited by
Eric Flint & Guy Gordon

A Logic Named Joe

Copyright © 2004 by the estate of Murray Leinster.

"The Fourth-Dimensional Demonstrator" was first published in *Astounding* in December 1935. "A Logic Named Joe" was first published in *Astounding* in March 1946, under Leinster's real name of Will F. Jenkins. *Gateway to Elsewhere* was first published in shorter form as "Jouney to Barkut" in *Startling Stories,* January 1952, and by Ace Books as a double novel in 1954 (coupled with A.E. Van Vogt's *The Weapon Shops of Isher*). *The Pirates of Zan* was first published in serialized form in *Astounding* in February–April 1959, under the title "The Pirates of Ersatz." It was reissued the same year by Ace Books as a double novel under the current title (coupled with Leinster's Med Ship story *The Mutant Weapon*). "Dear Charles" was first published in *Fantastic Story Magazine,* May 1953, and in book form in 1960 by Avon Books, as part of Leinster's anthology entitled *Twists in Time. The Duplicators* was first published in a shorter version in *Worlds of Tomorrow* in February 1964, under the title "Lord of the Uffts." The expanded version contained in this volume was reissued the same year by Ace Books as a double novel under the current title (coupled with Philip E. High's *No Truce With Terra*).

A Baen Book

Baen Publishing Enterprises
P.O. Box 1403
Riverdale, NY 10471
www.baen.com

ISBN: 0-7434-9910-7

Cover art by Kurt Miller

First printing, June 2005

Distributed by Simon & Schuster
1230 Avenue of the Americas
New York, NY 10020

Production by Windhaven Press, Auburn, NH (www.windhaven.com)
Printed in the United States of America

CONTENTS

CONTENTS

THE DEAN OF GLOUCESTER, VIRGINIA

by Barry N. Malzberg

"Murray Leinster" was the pen-name William F. Jenkins (1896–1975) used for his science fiction; his was one of the longest and most honorable careers the genre offered. The breadth of that career is astonishing; his first science fiction story, *The Runaway Skyscraper* was published in *Argosy* magazine in 1919, seven years before the science fiction genre inaugurated in the 4/26 issue of *Amazing Stories* had been established. And the short novel, *The Pirates of Zan*, included in this volume, was one of the last serials to appear in *Astounding Science Fiction* (February through April 1959) before, in February 1960, just after its 30th anniversary, it changed its name to *Analog*.

1

The January 1960 issue was the last one under the Astounding name, and Leinster was there with the short story *Attention Saint Patrick*, 30 years after his first appearance in the magazine.

This is a career and the career is only a part of Jenkins' contribution; he was also an inventor who obtained many patents. One of them, for the so-called "back-screen projector" used in movie theaters to this date, is that device which enables you or the annoying person in the row ahead of you at the Bijou to stand and leave the auditorium in mid-movie without casting a shadow on the screen. Jenkins who lived in Gloucester, Virginia, for most of his adult life, had four children, wrote much other than science fiction (appearing frequently in *Collier's*, *The Saturday Evening Post*, other mass circulation magazine of the 1940's and 1950's) but it is clearly the science fiction by which he will be remembered.

He wrote and wrote to great effect and is one of the very few writers to have contributed more than one short story to the canon regarded as famous and which reach far out of the genre of science fiction. (Arthur C. Clarke, author of *The Star* and *The Nine Billion Names of God*, is another; Ray Bradbury, author of *The Million Year Picnic* and *The Sound of Thunder* would also qualify.) *First Contact*, the first and still best story of humanity's first intersection in deep space with an intelligent, spacefaring alien race, was publishing in *Astounding* in 1945, reprinted hundreds of times and is regarded as not only an extraordinarily effective work of fiction and speculation but as a blueprint, a virtual manual, for how such contact might be accomplished safely and in a way which protects the parties who are alien to one another. The other story—which appears in this volume—is *A Logic Named Joe*, published in *Astounding* in early 1946, which brilliantly and with astonishing accuracy not only predicts but maps the contemporary Internet, Google searches, dial-up remedies and all. Like Arthur C. Clarke's communications satellite (virtually blueprinted by the young Clarke in 1945) this was here before the subject was here and not only the accuracy but overlap are remarkable. It is also, as you will note, a bitterly funny story.

There is a third work, *Sidewise in Time*, not nearly as skillfully written, which may be equally influential: published in the 1930's it is one of the earliest treatment of the alternate/parallel-universe theme in science fiction, the branching "real" worlds which would have existed had other choices been made and which adjoin our own. There is a science fiction award, the "Sidewise" for best annual treatment of the alternate-world concept, named in its honor.

Jenkins was always around; he was a major science fiction writer in the pre–John Campbell magazines of the 1930's, then was one of the very few writers to effortlessly manage the transition (with Campbell's installation as editor of *Astounding* in late 1937) to what we now call "modern science fiction." He was a constant presence in *Astounding* in the 1940's and 1950's, won his Hugo finally at the age of 60 with the 1956 *Astounding* novella *Exploration Team* (the Hugos were only instituted in 1953; science fiction had to catch up to Jenkins), wrote one of *Astounding*'s last serials, as I've noted, and continued publishing through most of the 1960's, most of this latter fiction being the Med Service stories (published in another volume of this reclamation of his work by Baen Books) and certainly had by the mid-sixties earned the not at all ironic sobriquet "The Dean of Science Fiction," which phrase in fact appeared in his obituary in the *New York Times*.

A remarkable figure, then, one of the central figures (as so noted in the Clute-Nicholls *Encyclopedia of Science Fiction*) of "magazine science fiction"—and it was magazine science fiction which drove the category, at least until the early seventies. Until then, virtually all important and influential science fiction appeared first in the magazines, only to reach book form later, and Jenkins was one of the ten or a dozen signal figures of the 1940's Campbell *Astounding* who were integral to the genre, which had reached its real maturity under Campbell. There is a consensus that Jenkins' novels were not at the level of his short fiction; certainly he published none which had a fraction of the reach and force enacted by *First Contact* or *A Logic Named Joe*, and most of the novels have been out of print for many years. The best of the shorter work is, however, unimpeachable and the span of the career, almost fifty years at or near the very top of the genre, is close to unparalleled. It should be added, and not parenthetically, that Jenkins also wrote mysteries and was the editor of an important early science fiction anthology.

A writer of significant range, Jenkins published two stories in Horace Gold's sardonic early-fifties Galaxy, *If You Was a Moklin* and *The Other Now*, which managed to embrace Gold's grim world-view in no less sprightly fashion than *First Contact* had embodied Campbell's more positive mien, and there is little doubt that a

Jenkins born fifty or seventy years later could have functioned very well on the cutting edge of contemporary science fiction. Surely *A Logic Named Joe* was as savagely innovative in 1946 as anything published in our celebrated cyberpunk eighties.

A remarkable, irreplaceable figure. Take him out of the history and as with Campbell that history might collapse. Fortunately we do not have to so speculate; he is here and we are lucky to have him. This collection is both celebratory and as absolutely contemporary as this great writer.

A LOGIC NAMED JOE

It was on the third day of August that Joe come off the assembly line, and on the fifth Laurine come into town, an' that afternoon I saved civilization. That's what I figure, anyhow. Laurine is a blonde that I was crazy about once—and crazy is the word—and Joe is a logic that I have stored away down in the cellar right now. I had to pay for him because I said I busted him, and sometimes I think about turning him on and sometimes I think about taking an ax to him. Sooner or later I'm gonna do one or the other. I kinda hope it's the ax. I could use a coupla million dollars—sure!—an' Joe'd tell me how to get or make 'em. He can do plenty! But so far I've been scared to take a chance. After all, I figure I really saved civilization by turnin' him off.

The way Laurine fits in is that she makes cold

shivers run up an' down my spine when I think about
her. You see, I've got a wife which I acquired after I
had parted from Laurine with much romantic despair.
She is a reasonable good wife, and I have some kids
which are hell-cats but I value 'em. If I have sense
enough to leave well enough alone, sooner or later I
will retire on a pension an' Social Security an' spend
the rest of my life fishin' contented an' lyin' about
what a great guy I used to be. But there's Joe. I'm
worried about Joe.

I'm a maintenance man for the Logics Company.
My job is servicing logics, and I admit modestly that
I am pretty good. I was servicing televisions before
that guy Carson invented his trick circuit that will
select any of 'steenteen million other circuits—in
theory there ain't no limit—and before the Logics
Company hooked it into the tank-and-integrator set-
up they were usin' 'em as business-machine service.
They added a vision screen for speed—an' they found
out they'd made logics. They were surprised an'
pleased. They're still findin' out what logics will do,
but everybody's got 'em.

I got Joe, after Laurine nearly got me. You know
the logics setup. You got a logic in your house. It
looks like a vision receiver used to, only it's got keys
instead of dials and you punch the keys for what
you wanna get. It's hooked in to the tank, which has
the Carson Circuit all fixed up with relays. Say you
punch "*Station SNAFU*" on your logic. Relays in the
tank take over an' whatever vision-program SNAFU
is telecastin' comes on your logic's screen. Or you
punch "*Sally Hancock's Phone*" an' the screen blinks
an' sputters an' you're hooked up with the logic in

her house an' if somebody answers you got a vision-phone connection. But besides that, if you punch for the weather forecast or who won today's race at Hialeah or who was mistress of the White House durin' Garfield's administration or what is PDQ and R sellin' for today, that comes on the screen too. The relays in the tank do it. The tank is a big buildin' full of all the facts in creation an' all the recorded telecasts that ever was made—an' it's hooked in with all the other tanks all over the country—an' everything you wanna know or see or hear, you punch for it an' you get it. Very convenient. Also it does math for you, an' keeps books, an' acts as consultin' chemist, physicist, astronomer, an' tea-leaf reader, with a "Advice to the Lovelorn" thrown in. The only thing it won't do is tell you exactly what your wife meant when she said, "Oh, you think so, do you?" in that peculiar kinda voice. Logics don't work good on women. Only on things that make sense.

Logics are all right, though. They changed civilization, the highbrows tell us. All on accounta the Carson Circuit. And Joe shoulda been a perfectly normal logic, keeping some family or other from wearin' out its brains doin' the kids' homework for 'em. But somethin' went wrong in the assembly line. It was somethin' so small that precision gauges didn't measure it, but it made Joe a individual. Maybe he didn't know it at first. Or maybe, bein' logical, he figured out that if he was to show he was different from other logics they'd scrap him. Which woulda been a brilliant idea. But anyhow, he come off the assembly-line, an' he went through the regular tests without anybody screamin' shrilly on findin' out what he was. And he went right on out an' was duly installed in the home of Mr. Thaddeus Korlanovitch at 119 East Seventh Street, second floor front. So far, everything was serene.

The installation happened late Saturday night. Sunday morning the Korlanovitch kids turned him on an' seen the Kiddie Shows. Around noon their parents peeled 'em away from him an' piled 'em in the car. Then they come back in the house for the lunch they'd forgot an' one of the kids sneaked back an' they found him punchin' keys for the Kiddie Shows of the week before. They dragged him out an' went off. But they left Joe turned on.

That was noon. Nothin' happened until two in the afternoon. It was the calm before the storm. Laurine wasn't in town yet, but she was comin'. I picture Joe sittin' there all by himself, buzzing meditative. Maybe he run Kiddie Shows in the empty apartment for awhile. But I think he went kinda remote-control exploring in the tank. There ain't any fact that can be said to be a fact that ain't on a data plate in some tank somewhere—unless it's one the technicians are diggin' out an' puttin' on a data plate now. Joe had plenty of material to work on. An' he musta started workin' right off the bat.

Joe ain't vicious, you understand. He ain't like one of these ambitious robots you read about that make up their minds the human race is inefficient and has got to be wiped out an' replaced by thinkin' machines. Joe's just got ambition. If you were a machine, you'd wanna work right, wouldn't you? That's Joe. He wants to work right. An' he's a logic. An' logics can do a lotta things that ain't been found out yet. So Joe, discoverin' the fact, begun to feel restless. He selects some things us dumb humans ain't thought of yet, an' begins to arrange so logics will be called on to do 'em.

That's all. That's everything. But, brother, it's enough!

Things are kinda quiet in the Maintenance Department about two in the afternoon. We are playing pinochle. Then one of the guys remembers he has to call up his wife. He goes to one of the bank of logics in Maintenance and punches the keys for his house. The screen sputters. Then a flash comes on the screen.

"Announcing new and improved logics service! Your logic is now equipped to give you not only consultive but directive service. If you want to do something and don't know how to do it—ask your logic!"

There's a pause. A kinda expectant pause. Then, as if reluctantly, his connection comes through. His wife answers an' gives him hell for somethin' or other. He takes it an' snaps off.

"Whadda you know?" he says when he comes back. He tells us about the flash. "We shoulda been warned about that. There's gonna be a lotta complaints. Suppose a fella asks how to get ridda his wife an' the censor circuits block the question?"

Somebody melds a hundred aces an' says:

"Why not punch for it an' see what happens?"

It's a gag, o' course. But the guy goes over. He punches keys. In theory, a censor block is gonna come on an' the screen will say severely, "Public Policy Forbids This Service." You hafta have censor blocks or the kiddies will be askin' detailed questions about things they're too young to know. And there are other reasons. As you will see.

This fella punches, "How can I get rid of my wife?" Just for the fun of it. The screen is blank for half a second. Then comes a flash. "Service question: Is she blonde or brunette?" He hollers to us an' we come look. He punches, "Blonde." There's another brief pause. Then the screen says, "Hexymetacryloaminoacetine is a constituent of green shoe polish. Take home a frozen meal including dried-pea soup. Color the soup with green shoe polish. It will appear to be green-pea soup. Hexymetacryloaminoacetine is a selective poison which is fatal to blond females but not to brunettes or males of any coloring. This fact has not been brought out by human experiment, but is a product of logics service. You cannot be convicted of murder. It is improbable that you will be suspected."

The screen goes blank, and we stare at each other. It's bound to be right. A logic workin' the Carson Circuit can no more make a mistake than any other kinda computin' machine. I call the tank in a hurry.

"Hey, you guys!" I yell. "Somethin's happened! Logics are givin' detailed instructions for wife-murder! Check your censor-circuits—but quick!"

That was close, I think. But little do I know. At that precise instant, over on Monroe Avenue, a drunk starts to punch for somethin' on a logic. The screen says "Announcing new and improved logics service! If you want to do something and don't know how to do it—ask your logic!" And the drunk says, owlish, "I'll do it!" So he cancels his first punching and fumbles around and says: "How can I keep my wife from finding out I've been drinking?" And the screen says, prompt: "Buy a bottle of Franine hair shampoo. It is harmless but contains a detergent which will neutralize ethyl alcohol immediately. Take one teaspoonful for each jigger of hundred-proof you have consumed."

This guy was plenty plastered—just plastered enough to stagger next door and obey instructions. An' five minutes later he was cold sober and writing down the information so he couldn't forget it. It was new, and it was big! He got rich offa that memo! He patented *"SOBUH, The Drink that Makes Happy Homes!"* You can top off any souse with a slug or two of it an' go home sober as a judge. The guy's cussin' income taxes right now!

You can't kick on stuff like that. But a ambitious young fourteen-year-old wanted to buy some kid stuff and his pop wouldn't fork over. He called up a friend to tell his troubles. And his logic says: "If you want to do something and don't know how to do it—ask your logic!" So this kid punches: "How can I make a lotta money, fast?"

His logic comes through with the simplest, neatest, and the most efficient counterfeitin' device yet known to science. You see, all the data was in the tank. The logic—since Joe had closed some relays here an' there in the tank—simply integrated the facts. That's all. The kid got caught up with three days later, havin' already spent two thousand credits an' havin' plenty more on hand. They hadda time tellin' his counterfeits from the real stuff, an' the only way they done it was that he changed his printer, kid fashion, not bein' able to let somethin' that was workin' right alone.

Those are what you might call samples. Nobody knows all that Joe done. But there was the bank president who got humorous when his logic flashed that "Ask your logic" spiel on him, and jestingly

asked how to rob his own bank. An' the logic told
him, brief and explicit but good! The bank president
hit the ceiling, hollering for cops. There musta been
plenty of that sorta thing. There was fifty-four more
robberies than usual in the next twenty-four hours,
all of them planned astute an' perfect. Some of 'em
they never did figure out how they'd been done. Joe,
he'd gone exploring in the tank and closed some
relays like a logic is supposed to do—but only when
required—and blocked all censor-circuits an' fixed
up this logics service which planned perfect crimes,
nourishing an' attractive meals, counterfeitin' machines,
an' new industries with a fine impartiality. He musta
been plenty happy, Joe must. He was functionin' swell,
buzzin' along to himself while the Korlanovitch kids
were off ridin' with their ma an' pa.

They come back at seven o'clock, the kids all happily
wore out with their afternoon of fightin' each other
in the car. Their folks put 'em to bed and sat down
to rest. They saw Joe's screen flickerin' meditative
from one subject to another an' old man Korlanovitch
had had enough excitement for one day. He turned
Joe off.

An' at that instant the pattern of relays that Joe
had turned on snapped off, all the offers of directive
service stopped flashin' on logic screens everywhere,
an' peace descended on the earth.

For everybody else. But for me—Laurine come to
town. I have often thanked Gawd fervent that she
didn't marry me when I thought I wanted her to.
In the intervenin' years she had progressed. She was
blonde an' fatal to begin with. She had got blonder and
fataler an' had had four husbands and one acquittal

for homicide an' had acquired a air of enthusiasm and self-confidence. That's just a sketch of the background. Laurine was not the kinda former girlfriend you like to have turning up in the same town with your wife. But she came to town, an' Monday morning she tuned right into the middle of Joe's second spasm of activity.

The Korlanovitch kids had turned him on again. I got these details later and kinda pieced 'em together. An' every logic in town was dutifully flashin' a notice, "If you want to do something and don't know how to do it—ask your logic!" every time they was turned on for use. More'n that, when people punched for the morning news, they got a full account of the previous afternoon's doin's. Which put 'em in a frame of mind to share in the party. One bright fella demands, "How can I make a perpetual motion machine?" And his logic sputters a while an' then comes up with a set-up usin' the Brownian movement to turn little wheels. If the wheels ain't bigger'n a eighth of an inch they'll turn, all right, an' practically it's perpetual motion. Another one asks for the secret of transmuting metals. The logic rakes back in the data plates an' integrates a strictly practical answer. It does take so much power that you can't make no profit except on radium, but that pays off good. An' from the fact that for a coupla years to come the police were turnin' up new and improved jimmies, knob-claws for gettin' at safe-innards, and all-purpose keys that'd open any known lock—why—there must have been other inquirers with a strictly practical viewpoint. Joe done a lot for technical progress!

But he done more in other lines. Educational, say.

None of my kids are old enough to be int'rested, but
Joe bypassed all censor-circuits because they hampered
the service he figured logics should give humanity.
So the kids an' teen-agers who wanted to know what
comes after the bees an' flowers found out. And there
is certain facts which men hope their wives won't do
more'n suspect, an' those facts are just what their
wives are really curious about. So when a woman
dials: "How can I tell if Oswald is true to me?" and
her logic tells her—you can figure out how many rows
got started that night when the men come home!

All this while Joe goes on buzzin' happy to himself,
showin' the Korlanovitch kids the animated funnies with
one circuit while with the others he remote-controls
the tank so that all the other logics can give people
what they ask for and thereby raise merry hell.

An' then Laurine gets onto the new service. She
turns on the logic in her hotel room, prob'ly to see
the week's style-forecast. But the logic says, dutiful:
"If you want to do something and don't know how
to do it—ask your logic!" So Laurine prob'ly looks
enthusiastic—she would!—and tries to figure out something to ask. She already knows all about everything
she cares about—ain't she had four husbands and shot
one?—so I occur to her. She knows this is the town I
live in. So she punches, "How can I find Ducky?"

O.K., guy! But that is what she used to call me.
She gets a service question. "Is Ducky known by any
other name?" So she gives my regular name. And the
logic can't find me. Because my logic ain't listed under
my name on account of I am in Maintenance and
don't want to be pestered when I'm home, and there
ain't any data plates on code-listed logics, because the

codes get changed so often—like a guy gets plastered
an' tells a redhead to call him up, an' on gettin' sober
hurriedly has the code changed before she reaches
his wife on the screen.

Well! Joe is stumped. That's prob'ly the first question
logics service hasn't been able to answer. "How can
I find Ducky?" Quite a problem! So Joe broods over
it while showin' the Korlanovitch kids the animated
comic about the cute little boy who carries sticks of
dynamite in his hip pocket an' plays practical jokes
on everybody. Then he gets the trick. Laurine's screen
suddenly flashes:

"Logics special service will work upon your question. Please punch your logic designation and leave
it turned on. You will be called back."

Laurine is merely mildly interested, but she punches
her hotel-room number and has a drink and takes a
nap. Joe sets to work. He has been given a idea.

My wife calls me at Maintenance and hollers. She
is fit to be tied. She says I got to do something. She
was gonna make a call to the butcher shop. Instead
of the butcher or even the "If you want to do something" flash, she got a new one. The screen says,
"Service question: What is your name?" She is kinda
puzzled, but she punches it. The screen sputters an'
then says: "Secretarial Service Demonstration! You—"
It reels off her name, address, age, sex, coloring, the
amounts of all her charge accounts in all the stores,
my name as her husband, how much I get a week,
the fact that I've been pinched three times—twice
was traffic stuff, and once for a argument I got in
with a guy—and the interestin' item that once when
she was mad with me she left me for three weeks an'

had her address changed to her folks' home. Then it says, brisk: "Logics Service will hereafter keep your personal accounts, take messages, and locate persons you may wish to get in touch with. This demonstration is to introduce the service." Then it connects her with the butcher.

But she don't want meat, then. She wants blood. She calls me.

"If it'll tell me all about myself," she says, fairly boilin', "it'll tell anybody else who punches my name! You've got to stop it!"

"Now, now, honey!" I says. "I didn't know about all this! It's new! But they musta fixed the tank so it won't give out information except to the logic where a person lives!"

"Nothing of the kind!" she tells me, furious. "I tried! And you know that Blossom woman who lives next door! She's been married three times and she's forty-two years old and she says she's only thirty! And Mrs. Hudson's had her husband arrested four times for nonsupport and once for beating her up. And—"

"Hey!" I says. "You mean the logic told you this?"

"Yes!" she wails. "It will tell anybody anything! You've got to stop it! How long will it take?"

"I'll call up the tank," I says. "It can't take long."

"Hurry!" she says, desperate, "before somebody punches my name! I'm going to see what it says about that hussy across the street."

She snaps off to gather what she can before it's stopped. So I punch for the tank and I get this new "What is your name?" flash. I got a morbid curiosity and I punch my name, and the screen says: "Were you ever called Ducky?" I blink. I ain't got no suspicions. I say, "Sure!" And the screen says, "There is a call for you."

Bingo! There's the inside of a hotel room and Laurine is reclinin' asleep on the bed. She'd been told to leave her logic turned on an' she done it. It is a hot day and she is trying to be cool. I would say that she oughta not suffer from the heat. Me, being human, I do not stay as cool as she looks. But there ain't no need to go into that. After I get my breath I say, "For Heaven's sake!" and she opens her eyes.

At first she looks puzzled, like she was thinking is she getting absent-minded and is this guy somebody she married lately. Then she grabs a sheet and drapes it around herself and beams at me.

"Ducky!" she says. "How marvelous!"

I say something like "Ugmph!" I am sweating.

She says: "I put in a call for you, Ducky, and here you are! Isn't it romantic? Where are you really, Ducky? And when can you come up? You've no idea how often I've thought of you!"

I am probably the only guy she ever knew real well that she has not been married to at some time or another.

I say "Ugmph!" again, and swallow.

"Can you come up instantly?" asks Laurine brightly.

"I'm . . . workin'," I say. "I'll . . . uh . . . call you back."

"I'm terribly lonesome," says Laurine. "Please make it quick, Ducky! I'll have a drink waiting for you. Have you ever thought of me?"

"Yeah," I say, feeble. "Plenty!"

"You darling!" says Laurine. "Here's a kiss to go on with until you get here! Hurry, Ducky!"

Then I sweat! I still don't know nothing about Joe, understand. I cuss out the guys at the tank because I blame them for this. If Laurine was just another blonde—well—when it comes to ordinary blondes I can leave 'em alone or leave 'em alone, either one. A married man gets that way or else. But Laurine has a look of unquenched enthusiasm that gives a man very strange weak sensations at the back of his knees. And she'd had four husbands and shot one and got acquitted.

So I punch the keys for the tank technical room, fumbling. And the screen says: "What is your name?" but I don't want any more. I punch the name of the old guy who's stock clerk in Maintenance. And the screen gives me some pretty interestin' dope—I never woulda thought the old fella had ever had that much pep—and winds up by mentionin' a unclaimed deposit now amountin' to two hundred eighty credits in the First National Bank, which he should look into. Then it spiels about the new secretarial service and gives me the tank at last.

I start to swear at the guy who looks at me. But he says, tired:

"Snap it off, fella. We got troubles an' you're just another. What are the logics doin' now?"

I tell him, and he laughs a hollow laugh.

"A light matter, fella," he says. "A very light matter! We just managed to clamp off all the data plates that give information on high explosives. The demand for instructions in counterfeiting is increasing minute by minute. We are also trying to shut off, by main force,

the relays that hook in to data plates that just barely
might give advice on the fine points of murder. So if
people will only keep busy getting the goods on each
other for a while, maybe we'll get a chance to stop
the circuits that are shifting credit-balances from bank
to bank before everybody's bankrupt except the guys
who thought of askin' how to get big bank accounts
in a hurry."

"Then," I says hoarse, "shut down the tank! Do
somethin'!"

"Shut down the tank?" he says, mirthless. "Does
it occur to you, fella, that the tank has been doin' all
the computin' for every business office for years? It's
been handlin' the distribution of ninety-four per cent
of all telecast programs, has given out all information
on weather, plane schedules, special sales, employment
opportunities and news; has handled all person-to-person
contacts over wires and recorded every business conversation and agreement— Listen, fella! Logics changed
civilization. Logics *are* civilization! If we shut off logics,
we go back to a kind of civilization we have forgotten
how to run! I'm getting hysterical myself and that's why
I'm talkin' like this! If my wife finds out my paycheck
is thirty credits a week more than I told her and starts
hunting for that redhead—"

He smiles a haggard smile at me and snaps off. And I
sit down and put my head in my hands. It's true. If something had happened back in cave days and they'd hadda
stop usin' fire— If they'd hadda stop usin' steam in the
nineteenth century or electricity in the twentieth— It's
like that. We got a very simple civilization. In the
nineteen hundreds a man would have to make use of a
typewriter, radio, telephone, teletypewriter, newspaper,

reference library, encyclopedias, office files, directories, plus messenger service and consulting lawyers, chemists, doctors, dieticians, filing clerks, secretaries—all to put down what he wanted to remember an' to tell him what other people had put down that he wanted to know; to report what he said to somebody else and to report to him what they said back. All we have to have is logics. Anything we want to know or see or hear, or anybody we want to talk to, we punch keys on a logic. Shut off logics and everything goes skiddoo. But Laurine—

Somethin' had happened. I still didn't know what it was. Nobody else knows, even yet. What had happened was Joe. What was the matter with him was that he wanted to work good. All this fuss he was raisin' was, actual, nothin' but stuff we shoulda thought of ourselves. Directive advice, tellin' us what we wanted to know to solve a problem, wasn't but a slight extension of logical-integrator service. Figurin' out a good way to poison a fella's wife was only different in degree from figurin' out a cube root or a guy's bank balance. It was gettin' the answer to a question. But things was goin' to pot because there was too many answers being given to too many questions.

One of the logics in Maintenance lights up. I go over, weary, to answer it. I punch the answer key. Laurine says:

"Ducky!"

It's the same hotel room. There's two glasses on the table with drinks in them. One is for me. Laurine's got on some kinda frothy hangin'-around-the-house-with-the-boy-friend outfit that automatic makes you strain your eyes to see if you actual see what you think. Laurine looks at me enthusiastic.

"Ducky!" says Laurine. "I'm lonesome! Why haven't you come up?"

"I . . . been busy," I say, strangling slightly.

"Pooh!" says Laurine. "Listen, Ducky! Do you remember how much in love we used to be?"

I gulp.

"Are you doin' anything this evening?" says Laurine.

I gulp again, because she is smiling at me in a way that a single man would maybe get dizzy, but it gives a old married man like me cold chills. When a dame looks at you possessive—

"Ducky!" says Laurine, impulsive. "I was so mean to you! Let's get married!"

Desperation gives me a voice.

"I . . . got married," I tell her, hoarse.

Laurine blinks. Then she says, courageous:

"Poor boy! But we'll get you outta that! Only it would be nice if we could be married today. Now we can only be engaged!"

"I . . . can't—"

"I'll call up your wife," says Laurine, happy, "and have a talk with her. You must have a code signal for your logic, darling. I tried to ring your house and noth—"

Click! That's my logic turned off. I turned it off. And I feel faint all over. I got nervous prostration. I got combat fatigue. I got anything you like. I got cold feet.

I beat it outta Maintenance, yellin' to somebody I got a emergency call. I'm gonna get out in a Maintenance car an' cruise around until it's plausible to go home. Then I'm gonna take the wife an' kids an' beat it for somewheres that Laurine won't ever find me. I don't wanna be' fifth in Laurine's series of husbands and maybe the second one she shoots in a moment of boredom. I got experience of blondes. I got experience of Laurine! And I'm scared to death!

I beat it out into traffic in the Maintenance car. There was a disconnected logic in the back, ready to substitute for one that hadda burned-out coil or something that it was easier to switch and fix back in the Maintenance shop. I drove crazy but automatic. It was kinda ironic, if you think of it. I was goin' hoopla over a strictly personal problem, while civilization was crackin' up all around me because other people were havin' their personal problems solved as fast as they could state 'em. It is a matter of record that part of the Mid-Western Electric research guys had been workin' on cold electron-emission for thirty years, to make vacuum tubes that wouldn't need a power source to heat the filament. And one of those fellas was intrigued by the "Ask your logic" flash. He asked how to get cold emission of electrons. And the logic integrates a few squintillion facts on the physics data plates and tells him. Just as casual as it told somebody over in the Fourth Ward how to serve left-over soup in a new attractive way, and somebody else on Mason Street how to dispose of a torso that somebody had left careless in his cellar after ceasing to use same.

Laurine wouldn't never have found me if it hadn't been for this new logics service. But now that it was started— Zowie! She'd shot one husband and got acquitted. Suppose she got impatient because I was still married an' asked logics service how to get me free an' in a spot where I'd have to marry her by 8:30

p.m.? It woulda told her! Just like it told that woman out in the suburbs how to make sure her husband wouldn't run around no more. *Br-r-r-r!* An' like it told that kid how to find some buried treasure. Remember? He was happy totin' home the gold reserve of the Hanoverian Bank and Trust Company when they caught on to it. The logic had told him how to make some kinda machine that nobody has been able to figure how it works even yet, only they guess it dodges around a couple extra dimensions. If Laurine was to start askin' questions with a technical aspect to them, that would be logics' service meat! And fella, I was scared! If you think a he-man oughtn't to be scared of just one blonde—you ain't met Laurine!

I'm drivin' blind when a social-conscious guy asks how to bring about his own particular system of social organization at once. He don't ask if it's best or if it'll work. He just wants to get it started. And the logic—or Joe—tells him! Simultaneous, there's a retired preacher asks how can the human race be cured of concupiscence. Bein' seventy, he's pretty safe himself, but he wants to remove the peril to the spiritual welfare of the rest of us. He finds out. It involves constructin' a sort of broadcastin' station to emit a certain wave-pattern an' turnin' it on. Just that. Nothing more. It's found out afterward, when he is solicitin' funds to construct it. Fortunate, he didn't think to ask logics how to finance it, or it woulda told him that, too, an' we woulda all been cured of the impulses we maybe regret afterward but never at the time. And there's another group of serious thinkers who are sure the human race would be a lot better off if everybody went back to nature an' lived in the woods with the ants an' poison ivy. They start askin' questions about how to cause humanity to abandon cities and artificial conditions of living. They practically got the answer in logics service!

Maybe it didn't strike you serious at the time, but while I was drivin' aimless, sweatin' blood over Laurine bein' after me, the fate of civilization hung in the balance. I ain't kiddin'. For instance, the Superior Man gang that sneers at the rest of us was quietly asking questions on what kinda weapons could be made by which Superior Men could take over and run things . . .

But I drove here an' there, sweatin' an' talkin' to myself.

"What I oughta do is ask this wacky logics service how to get outa this mess," I says. "But it'd just tell me a intricate and' foolproof way to bump Laurine off. I wanna have peace! I wanna grow comfortably old and brag to other old guys about what a hellion I used to be, without havin' to go through it an' lose my chance of livin' to be a elderly liar."

I turn a corner at random, there in the Maintenance car.

"It was a nice kinda world once," I says, bitter. "I could go home peaceful and not have belly-cramps wonderin' if a blonde has called up my wife to announce my engagement to her. I could punch keys on a logic without gazing into somebody's bedroom while she is giving her epidermis a air bath and being led to think things I gotta take out in thinkin'. I could—"

Then I groan, rememberin' that my wife, naturally, is gonna blame me for the fact that our private life ain't private any more if anybody has tried to peek into it.

"It was a swell world," I says, homesick for the dear dead days-before-yesterday. "We was playin' happy with our toys like little innocent children until somethin' happened. Like a guy named Joe come in and squashed all our mud pies."

Then it hit me. I got the whole thing in one flash. There ain't nothing in the tank set-up to start relays closin'. Relays are closed exclusive by logics, to get the information the keys are punched for. Nothin' but a logic coulda cooked up the relay patterns that constituted logics service. Humans wouldn't ha' been able to figure it out! Only a logic could integrate all the stuff that woulda made all the other logics work like this . . .

There was one answer. I drove into a restaurant and went over to a pay-logic an' dropped in a coin.

"Can a logic be modified," I spell out, "to cooperate in long-term planning which human brains are too limited in scope to do?"

The screen sputters. Then it says:

"Definitely yes."

"How great will the modifications be?" I punch.

"Microscopically slight. Changes in dimensions," says the screen. "Even modern precision gauges are not exact enough to check them, however. They can only come about under present manufacturing methods by an extremely improbable accident, which has only happened once."

"How can one get hold of that one accident which can do this highly necessary work?" I punch.

The screen sputters. Sweat broke out on me. I ain't got it figured out close, yet, but what I'm scared of is that whatever is Joe will be suspicious. But what

I'm askin' is strictly logical. And logics can't lie. They gotta be accurate. They can't help it.

"A complete logic capable of the work required," says the screen, "is now in ordinary family use in—"

And it gives me the Korlanovitch address and do I go over there! Do I go over there fast! I pull up the Maintenance car in front of the place, and I take the extra logic outta the back, and I stagger up the Korlanovitch fiat and I ring the bell. A kid answers the door.

"I'm from Logics Maintenance," I tell the kid. "An inspection record has shown that your logic is apt to break down any minute. I come to put in a new one before it does."

The kid says "O.K.!" real bright and runs back to the livin'-room where Joe—I got the habit of callin' him Joe later, through just meditatin' about him—is runnin' somethin' the kids wanna look at. I hook in the other logic an' turn it on, conscientious making sure it works. Then I say:

"Now kiddies, you punch this one for what you want. I'm gonna take the old one away before it breaks down."

And I glance at the screen. The kiddies have apparently said they wanna look at some real cannibals. So the screen is presenting a anthropological expedition scientific record film of the fertility dance of the Huba-Jouba tribe of West Africa. It is supposed to be restricted to anthropological professors an' post-graduate medical students. But there ain't any censor blocks workin' any more and it's on. The kids are much interested. Me, bein' a old married man, I blush.

I disconnect Joe. Careful. I turn to the other logic and punch keys for Maintenance. I do not get a services flash. I get Maintenance. I feel very good. I report that I am goin' home because I fell down a flight of steps an' hurt my leg. I add, inspired:

"An' say, I was carryin' the logic I replaced an' it's all busted. I left it for the dustman to pick up."

"If you don't turn 'em in," says Stock, "you gotta pay for 'em."

"Cheap at the price," I say.

I go home. Laurine ain't called. I put Joe down in the cellar, careful. If I turned him in, he'd be inspected an' his parts salvaged even if I busted somethin' on him. Whatever part was off-normal might be used again and everything start all over. I can't risk it. I pay for him and leave him be.

That's what happened. You might say I saved civilization an' not be far wrong. I know I ain't goin' to take a chance on havin' Joe in action again. Not while Laurine is livin'. An' there are other reasons. With all the nuts who wanna change the world to their own line o' thinkin', an' the ones that wanna bump people off, an' generally solve their problems— Yeah! Problems are bad, but I figure I better let sleepin' problems lie.

But on the other hand, if Joe could be tamed, somehow, and got to work just reasonable— He could make me a coupla million dollars, easy. But even if I got sense enough not to get rich, an' if I get retired and just loaf around fishin' an' lyin' to other old duffers about what a great guy I used to be— Maybe I'll like it, but maybe I won't. And after all, if I get fed up with bein' old and confined strictly to thinking—why

I could hook Joe in long enough to ask: "How can a old guy not stay old?" Joe'll be able to find out. An' he'll tell me.

That couldn't be allowed out general, of course. You gotta make room for kids to grow up. But it's a pretty good world, now Joe's turned off. Maybe I'll turn him on long enough to learn how to stay in it. But on the other hand, maybe—

DEAR CHARLES

To: CHARLES FABIUS GRANVER,
Sector 233, Zone 3, Home 1254, Radli.
The Thirty-Fourth Century, A.D.

My dear great-great-great-etc.-grandson Charles:

Your friend Hari Vans will discover this letter printed as a fiction story in an ancient, tattered book of still more ancient fiction stories in the rare-books stacks of the University Library. He will be astonished to see your name and still more astonished to read his own. He will be astounded to find your correct address in a volume printed when neither you nor your address existed. So he will show this letter to you, and in this way I can write you a very important message. The ordinary postal service could hardly be expected to deliver a letter after fourteen centuries, and I feel I must tell you about urgent family matters.

I need to arrange, through you, to meet and woo (and of course to win, despite your unfilial objections) your great-great-etc.-grandmother. When this letter is delivered, she will happen to be engaged to you, so I do not really count on your co-operation. The most I expect is a frantic effort on your part to prove that the whole business is pure lunacy. But that effort will be all I need, Charles, and I think that for the family's sake you should make it. It really is a family matter. As nearly as I can compute it on a basis of four generations to the century, you are my great-great-etc.-grandson some fifty-two times removed. This relationship exists because of a somewhat unusual series of events, and you need to know what to do to bring them about.

To make it clear . . . I imagine that in your day they still talk of time-travel as impossible because, so the argument runs, if one went back in time a hundred years, landed on his grandfather, and happened to kill him, he would make it impossible for himself to have been born. But of course if he wasn't born his grandfather wouldn't be killed. So he would be born. So he would kill his grandfather. So he wouldn't be born. *Ad infinitum.* I am sure you know this proof that time-travel is impossible.

However, I am your great-great-etc.-grandfather because of just the reverse of this classical paradox. It happens that when you read this, you are about to discover me as a visitor come forward from my time to yours. And in your time, with your extremely reluctant assistance, I shall woo and win your current girl friend and bring her contentedly back to my century to become your fifty-two-times-removed-grandmother.

I hardly expect you to approve the notion, Charles. You are inclined to be selfish. You will resist my great-grandparental authority, not caring about the consequences to the family. But I think you will flub it. After all, if you did manage to keep me from wooing and winning Ginny, you would not be born to stop me. So I would woo and win her, in which case you would be born to stop me. If you did such a thing, you would not be born. In short, I think I am going to marry Ginny. In fact, I already have, and now I want to arrange for it.

Let me clarify the situation a little. In my senior year at Collins University, my physics professor was Prof. Knut Hadley, Ph.D., M.A. etc., etc. He was a person with a sort of monorail mind, capable of following an idea tenaciously over dizzy heights of improbability and through fastnesses of opposing facts. In the previous semester he'd tracked an idea down. It was a dilly. As class-work, he had five of us seniors help him put together an incredibly complicated electronic gadget that he said would provide experimental proof of the verity of the Lorenz-Fitzgerald equation. His theory was—

No. I spare you that, Charles. Let's keep this simple. You just remember that if you manage to keep me from winning Ginny you won't be born to keep me from winning Ginny, so I will win her and you will be born to try and stop me—you see? Just bear that in mind if you get confused. It may help.

In any case, Professor Hadley's apparatus took a

splendid if incomprehensible form. We built it with elaborate care. And some two weeks before graduation it was finished. Professor Hadley was jubilant. Standing before us, he adjusted this and checked over that. He made sure of voltages and he measured micro-ohms of resistance. And then he got ready to turn it on.

For obvious reasons, I am not going to give you any clues to how it was made. As it turned out, this was the device by which I traveled to your century, and I wouldn't want you to make another and come back to kill your fifty-two-times-removed-grandfather. You will want to, Charles, but it would be most improper. All the intervening generations, of which I am the revered sire, would never exist. Out of consideration for them I can't allow it. My regards to your father, by the way, Charles. And your great-etc.-grandmother insists that I give you a message. She remembers you with an affection I cannot match, and hopes that you meet some nice girl and marry her and live happily ever after. I'm afraid I retain too much of my old antagonism toward Ginny's first suitor to wish you well.

In re the family business, though, Professor Hadley struck an enthusiastic attitude. He made a speech, in which he said that his device would demonstrate the theoretically undemonstrable. Dramatically, he flipped the switch over.

He was right about demonstrating the undemonstrable, all right! He didn't know his own genius or his own gadget. When he flipped over the switch a spark leaped, tubes lighted, insulation smoked . . .

And Professor Hadley, beaming, turned a rather pretty luminous puce color, and with every appearance of satisfaction faded quietly into thin air. Smiling happily and glowing like an off-color neon sign, he vanished deliberately before our eyes.

We stared, our mouths open. We blinked. And after about three seconds there was a sharp, somehow conclusive "snap," and the gadget burned itself out with enthusiastic thoroughness. It spat sparks. Its insulation caught fire. It definitely ceased to work. And Professor Hadley remained among the missing.

Your attention span is short, Charles, so I will not tell you of the disturbance caused by this event. We five witnesses to his disappearance, of course, were flatly disbelieved. The police hinted darkly of a multiple indictment for murder, but were stymied by the well-known rule of *corpus delicti*. Then they looked into his papers and found he was corresponding with seventeen female members of Lonely Hearts clubs. He had represented himself to them as a young and wealthy bachelor, and they were liars, too. The police began to investigate them, announced that an arrest could be expected in the near future, and the five of us were mysteriously clear of suspicion. But a diversion, about that time, helped to take attention away from us, too. On Graduation Morning the Dean of Women was discovered atop the statue of the University's Founder, celebrating the end of the academic year. She was standing on her head on the Founder's bronze top hat, singing A Robin in the Merry Month of May in parts—no mean feat for one woman—and she was wearing the Art Department's one prized Picasso neatly made over into a leotard. This tended to draw public attention from Professor Hadley's less spectacular disappearance.

I may say that the mystery has never been solved.

Nobody ever found out where he went. I think it possible, however, that his dentures may yet some day be found in some Upper Devonian fossil-bearing stratum. I say this because, while he was trying to prove the Lorenz-Fitzgerald hypothesis on purpose, I later found out that he had made a time-travel device by accident. And from my knowledge of Professor Hadley, I am sure he would have had it set up to run backward.

Here I have anticipated myself. I should say that I graduated some two weeks after the Professor disappeared, but with a commitment to jerk sodas during the summer session to pay up my senior-year bills. I remained in the small university town. Toothy schoolteachers swarmed in to absorb culture and get academic credits that would raise their pay if they didn't catch husbands. Time marched on.

Then Joe turned up. I call him Joe to spare him embarrassment. Joe was one of those scholastic triumphs nobody remembers. He was embracing a teaching career; he was magnificently learned; he was splendidly earnest. In his own way I am sure he was a perfectly swell guy—and nobody cared. He'd been grabbed in a hurry to teach Professor Hadley's subjects to the bespectacled summer students, and come fall he would be let go for somebody who knew less but counted more. It was too bad. I was brutal to Joe myself, finally, but—

Somebody told him what had happened to Professor Hadley. He thought it over. He came to me as a known witness. He said thoughtfully that Professor Hadley was a very able man, and, if he had thought he could prove the Lorenz-Fitzgerald theory, it was worth looking into. Would I help him reconstruct the burned-out gimmick and see what the trouble was? If he could find out, he could write a paper about it, and, if some scientific publication printed it, he might get a permanent instructorship. . . .

I felt sorry for him. Also, some of the schoolteachers were hanging around where I soda-jerked and happened to be walking my way when I quit.

I remembered the physics lab as a quiet place where one might peacefully drink a bottle of beer in the evenings. Or the mornings, for that matter. I agreed to help Joe. We began. And that is how fifty-two-times-removed-great-grandsons are born.

You are a result of all this, Charles.

Understand this, Charles, I have to tell my story as fiction in order to get it into print so Hari Vans will show it to you so you will yank on a piece of sash cord. . . . There is a paradox involved, Charles—if you haven't noticed. In my century and in my life, these things happened in June and July of a year ago. It's just about twenty-two months since Joe and I got Professor Hadley's gadget rebuilt and moved a safe distance away from it before we turned it on. But that device carried me into the thirty-fourth century, where Ginny was waiting interestedly to meet me because she'd read this letter. But twenty-two months ago I had not written it. Yet if you're to act in your typically impulsive way—and if Ginny is to regard me with the bright and fascinated eyes of a girl looking at the man she knows she's going to marry—I have to write it some time, don't I? So the things that have happened will take place?

Now let's talk about Professor Hadley's time-transporter instead. Shall we?

It was remarkably complicated to look at. There were coils and electron tubes. There were inductances, grid leaks and transistors, with dials, rheostats, feedbacks and assorted hardware. I didn't understand it, and even Joe grew more and more pained as we replaced one after another of the burned-out wires and condensers and whatnots, and it made progressively less sense to him. He knew his books, did Joe, but this was something else. Still, we got it rebuilt, and I could swear that it was exactly the way Professor Hadley'd had it put together, except with heavier wiring.

The Professor must have been pretty bright. He'd been absolutely sure the thing would demonstrate the Lorenz-Fitzgerald contraction, but it was much more remarkable than that. It was a time-transporter, moving objects from one temporal frame of reference to another.

Every scientist in history has said that can't be done. I hope the Professor, wherever he is—in the Upper Devonian or Jurassic or even the Lower Cretacious period—knows of his accidental triumph.

But Joe and I just sat and looked at it when it was done, Charles. We didn't know the next step to take. We had no idea what it would do, and neither of us was especially anxious to glow a luminous puce color and, however happily smiling, fade away into nothingness. We put a long extension-cord on the switch. From some distance away we turned the thing on. Nothing happened. We turned it off. I put an empty beer-bottle where Professor Hadley had stood and we turned the thing on. The beer-bottle glowed a pale pink and faded away. We turned the thing off. Nothing happened. The beer-bottle stayed gone.

We looked at each other. Joe looked very pained indeed. But then he muttered something about discovering the physical nature of the barrier. He tied a string to a beer-bottle. We vanished it. When we turned the gadget off it looked like the string was cut in half. But when Joe picked it up to look at the cut end, the beer-bottle came out of nowhere, still tied fast.

About that time I began to dither, Charles. I will be frank about it. There is much that I do not understand about Professor Hadley's time-transporter. It was the first one ever made, and I am quite sure there will never be another. If there is, it will be over my dead body. Right then, I opened a bottle of beer.

And Norton, the laboratory cat, came gloomily into the room. He was gaunt and seedy and with his usual hangover. I regret to tell you, Charles, that in my day some of the lower animals sank to near-human depths. Norton was notorious at Collins University for his intemperate habits. Believe it or not, he would pass up a sardine for a cocktail any day, and on the morning after a wet night he was frequently to be seen prowling about empty beer-cans trying to get a hair of the dog that bit him. Not that any dog would dare bite Norton, no! Norton was a mighty warrior, in his cups. One Christmas he got tanked up on egg-nog.

But that has nothing to do with you, Charles. This morning Norton came loping over to me with an imploring air, as one who would say feverishly: "Fella, give me one drink to straighten me out, and so help me I'm gonna join AA!" I gave him the drink. He lapped it up, broodingly. Then he burped, rolled over and went to sleep.

The same idea struck Joe and myself simultaneously.

You've guessed it. We waked Norton and tied a string to his collar, put him in the place from which the beer-bottle had gone into the wild blue yonder, and threw on the time-transporter switch. Norton was in the act of yawning as the current went on. His yawn continued undisturbed. He glowed, to be sure. Brilliantly. But he faded to invisibility in a sort of brownish-purple mist. The last we saw of him was his teeth just beginning to close in the insouciant manner so typical of him.

We turned off the time-transporter. Norton stayed gone. We discussed the matter at length. I went and pulled on the string. And Norton, tied to it, yielded to my tugging. He came protestingly out of nowhere, blinking reproachfully. He had every appearance of having been interrupted in a nap. He was unharmed and undisturbed save by our waking him. We put him down, and he curled up and went back to sleep.

Perhaps we were not conservative, Charles. After only one experiment with an animal, we probably should not have gone on immediately to a human subject. But we were enthusiastic. That is, I was enthusiastic, and Joe was pallidly grim. We solemnly matched to see who would fade out. I lost. Therefore I met your great-great-etc.-grandmother, through the help you are going to give me.

I rather like your numerously-great-grandmother, Charles. She's quite nice to have around. She's cuddly. We've been married for practically two years and I still approve of her. But of course in your time we haven't yet met. I know, though, that you will not fail me, my dear great-great-great-and-so-on-grandson!

As I understand the matter, Charles, your friend Harl will show you this letter in the book in which it is reprinted. You will read it and be enraged. You will profanely declare it nonsense. Harl will thereupon show it to your friends Stan and Laki—and of course to Ginny. And they will gang up on you. They will demand clamorously that you see if it is true. Ginny, in particular, will coax you—stamping her foot from time to time—and no descendant of mine—or of hers, if you can possibly grasp the idea—could possibly refuse Ginny anything.

Anyhow, on the morning after somebody named Dorlig wins the Lunar ground-to-ground race (your great-etc.-grandmother has dated it for me that way, Charles) your friends will descend upon you chanting demands for action. Stan will have bet his shirt on Dorlig on the authority of this fiction-tale. He will have won himself a nice piece of change. Harl will have bet more conservatively, but he'll be feeling pretty good too. Only you will have been too obstinate to wager a single coin on the winning of that race. And Ginny, knowing from the story what is to come next and halfway believing it, will be most especially irresistible. They will arrive in a group, creating a tumult and demanding to be introduced to your fifty-two-times-removed-great-grandfather. And you will growl at them and take them furiously down into the rumpus-room to prove to them that they are half-wits. Which they are not.

I would like to draw a dramatic picture of two concurrent scenes, here, of the events taking place at two so-widely-separated spots. In the physics lab of Collins University, away back in the twentieth century,

I sat. Joe had gone plodding over to a hardware store to buy a hank of sash cord. I wouldn't trust to the string that had sufficed for Norton. I sat in the dusty, hot laboratory, listening to the buzzing of a fly, and Norton, snoring off in the corner, and the gay laughter of bespectacled schoolteachers being charming and girlish out on the campus. All was peace. All was tranquility. I was genuinely thrilled by what had happened to Norton and was about to happen to me, but I didn't know Ginny was in my immediate future. If I had, I'd have been in a hurry.

And far, far away in time, you, Charles, scowlingly led a gay party down into your family's rumpus-room. Its walls glowed faintly with the changing forms and movements of the dynamic decorations. You picked out those decorations, and they are pretty corny. That sequence in which a spacesuited figure with your face slaughters grymvals —the batlike things with jet propulsion—while a rather sappy-looking blonde watches admiringly. That smacks of vainglory, but let it go.

You showed them the rumpus-room, conspicuously bereft of me. Laki—a nice girl, Laki, if you go for brunettes—giggled excitedly.

Stan poured coins cheerfully from one hand to another to show you how dumb you were not to be on a sure thing straight from your great-etc.-grandfather's own lips. Hari jingled coins, a bit rueful for not having bet with more nerve. And Ginny waited radiantly to see the man whom she knew from this letter was going to take her back to the strange, remote, primitive days when pictures were two-dimensional and all the food that people ate was grown in fields right here on Earth.

Ginny wore green, with a necklace of glittering synthetic stones—not valuable, only carbon crystals—about her neck. Her tiny feet—but why should I describe Ginny to you, Charles? You've seen her, and you probably have a hard enough time following these ideas without being disconcerted by Ginny. The marvelous thing about Ginny was her superb confidence of knowing exactly how I was going to feel about her (indirectly, in my own clever way, I'm telling her now) plus the satisfaction that I did not know anything about it yet. Because, of course, when all this happens, none of it will have taken place so far as I am concerned—if you grasp my meaning—and I'm going to write this letter afterward, but Ginny is going to read it ahead of time. I tenderly hope this doesn't make you dizzy, Charles. You will need to be your usual, absent-minded self. A tense pause occurred.

Back in the physics laboratory Joe returned with the sash cord. There were more cries of merry laughter out on the campus. Flies buzzed on and Norton dreamed of cocktails and sardine canapes. All was peace. The world trundled on, unaware of the unparalleled and never-to-be-duplicated event about to take place.

It was a tense moment indeed. We prepared for my splendid journey. I cut off a length of sash cord. Then I felt Joe hauling at my belt. He was tying the other end of the sash cord to it. He'd accomplished it when I realized. But I objected. I would trust my pants to a belt, but not my life. I hadn't lost my nerve, but I wasn't going to take any unnecessary chances, either. I tied my end of the sash cord around my ankle with a firm, double-knotted diamond hitch.

Then I said, "Tie the other end to something, Joe."

I watched him tie the cord's end firmly to a steam-radiator.

I felt prickles down my spine, but I said, "I will not let Norton lead where I dare not follow! Let'er go, Joe!"

And Joe retreated to the extension-cord switch. He gulped, and looked unhappy, and threw the switch over.

He and the laboratory, the floor, the ceiling, the steam-radiator and all the world I knew, vanished in a luminous puce-colored mist. I stood still. Nothing happened. There I was. Apparently, that was all there was to it. About me there was merely a brownish-purple nothing-in-particular. There was no sound or movement of any sort. True, I no longer heard the glad cries of the summer-session school-teachers on the campus, but aside from a feeling that I'd crawled into a puce-colored hole and pulled it in after me, there was no sensation at all. I thought to look for the beer-bottle that had vanished permanently. I did not see it. I did not see anything. I might as well be nowhere. I very probably was.

It did not strike me as high adventure. It did not really strike me as anything at all. I was distinctly disappointed. I began to wish that Joe would haul on the sash cord tied to my ankle and get me out. Of course I could have walked off in the mist to see if it was different anywhere else, but I had an innate conviction that I'd better stay where I was. At that point I was very calm, Charles. Extremely calm. But as minute after minute passed by and absolutely nothing happened, I began to sweat slightly.

I endured it as long as I could, and then I bent down and picked up the sash cord tied to my leg. I waggled it, as a signal to Joe to pull me out of wherever I was, if anywhere. He did not respond. I pulled on the cord, to stretch it taut so Joe would recognize that it was time for him to do something practical.

It didn't get taut. Because here, my dear Charles, I was faced with a small error of judgment on my own part. But it was an error over which I shall rejoice forever. It was an inspired fuzzy-mindedness which brought about the rest. When Joe and I were preparing for me to vanish in a puce-colored mist, Charles, Joe had prepared to fasten the sash cord to my belt. It was not an especially sound idea, but I bless him for it. At the time, though, I'd protested. I'd cut off a length of sash cord to tie to my ankle. To my ankle I tied it. Firmly. This, I considered, was my lifeline. This was the cord I thought I'd seen Joe tie to a steam-radiator. But he'd tied the other cord instead—and somehow I did not notice. It was an error on my part, and a singularly happy one.

But not at the moment. I hauled on the cord from my ankle instead of the one fastened—I didn't know how inadequately—to my belt. The rope from my ankle was fastened only there. The other end came unresistingly as I pulled. The cut-off place came into the brownish-purple mist with me. And when I saw it, I knew a moment of such anguish as I would not wish even on you, my erstwhile rival and great-etc. Every hair on my head stood on end and cracked like a whiplash. My eyes bugged out. I was in a place that can only be described as nowhere. I wanted to get out. But I'd pulled into the hole with me what I thought was my only link to a world of schoolteachers, alcoholic cats and—Joe.

I felt a pure, hysterical aversion to the end of that cord. I hadn't meant to pull it to where Joe couldn't yank it back. I had. I had a frenzied impulse to return it to him. So I threw that cord hysterically away from me, into the puce-colored mist

And it tickled you on the back of your neck.

This is the crucial moment, Charles. When you and Laki and Stan and Hari and of course Ginny stand in your cellar rumpus room, everybody will have read this narrative. But you, Charles, will be savagely determined to prove it sheer nonsense. And your friends have often displayed what you consider peculiar ideas of humor. When you have pointed out the conspicuous absence of anybody from an earlier age in the room, and are pointing out triumphantly to them that this story is all eyewash and that your great-great-etc.-grandfather is not going to visit you that morning from fourteen centuries previous. When you have done all that, Charles, the rope will tickle the back of your neck.

You will whirl. You will see an unfamiliar type of cordage in mid-air. You will suspect Hari and Stan of a practical joke. Your face will turn purple and you will yank at the rope, while you howl that it is all blank-blank foolishness.

And at that moment I will fall on your head out of the thin air above you, and wind up sitting on your stomach as you flop on the floor. Nearly the only gratitude I feel toward you, Charles, is for breaking my fall in that way. I might have bumped myself in a six-foot fall for which I was—will be—unprepared. Doubtless this would be an appropriate place to speculate on why, when I pulled a piece of sash cord from the twentieth century and heaved it from me in horror, it should tickle your neck in the thirty-fourth century. But I admit candidly that I haven't any ideas on the subject. Professor Hadley's inadvertent time-transporter worked that way. I'm going to let it go at that.

I sat up and gazed blankly at you. You thought I was a practical joker, hired or persuaded to play a part. You panted at me. And I was a bit embarrassed. You weren't Joe, whom I'd hoped would pull me out of nowhere. You were a stranger to me then. You were a red-faced, rather foolish-looking stranger, drawing in your breath to swear.

So I said politely, "Doctor Livingstone, I presume?"

To you this was further evidence of a put-up job. You heaved up mightily, gasping. I got off your stomach and tried to help you up with proper courtesy. But you swung wildly, connected, and I went banging into the wall. Then, your great-great-etc.-grandmother tells me indignantly, you grabbed a chair and prepared to commit mayhem on me. Hardly the way to treat a distinguished progenitor, Charles, let me tell you.

This was the first moment when your great-and-so-on-grandmother felt really certain you were not the gentle soul she had hoped. Moreover, knowing that I was destined to woo and win her, she forestalled any hindrance to her tender dreamings by swinging on you with a hartlegame bat from the rumpus-room equipment nearby. And when you collapsed, she, with the fine competence of which small and beautiful women are capable in emergencies, discovered a piece of sash cord fastened to my belt in the back, untied it, and deftly knotted it to a piece of furniture for later reference.

Here, perhaps, my letter to you could end. The other events in your rumpus-room, your time, your historical period, followed an absolutely inevitable pattern.

Laki screamed piercingly. Your father heard, and came rushing with a first-aid kit. He arrived to view Ginny—bless her—standing embattled above me with the hartlegame bat in her hand and blood in her eye. You were collapsed on the floor.

Your father gasped: "Wha—what—"

And Ginny said in a level and determined tone, "He's Charles's fifty-second-great-grandfather, sir, and Charles hit him. It wasn't respectful—so I clobbered him."

The word "clobbered" is not in thirty-fourth century common speech. Ginny had learned it from the reading of this missive to you. She had not known what it meant, but when the emergency arrived she not only knew what to do, but had the word for it. Your great-great-great-etc.-ancestress is a remarkable woman, Charles! She has brains, determination, intuition, clarity of thought, and she is deliciously cuddlesome besides. Even after having been married to her for a considerable time, I like her very, very much!

"What's that?" demanded your father dazedly. "Great-great—"

Hari and Stan tried to explain, together. I opened my eyes and saw Ginny. My last previous view had been of a hamlike fist gaining momentum before my nose. Ginny was a welcome change. I sat up, staring at her. My mouth dropped open.

I heard myself saying earnestly: "Look, angel! It's not true there's no marrying in Heaven, is it? With you around that would be a dirty trick."

And Ginny kissed me. It was quite proper. She had read this letter, and she knew that she was going to marry me—knew it in fact the instant she saw me—and even that nearly two years later I would still be bragging about it. In fact, I would be—I am—gloating over it in a quite unseemly manner. So her engagement to you, Charles, was automatically terminated by my arrival. In its place an arrangement of much longer standing matured. And while I do not believe in long engagements as a rule, Ginny's and mine of some fourteen centuries' duration has worked out all right.

You stirred and rose. I was still there. Ginny was very close to me. You howled and leaped toward me again. I got in one gratifying punch on the nose—which does resemble mine, by the way—and then Harl and Stan and your father grabbed you, and Ginny grabbed me. When she touched me, all my belligerent impulses died. I felt infinite love for all the world. I might even have forgiven you, Charles, temporarily, for being my rival as well as my fifty-two-times removed grandson.

Your father said desperately, "Let me understand this thing!" He pushed you into a chair and looked unhappily at me. My costume was eccentric. Harl and Stan again tried to explain.

But you, Charles, bellowed, "It's a lie! It's a trick! It's a stupid practical joke! I'll kill—"

Laki said shakily, "Suppose we let the police settle it. If he really is who the book says—"

You bounced up and roared, "I'll get 'em! You hold that faker here, Father, and I'll teach these idiots to play jokes." You rushed out. Your father mopped his face.

I said mildly to Ginny, still standing close by me, "Where am I, anyhow? Not that it matters."

Ginny reached out her hand to Stan. As if somnambulistically, he handed her a book. It was an ancient, crumbling, tattered volume of fiction. Ginny opened it with fingers that trembled only a very little. I read:

> To: *Charles Fabius Granver*
> *Sector 233, Zone 3, Home 1254, Radii.*
> *The Thirty-Fourth Century,* A.D.
> *My dear great-great-great-etc.-grandson*
>   *Charles:*

Ginny said softly in my ear, "Read it! Fast!"

I read.

I heard your father saying harassedly, "His face does look familiar. . . ."

I handed him the book and bowed benignly. I said, "Sir, I am very happy to have met you. It is a rare privilege."

And so it was. And will be. One does not meet even a fifty-one-times-removed grandson every day.

There was a scraping sound. Hari turned pale. Stan jumped. Somehow, I think that up to this moment they had not quite fully believed. But that scraping sound . . . Ginny had competently untied a piece of sash cord from my belt in the back and fastened it to a chair. It had reached up to the ceiling. Having admitted my failure to notice that Joe—back in the laboratory—had tied a cord to my belt with a very clumsy granny-knot, I don't feel I have to justify my not connecting the facts of time-travel with that piece of rope. Not up to this moment. But Ginny had realized from the beginning. She'd been previously informed. I'm informing her now. She'd tied the cord to a chair, and some fourteen centuries away my colleague Joe was dragging on the cord. He'd taken his time about it!

Ginny said shakily, "I—guess we'd better hurry. . . ."

She was a little bit scared. To tell the truth, so was I. I said somehow hoarsely, "I'll stay here if you'd rather—"

But I'd read this letter. And I felt—well, Charles, perhaps you can never understand how magnificent I felt when Ginny smiled at me and put her hand in mine and said to Laki, "You might try to explain to Uncle Seri for me."

The chair tied to the sash cord stirred again. I lifted Ginny to a table and climbed up beside her. Harl—again somnambulistically—handed me a chair. I twisted the sash cord about myself very carefully. I made a good strong knot—much better than Ginny had untied—and Ginny, trembling, let me pick her up in my arms. I stood on the chair on the table and jerked at the sash cord.

Your father, Harl, Stan, Laki—she seemed a very nice girl—the rumpus-room, the dynamic mural and the hartlegame bat—all vanished in a luminous puce-colored mist. I still felt a tugging at my waist. But for a moment Ginny and I were private in the brownish-purple mist that is characteristic of—hmmm—let us say "nowhere." And in that moment I kissed Ginny and she kissed me back.

Then I walked out into the laboratory with Ginny in my arms and said thoughtfully to Joe—whose jaw dropped down to here—"Joe, this hurts me more than it does you."

And then I smashed Professor Hadley's time-transporter. I stamped on it, while Joe gazed stupidly at Ginny. I had reason to smash the device. Naturally! If anybody else traveled in time, they might not be as smart as I am, or their descendants might not be as dumb as you, Charles. Something might get messed up. Somebody might marry the wrong person somewhere in the next fourteen centuries, and Ginny might not get born. I wouldn't risk that!

So, Charles, I am happy to report that everything ended nicely, or will end nicely. For everybody but you, and I must apologize for that. But surely you can understand that it is all for the best, can't you, Charles? It would have been interesting to have gone beyond your rumpus-room in the thirty-fourth century, and see what a city of your time was like, and I'd like to see the spaceships and the ground-cars and the little personal fliers Ginny has been telling me about. But it doesn't matter.

You look at them, Charles. I'll look at Ginny.

You needn't worry about her, though. That gal has brains! She only halfway believed this story until I fell on your head. But because she halfway believed, the morning she comes to your house with Harl and Stan and Laki, she'll have made some tentative precautions.

She brought along a whole bag full of crystallized carbon—all the costume jewelry around the house with carbon crystals in it. Merely trinkets, of course. You can buy them by the pound. Pretty beads. But back in the twentieth century they're called diamonds and we don't know how to make them yet. She even picked up a paperbacked book on electronics for beginners, aimed at ten-year-old kids. Some of it is over my head so far, but it's pretty useful. With diamonds to start on and super-duper electronic principles to go on with, Ginny and I are in no danger of starving, even in these primitive times.

We've got a primitive house with old-style hot-and-cold water and a quaint old electric furnace, and we listen to our antique radio and watch primeval television, and we drive a car that burns that quaint old stuff called gasoline in its cylinders ! But we manage. We don't mind hardships. We have each other.

I was just finishing this letter, Charles, when Ginny came in. Somehow I find it very satisfactory to be married to Ginny. Lately it's gotten even better. And she came in with something to show me that enables me to finish this note with an item of news that is highly important to all the family.

Ginny, beaming, took my finger and made me feel. And it's so! We have a son, Charles. He looks like me, but Ginny seems pleased. And the thing I felt—Charles, just as I finished this letter, Ginny showed me that your great-great-great-grandfather fifty-one times removed, at the age of seven months and one week, has just cut his first tooth!

I'm sure you will be pleased!

GATEWAY TO ELSEWHERE

Chapter 1

This is the story of what happened to Tony Gregg after he had learned about the fourth dimension—or maybe it was the fifth or sixth—in a *shishkebab* restaurant in the Syrian quarter on lower East Broadway, New York.

He didn't go to the restaurant originally to learn about the fourth dimension. His first visit was simply for *shishkebab*, which is a wonderful dish of lamb cubes skewered on small round sticks and cooked with an unlikely sauce containing grape leaves. It was quite accidental that he asked the owner of the restaurant about a coin that he—Tony—carried as a luck-piece.

Tony had bought it for a lucky charm in one of

those tiny shops on side-streets in New York, where antique jewelry and ivory chessmen and similar wares are on display in the windows. He picked it out because it looked odd. His conscience—he had been raised with a very articulate conscience—reluctantly consented to the purchase because the coin was very heavy for its size and might be gold. (It certainly wasn't a medal, and therefore had to be a coin.) It bore an inscription in conventionalized Arabic script on one side, and something on the other that looked like an elaborate throne without anybody sitting on it. But when Tony tried to look it up, there simply wasn't any record in any numismatic catalogue of any coinage even resembling it.

One night—this was his first visit, not the later one when he learned about the fourth dimension—he went down on East Broadway for *shishkebab*, and it occurred to him to ask the Syrian restaurant-keeper what the Arabic inscription might say. The Syrian read it, frowned darkly, and told Tony that the coin was a ten-dirhim piece, that the inscription said it was a coin of Barkutand, that he had never heard of any place called Barkut. Neither had Tony. So Tony got a little curious about it, and the next day spent half an hour in the Fifth Avenue library trying to find out something about either the coin or the country it came from. But as far as the library was concerned, there wasn't any place called Barkut. Never had been.

The coin was solid gold, though. A jeweler verified that. At bullion, it was worth somewhere around six dollars. And since Tony had paid only a dollar and a half for it, he was rather pleased. Even his conscience smugly approved. It isn't often that you pick up anything in an antique shop that you can sell for more than you paid for it, no matter what people tell you. So Tony kept it for a luck-piece, and every night on the way home from the office he paused outside Paddy Scanlon's Bar and Grill and gravely tossed the coin to see whether he should have a drink or not. Which was a pretty good way of being neither too abstemious nor too regular in such matters. His conscience approved of this, too.

He didn't really think the coin brought him good luck, but the small mystery of it intrigued him. He was a rather ordinary young man, was Tony. He'd enlisted in the Second World War, but had never got beyond a base camp although he'd howled for action. Instead, he sat on his rear and pounded a typewriter for three long years. Then he was discharged and got his old job back—at the same old salary—and went back to his old lodging house—at a bright new rate per week. Kind of a sour deal all around. So now he was glad he had the coin—because he liked to imagine things. His conscience sternly and constantly reminded him that he should be polite, attentive to his duties, efficient and no clock-watcher; and the radio reminded him every morning while he was dressing that he'd better use a specific tooth paste, hair stickum, breath deodorant, and brand of popular-priced suits. It was pleasant, therefore, to have something vague and mysterious around, like the coin.

It couldn't have been made as a novelty or anything like that. Not when it was gold. But it came from no country anyone had ever heard of. He liked to think that there was some mystery about its having reached his hands; some significance in the fact that he had come to own it and no one else. To make it seem more significant, probably, he got into the habit of tossing it for all decisions of no particular moment. Whether to go to a ball game or not. Whether or not to eat at his regular restaurant. On this excess, his conscience dourly reserved decision.

He'd owned the coin two months, and the habit of using it to make small decisions had become fixed, when one evening he tossed it to see whether or not he should go to his regular restaurant for dinner. It came tails. No. He was mildly amused. To another restaurant uptown? Tails again. He flipped and flipped and flipped. His common sense told him that he was simply running into a long sequence of tails. But he liked to think that the decisions of the coin were mysterious and significant. Tonight he got a little excited when one place after another was negatived. He ran out of restaurants he could remember having dined in. So he tossed his coin with the mental note that if it came heads he'd try a new restaurant, where he'd never dined before. But the coin came tails. Negative. Then he really racked his brains—and remembered the little Syrian restaurant down on lower East Broadway. He flipped for that. And the coin came heads.

He got on the subway and rode downtown, while his conscience made scornful comments about superstition. He went into the small converted store with something of an anticipatory thrill. His way of life was just about as unexciting as anybody's life could be. He had been pretty well tamed by the way he was raised, which had created a conscience with a mind of its own and usually discouraging opinions. His conscience now spoke acidly, and he had to assure it that he didn't really believe that the coin meant anything, but that he only liked to pretend it did.

So he sat down at a table and automatically flipped the coin to see whether he should order *shishkebab* or not. The swarthy, slick-haired proprietor grinned at him. There was a bald-headed man at a table in the back—a man in impeccably tailored clothing, with gold-rimmed eyeglasses and the definite dark dignity of a Levantine of some sort.

"Say," said the proprietor, in wholly colloquial English. "You showed me a funny goldpiece last time you were here. Is it that? Mr. Emurian, back there, he knows a lot about that stuff. A very educated man! You want I should ask him about it?"

This seemed to Tony a mysterious coincidence. He agreed eagerly. The restaurant-keeper took the coin. He showed it to the bald-headed man. They talked at length, not in English. The restaurant-keeper came back.

"He never seen one like it," he reported. "And he never heard of Barkut, where it says it come from. But he says there's a kinda story about coins and things like that—things that come from places that nobody ever heard of. He'll tell you if you want."

"Please!" said Tony. He found his heart beating faster. "If he'll join me—"

"Oh, he'll have a cuppa coffee, maybe," said the restaurant-keeper. "On the house. He's a very educated man, Mr. Emurian is."

He went back. The bald-headed man rose and came with easy dignity toward Tony's table. His eyes twinkled. Tony was flustered because this Mr. Emurian looked so foreign and spoke such perfect English and was so perfectly at ease.

"There is a legend," he told Tony humorously, "which might amuse you—if I may put down my coffee cup? Thank you." He sat. "It is an old wives' tale, and yet it fits oddly into the theories of Mr. Einstein and other learned men. But I know a man in Ispahan who would give you a great sum for that coin because of the legend. Would you wish to sell?"

Tony shook his head.

"Say—five hundred dollars?" asked Mr. Emurian, smiling behind his eyeglasses. "No? Not even a thousand? I will give you the address of the man who would buy it, if you ever wish to sell."

Tony was too flabbergasted to even shake his head.

Mr. Emurian laughed. "This man," he explained amiably, "would say that the coin comes from a country which is not upon our maps because it is unapproachable by any ordinary means. Yet it is wholly real and actually has a certain commerce with us. It is—hm—have you ever heard of worlds supposed to be like ours, but in other—ah—dimensions, say, or in parallel but not identical times?"

"I've read Wells' *Time Machine*," said Tony awkwardly.

"Not at all the same," the dark man assured him. "And notions of startling new machines for traveling between sets of dimensions or in time itself are quite absurd. Discoveries of that sort are never drastic! When electricity was discovered, it was your own Franklin who observed that it was no new force, but quite commonplace. Every thunderstorm since time began had demonstrated it. Similarly, if travel between worlds or to other times should ever become really practical, it is certain that the discovery will not be dramatic. It will turn out that people have been doing it for centuries as a matter of course, without ever realizing it."

"You mean—" Tony stopped.

"The legend," said Mr. Emurian, "suggests that your coin came from a world not our own. That it came from a world where history quite truthfully denies much of the history we truthfully teach to children." He regarded Tony zestfully and said, "Ordinarily, two things which are equal to the same thing are equal to each other. But two places which are exactly equal to each other are identical—are the same place. Now consider! Suppose that somewhere there existed a world in which Aladdin's lamp existed and was in good working order. Suppose that upon that world there was a place which was absolutely identical with a place in this world. It would have to be a place where the working or not working of Aladdin's lamp made absolutely no difference. Now, according to the legend, those two places, on two worlds, would actually be one place which was on both worlds, and which would serve as a perfectly practical gateway between them. Travelers would pass casually through it without ever noticing it. You and I perhaps, pass through such gateways every day without the least realization."

The dark man seemed to find amused satisfaction in the look of mystified enthusiasm on Tony's face. He waved a manicured hand.

"Look at this restaurant. Here. Tonight," he said, beaming. "Today, for example, Calcutta could have vanished in a tidal wave and be sunk forever under the sea. Or it could not. Here and now, we knowing nothing about it, such an event would still have made no slightest difference. So that from this restaurant tonight we could walk out into two different worlds—you into the one where such an event had taken place, and I into the world where it did not. And I might go and live peacefully and die of old age in the Calcutta which to you was utterly destroyed."

"But we are in the same world!" protested Tony. "We'll stay in the same world!"

"Probably, but are you sure?" Mr. Emurian twinkled through his glasses. "We have never seen each other before. How do you know that I have always lived in this particular world? How do you know that the history of the world in which I was born is the same? I was surely not taught the same history! And if we separate here tonight, and you never see or hear of me again, how will you know that I remain in the world you inhabit?"

Tony said painfully, but with his heart beating fast:

"I—guess I won't. But there's no proof, either, that—"

"We agree," said Mr. Emurian, nodding. "There can be no proof. I have told you a legend. It says that there are other worlds. They are not quite real to us, because we cannot reach them at will. But according to legend they touch each other at many places, and it is possible to travel from one to another, and in fact we constantly visit the frontier cities of other worlds without ever knowing it. We do not know it, because we are a part of our own world, and there is an attraction; a magnetism; a gravitation, perhaps; which draws us back before we stray far through the gateway of a world which is not our own."

He regarded Tony benevolently through his eyeglasses.

"As for your coin—sometimes that gravitation or that attraction is not enough. We stray deep into other worlds and doubtless we are very unhappy. Or an object from another world strays into ours. But always the gravitation or the magnetism remains to some degree. That is what my friend in Ispahan believes—so firmly that he might be willing to pay you as much as two thousand dollars for the coin in your hand."

Tony looked at the coin with deep respect. He had never in all his life before owned anything worth even a fraction of two thousand dollars. His conscience spoke in no uncertain terms. He said slowly:

"I—suppose I ought to sell it, then. I can't really afford to carry around a luck-piece as valuable as that. I—might lose it." After a moment, he said wistfully: "I suppose your friend is a coin collector?"

"Not at all," said Mr. Emurian. "He is a businessman. He would use the coin, I am sure, to get into this other world and set up a branch of his business there. He would import Barkutian dates or dried figs or rugs, or possibly gold and frankincense and myrrh. He might deal in ivory and apes and peacocks in exchange for Birmingham cutlery, printed cotton cloth, and kerosene lamps. And if the atmosphere were congenial he might establish a residence there, staffed with pretty slave girls and Mameluke guards, and settle down to a life of comfortable luxury with no fear of atomic bombs and Communism."

Tony said more wistfully still:

"How would the coin guide him to Barkut?"

Mr. Emurian gently shook an admonitory finger.

"You accept my legend as fact, my dear sir! You are a romantic!" Then he added comfortably: "I do not know how he would use the coin as a guide. I do know that he would consider that it was not quite real in this world, and hence should be exempt from some physical laws. He would expect it to have some tendency to become more real, which it could only do by returning to its own time and place. How the tendency would show itself, I cannot guess. But I will write down my friend's name and address. I promise that he will pay you a high price for your token."

Tony Gregg looked almost hungrily at the coin. An idea came into his head. His conscience, its eyes on that two thousand, protested indignantly.

"I'll let the coin decide," he said unhappily. "Heads I sell it, tails I don't."

He tossed. The coin thumped on the table. Tails. He gulped in relief and pushed back his chair.

"It's settled," he said, flushing a little in his excitement. "And—and I won't take your friend's address because I—don't want to be able to change my mind."

Mr. Emurian beamed.

"A romantic!" he said approvingly. "It is admirable! I wish you good fortune, sir!"

Tony thanked him confusedly and paid his bill and departed.

Outside, in the spottily lighted street, he felt more or less dazed; his conscience prodded him, bitingly reproachful, demanding that he go back and get the address he had just refused. This was in the Syrian quarter, on lower East Broadway, with signs in Arabic in those scattered shop windows still lighted. Most of the buildings about were dark and silent, and there were only very occasional lumbering trucks for traffic. The atmosphere was a compound of the exotic and the commonplace that did not make for clear thinking. The facts were staggering, too. If the coin in Tony's pocket was worth two thousand dollars, that in itself was enough to make him dizzy. He had never carried more than a week's salary in his pocket at any time, and never that for long.

So he rode uptown on a subway train which had come from Atlantic Avenue, Brooklyn, and would go uptown only to Times Square. At Times Square he changed trains like a sleepwalker and went further uptown still. He was lost in excited, dazzled speculation which hardly let him notice his surroundings. He had come up from the subway exit and was walking toward his lodging when he realized he'd been too agitated to eat the *shishkebab* he'd paid for. He came to a diner, and was still hungry. He automatically flipped the coin. It came heads. He went into the diner. The man at the stool next to him got up and went out. He left a paper that he'd stuck under him when he finished with it. Tony thriftily retrieved it while waiting for his hamburger and coffee. Then a thrill went all the way down his backbone and he nearly choked. The paper was *Racing Form*.

On the way uptown Tony'd had a bitter argument with his infuriated conscience. He'd insisted defensively that if an importer of dates and dried figs and rugs in Ispahan could find profit in a journey to Barkut, why couldn't an up-and-coming young American do even better? Tony was no businessman, but he'd been trained to believe that anybody who did not desire above all things to be a brisk young executive had something wrong with him. So he'd been insisting feverishly that commerce in electric refrigerators, nylon stockings, fertilizer, lipstick and bubble gum was his life's ambition, and this was his chance. But actually, his mind had kept slipping off sidewise to visions of white-walled cities under a blazing sun, and of lustrous-eyed slave girls and Mamelukes armed with scimitars, and of camel caravans winding over desert wastes.

It was in a hopeless confusion of such images that he left the diner and went to his room, clutching *Racing Form* fast. He sat up till long past midnight, flipping the coin and charting out a crucial test of its virtues. He dreamed chaotically all night, and when morning came he awoke with common sense—i.e., his conscience—reviling him bitterly for his plans.

But he would not be shamed out of them. His conscience grew strident and then almost hysterical, but he sneaked out of the house with a hangdog air as if to avoid his own eyes, and rode to Belmont Racetrack with his hat pulled down over his forehead. When he put down the first two dollars at the betting window his conscience had been reduced to the point of simply jeering at him for a fool and a romantic, refusing a chance to sell a crazy luck-piece for two thousand dollars so he could use it to guide him in making two-dollar bets! A horse named Rainy Sunday? said his conscience derisively. Tomorrow would be Black Friday when he was fired for taking an unauthorized day off!

But Rainy Sunday won, paying six for two. Then Occiput paid off. Then, in order, Slipstream, and Miss Inflation, and Quiz Kid, and Armageddon . . . and the daily double . . .

Tony rode back to town in a sort of stunned composure. He had a trifle—a few hundred—more than eleven thousand dollars in his pocket. His conscience told him with icy disapproval that it had all been coincidence, and that now the proper thing for him to do was put that eleven thousand dollars in good, conservative securities, and never go near a race track again.

So Tony went up to his room and packed in feverish haste while his conscience yammered at him in mounting agitation, paid his rooming-house bill, and went out and flagged a taxi while the mood of resolution—and escape—was upon him. In the taxi he flipped the coin to see where he should head in order to take the coin nearer to Barkut. If there was a mysterious attraction trying to pull the coin back to its own world, it would obviously work on probability, operating to cause coincidences that would take it home. And if somebody was letting it guide him by flipping it for heads and tails . . .

Well, there was eleven thousand dollars to make the theory seem likely.

A couple of weeks later Tony considered the theory proved. At that time he had reached, he was fairly sure, a place well off any imaginable map of the world he had been born in. He stood on a sandy beach with blue sea to his left and desert on all other sides. A middle-sized whirlwind or sand-devil spun meditatively in one place a quarter-mile away, seeming to watch.

Tony had one desert Arab, very much unwashed, squirming under his right foot, and two other equally unwashed scoundrels coming furiously at him with spears from right and left. At this moment he thought irrelevantly, but not at all regretfully, of the tossings of the coin that had begun his journey.

He did not have time for philosophizing, however. So he swung the long, curved scimitar in his hand, pulled his belted-in-the-back topcoat out of the way with his left hand, and faced his would-be assassins.

Chapter 2

It could have been a very happy journey—up to the unwashed scoundrels, at least—but Tony's conscience had tried to spoil everything. It spoke with an inflection very much like the maiden aunt who'd raised him. Tony would get into trouble, said his conscience gloomily, for slipping off without a passport, and actually bribing somebody to help him do it. He should have paid the income tax on that eleven thousand dollars and put the rest in gilt-edged bonds. He should not have flown across the South Atlantic in a plane of such antiquity, to a flying field in Tunisia instead of to a proper airport where he would have been arrested for not having proper papers. He should not have slugged the Tunisian customs official who was planning to arrest him anyhow, even though the coin had blithely come heads when tossed for the decision. And certainly, having done so, he should not have tucked a hundred-dollar bill in officialdom's fingers for the man to find when he came to. To be sure, the official had pocketed the bill and kept his mouth shut, but fifty would have been enough. After all, where was more money coming from when this was gone, and what was Tony gaining in exchange for wasted cash?

So said Tony's conscience, which was a born killjoy. He ignored it as much as he could. It was exhilarating to dodge regulations and red tape after a lifetime subject to them. His conscience said aggrievedly that he was now a felon and would presently be confined in a jail with primitive sanitary arrangements. Tony's maiden aunt, who had formed his conscience, had been hell on sanitation.

But Tony paid no heed. He spent money lavishly and got in return things which he prized highly. A sight of the sun setting on the desert. Once a bare glimpse of a dusky Arab damsel's face when the wind blew aside her veil. The smell of horses and camels and the East generally—concentrated it was bad, but when sufficiently diluted it was delectable—and that gorgeous time near the end of his journeying when a skinny thief tried to rob him in the bazaar at Suakim on the Red Sea and Tony grandly rescued him from the blows of indignant merchants who had meant to rob Tony in another manner. Afterward, too, he'd hired the thief to be his guide and interpreter. The coin came heads when he tossed it for the decision.

These things gave him satisfactions not to be obtained from the actions approved by common sense and the code of conduct a right-thinking young future executive should abide by. Tony thrived on them. He put on weight. He grew sunburned. Contentedly going where the toss of a coin suggested, knowing nothing of what the next instant would bring except that it would be unexpected, he straightened up from what had been an incipient bookkeeper's stoop. He walked with a freer motion and looked—this was the odd part—a much more likely prospect for a young executive's job than he had ever looked before.

His conscience grudgingly conceded as much, but waxed ever more bitter as Tony spent his funds lavishly for progress toward whatever unknown destination the supposedly homing coin would lead him to. Curiously, the coin did come an almost mathematically exact even number of heads and tails over a reasonable period of time. The laws of chance were not broken by an excess of heads, or tails, or excessively long runs of either. There could be absolutely no guarantee that Tony's travels were guided by anything but purest arbitrary chance. But his journeying was convincingly direct, when he plotted it on a map. He'd come as straight as transportation facilities would allow to Suakim on the Red Sea.

Suakim is and always will be a hot and sleepy and odorous town full of Arabs, Tamils, Somalis, and other persons who regard non-Moslems—their official rulers included—as the destined and legitimate prey of the Faithful. Tony's newly hired interpreter considered Tony his express and particular prey. For a time he tried valiantly to collect by wheedling Tony to make purchases on which he—the interpreter—would collect commissions of from fifty to seventy-five percent. For one long night he waited hopefully for Tony to snore, so that he could rob his baggage. But Tony slept dreamlessly and silently, like a child.

Then the interpreter's opportunity came.

On the third day of Tony's stay in Suakim—the coin came invariably tails at any suggestion of departure—Tony made some small purchase in the bazaar. He gave an Egyptian pound in payment. In the change there was a small silver coin with an inscription in conventionalized Arabic script on one side, and an ornate, empty throne on the other. Tony regarded it with apparent calm. He showed it to his hired thief.

"This is a coin of Barkut," he told the man who was itching to rob him. "It is my desire to go to Barkut. Arrange it."

He went back to the fly-infested hotel, where he paid nine prices for his lodging. He spent some time flipping the coin. He had changed a good deal inside as well as out, once he'd learned how to grow really stern with his conscience. The coin turned up some heads and some tails. If it actually had a homing instinct, it gave him essential information. If everything had been a matter of chance up to now, and the series of coincidences between fact and the heads-and-tails decisions of the coin were about to end, it simply led him to preparations for an over-elaborate suicide.

Within the hour, his interpreter came back to the hotel with voluble assurances that he had engaged a *bakhil* to carry Tony to Barkut. It was taking on the last of its cargo now. It would put out into the harbor at sunset, and Tony must board it secretly during the night because of harbor regulations.

Tony packed. He was reasonably well outfitted, now. He dressed for his journey in the absolute ultimate of the inappropriate. He wore a soft felt hat, brightly polished brown shoes, and a camel's-hair topcoat with a belt in the back. He slipped a revolver in his pocket.

Night fell. Tony dined, as well as the resources of Suakim would permit, and felt expansive and contented and anticipative. Two hours after dark, his interpreter returned with news that the *bakhil* was out in the harbor and awaited his coming. Tony went down to the water front of Suakim—a not too cautious move in itself, alone and at night. He climbed down a ladder into a small boat and placidly let himself be rowed out into the darkness. The night was black, save that stars glowed enormously against a sky like velvet. The sleepy, murmurous sounds of the city were very romantic indeed. There was the lapping of waves, and somewhere a wraith of string music where revelers made merry, and somewhere a dog barked indignantly in the darkness. That was all, except the sound of the oars.

Presently a dark form loomed ahead. The *bakhil* was an ungainly shape some seventy or eighty feet long, with the stubby thick mast and colossal boom on her lateen rig. Tony's interpreter hailed. A guttural voice replied. The small boat came alongside the *bakhil* and the interpreter steadied it for Tony to step on board. He climbed to the deck. The *bakhil* stank glamorously of fish and pearl oysters and goat hides and kerosene and tar and bilge water and humanity. Its deck was an impenetrable maze of shadows in the starlight. Tony drew a deep breath of complete satisfaction. He moved aside to be out of the way.

Then there was an infuriated howl, plus the sound of oars being worked at most enthusiastic speed. Tony's interpreter and guide had obsequiously held the small boat to allow him to board the *bakhil*. The unwashed cutthroats of its crew had prepared to receive Tony's baggage. Instead, they saw and heard the shore boat being rowed away at the topmost speed of which the interpreter was capable.

The *bakhil's* crew howled with rage, which was not righteous indignation at the witnessing of a theft, but the much greater rage of being cheated of the privilege of stealing Tony's possessions for themselves. Men raved up and down the deck, uttering deep-throated maledictions at the top of their voices. Then, forward, the loudest voice shouted down the others. A small boat from the *bakhil* splashed overside. It went cursing after the racing oar strokes of the boat with Tony's baggage in it.

Tony stepped delicately to the stern and ensconced himself against the rail. He got a cigarette lighter and lighted a cigarette and smoked it happily, still holding the lighter in his hand. This event had been implied in the series of heads and tails the golden coin of Barkut had turned up when he spun it for decisions on how he should prepare for the trip by sea. All this uproar was consoling confirmation of the homing tendency of the ten-dirhim piece. He smoked beatifically, while out on the dark harbor water one small boat manned by cutthroats went raging after another small boat manned by a sneak thief, and the crew of the *bakhil* listened between cursings to the sounds on the water.

Far off, there was a howl of fury. Still farther, a triumphant yell of derision. The small boat of the *bakhil* came back in a thick fog of sulphurous language,

Tony's late interpreter evidently having made the shore and gotten away with his loot.

The boat's crew scrambled to the deck. The boat itself was made fast overside. There was much muttered talk. Then men came astern to where Tony smoked in blissful excitement. They circled him deliberately. He snapped his cigarette lighter. Its glow showed him the villainous bearded faces of the *bakhil's* crew. Hairy chests and ragged garments. Knives gleaming and ready.

And the lighter's flame showed them Tony, puffing joyously on a cigarette, with one hand holding the lighter with its flickering flame, and the other holding a cocked revolver.

There was a pause without words.

Then a launch's internal combustion engine caught somewhere. It began to run with a sort of purring roar. A harbor launch. A police launch, probably, ready to investigate the howls of fury on the harbor's dark waters. If Tony were murdered here and now, his body might have to be slid overboard still unrobbed, and even that would be dangerous. More, he might kill somebody first.

The sound of the police-launch motor moved across the harbor. A voice grunted urgently on the *bakhil's* deck, and the group before Tony melted. Men swarmed to ropes and spars. The great lateen sail rose creaking against the sky, and forward, men hauled feverishly at a crude windlass to lift the *bakhil's* anchor. Then slowly, slowly, slowly, in what were hardly catspaws of wind off the land, the *bakhil* gathered way.

It moved creakingly but very smoothly over the water. When the police launch was at its nearest, Tony

tossed his cigarette overboard and blandly watched
it go by. He was contentedly confident that all went
well.

But his conscience wailed, as the police launch
departed. Now he would be killed, and there would be
nobody in all the world who would ever admit to the
least idea of his fate. He could be traced—perhaps!—to
Suakim, though even that was unlikely. But from
Suakim on he would seem to have evaporated. With
dawn, the *bakhil* would be remote from all witnesses
to happenings on its deck. Tony would be murdered
and robbed, and his few remaining possessions divided
among these cutthroats who had surely no intention
of taking him to any agreed-on destination! And what
good had he done, or even tried to do? Even if he
unthinkably escaped murder, now, he had not even
pretended to make inquiries in Suakim on the probable
products of Barkut, of the market it might offer for
imports, or even of the possible profit in import-export
trade! He had thrown away his life, and more—here
Tony's conscience grew acrimonious—he had not made
one single move that a brisk young executive would
have made first of all!

Chapter 3

The *bakhil* cleared the harbor. The wind freshened,
and she bent to the breeze and her forefoot cut into
the swells. Tony smoked contentedly. He reflected
that something like this untraceability was necessary

for a journey to Barkut and other places not on topo-
graphic surveys. If the area about a gateway were ever
searched for a person who had gone through it, that
very search would change it, so that somehow it would
cease to be identical in the two worlds, and so would
cease to be a gateway. In ancient days, when news
traveled slowly and searches for missing persons were
unthought of, there must have been many gateways
indeed. That would account for the wild fables which
none believed, nowadays, but which were probably
history in some world or other. There was probably a
brisk trade between places where magic lamps were
functional devices, and prosaic places like the world
of Tony's youth. Now gateways were probably rare
and trade almost nonexistent. But not quite. He had
the proof of that!

So Tony grinned happily to himself in the starlight
at the *bakhil's* stern. He let his imagination run riot
in pictures of white-walled cities under a brazen sky,
and camel caravans in slow motion over fabled sands,
and—to be honest about it—he meditated with some
interest upon the possibility of lustrous-eyed slave
girls whose sense of duty to their master might make
them very interesting companions—if one happened
to be their master.

When the sun rose he was still thinking about the
sort of residence a successful young executive might
set up in Barkut if that land were as uninhabited as
the bald-headed man had suggested in the *shishkebab*
restaurant. But about him there was no sign of any
sort of civilization. The *bakhil* glided smoothly over
waves that were neither high nor negligible. The sea
was of an improbable but fascinating color. The sky

was lapis lazuli, and the *bakhil* was sheer archaic clumsiness. The heavy, bending boom which carried her mainsail seemed about to crack with the burden of patched canvas and wind which strained it. The crew was as unsavory a gang of cutthroats as ever a director sought in vain for a motion picture. There was not a man who did not carry a knife in plain view, and few who had not been liberally scarred by the knives of others. The captain's face looked very like a rough sketch for a crossword puzzle blank.

None spoke a word to Tony. All glowered when he met their eyes. The *bakhil* sailed on a course Tony could not determine, toward a destination he could not guess—except that it surely was not Barkut—and there was apparently no soul on board but himself who spoke English or had any feeling but that of murderous antipathy toward him.

He flipped the golden ten-dirhim piece and felt exceeding peace fill all his being. Crew members saw the glint of gold in the sunshine. If Tony moved from the rail and one of them could get behind him, the result would be final. If he dozed, he would wake in another world, but not very likely Barkut. His life hung upon the fact that he had a revolver, and that it might cost lives to kill him. He waited contentedly all through the baking-hot day for nightfall, quite well aware that with the darkness plans would take effect to abate the nuisance of his living presence.

Came the sunset. Glorious reds and golds. The surface of the sea looked like molten aureate metal. The whiskered villains of the *bakhil*'s crew prostrated themselves in pious prayer unto Allah, and then began low-toned discussions over the most practical way of inserting some six or seven inches of steel into Tony's liver.

He beamed. He was alive. This was life and zest and adventure such as he had never known or dreamed of before. His conscience was despairingly silent. Tony would not have changed places with anyone on earth.

The sun sank below the horizon. Darkness seemed to flow over the world from the horizon on every hand. Obscurity blotted out the edge of the world, and shadows appeared and grew opaque upon the *bakhil's* deck, and Suhail, the great star, shone brightly in a dimming sky. Then it was night.

Men gathered forward. And Tony tossed overboard his twentieth cigarette of the day, and heard it hiss briefly as it touched the water. He moved briskly, silently.

The helmsman closed his eyes and sank to the deck. Darkness hid his sorrow. He had been the victim of a scientific gun-whipping learned by Tony in a neighborhood movie palace on Amsterdam Avenue, while watching Randolph Scott in the role of a frontier marshal. Tony re-pocketed the revolver, hauled the trailing small boat close under the *bakhil's* stern; then he pushed the great tiller hard over. The lubberly *bakhil* came heavily up into the wind and hung there. Its lateen sail flapped crazily. The ship careened, the massive boom swung over and increased its heel, and then the *bakhil* seemed simply to shiver irresolutely, dead in the water, all way gone.

Tony slipped over the stern into the small boat. He took to the oars as a displeased outcry arose on deck. He pulled off into the darkness. He had no idea where he might be, save that he was roughly twenty hours slow sail from Suakim. He might be anywhere along the African eastern coast, or along either of two shores of Arabia. The essential thing was to get away from the *bakhil* where his murder was at the moment being loudly promised.

He got away. When some sort of order seemed to be restored on the ship, he ceased his rowing and muffled his oars. Then he went back to work, pulling sturdily up-wind. The *bakhil* had somewhat less than the sailing properties of an ordinary washtub. Pulling upwind from her, he might progress faster to windward by manpower than she could by sail. Certainly, once he was lost in the darkness she would never find him again.

She did not. After half an hour, Tony Gregg—clad in soft felt hat, highly polished brown shoes, and a camel's-hair topcoat belted in the back—curled himself up on the bottom-boards of the little boat and went contentedly to sleep. His last conscious thought was a mild wonderment that even this landing-boat had a pervading aroma of fish, pearl oysters, goat hides, bilge water, kerosene, and the unwashed humanity that occupied it recently.

Bumpings awakened him. The boat's keel thumped on a sandy bottom. He opened his eyes and saw a colossal, amiably stupid face gazing open-mouthed down at him. He knew immediately that it was an illusion, because it was five feet from ear to ear and definitely on the misty side—a countenance formed in vapor. He closed his eyes resolutely and told himself to wake up. When he opened them again there was naturally nothing in sight but very blue, very clear sky above the gunwale. But the boat bumped again. Tony sat up and saw a sandy shore and a sandy beach and a sandy stretch of pure barrenness beyond. There was no surf. Fairly gentle waves bumped the small boat, and bumped it again, and gradually edged it toward the strand on which the swells broke in half-hearted foaming.

There was just one really curious feature about the world he saw. That oddity was a minor, dark-colored whirlwind—actually a sand devil—which wavered its way along the beach a hundred yards away. It looked—the thought was fanciful—rather like the picture of a *djinn* coming out of a bottle that had been in a copy of the *Arabian Nights* Tony had owned as a small boy. He noted the resemblance, but of course thought no more of it. For one thing, there was no bottle. For another, this small whirlwind traveled in a wholly natural fashion. It went a couple of hundred yards further and then seemed to stop, spinning in a meditative fashion.

Tony sat at ease until the boat finally grounded. Then he seized the moment of a receding wave to step overside and walk smartly ashore without wetting more than the soles of his low-cut shoes. Safely on land, he was—and almost infinitely alone. There was sea on the one hand, and sand on the other. That was all. There was not even a sea bird flapping over the waves. Only the whirling sand devil remained to break stillness. It was rather peculiar that it was so dark, when whirling above such white sand. It looked rather like smoke.

He flipped the ten-dirhim piece. He marched valiantly along the shore in obedience to its decision.

He covered half a mile. The whirlwind persisted. It moved inland. It grew taller, as if to keep him in view. Odd . . .

Then three men on camels came over the crest of a sand dune and halted, regarding him. He waved to them. They came toward him, shading their eyes to search for possible companions beyond and behind him. But he was patently alone. They gobbled in low tones at one another.

They came closer and dismounted and regarded him, with cat-in-canary-cage smiles. They were whiskered, they were dirty, and they were almost certainly verminous. One, short and fat, fingered a scimitar suggestively. The other two carried spears. The small whirlwind moved restlessly, half a mile away. The three men ignored it.

Tony flipped the ten-dirhim piece. It glittered goldenly in the sunshine. The expressions of the trio changed from merely ominous greed to resolution. The short man with the scimitar swaggered up to Tony. The two others watched with glittering eyes. The short man said something that probably meant "Gimme!" Tony flipped the ten-dirhim piece. The man with the scimitar scowled and grabbed. Tony swung. Hard, to the whiskers. He felt a certain naive pride when the whiskered man went flat on his back, wheezing in astonishment. He snatched up the scimitar and said sternly to the others:

"I'm on my way to Barkut. But I'll be glad to pay you—"

The other two men came for him at a run. They had very practical spears, which they carried in an accustomed manner. They made for him from two sides, one from the right and one from the left. A scimitar is not a weapon for use against spear. Moreover, Tony found it necessary to keep his foot on the wriggling, wheezing fat man to keep him still. These were desert Arabs—Bedouin—to whom the possession of goods is a sign of luck but by no means of inviolate personal ownership. If somebody has something they want and they can with reasonable safety take it, they do so, rejoicing.

Tony learned this fact later. At the moment he was only aware that they meant definitely to kill him for the ten-dirhim piece whose glint in the sunshine had roused their cupidity. They were remote from all law or other reasons for restraint. The spearmen plunged for him, eyes intent. Tony thought, in one masterpiece of irrelevant reflection, of the moment when he had begun this journey by flipping a coin. But still he would not have changed places with anybody in the world.

He took action. It was pure instinct. The scimitar in his hand had a good deal of the feel of a slightly heavy tennis racquet. It even balanced like a racquet. The left-hand spearman was nearest.

Tony swung the scimitar as for a neat back-hand return-volley stroke. The head of the spear sprang off. Quickly he turned and with the scimitar served a fast though imaginary ball straight over the net. He followed through. The second spearman got in the way. Tony still followed through. He saw his victim with unforgettable clarity—pure, bearded villainy with one eye and a sword-split nose. Then the scimitar landed. The result was colorful—mostly red—and unquestionably lethal. Tony wanted to be sick, and to avoid it he turned on his two remaining foes. The short fat man was on his feet now, still wheezing. The spearman looked dazed. They ran. Tony chased them with his reddened scimitar. They headed at first straight for the whirlwind, but then swerved around it, almost warily; just as it obligingly started to get out of their way. They vanished over sand hills.

Tony stopped, panting. He went back to the scene of the conflict. He carefully did not look at the man he'd hit with the scimitar. There were three camels, still kneeling. Tony wanted to get away from there. He tethered two of them to the third, and mounted that one. Nothing happened. He kicked it.

The camel, offensively chewing a reeking cud, got up hind-end first, and Tony nearly fell off. Then it resignedly began to move in some indefinite direction. The other two camels followed docilely. The whirlwind moved companionably along with them—never very near, but never quite out of sight. At times it was a mile away and of respectable size. Sometimes it was only a couple of hundred yards off, and not more than twenty or thirty feet high. But it followed persistently, rather like an interested stray dog following a man whose smell fascinates it.

Hours later—many hours later—a white-walled city appeared in the distance. Date groves surrounded it. There were minarets within the wall, and a lacy structure comparable for beauty of design to the Taj Mahal—only the Taj Mahal is a tomb. A camel caravan moved unhurriedly away from its gates, bound for some place of mystery on beyond.

The whirlwind fell behind, as if bashful. It stretched

upward and upward—again as if to keep Tony in sight—until it was merely the most tenuous of mistinesses. That was when he was almost at the edge of the oasis. Then it vanished suddenly, as if it had collapsed.

Tony Gregg rode up to the nearest city gate and slid down his camel's off foreleg, which stank. Soldiers in turbans and slippers and carrying flintlock muskets looked at him in lively suspicion. He essayed to speak. They essayed to speak. Then they all stared. Presently two of them took him gingerly by the arm and led him through the city streets.

The smells and sights and sounds he encountered were those of a dream city—though the smells were not altogether those of a pretty dream. There were flat-topped houses and veiled women and proud camels and bearded men. There were barred, narrow windows and metal-studded doors, and projecting upper stories to the houses which leaned out above the narrow streets and nearly blotted out the sky.

The two soldiers led Tony, thrilled and satisfied, into a dark doorway. They released him. They stepped back. There was a conclusive *clang*. And Tony saw that the doorway was completely filled by a grille of very solid and very heavy grim iron bars, through which he and the soldiers blinked at each other. He was in a prison. He was in a partially open-air dungeon. He was, in fact, in the clink.

This was the manner of his arrival in Barkut.

Chapter 4

Three weeks later, in mid-morning, Tony sat comfortably in the shady part of the courtyard and looked more or less dreamily at the slave girl Ghail's legs. She had nice legs, and rather a lot of them was on display. They were slim, as a girl's legs ought to be, and they tapered nicely to the knee, and then they flared just the right amount at just the right place below them, and went down to very nice ankles, and below them to small bare feet—very dusty at the moment—one of which tapped ominously on the floor of the courtyard. He was still kept behind a locked iron grate, technically imprisoned, and his conscience had had a swell time pointing out to him how completely irresponsible and harebrained and half-witted all his actions had been. He was, however, unworried except over the reaction that tapping foot might presage.

At first, of course, he'd been totally unable to speak Arabic, and nobody in Barkut seemed to be able to speak English. He'd tried to communicate from his original prison cell with the help of a dog-eared guide book he'd picked up second-hand in Suez. The vocabulary it offered, however, was limited. It gave the phrases for complaining that prices were too high, that the food was overripe, and that the speaker wanted to go back to his hotel. But in Barkut Tony had been charged nothing, the food was good if monotonous—though fresh ripe dates had been a revelation to him—and he was in jail and had no hotel. After two days of this unsatisfactory conversation, he'd been moved to a convenient cell-and-courtyard in the palace. He'd been inspected by various whiskered people he thought were officials, and then the slave girl Ghail had appeared and resolutely set to work to teach him to talk.

That was the way she undoubtedly looked at it. Tony was presumably an adult male, but he babbled only a few Arabic words, and those with a vile accent. The slave girl had settled down to the job with something like a scowl. She had an imperial carriage, which Tony recalled vaguely could be credited to the carriage of burdens on her head as a child. She was long-legged and lissome and had an air of firm competence, and he knew she was a slave girl because married women and the marriageable daughters of citizens walked the streets—if at all—only when swathed in voluminous robes and with veils which complied with the strictest of Moslem traditions. This girl Ghail was not swathed to speak of, and she was not veiled at all, and she was distinctly pretty and very far from shapeless. And she regarded Tony with a scowling disparagement which made him work earnestly to learn to carry on a conversation.

Matters had progressed nicely in three weeks, and Tony found himself possessed of a talent for languages. But now she tapped her foot ominously on the floor of his comfortable prison. She said, in measured calm:

"Now, just what do you mean by that?"

Tony spoke apologetically. But he was pleased with the fluency he displayed in the Arabic she had taught him.

"I wanted to know."

"And just why did you want to know the name of

my owner and the value in money that is placed upon me?" demanded the girl.

"Sooner or later," explained Tony, trying hard to be convincing, "I shall be questioned by the rulers of this place. I think that is why you have been set to teach me the language. When I am questioned and can explain myself, I shall become high in favor, and rich. It was my thought that then—Allah permitting—I would purchase you from your owner."

The slave girl's foot tapped more forbiddingly still.

"And for what purpose," she demanded icily, "would you wish to purchase me?"

Tony looked at her in pained astonishment. His conscience mentioned acidly that this conversation was not only improper but indiscreet. A brisk young executive would never . . . To which Tony replied that he wouldn't have much fun, then. When his conscience began a heated rejoinder, he cut it short.

"Truly," said Tony in false piety, "somebody has undoubtedly said that the desires of a man's heart are many, but that if there is not one woman more desirable than all else, he is not human."

His Arabic was still sketchy, but he put it over. The girl's eyes, however, instead of warming, burned angrily. "You are human?" she demanded.

"All too human," admitted Tony, "what else?"

She stood up in queenly indignation. She smiled— but painfully and with contempt, like someone speaking to a half-wit or worse.

"You came across the desert from the sea," she said tolerantly, "riding one camel and leading two others. But an hour before your coming, one of the watchers on the city wall had seen a *djinn* in the desert. When you came, so stupid that you could not even speak the language of humans, do you think we did not know you for what you are—a *djinn*?"

"A *djinn*," said Tony blankly. The word was one of the very few—alcohol was another—which would be the same in Arabic and English. "Do you mean those creatures of the Thousand and One Nights?"

"Of history, yes." Ghail's tone was bitingly scornful. "And if we had doubted, within the hour there came a Bedouin to the city gate, a one-eyed man with a sword-slit nose, who told us of your taking the form of a bale of rich silk, torn open upon the beach of the sea. When he and his companions alighted from their camels to gather up the wealth, you changed instantly to the likeness of a young man strangely garbed and ran swiftly to their camels and flogged them away faster than the men could follow. The man demanded his camels, and they were those you brought to the gates of the city. So they were yielded to him. Do you deny now that you are of the *djinn*?"

Tony swallowed, hard. A one-eyed man with sword-slit nose? That was the man he had killed, back at the seashore! He'd been trying hard to forget the encounter, though if he'd ever had to pick out anybody on looks alone to be worked over with a scimitar, that man would have been the one. But—he could not have come and demanded the camels! It was not possible! Tony had left him an exceedingly messy object on the sand, and had chased his two companions with the scimitar as much in horror of his first dead man as out of any sort of anger. He swallowed again, very pale.

"You could not speak our human language." Ghail was tolerant, and scornful, and amused. "So I taught it to you. We hoped to make a bargain with you, because some of you *djinn* are willing to be traitors to your race. Perhaps you are ready to make such a bargain. But it is insolence for one of the *djinn* to think of purchasing a human slave!"

Even Tony's conscience was stunned, now.

"L-look!" he said desperately. "In my world, *djinns* are only fables! What do they look like?"

"When the watcher on the city wall saw you on the desert, you had the form of a whirlwind. Why not? Is not that the way in which you travel?"

Tony swallowed yet again. His conscience had made a quick recovery. Now it began to say something piously satisfied about now look what a jam he'd gotten himself to, actually thinking romantic thoughts about an idiot girl who believed in imaginary creatures like *djinns* and *efreets!* But Tony shut it up. He saw implications of the theory of multiple worlds that he hadn't realized before. What is true in one world is not necessarily true in another. What is false in one world, also, is not invariably false in another. Actually, if there are enough worlds, anything must be true somewhere. Anything!

And he remembered—and flinched at remembering— his impression of a huge, vaporous, open-mouthed face which had been looking down at him in the small boat when he waked on the shore. He remembered the sand devil, the whirlwind, which had looked like dark smoke in spite of the fact that it was whirling over white sand. It had kept pace with him as he went to meet the Bedouin and their attempt to kill him. It had hovered interestedly near during that encounter. And it had wavered hopefully after him all the way across the desert to this city.

He gulped audibly. The inference was crazy—but if this was a world in which *djinns* were real, then craziness was sense. And then something else occurred to him.

"How long after my arrival did the one-eyed man come to claim the camels?" he demanded.

The slave girl shrugged. "One hour. No more. That was why we were sure."

"And the camels were stolen by the seashore."

"You stole them! They were stolen by the sea."

"I traveled some hours by camel," said Tony grimly. "He must have followed their footprints in the sand—if he knew where to demand them. So he traveled as far on foot as I did on camel-back—if he tells the truth! But it took me five hours to reach the city from the sea on camel-back. Yet he made the journey on foot in only one hour more. How fast does the one-eyed man walk? As fast as a camel, even trailing?"

The girl Ghail stared at him. Her face went blank. It was a five-hour journey from the sea to the city. She knew it as well as Tony. That was by camel. On foot it would take a man ten hours or better. If the one-eyed man had trailed the camels, he could not possibly have arrived so soon. Not possibly.

"A whirlwind followed me all the way," said Tony, swallowing. "And—I killed a one-eyed man with a slit nose as he and two companions tried to rob me. Somehow, I think that the one-eyed man who got the three camels sometimes doubles as a whirlwind."

His conscience was strickenly silent. But Ghail

knitted her brows and stamped her bare feet and snapped a number of Arabic words she had never taught Tony. They crackled. They sparked. They seemed to have blue fire around the edges.

"The misbegotten!" she cried furiously: "The accursed of Allah! From his own mouth came the proof that he lied! And we saw it not! *He* was the *djinn!* He has made mock of the wisdom of men! How he will laugh, and all his fellows!"

She turned upon Tony. "And you—you are as stupid as the *djinn!* Why did you never ask about your camels?" She paused suspiciously. "But—were they camels? Perhaps they also were *djinn!* Perhaps it is all a trick! You may be another *djinn!* This might be—"

Tony threw up his hands. "In my world," he said helplessly, "*djinn* are fables."

"Your world?" snapped the girl. "How many worlds did Allah make? And if *djinn* are fables, why is the throne of Barkut empty?"

"On the coins?" asked Tony as helplessly as before.

She stamped her foot once more. "On the coins and in the palace! What sort of fool are you? You say you are human? Will you drink of the *lasf* plant?"

She fairly blazed scorn at him; scorn and vexation and at least the beginning of bewilderment. Tony tried to placate her.

"If *lasf* is not something spelled backwards with added vitamins, and if other humans drink it, I have no objection at all!"

She jumped to her feet and hurried to the barred gateway of the courtyard adjoining his cell. She spoke imperiously through the bars. Even a slave girl can be imperious to other slaves, on occasion. And there was always somebody passing that barred gateway, with full freedom to look in. Tony had chafed at the fact—and been reproached by his conscience for chafing—when Ghail first began her daily lessons in Arabic. Lately he had become resigned. But he still wished stubbornly that things were different.

She came back with a polished brass goblet containing a liquid. She tasted it carefully, as if its contents might be doubtful, and then offered it to Tony.

"This is *lasf*," she said sternly. "It is poisonous to the *djinns*. If you drink, it will be of your own will."

Tony drank it. From the expression on her face, it seemed to be an action of extraordinary importance. He was tempted to make a flourish, but made a face instead. It was not wholly bad. It had a faintly reminiscent flavor, as of something he had drunk before. It tasted a little like some of the herb teas his maiden aunt had dosed him with as a child. From experience he knew that the flavor would last. He would keep tasting it all day, and it ought to be good for something or other, but he could not guess what.

He handed back the goblet.

"I wouldn't say," he remarked, "that it would be a popular soft drink back home, but I have tasted some almost as bad."

Chapter 5

The girl Ghail stared at him in seeming stupefaction. Then, as he regarded her expectantly, she suddenly began to flush. The red came into her cheeks and spread to her temples, and then ran down her throat. He followed its further spread with interest. When it had reached her legs she abruptly ran to the gate and hammered on it, crying out fiercely. Soldiers with whiskers and flintlock muskets appeared instantly, as if they had been kept posted out of sight for an emergency which could only be created by Tony Gregg. They let her out, scowling at him.

He sat down and breathed deeply, staring at the stone wall of his dungeon-courtyard. She'd believed him a *djinn*, eh? *Djinns* were creatures of Arabian mythology. They were able to take any form, and sometimes were doomed to obey the commands of anybody possessing a talisman such as a magic ring or lamp. At other times they could scare the pants off of even a True Believer not so equipped. They kidnapped princesses, whom the heroes of the Arabian Nights unfailingly rescued, and they fought wars among themselves, and they were not quite the same as *efreets*, who were always repulsive, while *djinns* might take the form of very personable humans. They were also not quite so dreadful as *ghuls*—from which the English word "ghoul" is derived—who lived on human flesh.

There was a wooden bench against the wall, at which Tony stared abstractedly. He became aware that it was oscillating vaguely. It thumped this way, and that, and just as the oddity of its behavior really caught his attention, the bench fell over. It tumbled sidewise with a heavy "bump" to the hard-baked clay floor.

Tony looked startled. Then he got up and went

over to the bench. At a moment when *djinns* were
recently made plausible, erratic behavior of furniture
suggesting ghosts was practically prosaic. He examined
the overturned object. There was a minor quivering
of the wood as he touched it. It felt almost alive.

He heaved it up, so completely off base mentally
that he acted in a perfectly normal manner. He was
actually too dazed to do anything else. The quivering
of the bench stopped. He saw a bug on the hard-
baked clay—a beetle, lying on its back and wriggling
its legs frantically. It was pressed solidly into the
clay, as if the full weight of the bench had thrust it
down without crushing it. It was a trivial matter. An
absurd matter. It was insane to bother about a bug
on the ground

But as he looked down at the wriggling black
thing, its outlines misted. A little dustiness appeared
in mid-air, down by the floor. Then Tony Gregg's hair
stood up straight on end, so abruptly that it seemed
that each separate hair should have cracked like a
whiplash. He backed away, goggling.

And a tiny whirlwind appeared, and rose until it was
his own height or maybe a little more, and then an
amiable but unintelligent female face appeared at the
top of it. The face was two feet wide from ear to ear. It
was a bovine, contentedly moronic face with no claim
whatever to beauty. It beamed at him and said:

"Sh-h-h-h-h!"

Tony said:

"Huh?"

"There is danger for me here," said the female face,
beaming. "I have hidden here for days. I was"—it
giggled—"that beetle under the bench. Before that I

was a fly on the wall. My name is Nasim. Please do not tell that I am here!"

Tony gulped. He clenched his hands and stared at the swirl of dust on the courtyard floor. It tapered down practically to a point where he had seen the bug pressed in the clay, but at his own shoulder height it was almost a yard across, like an elongated, unsubstantial top which swayed back and forth above its point of support.

"You are—" Tony gulped. "A—*djinn?*"

"I am a *djinnee*," said the beaming face coyly. Tony gulped again.

"Oh. . . ."

The face regarded him sentimentally. It sighed gustily.

"Do I frighten you in this shape?" it asked, even more coyly than before. "Would you like to see me in human form?"

Tony made an inarticulate noise. The face atop the whirlwind giggled. The mist thickened. Substance seemed to flow upward into it from the ground. A human form appeared in increasing substantiality in the mist. The round face shrank and appeared in more normal size and proportion on the materializing human figure. Tony's mouth dropped open. He abruptly ceased to disbelieve in the existence of *djinns*. He was prepared to concede also the existence of *efreets, ghuls,* leprechauns, ha'nts, Big Chief Bowlegs, the spirit control, and practically anything anybody cared to mention. Because from the small whirlwind a convincingly human female form had condensed

The pink-skinned, rather pudgy, quite unclothed figure cast a look of arch coyness upon Tony.

"Do you prefer me as a human woman?" asked the figure, giggling. "I would like for you to like me. . . ." Tony caught his breath with difficulty.

"Why—er—yes, of course. But—just in case somebody looks in the gate, hadn't you better put some clothes on?"

The *djinnee* who called herself Nasim looked down at her human body and said placidly:

"Oh. I forgot."

Garments began to materialize. And then there was a clanking at the gate, and then a howl of fury, and a flintlock musket boomed thunderously in the confined space of the courtyard. The pink-skinned, pudgy female form seemed to rush outward in all directions. There was a roaring of wind. A dark whirlwind, giggling excitedly, sped upward and fled away. Even in flight, and in the form of a whirlwind, it looked somehow rotund and it looked somehow sentimental.

Then Tony was almost trampled down by half a dozen soldiers with baggy trousers and slippers and flintlock guns which banged and smoked futilely at the vanishing patch of smoke in the sky. And there was a fat man with a purple-dyed beard, and there was Ghail, the slave girl, with a good deal more clothes on than before. She looked at Tony with a distinctly unpleasant expression on her face.

"Now," said Ghail ominously, "would you tell me the meaning of the *djinn* hussy, without any clothes on, in the very palace of Barkut?"

Tony's conscience caught its breath, and began to express its highly unfavorable opinion of things in general, and of Tony in particular.

Chapter 6

Tony Gregg's conscience, as has been noted, was
the creation of the worthy spinster aunt who raised
him. Having no more normal outlet for the creative
instinct, she had labored over Tony's conscience. And
following a celebrated precedent, she made it in her
own image. In consequence, Tony often had a rather
bad time.

That night his conscience, which seemed almost to
be pacing the floor in anguish beside his bed, gave
him the works. Horrible! Horrible! said his conscience.
Here it had spent the best part of his life trying to
make him into a person who, in thirty or forty years
of devotion, scrupulous attention to his duties, and a
virtuous and proper life, would attain to the status of
a brisk young executive. Tony's conscience conveniently
ignored the fact that after thirty or forty years of
virtue and scrupulosity, Tony would neither be young
nor brisk. And what had Tony done? demanded his
conscience bitterly. He had won more than eleven
thousand dollars in the low and disreputable practice
of betting on horse races. But had he invested that
windfall in gilt-edged securities? He had not. He'd
come on a wild-goose chase across half the world, to
arrive at this completely immoral and utterly preposterous place of Barkut! He had spent three weeks in jail!
His conscience metaphorically wrung its hands. And
now—now a slave girl who showed her legs aroused
his amorous fancy. Worse, a female *djinn* with no
modesty whatever—

Tony yawned. He felt somewhat apprehensive

about the *djinnee* who said her name was Nasim, but he was certainly not allured. He was even almost grateful, because the slave girl Ghail had been in the sort of rage a girl does not feel over the misdeeds of a man she cares nothing about. And Tony felt a very warm approval of Ghail. It was not only that she had nice legs. Oh, definitely not! He approved of many other things about her. And besides, she was a nice person. She treated him like an individual human being, and during all his life heretofore, Tony had been surveyed as a possible date, or a possible husband if nothing better turned up, but rarely as a simple human being.

He turned over in bed. He was no longer in his cell, but in something like a bridal or royal suite in the palace. It was so huge that he felt a bit lonely. The ceiling of his bedroom was all of twenty feel tall, and arched, with those sculptured icicles he had seen in pictures of the Alhambra in Spain. The floor was of cool marble tiles, with rugs here and there. The bed itself was hardly more than a pallet upon a stand of black wood ornamented in what certainly looked like gold. The coverings were silk. There was a pitcher of some cooling drink by his elbow, and if he pulled a silken bell cord a slave—male—would come in and pour it out for him.

His position in Barkut had changed remarkably during the day. At the moment of the excitement over Nasim, Ghail had brought a chamberlain with a purple-dyed beard to explain that his imprisonment had been all a mistake. He had been believed a *djinn,* clad in human form for subversive political activity within the city. Since he wasn't a *djinn*—and drinking the *lasf* proved without doubt that he was not—and since he had told the girl Ghail that when he talked to the rulers he would be high in favor and rich, the rulers were naturally anxious to know what he had to offer in exchange for favor and riches. Also—the slave-girl put this in a bit sullenly—if the king of the *djinn* of these parts had sent a *djinnee* at great risk into Barkut to beguile Tony, it was evident that the *djinn* also attached great importance to him. So the rulers of Barkut wanted also to know what that importance was.

Tony had been led to a great hall with zodiacal figures in brass laid flush in the black marble floor. The throne of Barkut stood beneath its canopy against the far wall. It was empty. There were six ancient men seated on rugs before it, smoking water pipes. They smoked and coughed and wheezed and looked unanimously crabbed and old and ineffective. But their red-rimmed eyes inspected the slave girl before they turned to Tony, so he felt that there was some life somewhere in them yet.

They greeted him with fussy politeness and had him sit and then wheezingly asked him who he was and where he came from, and generally what the hell the shooting was about.

The slave girl Ghail intervened before he could answer. She explained that Tony came from a far country, and that he had crossed the farthest ocean on a great flying bird. Tony had told her as much, lacking an exact Arabic term for a transatlantic plane or even for a converted four-motored bomber. He had traveled farther, Ghail added, in a boat of steel with fire in its innards. This was a repetition of Tony's description of the somewhat decrepit steamer from Suez to Suakim. And these things, Ghail said firmly, she had believed to be lies from a more than usually stupid *djinn*. But since Tony was no *djinn* but a human, who was inexplicably sought after by the local *djinn* king, she believed them absolutely.

The six councilors smoked and coughed and made other elderly noises. Tony opened his mouth to speak, and again the slave girl forestalled him.

In his home land, said Ghail truculently, Tony was of a rank second to none. This was her interpretation of his attempt to explain that nobody in America was of higher rank than even he was, as a citizen. He was a prince, Ghail elaborated, journeying in quest of adventure and to see the peoples of the earth—an activity considered highly appropriate in princes. His people had so subdued the *djinn* that they, though only humans, rode in the air with ease and safety, and spake to each other privately though a thousand miles apart, and traveled in personal vehicles with the power of forty and fifty and a hundred horses, and were mightier in war than any other people under the sun.

These statements also Tony had made in the course of his language lessons. He had thought Ghail impressed, then, and she was not an easy person to awe; and now she repeated them parrot-like, with a belligerent air, as if daring anybody to question them. In short, she said, Tony was a very dangerous person. On the side of Barkut he would be dangerous to the *djinn*. On the side of the *djinn*—and the king of the *djinn* had already tried to allure him by the charms of a *djinnee*—he would be dangerous to Barkut. Therefore he should either be secured as an ally of Barkut, or else executed immediately before he could set out to help the *djinn*.

Tony said feebly, "But—"

"Did you not tell me that you were in the greatest of all wars?" Ghail demanded. "In which millions of humans were killed? Did you not say that your nation ended the war by destroying cities instantly, in flame hotter than the hottest fire?"

Tony had unquestionably mentioned atomic bombs. He had also said that he was in the war. He had not mentioned that he spent it at a typewriter—because, of course, Ghail would not know what a typewriter was.

"So you," said the slave girl firmly, "will swear by the beard of the Prophet to lead the armies of Barkut to victory over the *djinn*—or else—"

Ultimately he swore, gloomily and at length, on a book with a binding of marvelously ornamented richness. It was a Koran, and he had never read it and did not believe its contents. More, he did not know what sort of beard the Prophet had affected, so it could not be said that there was a meeting of minds, and possibly the contract was not really valid. But he felt an obligation, nevertheless.

Late that night, unable to sleep, it recurred. The ancient men of the Council of Regents of Barkut had given him their confidence out of the direness of their need. The slave girl Ghail counted on him, because there was no one else to turn to. The danger to Barkut from the *djinn*, he gathered, was extreme. The plant *lasf* was a partial protection against the *djinn*, but bullets merely stung them, and *lasf* grew constantly more difficult to come by, and the *djinn* grew bolder and bolder as the humans in Barkut ran into the technological difficulties inherent in a shortage of *lasf*. Four years ago, the king of the local *djinn* had, in person, kidnapped the authentic queen of Barkut and now held her prisoner. Hence the empty throne and the Council of Regents. For some reason not clear to Tony, the ruler of Barkut could not actually be injured by a *djinn*, though her subjects were not so fortunate. Therefore the Queen's only sufferings were imprisonment and the ardent courtship of the *djinn* king. Still . . .

Lying wakeful in bed in the royal suite of the palace, Tony surveyed this statement of the situation with distrust. It sounded naive and improbable, like something out of the Arabian Nights. It was. Like all the events stemming from his purchase of a ten-dirhim piece in an antique shop on West 45th Street, New York, it was so preposterous that he pinched himself for assurance that his present surroundings were real.

They were. The pinch hurt like the devil. He rubbed it, scowling. Then he heard a thud on the windowsill of his bedroom. He got out of bed, suspicious. He went to the window. Nothing. It looked out upon a small garden, there to please the occupants of this suite. There were grass and shrubbery and small trees and a fountain playing in the starlight. It smelled inviting. Beyond lay the palace, and beyond that the city, and beyond that the oasis and the desert. And somewhere—somewhere unguessable—lay the dominions and the stronghold of the *djinn* beyond the desert.

His conscience wrung its hands. In the fix he was in, to be thinking about *djinns* and captive queens and such lunatic items! How about those fine plans for an import-export business between Barkut and New York? What had he learned about the commercial products of Barkut? What was the possible market for American goods? If he went, with no more than he now knew, to an established firm in New York to get them to take up the matter, what information could he give them that would justify them in offering him an executive position? Why, if he'd only confined his attention to proper subjects like exports and imports instead of trying to rouse the romantic interest of a long-legged slave girl, nobody would ever have thought of asking him to lead an army

Rubbing his leg where it hurt, he gazed out into the garden and rudely thrust his conscience aside. That garden looked romantic in the starlight. He wouldn't mind being out there right now with Ghail . . .

Something stirred on the windowsill almost beside his hand. He started, and in starting dislodged one of the soft silken cushions that were everywhere about this place. It fell to the floor. He saw a tiny dark shape on the sill, like a frog. He groped for a shoe to swat it with, and it jumped smartly into the room. It *was* a frog. He could tell by the way it jumped . . . but it landed on the cushion with a whacking, smacking "thud" such as no frog should make. It sounded like a couple of hundred pounds of steel mashing a pillow flat and banging against the floor beneath. The pillow, in fact, burst under the impact. Stray particles of stuffing flew here and there. The frog disappeared within. From the interior of the burst cushion came explosive swearing in a deep bass voice.

Then the split silken covering inflated and burst anew, and a swirling luminous mist congealed into a solid shape, and Tony found himself staring at an essentially human form. It had the most muscle-bound arms and shoulders he had ever seen, however, and a chest like a wine cask, and a wrestler's knotty legs. Its head and face were of normal size; but it took no effort whatever to realize that the features were those of a *djinn*. The slanting, feral eyes, the white tusks projecting slightly from between the lips, the pointed ears—it was a *djinn*, all right, and a *djinn* in a terrible temper.

"Mortal!" it roared. "You are that strange prince who came across the desert!"

Tony swallowed.

The creature revealed additional inches of tusk.

"You are that creature, that mere human, who ensnared the love of Nasim, the jewel among *djinnees!*" It pounded its chest, which resounded like a tympany. "Know, mortal, that I am Es-Souk, her betrothed! I have come to tear you limb from limb!"

Tony's conscience said acidly that it had told him so. He was not aware of any other mental process. He simply stared, open-mouthed. And the *djinn* leaped on him with incredible agility.

Sinewy, irresistible powerful hands seized his throat. They tightened, and then relaxed as the *djinn* said gloatingly:

"You shall die slowly!"

Then the hands tightened again, bit by bit.

Tony had not lately taken any systematic exercise greater than that of punching buttons in an automat restaurant. It was hardly adequate preparation for a knock-down, drag-out with a *djinn*. He clawed at the strangling hands with complete futility. Then a strange calmness came to him. Perhaps it was resignation. Possibly it was a lurking unbelief in the reality of his experiences, somewhere in the back of his mind. But being strangled, even if it were illusion, was extremely uncomfortable. He remembered a part of the basic combat training he had received before being assigned to sit at a typewriter for the glory of his country's flag. An axiom of that training was that nobody can strangle you if you only keep your head. All you have to do—

Tony did it. Because being strangled is painful.

He reached up with both hands, and in each hand took one—just one—of the *djinn's* sinewy fingers. One complete human hand is stronger than the single finger of even a *djinn*. Tony peeled the single fingers ruthlessly backward. Something snapped.

The *djinn* howled and hooted like an ambulance. Tony hastily repeated the process. Something else cracked. The *djinn* howled louder, and let go. There were dim shoutings and rushing in the corridors of the palace. But Tony remained alone, gasping for breath, in the high-ceilinged room with this creature who said he was Es-Souk the betrothed of Nasim. By now Tony remembered Nasim only as a beaming misty face and a pudgy human figure which had seemed exclusively pink skin. Es-Souk swelled to the size of an elephant, beating his breast and hollering.

Tony coughed. His throat hurt. He coughed again, rackingly.

The monstrous, and now unhuman, figure sneezed. The blast of air practically knocked Tony off his feet. Then Es-Souk uttered cries which were suddenly bellowings of terror. He sneezed again, and the silken bed sheets flapped crazily to the far corners of the room.

Then the *djinn*'s figure melted swiftly into a dark whirlwind which poured through the window. There were poundings on the door, but Tony paid no attention to them. He reeled to the window and stared out.

A shape fled in panic among the stars. It was a whirlwind of dark smokiness, but the stars were very bright. It showed. The whirlwind which was the *djinn* Es-Souk fled in mortal terror—or perhaps immortal terror—from the neighborhood of the palace of Barkut. And as it fled, it paused and underwent a truly terrific convulsion. Lightnings flashed in it. Thunder roared in it. The whole sky and the countryside were lighted by the flashings.

When a whirlwind sneezes, the results are impressive.

Chapter 7

Tony was wakened by the firing of cannon. His heart sank. An attack of some sort upon the city of Barkut? His conscience expressed bitter satisfaction at the possible impending consequences of his misdeeds, all done against his conscience's advice. But Tony listened to the cannon-shots. They were fired at regular

intervals. Which might mean a salute, or might mean
something of a ceremonial nature, but certainly didn't
mean guns being aimed and fired as fast as they bore
on their targets.

He got out of bed and dressed. He had folded his
trousers carefully and put them under the mattress of
his bed. The result would not have satisfied him in New
York, but here it was the nearest approach to a crease
in his pants he'd had since his arrival. He put them on.
He felt better. He began to tuck in his shirt tails.

The door opened. His breakfast, evidently. Two
dark-skinned slaves carried a gigantic silver platter on
which was piled the better part of a roasted sheep.
Fruit. Coffee. Bread, which was in thin, flexible, doughy
sheets more suited for the wrapping of packages than
the making of breakfast toast. With the two male slaves
came two slave girls in garments quite appropriate
for indoors in a hot climate. They were gauzy and
not extensive. One of the girls carried some kind of
musical instrument. They smiled warmly upon Tony
as he finished tucking in his shirt.

"Your breakfast, lord," said one of them brightly.
"The City rejoices in your victory."

"Victory?" said Tony. "What victory?"

"The defeat, lord," said the prettier of the two slave
girls, "of the *djinn* who was sent to slay you who are
the hope of Barkut. The cannons fire and the people
dance in the streets. There will be decorations and
fireworks."

Tony's conscience was skeptical. He shared its view.
But the cannon boomed, nevertheless. Tony's neck
was sore this morning, and he had cold chills down
his back at odd moments. Breaking the *djinn's* fingers

had been a sound Army trick, but this Es-Souk had immediately afterward swelled to the size of at least a hippopotamus, and as soon as he stopped roaring he'd have tackled Tony again, and then there'd have been nothing but a blot left of Tony. Tony still didn't know what had made Es-Souk sneeze or flee in such palpable bellowing terror. Tony's conscience said, with something of the bite of vitriol, that the *djinn* had doubtless sneezed from an incipient cold, and that these two slave girls weren't any too well protected against draughts, either.

He regarded them interestedly as the great silver platter came to rest on folding legs, convenient to his bedside. The two male slaves bowed deeply and departed. The booming of cannon continued. The two girls stayed.

"Hm . . ." said Tony. "You two—"

"We serve you, lord," said the girl with the musical instrument. She seemed quite happy about it. "I play and Esim dances, or she plays and I dance, and both of us carve your meat and pour your sherbet and serve you in all ways."

Tony regarded them again. Slave girls. Unveiled. Very sketchily attired. Very pretty. A charming idea of hospitality. Ghail had nicer legs, but—

His conscience snarled at him.

"So the cannon fire because of my victory!" he observed, reaching out for coffee.

One of them passed it to him, reverently.

"Aye, lord," she said brightly. "Never before in the history of Barkut has a man defeated a *djinn* in single combat. Were they not so stupid, we had been their subjects long ago."

He drank the coffee. So nobody before had ever defeated a *djinn* in single combat? In that case, maybe some sort of celebration was in order. But he gloomily wished he knew how he'd done it. He scowled.

"You seem sad, lord," said the one called Esir, anxiously. "Esim has made a song of your victory. Would you wish that she sing to cheer you?"

Tony grunted. His conscience observed warningly that he did not know anything about the local domestic habits. Perhaps, despite the veils and swathing robes women wore in the streets, it was an old Arabic custom to provide strictly musical entertainment with breakfast in a guest's bedroom.

"You two are slaves?" he asked, as one of them anticipated his reach for an orange and swiftly halved it for him and handed it to him with a tiny golden spoon for him to eat it with.

"Aye, lord. Your slaves," said the two in unison, beaming.

Tony strangled on his first spoonful of orange pulp. They pounded his back anxiously. He coughed and blinked at them.

"You mean—"

"You came to Barkut without attendant, lord," said Esir, happily, "and it was not fitting. So the Council gave us to you, with horses and other slaves, that you might be suitably served. And all of us, your slaves, wished to kneel to you immediately, but Ghail the slave girl said that you had told her you did not wish to be disturbed last night, and therefore we only waited your summons—which did not come."

Tony absorbed the statement. It required considerable absorbing. He opened his mouth, and they hung upon his impending words, and he closed it without saying anything. So, Ghail had kept him from having these two girls to dance and sing for him last night, eh? His conscience said something half-hearted about Ghail doubtless having his best interests at heart, but it had said too much in the past about her nonchalantly displayed bare legs. He did not heed it.

"Tonight," said Tony with decision, "things will be different."

They gave him the brightest and most joyous of smiles.

"And may we watch, lord," said Esim hopefully, "when you slay the other *djinns* who will doubtless be sent to murder you tonight?

Tony choked again. That was something he had been trying not to think about. The people of Barkut were, apparently, rather casual about *djinns* in spite of the long-continued war and the captivity of their official ruler. On the two occasions when *djinns* had turned up to Tony's knowledge, the people had not run away, but had come howling with rage to attack them. Flintlock muskets had bellowed after the *djinnee* Nasim as she fled in the form of a whirlwind. Palace guards had been spoiling for a fight and were actually breaking down the door of Tony's apartment when he opened it for them after Es-Souk's departure. These people would put up a battle, and were not averse to it. But still they said that no one man had ever before conquered a *djinn* in single combat.

It was something that needed to be looked into. And then Tony had an idea. Rather strangely, he had altogether failed to use his ten-dirhim piece for guidance since his arrival in the city of Barkut itself. The reason was simply that he hadn't needed it to decide anything. He'd been quite content with things as they were. Even imprisonment in the dungeon-and-courtyard had not been bad. He'd been busy learning Arabic, with Ghail around to look at appreciatively—

But now the *djinns* were after his neck. Now he needed to know what to do.

He finished his breakfast and stood up. The two girls brought him a golden basin and water to wash his hands. They watched his every movement with a breathless absorption which was almost childlike and was certainly flattering. Dismissing them, he patted one on her bare shoulder. She made a little movement as if cuddling against his hand while she smiled at him. He patted the other—

They went out the door, smiling worshipfully back at him. He found himself whistling as he dug in his pocket for the ten-dirhim piece. He regarded it affectionately. When he was a brisk young executive with a residence in Barkut suitably staffed with male and female slaves, it would all be due to this coin! And now this coin would give him some needed advice.

He flipped it. He flipped it again. And again and again.

Half an hour later, when Ghail came into his apartment—and he noted disapprovingly that she was wearing more clothes than ever—he was sunk in abysmal gloom. The ten-dirhim piece was no longer informative. It turned up heads and tails completely at random. It contradicted itself. It had no longer any special quality at all. It was at home. It was in its own world. The attraction; the gravitation; the singular force which prevented the indiscriminate mixing-up of objects of different worlds by causing coincidences which kept them at home—that force was gone. Because the coin was back where it belonged and was no longer endowed with any property urging its return.

Ghail regarded Tony with an enigmatic expression.

"Greeting, lord," she said in a tone which had all the earmarks of suitable slave-girl humility, but somehow was not humble at all, "there is news of great moment."

Tony felt inclined to groan. Among other things, he foresaw that he would be in for a bad time with his conscience presently.

"What is the news?" he asked drearily.

"The King of *djinns* has sent an embassy," Ghail told him. "He offers greetings to the prince beyond the farthest sea. He admires your prowess and desires to look upon the champion who defeated Es-Souk in single combat. He has punished Es-Souk for attempting to slay a human in a merely private quarrel. He offers a truce, safe conduct, and an escort of his private guard."

Tony's conscience said indignantly that when an important message like this was at hand, Tony should be ashamed to be looking at Ghail and mooning about how much better looking she was in less costume.

"What should I do?" asked Tony. "As I recall it, I pledged myself to destroy him, the other day. Yesterday, in fact. Do I tell him I'm in conference?"

Ghail shook her head frigidly.

"You should accept," she told him with no cordiality at all. "If you refused, he would think you were afraid."

"To be honest about it," said Tony, "I am. Have you any idea how I chased that *djinn* away last night?"

She looked at him in amazement.

"I haven't either," said Tony. "He was strangling me, so I broke a couple of his fingers and he let go, howling. Then he swelled up to the size of a gigantosaurus, bellowing, while I coughed my head off. He was just about to come for me again when he started to sneeze, and he went into a panic and flew out the window like his tail was on fire. I haven't the least idea why."

The slave girl looked at him strangely.

"He sneezed? But *lasf* sometimes causes that! Not always, but sometimes. Had you *lasf?*"

"Not unless it was on my breath—which isn't unlikely," Tony said gloomily. "It's foul stuff and the aroma lingers on. I had a drink of it yesterday. You gave it to me."

"*Lasf* is poisonous to the *djinn* but not to human beings," said Ghail with some reserve. "We anoint our weapons and bullets with it before we go out to fight the *djinn*. It is very poisonous to them. They run away. Sometimes they sneeze. But *lasf* is very rare. The *djinn* pay the Bedouin of the desert to uproot and destroy it wherever they find it."

"Like DDT," said Tony morbidly, "with bugs hiring rabbits to sabotage the whole business." He had to use English words where he did not know the Arabic equivalents. She listened, uncomprehending. "Never mind. If you don't know how I did it, nobody knows, so that's that. So—I have to visit this *djinn* king, eh? If it's under safe-conduct, I suppose I'm safe from further strangling until I get back?"

"Oh, yes," said Ghail. "You and your attendants are safe until you return. Of course you will be offered bribes to betray us, and persuasion, and he may try to frighten you, and"—her voice grew suddenly angry—"he will have his *djinnees* try to beguile you. He does not want you to lead our armies against him."

"I'll try to resist the bribes and the beguilings, too," said Tony. Then he shuddered. "If what I had yesterday was a fair sample . . . Tell me, where do I get this reputation as a general?"

Ghail said coldly: "I told the Council about the war you were in. Also, that *djinnee* in the courtyard may have been listening for days. One way or another, it would get back to the *djinns*."

Chapter 8

Tony had been standing. Now he sat down. He looked at Ghail. He said, changing the subject:

"What's the matter, Ghail? You act as if I had bleeding gums or something equally repulsive. When you thought I was a *djinn* you didn't act this way."

Ghail said: "There's nothing the matter." Then she added pointedly, "Did you enjoy your breakfast this morning?"

"That roasted sheep wasn't necessary," admitted Tony. "The coffee and fruit would have been enough. Did you arrange it?"

"It was thought," said Ghail coldly, "that since I had talked to you often I might know your likes and dislikes."

"Hm. . . ." said Tony. "You picked out those slaves—

the two girls who were part of the present made by the Council?"

Her lips tensed. "I did. I hope they please you."

"It evidently didn't occur to you," said Tony in gentle reproach, "that you could have included yourself in the gift. That is the only criticism I could offer."

She stamped her foot.

"I am the personal property of the Queen!" she snapped. "The Queen is a prisoner of the *djinn*. I cannot be bought or given save of the Queen!"

"It would be nice," Tony submitted, "if you could be persuaded."

She turned her back on him and started for the door. Tony said: "By the way—when do I start for the *djinn* king's court? And you said the safe-conduct includes my attendants. Do I tell Esir and Esim to pack up for a trip?"

"You do not!" Ghail said shortly. "You will have but one attendant. You will start before nightfall. The *djinn* will provide mounts and accommodation for you and one other only!"

"I suppose—"

"You will go," Ghail said shortly, "because the *djinn* king invited you. I go as your pretended slave, but actually to take necessities to our captive Queen."

Tony looked at her. He raised his eyebrows.

"The journey," said Ghail haughtily, "will be made on the camels of the *djinn,* which are actually *djinn* in the form of camels. They travel like the wind. What would be four days' journey by human travel will be accomplished in no more than three hours."

"I was sure," said Tony in some regret, "that

somehow you would manage to make it unsatisfactory. All right! Thank you."

He watched gloomily as she went out the door. Life, he reflected, had been a great deal more simple when he was a prisoner in a dungeon with a courtyard, instead of a general of armies he hadn't seen yet and a prince who had to make journeys to the courts of nonhuman entities he hadn't believed in before yesterday morning. At least, while he was a prisoner, Ghail had been around a lot, in a costume of limited area, and she'd been interested in him, if scornful. Now she seemed scornful of him and not interested. She rather resembled his conscience.

His conscience said sternly that though an untutored slave girl, reared in a highly unfavorable atmosphere, she at least showed a devotion to duty and a sense of moral values which Tony was not displaying. Only Heaven knew, said Tony's conscience, what enormities he might commit at any time, now that he had ceased to heed his proper mentor—it was fortunate that this poor slave girl had a sense of duty!

To this Tony replied that Ghail's sense of duty had led her to pick out two very attractive slave girls as presents for him, and since he was going off somewhere and didn't know when he'd be back, he might as well call them in and have some music while he waited.

He stood up to pull the bell cord.

Then he saw a stirring down at floor level out of the corner of his eye. He whirled with something like a gasp. After the affair of the dungeon courtyard and the windowsill last night, he was becoming jumpy when bugs and frogs and other small objects moved in his neighborhood.

Two of the marble tiles of the floor were rising where they joined, as if something swelled beneath them. Tony stared, momentarily paralyzed. A green shoot appeared and grew. Leaves appeared at its tip as he watched. Branches spread out, and more leaves, and then a bud. The bud swelled. It opened into an enormous lush blossom of a violent magenta hue. And then the flower rearranged itself. It became a miniature head—and there was the beaming, sentimental face of Nasim the *djinnee*, wearing her explicitly minus-I.Q. expression of amiability.

"Sh-h-h-h!" said the face in the flower, coyly.

Tony gulped. "I'm sh-sh-h-h-shed," he said. "What's up?"

"I'm sorry about Es-Souk," said the *djinnee*, beaming. "He's so jealous! He can't help it, poor thing! The king has put him in jail and it serves him right!"

Tony said: "Oh!"

"I felt that I had to tell you I was sorry," said the *djinnee*, almost simpering. "You're not angry with me?"

"Oh, no," said Tony. "It wasn't your fault."

"That's so good of you!" said Nasim. She regarded him with adoring, cowlike eyes from the flower bush. "I've been hiding in a crack as a little moth's egg, waiting to tell you how sorry I am. But there's been somebody around all the time."

"Yes," said Tony. "There has been."

"Would you like me to take the form of a human woman?" asked Nasim hopefully—and giggling—"for a while?"

"You'd better wear some clo—" began Tony in apprehension. Then he said desperately, "Better not. Somebody might come in."

Nasim beamed. "All right. But you're going to our king's court. I'll see you there! I'll be around!"

"I'm sure you will be," said Tony dismally.

"I'm watching over you," said Nasim beatifically. "Since I heard about what Es-Souk tried to do on my account, I made up my mind to watch over you night and day. And I will! Night and day!"

Tony stared at her, appalled. There was a small noise outside the door. Nasim said sentimentally:

"I hate to go like this, but somebody's coming." She beamed. "I'll be a little grease spot on the floor. Mind, now," she added archly, "don't step on me!"

The flower and blossom and all the leaves and branches seemed to contract smoothly. Suddenly they were not. The marble floor tiles fell together with a clink.

A delicate tapping on the door. Esir and Esim poked their heads around the door frame. Their faces were hopeful, and at the same time distressed.

"Lord!" said Esir plaintively. "We hear that you go on a journey! Do we go too?"

Tony sighed.

"I'm afraid not," he admitted. "Affairs of state, and all that. I'm taking only one attendant, and I've not choice of that one."

"But, lord," protested Esim, "we have just been given to you and we do not even know if we please you or not!"

They came into the room. They were young and shapely. They pleased him very much. They were openly eager for experimental evidence of this fact, and looked at him imploringly.

I like you both very much," said Tony. "In fact—" He thought back along a lifetime in New York, spent on subways and in automats and over double-entry ledgers, with only one interlude pounding a typewriter in an army camp. "In fact, I think I could be perfectly happy here in Barkut but for one thing."

They said anxiously: "Lord, what is it that keeps you from happiness?"

Tony sighed deeply. He said in deepest gloom: "Dammit, there's no privacy!"

Chapter 9

The *djinn* camel was twenty feet tall, and it ambled through the night over the desert with monstrous strides. There were bright stars overhead, and a low-hung moon to cast long shadows; there was a camel-guard of *djinns* riding other *djinn* camels on every hand. Altogether the picture was one of barbaric magnificence. Wind swept past the contrivance which did duty as a cabin on the huge ship of the desert. The contrivance reminded Tony forcibly of the inside of a British miniature car, minus the instrument board. But it did not ride so smoothly. The size of the camel did not change the nature of its gait, and it would not be wise to burp while the animal was in motion.

Tony looked out a window at their escort. Ten-foot

djinns on twenty-foot camels. Bearded, mustachioed, tusked and pointed-eared monstrosities, with spears as tall as their camels, with monstrous scimitars as tall as Tony himself, with garments of silk and velvet and garnished with gigantic precious stones which gleamed even in the moonlight. A hundred of them, no less, keeping close formation about the beast on which Tony and Ghail the slave girl rode.

In the moonlight, the *djinn* guard looked bored. It probably was boring, Tony reflected abstractedly, to be plodding at a mere forty miles an hour over endless sand, on the back of an acquaintance metamorphosized into a camel who would presently expect you to change places with him. This kind of exchange was taking place with some regularity. At least camels and their riders dropped out of formation and fell behind, and presently new camels and new riders came hurrying up from the rear to resume the place that had been vacated.

A lurching of the camel threw Ghail against him. She was veiled, now, and swathed in all the drapery of a woman dressed for travel or the street. She was singularly remote, too. Back at Barkut's city gate, she had climbed the ladder to the camel cabin—at the height of a second-story window—with an air of extreme aloofness, ignoring the demoniac *djinn* guardsmen waiting about. Tony had been unable to match her dignity as he scrambled up and joined her in the small, close coupe. The guard had formed up about them and they had gone sweeping away into the desert darkness, leaving the city's faint and twinkling light behind. Ghail had spoken no word then, and she did not speak now. The silence was burdensome.

A moment later the camel lurched again. Tony was thrown almost into her lap.

"I'm sorry," he said politely. "Bad road, this."

"There is no road," said Ghail composedly. "We have reached the foothills of the mountains, and the *djinn* are not used to walking. They wished to carry us in whirlwinds, but in your name I declined."

"I suppose," agreed Tony, "we'd have gotten dizzy."

He fell silent again. Another monstrous lurch, and Ghail landed almost exactly on his knee. He helped her back into her own place again and said:

"Look here! We'd better have some system about this! I know you disapprove of me thoroughly, but in default of safety-belts I'd better put my arm around you."

The camel seemed to stumble and Tony grabbed. They were suddenly upright again, and his arm was firmly around her and she made no protest.

"I don't disapprove of you especially," she said with some primness, "but all men are alike."

"The observation is remarkably original," he told her. "I suppose you are also prepared to tell me that I do not respect you?"

She turned her head. Her lips were close to his ear. She whispered fiercely:

The camel is a djinn! It's listening!

"True," said Tony. "Damn! No privacy even here!"

He stared gloomily out at the moonlit foothills which now had arisen from the desert and seemed to lead on through deeply shadowed moonlight toward mountains which also were alternately shadowed and shining ahead. He suddenly felt a soft hand groping for his. It pressed his fingers meaningfully. He squeezed back, encouraged beyond expectation. But the hand was snatched away.

Soft warm breath on his neck. A furious whisper in his ear:

"*I wanted to tell you something! Here is* lasf. *In tiny glass phials you can break in case of need. Then no* djinn *will come near you. It is for your protection!*"

Tony put out his hand again. One very small smooth glass object, the size of his thumb or smaller. He put it away. He reached again. Another. A third. He put them in separate pockets to avoid the danger of breaking them against each other. He put his lips to her ear.

"*Thanks. Have you some for yourself?*"

"*Of course! And some for the Queen, to protect her when you lead our armies to her rescue—when you are ready to destroy the* djinn. *Now you had better talk, since you have begun!*"

He leaned back, as well as he could considering the violent and erratic movements of the *djinn* camel's gait. He suddenly began to feel better. After all, qualified privacy on a *djinn*'s back might have its points.

"Hm. . . ." he said aloud. "In my country the *djinn* have been subdued so long—they're kept on reservations—that humans don't bother about them any more. I've even forgotten the stuff one learns about them in first grade at school. It seems extraordinary to me that they can change their size so much. Their shape, yes. In my country even human women can do remarkable things to their shapes with girdles and falsies. You'd hardly believe! And of course they change their coloring. But size, absolute size, no. . . ."

Ghail stirred uneasily. But she spoke as primly as before.

"*Djinns* are elastic," she said. "With the same amount of substance they can be as large as a whirlwind. Or as small as a grain of sand, though no one could possibly pick them up—for always they weigh the same."

"You mean," asked Tony, with interest, "that a *djinn* in the shape of a bug or—hm—a moth's egg, weighs as much as when he or she is a camel and that sort of thing?"

Ghail caught hold of his right hand, and held it firmly. "That is it, yes," she said shortly.

"Then that," said Tony blithely, "explains why the bench in the courtyard turned over. A *djinn* beetle was climbing on it. It explains a lot of things."

Ghail held his left hand. She ground her teeth. "Thanks," said Tony. "Since we don't get thrown around so much this ride is much more fun, isn't it?"

Ghail turned her head and whispered in his ear, strangling with fury:

"*As soon as you have destroyed the* djinn *I am going to kill you!*"

Tony beamed in the darkness inside the small cabin on top of the lurching camel. Ghail held his hands, muttering fiercely. His arm was about her shoulders. The combination made the bumping and swaying and unholy undulations of the beast not at all annoying—to Tony.

"There's another thing I'd like to ask about," he said cheerfully. "When you were teaching me to speak your language, you wore a very sensible hot-weather costume. I mean, there wasn't too much of it. About like the bathing suits girls wear back at home. And you very properly didn't seem embarrassed. But that was only when you thought I was a *djinn.* As soon as you found out I wasn't, you got all bothered. In fact, you blushed in the most unlikely places. . . . Why?"

She said through clenched teeth:

"*Djinns* are not human. I would not be embarrassed before a cat, either. Or a slave. But a man, yes!"

"Yet Esir and Esim—"

"They would have been embarrassed too, before they were given to you and were your slaves." Her voice quivered with fury. "I am dressed as I am because I travel with you."

Then she hissed into his ear:

"*When this is over I will see that you are boiled in oil! You will be fed to dogs! You will be torn into little pieces—*"

Tony's ear tingled pleasantly. He continued to beam in the darkness as the twenty-foot camel which was actually a *djinn* went swaying and lurching through the night.

It had been two hours' journey across the desert proper—a caravan might make forty miles a day if pressed, but this camel made that much in an hour— and it was another hour before the *djinn* king's court appeared to be nearing. The evidence of approach was fairly obvious. The troop of *djinn* guards approached a narrow pass between precipitous cliffs. It was guarded by two colossal shapes with flaming eyes. They stood forty feet high, in gleaming armor, and they carried battle-axes whose blades were more than a man-height wide, with shafts the size of palm trees. They challenged in voices like thunder. The cavalcade halted. A guttural voice gave a countersign. The gigantic guards drew back. Tony watched with interest.

"Very impressive," he said judicially. "But actually, you tell me these are simply *djinn* who have extended themselves—decompressed themselves, you might say—to reach those rather excessive dimensions. At that size they're not much more substantial than so much fog, are they? How can they handle such axes?"

"The axes," said Ghail shortly, "are a part of themselves. *Djinns* can take the appearance of a chest of coins or jewels, which seem like many objects. But to pull away one coin or jewel would be to pull away a part of the *djinn*. You could not. The axes are a part of their form. So are their garments and the ornaments they wear."

"Hm," said Tony, "I see."

The cavalcade went on. The pass through the mountains grew more narrow and more straight. The cliffs above it grew steeper, until the giant camels with their giant riders rode in utter darkness with only a ribbon of star-studded sky above them. Then the pass turned, and widened a little and narrowed again. The entrance to the farther and still narrower part of the pass was completely closed by something only bright starlight enabled Tony to believe he saw. It was the head of a dragon with closed eyes, seemingly dozing. It completely filled the pass. Great nostrils the size of subway tunnels gave out leisurely puffs of smoke the size of subway trains.

The caravan moved up to it and halted. The leader of the guard bellowed. The great eyes of the dragon's head opened. Each was as large—so Tony estimated—as one of Macy's plate-glass windows. They looked balefully down at the *djinn* trooper.

He bellowed again. The nostrils puffed. Then the gigantic mouth opened. It looked rather like the raising of a drawbridge for the passage of a tow of coal barges. It gaped wide. Flames played luridly, far down the exposed throat.

The caravan moved smartly into the wide-held jaws. It went comfortably down into the flame-lined maw—

And suddenly the low-hanging moon shone brightly on a wide valley with the palace of the *djinn* king in the distance. It was huge. It was ablaze with lights. And the passageway to it was lined with giants whose feet, only, were visible. Legs thicker than the thickest tree trunks rose overhead. Bellies protruded rather like fleshy stratocumuli, hundreds of feet above the camels of the caravan. The heads of the giants were invisible. Tony felt very small. To reassure himself he said amiably to Ghail:

"It must be a fairly calm night. If not, expanded as they are, even a light breeze would make these giants wobble all over the place like captive balloons."

Ghail put Tony's right hand firmly in front of him. She released it. She took his left arm and removed it firmly from her shoulders.

"We are almost there," she said shortly. "You will ask that I be taken to our Queen in her prison, that she may have the solace of a human woman to weep with her in her captivity."

There was sudden uneasiness, even anxiety, in her voice. In fact, it wavered a little. And Tony knew why she was frightened. She traveled as his slave. Here, among the *djinn*—

"I'll do that," he told her almost remorsefully. "I've been pretty much of a beast, haven't I? But I'll see that you're toddled off to your Queen while I see the king and listen to his offers of bribes."

She adjusted her veil and swathing robes.

"You will not see him tonight!" she said bitterly. "You will be shown to your apartment, and there he will send refreshments and entertainment to beguile you so that you will wish alliance with him instead of Barkut! There will be wine, and *djinnees* in the form of women, and everything that is disreputable to appeal to a man!"

Tony managed to look shocked. Actually, it sounded interesting.

"You mean that *djinn* are as immoral as all that?"

"Of course!" she said more bitterly still. "They are stupid! They are unbelievably stupid! So of course they are immoral! And if they were not stupid, and probably if they were not immoral, we humans would have no chance against them at all! And it is because men are so stupid that they are so immoral, and—and—"

Suddenly, she was crying. And Tony patted her shoulder comfortingly, and took aside her veil and wiped her eyes. And as suddenly she was not crying at all, but looking at him very strangely.

"What—what do you think of me now?" she asked in a small voice.

"My dear," said Tony with a sigh, "I think you are probably the most intelligent girl I ever met in my life."

The caravan halted before the intricately sculptured gateway of the *djinn* king's palace, and there was no more time for even semiprivate conversation.

Tony descended from the camel in a very stately fashion. To the gorgeously robed *djinn* chamberlain who greeted him in the king's name, he relayed Ghail's request—that she be allowed to share the captivity of the Queen of Barkut during his visit. Shortly, Ghail went away behind a *djinnee* who was at the moment some twelve feet tall, of a greenish complexion, and wearing a necklace of diamonds each one of which was a good deal larger than a baseball. Tony chatted amiably with the chamberlain who greeted him as a prince and a general of Barkut.

"A most comfortable journey!" said Tony, as a procession formed up to escort him to his quarters. "Your camels, in particular, arouse my admiration!"

He swaggered in exactly the manner of the solitary general he had come in contact with in the greatest war of the human race.

"Admirable!" he repeated in that general's very tones. "The one who carried me is a very pearl among camels!" The camel he had ridden turned its head. It looked at him sentimentally. It sighed gustily. It giggled.

Nasim.

Chapter 10

Tony was, he admitted regretfully, disappointed. He'd marched to his assigned quarters in the palace between long lines of *djinn* courtiers, who should have dazzled him with their silks, satins, jewels, and furs. But once a slight noise behind him made him turn his head, and he discovered that the courtiers he had just passed were sneaking away hastily, and he strongly suspected that they were running around ahead of him to assume new forms—including new costumes and jewels—and stand in line again. And, since in assuming a new form they also provided themselves with the costumes and ornaments that went with it, he remained undazzled even by ropes of pearls as big as hen's eggs, and rubies as big as grapefruit, and so on and on. Jewels of that sort, he was able to remark to his alert and highly suspicious conscience, were in rather bad taste. If you tried to pull one off—though that would be bad taste too—it would be like trying to take away somebody's nose or ear. The jewels were, in fact, not marketable commodities. They were in effect paste, and therefore showed a lamentable lack of imagination.

His conscience bitterly reminded him of Ghail's forecasts of libidinous entertainment waiting to refresh him after his journey. Tony brightened. He was more than a little tired, but he had often wondered—as who has not?—whether what the censors cut was one-half so lurid as the stuff they passed.

There was a guard of honor in the anteroom before his suite. Tony went through the motions of inspecting it.

Twelve-foot giants looked down at him through yellow cat's-eyes with airs of truculence. The commander of the guard grandly asked for the countersign for Tony's personal guard for the night. Tony thought of Ghail.

"The word," he said, "is 'Solitude.' "

Then he went to look at his bedroom.

Like the rest of his lodging it was on a scale of lavishness to be found only in three-million-dollar-budget motion pictures. His bed had apparently been carved from a tremendous limpet-shell; the walls were iridescent; the furniture was onyx and gold; his quarters in the palace in Barkut were practically sub-minimal housing by comparison—yet he could not find a thrill in it. Ghail had spoiled everything by that unfortunate comment on the ability of *djinns* to take any form they wished, including chests of coins and jewels. It spoiled things for him. It spoiled even the effect of the utterly lavish, super-tremendous banquet hall to which he was presently taken for refreshment.

He was very hopeful as the affair began, but he fell into gentle melancholy as the *djinns* gave him the works. They intended, evidently, to give him the sort of evening that would be a True Believer's dream. And from their standpoint it was undoubtedly total entertainment without even the sky as a limit. But Tony derived only a morbid pleasure from the anguished moans of his conscience as the floor show progressed. To a citizen of the United States, accustomed to a nineteen-dollar radio for music, TV girl-shows and the Radio City Music Hall as seen from a dollar-forty seat, practically any bathing beach in summer, and an occasional burlesque show over in New Jersey, the thing was pathetic.

A normal male inhabitant of Barkut might have been ravished—in several senses—by the crystal bowl of wine which was big enough for several girls to swim in, and by the girls who did swim in it. But

Tony had seen colored movies of an All-American girls' swimming meet. An unsophisticated Arab might have been enchanted by the *djinnees* who wore human forms and practically nothing else and who sang lustily and danced enthusiastically for Tony's benefit. But he had seen precision dancers both in person and on the stage. Also, these *djinnees* misguidedly strove for beauty after Arab notions, and in consequence were markedly steatopygian, which is to say, bell-bottomed. So that when by *djinn* standards the performance was at its hottest, Tony was moved to homesickness. There is an art in doing the bumps. There is a definite technique to the striptease. And the *djinnees*, willing workers as they were, didn't have it.

Tony's conscience screamed shrilly at the beginning, when he failed to rise and depart amid blushes. But as he sat, a sad and lonely and a disappointed figure, immune to the lavish immorality of the *djinns*, his conscience was amazed. It had been prepared for the battle of its existence, and was girded for it. But antibodies to vice had been generated in Tony's system—so he assured his conscience—by the various forms of entertainment passed by boards of censorship in the United States. He was unaffected by the temptations of the *djinns* because—via technicolor—he had been tempted by professionals against whom the *djinnees* simply did not stand up. In fact, Tony assured his conscience regretfully, it seemed that where *djinnees* were concerned, he simply couldn't take yes for an answer.

By midnight he was yawning. At half-past midnight he could keep his eyes open only with difficulty. At one he went apologetically, and alone, to bed. His conscience could hardly believe it. And when at last it ventured upon those sternly virtuous commendations which, coming from a good conscience, are supposed to be the most precious things in life, Tony yawned again.

But no conscience is approving for more than the briefest of intervals. Tony's almost instantly afterward observed that it was outrageous for him to think of sleeping in his clothes! He hadn't drunk enough for that! He opened boredom-bleared eyes and looked wearily around the magnificence of his sleeping apartment, and regarded the bed which was surely large enough for more than one person. He had had his lesson. He saw nothing but seemingly insensate furniture. But he knew better. Benches might totter and fall at any instant. Floor tiles might crack. And he confessed, to his conscience, what may have been the true reason for his insensibility:

"I just feel," he said drearily, "that I haven't any privacy."

And then he slept.

Came the dawn. And with the dawn came Nasim. It was so early that Tony had barely opened his eyes. He was thinking those more or less gloomy thoughts with which a man customarily greets a new day, when a small whirlwind some three and a half feet high came in through the doorway of his room. Atop it, Nasim's beaming countenance glowed with excitement. Tony turned over and realized that he had slept fully dressed, including his shoes. He sat up wearily.

"Hello, Nasim. Thanks for the camel ride. That was you, wasn't it?"

She giggled. "I asked to do it. I said it would be

a privilege. It was!" Then she said, "That slave girl doesn't like you! It's terrible! A slave girl not liking her master! And you don't like her either. You said she was intelligent. I'm glad I found out! I was going to make a study of her so I could take her form and fool you some day. It would have been a good joke on you! But now I won't."

For some reason, Tony's hair tended to stand up all over his head. But he yawned.

"No," he said. "I wouldn't, if I were you. It wouldn't be amusing." Then he asked, "How'd you get past the guards? Somebody told you the countersign?"

She giggled again. "I was a little centipede running along the floor. They didn't see me. Anyhow, the king wants me to find out why you were bored last night. Were you"—she sighed and looked at him hopefully—"were you being true to me?"

Tony felt a sort of inward jolt. Nasim, in his mind, was associated with beetles and moth eggs and grease spots. Now centipedes, too.

"I guess that was a sort of—mm—by-product of something else, Nasim," he said forlornly. "I just didn't feel romantic last night. That's all. Did the king say anything else about me?"

"He's going to execute Es-Souk for trying to kill somebody he's decided he wants to be friends with," said Nasim virtuously. "And he wants you to watch. I feel sorry for poor Es-Souk! He couldn't help being jealous of me! And also the king's terribly anxious to find out how to make you his friend instead of a general for Barkut."

"Do you know," said Tony, "I'd give a lot to know why he's so anxious!"

Nasim beamed at him; just a plump little whirlwind three and a half feet tall, spinning in the middle of Tony's bedroom, which itself looked something like the foyer of a super-plushy hotel at thirty-five dollars a day without bath. She looked, Tony reflected dismally, rather cute for a whirlwind. A bit on the chubby side, to be sure, but anybody who cared for whirlwinds would appreciate Nasim. Such a person would be eager to have her for a pet. Still—

"I'm going to whisper in your ear," said Nasim coyly. "And I'll have to take human form to get close enough."

The whirlwind enlarged a little. Tony watched in alarm as a human figure began to show pinkly through the mist which was Nasim as a whirlwind. He grew apprehensive. He called anxiously:

"Clothes, Nasim!"

His cry came almost too late, but not quite. The very last of the mist which was her whirlwind form materialized about her as a Mother Hubbard wrapper of absolute shapelessness. Then she beamed at him breathlessly.

"I always forget, don't I?"

Even in human form, Nasim was chubby. Her eyes were not the elongated animal eyes of male djinns, though, and apparently she had remembered with some care not to have her ears pointed. But Nasim, naturally, could not imagine an expression which was not intellectually *kaput*. She came coyly and sat down on the bed close to Tony. The bed yielded surprisingly under her weight, which gave Tony something to think about.

"I'm going to whisper," she said archly. She bent close—

Ghail, whispering in his ear on camel-back last night, had provided a very pleasant sensation; but somehow Nasim was different.

"The king wants you for a friend because of the way your nation destroys cities in war," she whispered. *"In just a bit of a second, in flames hotter than the hottest fire."* She drew back and beamed at him. "Now, isn't that nice of me?" she demanded aloud. "Listen again!"

She bent over. Tony listened, trying to think what meaning atomic bombs could possibly have to a king of the *djinn*.

"When Es-Souk is executed, it will be like that," the coy voice whispered. *"They'll explode poor Es-Souk, and he will be just a terrible explosion hotter than the hottest flame. And I told the king that you told the slave girl your country keeps* djinn *on reservations. So the king knows that your country must explode* djinns *to destroy your enemies' cities, and he's afraid you'll tell the people of Barkut how to do it too."*

Tony's flesh crawled. It was not altogether the discovery that when a *djinn* was executed he exploded. Any creature which could change its size from that of a grain of sand to a whirlwind . . . such a creature could not be ordinary matter. Not flesh and blood with sex-hormones and mineral salts to taste. It would have to be something different. A mixture of loosely knit neutrons and electrons and positrons and so on—Tony's knowledge of nuclear physics came from the Sunday supplements—and even that was startling enough, but not horrifying. The thing that made Tony's flesh crawl was that every *djinn* and *djinnee* must be in effect an atomic bomb. Which could be set off.

They'd avoid it if possible, of course. The *djinn* king was scared to death of the bare idea. But no human could feel comfortable sitting on a large bed with an atomic bomb next to him. Especially, perhaps, when the bomb was wearing nothing but a Mother Hubbard wrapper and felt romantic.

Tony got up hastily. Nasim looked reproachfully at him.

"That's not nice!" she pouted. "I tell you nice things and you jump up! Now you sit right back down here and whisper something nice to me!"

Tony shivered. He racked his brains for a suitable thing to say which would be romantic enough and yet not commit him. He bent over.

"*You know other* djinns *are listening.*" he said, dry-throated. "*So, of course . . .*" Then he swallowed and went on: "*I'm going to ask the king for Es-Souk's life. I don't want him to die on my account. I*"—he gulped audibly—"*I can fight my own battles.*" Against atomic bombs, too! his conscience added acidly.

Nasim looked at him in disappointment. "I suppose that's noble of you," she said plaintively, "but it isn't very romantic! You aren't nice to me! You get angry when I forget about wearing clothes, and—"

"I said only last night that you were a pearl among camels, didn't I?" demanded Tony harassedly. "After all, you don't want to rouse the beast in me, do you?"

She giggled, and he added desperately: "—In public?"

"Well . . ." she said forgivingly, "I hadn't thought of that. I understand now. I'll think of something. And I guess I'll go now."

She got up and trailed toward the door, a dumpy,

rotund little figure in a wrapper that dragged lopsid-
edly on the floor behind her. At the door she stopped
and giggled again.

"You saying something about a beast just reminded
me," she said brightly. "That slave girl you brought
with you sent a message. She said that if you can
spare time from your beastly amusements, the Queen
of Barkut wants to talk to you."

Tony tensed all over.

"How the hell do I ring for somebody to guide me
around this place?" he demanded feverishly. "She and
Ghail are waiting!"

"Anybody'll show you," said Nasim. "Just ask your
servants."

"I haven't any servants," said Tony agitatedly. "Only
those guards outside."

"Oh, yes, you've got servants," Nasim insisted. "The
king told them not to intrude on you but to be on
hand if you wanted them. I'm sure he appointed a
friend of mine to be your valet. Abdul! Abdul! Where
are you?"

Out of the corner of his eye, Tony saw an infinitesimal stirring up near the ceiling. He spun to face
it. A cockroach—quite a large cockroach—appeared
on top of the drapes by a window. It waggled its
feelers at them.

"Hello, Abdul!" said Nasim. "The great prince who
is the king's guest wants to see the Queen of Barkut
in her dungeon. Will you take him there?"

A sudden, geyserlike stream of water spouted out
from where the cockroach stood. Hard and powerful,
like a three-inch jet from a fire hose. It arched across
the room, hit the farther side and splashed loudly,

ran down the wall to the floor, and there suddenly jetted upward again in a waterspout which, in turn, solidified into a swaggering short stout *djinn* with a purple turban.

He bowed to the ground before Tony.

"This way, lord," he said profoundly, "to the Queen of Barkut."

Glassy-eyed, Tony followed him out of the door.

Chapter 11

He followed the *djinn* Abdul out the door. Then he stared. There had been a vast anteroom before his suite. He had gone through the motions of inspecting his guard of honor in it. Now there was an enormous swimming pool in its place, with beyond it a luxuriant jungle of hot-house trees. Tony examined it with startled attention.

"It seems to me that this was a little bit different, last night," he observed.

"Aye, lord," said the *djinn* solemnly.

He led the way along the swimming pool's rim. Tony followed. He was worried about the message from Ghail, of course. The night he had just spent had been even aggressively innocent, but somehow he felt that Ghail was not likely to believe it. Her request for him to come to the Queen was not phrased in a way to indicate great confidence in him. But there was not much that he could do about it.

"Interior decoration among the *djinn*," said Tony,

frowning, "is evidently not static art. Things change over-night, eh?"

"Aye, lord. And oftener," said Abdul solemnly. "We *djinn* have much trouble with boredom. We are the most powerful of created things. There is nothing that we can desire that we cannot have. So we suffer from tedium. Someone grew bored with the anteroom and changed the design."

Tony raised his eyebrows. "I have a glass phial in my pocket," he observed. "Can you change the design of that?"

"It is a human object, lord," said Abdul with an air of contempt.

Tony grinned. During the night—during his sleep—his conscience had reached some highly moral conclusions which he was inclined to accept. One was that *djinn* were different in kind from humans, but they were not for that reason akin to the angels. Tony went right along with this decision, recalling the floor show of the night before. More, they were but matter, said his conscience firmly—unstable matter, perhaps, with probably some Uranium 235 somewhere in their constitutions, and in the United States the Atomic Energy Commission would take action against them on the ground of national security. But they were not spirits.

They were material. Grossly material. They knew only what they saw, felt, smelled, and heard. They were limited to the senses humans had. Tony had referred to the glass phials in his pocket. Abdul plainly knew nothing about them and could not mystically determine their contents, or he would have been scared to death. They contained *lasf*. So it was not impossible to keep a secret from a *djinn*. It was not impossible to fool them. It might not be impossible to bluff them.

These were encouraging thoughts. *Djinns* were creatures, and therefore had limitations. They changed massive architectural features of the *djinn* king's palace overnight, but they could not—it was a reasonable inference—change the form of a human artifact. Therefore it was probable that the things they could change were of the same kind of matter as themselves

Tony's guide opened a door. It should have given upon a passageway of snowy white. Its walls should have been of ivory, perhaps mastodon tusks, most intricately carved in not very original designs. Instead, beyond the door Tony found a corridor which was an unusually lavish aquarium. It had walls of crystal with unlikely tropical fish swimming behind them. The fish wore golden collars and were equipped with pearl-studded underwater castles to suffer ennui in.

Which was a clue. It occurred to Tony that he had not yet seen one trace of a civilization which could be termed *djinnian*, as opposed to human. Everything he had seen was merely an elaboration, a magnification, an over-lavish complication, of the designs and possessions of men. Humans wore clothes, so the *djinn* wore garments made after human patterns only more lavish and improbable. Humans had palaces, so the *djinn* king had a palace which out-palaced anything mere humans could contrive. But the riches of the *djinn* were unstable, their lavishness had no meaning, and they had no originality at all. In his home world, Tony reflected, *djinns* would only really fit in Hollywood.

He cheered up enormously. In his pocket he had three phials of *lasf*. If his opinion was correct, the palace was constructed of the same material as the dragon in the narrow pass, the two colossi before that, and the row of giants on the final lap to the palace gateway. If he uncorked one of the phials, it was probable that the walls about him would begin to sneeze and flee away in the form of whirlwinds—one whirlwind for each unit of the edifice. The *djinn* palace had an exact analogy in the living structures of the army ants of Central America, which cling together to form a shelter and a palace—complete with roof, walls, floors, and passage-ways—for the army-ant queen whenever she feels in the mood to lay some eggs. But the *djinn* were not sexless like the army ants. Nasim's romantic impulses seemed proof enough of that. And besides—well—the *djinnees* who had danced for him last night had displayed an enthusiasm which simply wasn't all synthetic. They had something more than a theoretic knowledge of what it was all about. What they had lacked was art.

It was with an increasing feeling of competence, then, that Tony strode off to answer Ghail's summons. He began to anticipate his audience with the king of the *djinn* with less aversion. And somehow, the atomic-bomb aspect of the *djinn* tended to fade away. Ghail had never mentioned anything of the kind. Humans, apparently, did not know that *djinn* were fissionable. So it was unlikely that they could be set off by accident. But it was still hard to imagine getting romantic with an atomic bomb, even if it wasn't fused.

More doorways. They passed through parts of the palace with which Tony was naturally unfamiliar, and whose features as of today he could not compare with yesterday's. Then they reached a quite small, quite inconspicuous doorway, and the *djinn* Abdul stopped before it and bowed low again.

"The residence of the Queen of Barkut, lord," he said blandly.

Tony stepped out-of-doors, onto a sort of dry meadow with patches of parched grass here and there. The sun shone brightly. He heard a bird singing rather monotonously, and he assured himself that no *djinn* was making that noise! A hundred-odd yards away there was a clump of trees and among the trees a small group of mud-walled houses which were plainly human buildings, not too expertly made, with completely human implements about them.

Tony advanced. Someone waved to him, and he felt his heart pound ridiculously faster. But as he drew nearer yet, he saw that it wasn't Ghail. It was a stout, motherly woman with her gown tucked up to reveal sturdy, sun-browned calves. She seemed to have been working in a garden. He saw a neatly hoed patch of melons, and a field of onions and other vegetables. The woman beamed at Tony and said:

"The Queen is in there. You are the Lord Toni?"

Tony nodded. Abdul looked oddly uncomfortable.

"When you go back to Barkut," said the woman, "do try to get them to send us some sweets! We haven't had any sweets for months!" Then she said tolerantly to Abdul: "Not that you don't try, of course."

Abdul wriggled unhappily. "I will wait here, lord," he said sadly. "It is not fitting for a *djinn*, of the most powerful of created beings, to be made mock of by a mere human. Perhaps I will go back and wait by the door."

Ghail came out of the largest building—it would have no more than two or three rooms, and was of a single story—and regarded Tony with a deliberately icy air. She said:

"Greetings, lord."

Just then the motherly woman said comfortingly to the short stout *djinn:*

"Oh, don't go away, Abdul! I'll watch your magic tricks for a while—if they're good ones."

Abdul wavered. Tony grinned at Ghail. He said critically:

"Of the two of us, you look most like you had a hang-over. Have you been crying?"

"With my Queen," said Ghail with dignity, "over the sadness of her captivity."

Then a pleasant slender sun-browned woman came out beside Ghail and nodded in a friendly fashion to Tony. He gaped at her. She had the comfortable air of an unmarried woman who is quite content to be unmarried. Which is not in the least like a queen. The palace of the *djinn* king loomed up on all sides, but here in the center things were different. These houses did not look like a dungeon, to be sure. Here was a meadow half a mile this way by half a mile that, with these buildings and gardens in the center so that it looked like a small farm. The contrast between these structures and the magnificence of the palace was odd enough. The atmosphere of reasonably complete contentment was stranger still. The Queen looked as if she were having a perfectly comfortable time here, and was as well-satisfied as anybody ought to be.

"This," said Ghail stiltedly, "is the Lord Toni."

Chapter 12

The Queen smiled. There was flour on her hands, as if she had been cooking something.

"Have you breakfasted, Lord Toni?" she asked.

"Well—no," admitted Tony.

"Then come in," said the Queen, "and we will talk while you do."

They entered a small room, an almost bare room, a peasant's general-purpose room which had the shining neatness of a house with no man in it to mess it up. But this had not the fussy preciosity of too many possessions. There was a small fire burning on a raised hearth, giving off a distinctly acrid smell which yet was not unpleasant.

"You will have coffee," said the Queen, "and whatever else we can find. We are a little straitened for food today, because so much went for your meal last night."

Tony had been dazed, but this was a jolt which showed in his expression. The Queen laughed.

"The *djinns* have their own foods," she explained. "But no human being can eat of their dainties. When I was first made prisoner the king used to raid caravans to get food for me, but it was very tedious! So now I have my own garden, and someone—I think it was

Abdul—stole chickens for me. When you came as a guest they asked me for food for you, and I gave it. Of course. You probably did not notice, but no matter what you pointed to in all the dishes they paraded before you, you actually got—" she chuckled—"no more than flesh of chicken, and eggs, and cheese and dates and salad! That was all I had for you."

Tony said: "Majesty, I think I ought to make some appropriate speech. But I don't know what to say!"

She busied herself at the fireplace, and Ghail went quickly to help. The two of them gave Tony his coffee, and a melon, and eggs. It went very well.

"You are going to defeat the *djinns,* Ghail tells me," the Queen said practically. "She assures me you will destroy them to the last small *djinnling.* I hope not."

Tony goggled at her. "But—"

"Oh, I know!" said the Queen. "I am their prisoner, and so on. But in their way they're rather cute." Tony stared.

"I've lived among them four years," the Queen said briskly. "I've had them around all the time. They're a little bit like men, and a good deal more like children, and quite a lot like kittens. I suppose you'd say that I've made pets of them. Of course they won't let me go home, but it isn't bad."

Tony chewed and swallowed, and then said carefully: "I'm afraid I don't quite understand."

The Queen shrugged. "They're terribly vain, like men. If possible, more so. You can do anything with a *djinn* if you flatter him. They're terrible show-offs, like children. My maid outside can wind Abdul around her little finger any time. He loves to show off his

transformations, and she watches him. The other
djinns won't. And they're like kittens because they're
so completely selfish. But that's very much like men
and children, too."

Tony said in astonishment:

"But they're a menace to Barkut—"

"Of course!" the Queen conceded impatiently.
"They're dangerous to Barkut in the same way that
a troop of—say—wild apes would be dangerous to a
village near where they lived. They steal, and they
destroy, and they probably kill people now and then.
But it's because they can't understand people and
people can't understand them."

"There's a war—" began Tony.

"Oh, the war!" The Queen dismissed it scornfully.
"That's what all wars are about! Misunderstandings!
Marriages are too, probably. Men are so absurd! That's
why I have to stay a prisoner."

Ghail said warningly: "Majesty!"

The Queen regarded Ghail with impatience.

"My dear, you cannot deny that I am patriotic! I
have no children, so I can be patriotic! But for the
same reason I haven't any particular prejudice against
the *djinns*. Do you remember how I used to adore
horses? I've come to like the *djinns* as well, that's
all. I admit that it seems terribly silly to me that I
have to stay here because the *djinn* king's vanity is
involved in holding me prisoner! If I were to escape
and go back to Barkut, he'd feel that he had to attack
it furiously to recapture me. So I can't go home until
he's conquered. So I simply want the Lord Toni to
realize that as far as I am concerned—"

Ghail said again: "Majesty!"

Tony looked sharply at Ghail and at the Queen. Ghail was young and very desirable. The Queen was less young and contentedly undesirous. She laughed frankly.

"Very well, Ghail!" And to Tony she said: "I think that even as a captive queen, though, I can amend my council's orders to say that it will not be necessary to exterminate the *djinns* completely! I should think, in fact, that if they were suitably subdued, a few tame ones kept around the palace would be quite pleasant. They'd be excellent for the prestige of the throne of Barkut, too!"

Tony said painfully: "Majesty—"

"It's really too bad you came to Barkut at all," the Queen said, though with no unfriendliness. "Humans and *djinns* alike believe that if anybody can bring about a human victory, you can. So the humans won't consent to a compromise until they've tried for conquest. And if they would, the *djinns* would be sure they knew they couldn't win, and they wouldn't compromise until they'd tried for conquest. It's so silly! We really could get along without fighting, if we tried! I've been working on the *djinn* king. He was willing to come to a compromise, but—male vanity again!—only on condition that the Queen of Barkut married him. And that seemed to be out of the question."

"It was out of the question!" snapped Ghail, her eyes angry.

"I was wearing him down," protested the Queen. "After all, if he had his harem of *djinnees*, a private agreement that his marriage to a human queen would be a form and not a fact—"

"Absolutely out of the question!" repeated Ghail, her color high. "Absolutely!"

The Queen sighed.

"I know it is, my dear . . . and it's too late now, anyhow. The Lord Toni has come. The humans think he's going to lead them to victory. The *djinns* are sure that if he can't, the war goes to them." She looked at Tony, frowning. "Of course you've got to win, Lord Toni! Of course! Humans as the slaves of *djinns* would be in a terrible state! It would be like enslaved by apes or—children! And apes make nice pets—I had one once—and children are doubtless very well, but apes or children or *djinns* would be horrible masters! But the *djinns* are so amusing—"

"I'm getting a trifle confused," admitted Tony.

The Queen nodded kindly.

"I know," she said condescendingly. "You men only really talk to each other. You don't often see things straight. If you only talked to women more . . . about things that really matter, that is—"

"May Allah forbid!" said Tony grimly. "I've never yet talked to a woman who didn't try to make me apologize for being a man, or any who'd have bothered to talk to me if I hadn't been! You are a queen, Majesty, and you're giving me what I take to be rather complicated instructions. I'm only a man. So whatever I do—because I'm a man—you will explain should have been done differently. No man can ever do anything exactly the way a woman would like him to, but whatever he does, women will make the best of it. So I'm not going to try to do whatever it is you're trying to command. I'm going to handle this my way!"

He spoke hotly, through a natural association of their viewpoint with that of his conscience. Which had reason behind it, at that. But at the same time, he wondered rather desperately what his own way would be.

The Queen regarded him complacently.

"I know. Men are like that." Then she added, "I think you and Ghail will be very happy."

Ghail turned crimson. She stamped her foot furiously. "Majesty—" she cried. "You go too far—"

There was a small-sized uproar outside. The voice of the stout woman, in alarm:

"Abdul! Abdul! You can't do things like that!"

Tony plunged to the door. At the foot of the wall which was the *djinn* king's palace, almost a quarter of a mile away, there was a twelve-foot soldier-*djinn* who by his gestures had just communicated some message of importance. In the stretch between the wall and the farmhouse, a charging rhinoceros raced at top speed. It plunged toward the small group of buildings. Fifty yards away it seemed to stumble, crash, and in mid-air turned into a round ball with spiral red-and-white stripes which made a dizzying spectacle as it rolled. It was five feet in diameter. It checked abruptly two yards from the Queen's door and there abruptly wrinkled itself, changed color, and collapsed into the short, fat, swaggering *djinn* with a turban who was Tony's guide to this place, who was Nasim's friend Abdul, and who had awaited a summons to duty as a valet in the form of a cockroach atop the window hangings of Tony's bedroom.

He bowed profoundly.

"Lord," he said, "there is a message from the king.

Es-Souk, who was to have been executed today for your amusement, has escaped from his prison. He undoubtedly seeks you, lord, to attempt your murder before his own death, since he cannot live under the king's displeasure."

Tony felt himself growing just a little pale. He remembered fingers closing on his throat, and an elephant-sized monster in his bedroom in the palace at Barkut, beating its breast before falling upon him to demolish him utterly.

That—irrelevantly—suggested the only possible source of action. Tony gulped and said:

"Thank you, Abdul. Tell the king I am very much obliged for the warning. But tell him not to worry about it. I won't need any extra guards. I'll handle Es-Souk. In fact, I'll help hunt for him as soon as I've—as soon as I've refilled my cigarette lighter."

Chapter 13

He went back into the house. His knees felt queer. He fumbled in his pockets. He brought out the lighter, and then brought out one of the small glass phials Ghail had given him in the camel cabin on the way across the desert—one of those containing *lasf*.

Ghail looked pale, too.

"What are you going to do?" she demanded. Her voice trembled.

"Attend to Es-Souk, I hope," said Tony, with quite unnatural calm. To the Queen he said: "Your Majesty, if you have any pet *djinns* around at the moment, you'd better chase them out. I'm opening up a phial of *lasf.*"

"But—"

"I've got an idea." said Tony. "It doesn't make sense, but nothing makes much sense any more. I'm going to take advantage of what I think is a generally occurring allergic reaction among *djinns.*" The words "allergic reaction" had no Arabic equivalent, so he had to use the English ones, and to Ghail and the Queen of Barkut they sounded remarkably learned and mysterious. "And just to make sure, I'd appreciate it enormously if you'd draw me a picture of the leaf of the *lasf* plant."

He unscrewed the seal of the cigarette-lighter tank. It was bone-dry of fluid, of course. It hadn't been filled since Suakim. And while confined in his later cell it had been extremely annoying to have to get a light for an occasional cigarette, rolled from local tobacco, from a brazier kept burning by the guards outside his gate. Now the lighter was a godsend. If he was right about *lasf,* a cigarette lighter was the ideal weapon in which to use it.

He extracted the stopper of the small glass phial. With not especially steady fingers he poured the liquid into the tank. It soaked up and soaked up. Its odor was noticeable. Presently the wick was moist. He re-sealed the tank and snapped down the lighter's cover. He re-stoppered the phial and put it away.

"Now I'd like to wash my hands," he said unhappily, "and—is that the picture of the *lasf* leaf?"

The Queen had stooped and traced an outline on the clay floor of her dwelling. She said:

"I'm quite sure. Yes."

Tony stared at it and sighed in enormous relief. Ghail brought a bowl of water. He washed his hands with meticulous care. He dried them on a cloth she handed him.

"If you keep pet *djinns* around," he observed, "better burn that cloth. Right away. And I'd empty the water on soft earth and throw more earth on top of it. No use revealing that you've got *lasf* around, until you need it. The faintest whiff would give it away to them."

Ghail said again:

"But wh-what are you going to do?"

"I'm going to hunt Es-Souk," said Tony. "I think the *djinn* king is putting something over on me. I had a fight with Es-Souk in my bedroom in Barkut. He ran away. There's been talk of atomic bombs and the king thinks I can make them. But he wants to make sure. I'm under safe-conduct, of course, but if a condemned criminal—Es-Souk—breaks loose and kills me, the king can't be blamed. He'll apologize all over the place, of course. He'll probably offer to pay reparations and indemnity, and salute the Barkutian flag, and all that. But I'll be dead. And the war will go on merrily. You see?"

"But that's—dishonorable!" protested Ghail.

"Nothing's dishonorable," said Tony, gloomily, "unless you can prove it. And you'd never prove that! Just helping hunt for Es-Souk is no good. I've got to meet him in single combat, somehow, and whip him again so the king will know I do it without mirrors or outside help. If I do that, maybe we'll get somewhere."

He turned to go out the door. Ghail caught at his sleeve.

"P-please!" she said shakily. Her eyes were brimming. Tony saw the Queen regarding them critically. He was embarrassed.

"What is it?" he asked.

"Last—last night—"

Tony sighed deeply.

"Listen," he said. "If you want to sign a pledge that the lips that touch *djinnees*, shall never touch yours, you go right ahead! It won't interfere with my plans in the least. Is that satisfactory?"

"I—don't understand," said Ghail faintly.

Tony regarded her in weary gloom.

"Oh, all right!" He spread out his hands, holding the cigarette lighter in one of them. "Maybe you don't. But I'll bet Esir and Esim would!"

He went out the door to find Abdul waiting for him expectantly. Behind the door he heard Ghail sob. He marched heavily off toward the palace door, a quarter of a mile away. Abdul followed interestedly. Tony's conscience spoke to him acidly, mentioning his discourtesy to Ghail and the fact that he hadn't even said good-by to the Queen of Barkut. He snarled at it, out loud. In consequence he did not hear Ghail say, between weeping and fury:

"The—b-beast! Oh-h-h-h, the *beast!*"

Nor did he hear the Queen say approvingly:

"I'm sure you're going to be very happy with him, my dear! You'll never quite know what he's going to do next!"

This was, however, one of the few times when Tony himself did know what he was going to do.

He was angry. He grew angrier. The whole affair was simply too pat. It was too perfectly coincidental. It was exactly the sort of thing that the heads of nations in his own world—the heads of some nations, at any rate—had pulled off too many times. Tony had not yet met the *djinn* king, but he felt that he was being manipulated with the sort of smug clumsiness characteristic of power politicians. The *djinn* king in all his official acts was ineffably virtuous and chivalrous. He'd invited Tony to visit him under safe-conduct, he'd provided him with a guard, with entertainment, he'd paid him extravagant honors—and he was arranging for him to be assassinated by someone whom he could afterward execute with every expression of horror for his crime.

"He's a damned—he's a damned totalitarian," Tony growled.

He stamped into the palace, too angry to be scared any longer. There is a certain indignation of the naive and the imaginative which practical men and politicians never understand. The innocent common citizen who believes in hair tonics and television commercials and the capitalist system, believes most firmly of all that justice and decency are going to triumph. He will endure with infinite patience as long as that belief is not challenged. But let him see injustice fortifying itself for a permanent reign; let him see deceit become frankly self-confident; then he explodes! More tyrants and dictators have been overthrown for trying to make their regimes permanent than for all their crimes. In all that had gone before, Tony had been less active than acted-upon. But now he was furious.

He found the fifteen-foot captain of his personal

guard of honor. He said harshly to that cat-eyed giant:

"Captain! You will take a message immediately to your king! Say to him that as his guest, I request a favor of the highest importance! I wish a proclamation to be made everywhere within the palace saying that I, your king's guest, have been insulted by one Es-Souk, who after attempting to assassinate me while I slept, fled in terror when I grappled with him. The proclamation is to say that I had intended to ask the king to pardon him so that he could accept my challenge, and that now I have demanded of the king that I still be allowed to do battle with Es-Souk unless he is afraid to fight me. The king, therefore, grants safe-conduct to Es-Souk to an appointed place of single combat, and that the king commands his presence there because of the disgrace to all the *djinn* folk if one of them is too much of a coward to fight a single man. And you will tell the king that if Es-Souk is afraid to fight me—as I believe—then I demand that some other *djinn* take his place unless all *djinns* are afraid of me!"

The guard-captain towered over Tony, more than twice his height. For the honorable post of official guardian of the king's guest's safety, he had chosen a form neatly combining impressiveness and ferocity. He looked remarkably like an oversized black leopard walking on his hind legs and wearing a green-and-gold velvet uniform. Now his cat-eyes glared down into Tony's. But Tony, staring up, stared him down.

"Incidentally," snarled Tony, "you can tell the king that I'm quite aware that I'm being insulting, and that nobody will blame him if I get killed in single combat of this sort!"

"Lord," purred the *djinn* captain of the guard, "I shall give the king your message."

He saluted and walked with feline grace toward the nearest doorway. There, however, he was momentarily stalled, because some other *djinn* assigned to being a part of the palace had grown bored with the design of his part of the structure, and had changed the door sizes. The captain of the guard had to stoop and crawl through a doorway to go on his errand.

Tony paced up and down, growing angrier by the second. He had never fancied himself as a fighting man, and he did not fancy himself as one now. He simply felt the consuming fury of a man who feels that somebody is trying to make a sucker out of him. He fairly steamed with fury.

His valet, Abdul, watched him with wide eyes. He saw Tony muttering to himself, white with the anger which filled him. He said unhappily:

"Lord—"

Tony whirled on him.

"What is it?" he demanded savagely.

"You are very angry," said Abdul. "And—lord, created beings do not grow angry when they are afraid. You are not afraid."

"Is that all?" demanded Tony.

Abdul squirmed as if embarrassed. As if embarrassed, too, his whole body rippled in the beginning of a transformation into something else. He repressed it and returned to the appearance of a short, stout, swaggering *djinn* with a turban. But he was not swaggering now.

"It appears, lord," he said apologetically, "that you know you can destroy Es-Souk, or whatever other champion appears to do battle with you."

Tony glared at him. He thought he could, but he was not sure. His line of reasoning was tenuous, but he believed it enough, certainly, to risk his life on it. Yet he could not have managed that belief, at all, without his hot anger at the clumsily smart trick the *djinn* king had so obviously contrived. It was not fair. It was too smart. And it was complacent. The complacency may have been the most enraging part of the whole thing.

"I am quite willing," said Tony, strangling with fury, "to take on the whole damned *djinn* nation, beginning now, and including your fellow-*djinns* who happen to be the floors and walls of this room!"

Abdul said tentatively:

"Lord, we *djinn* are the most powerful of created beings. Therefore we can only have as our ruler the most powerful of created beings. Any less—any whom we could destroy—it would be beneath our dignity to obey."

Tony turned his back. He paced up and down. There was a pause. Then:

"I take a great risk," said Abdul plaintively. "Lord, will you permit me to obey you?"

"No!" snapped Tony. "Go to the devil! Get out!"

Abdul sighed. Mournfully, but elegantly, he turned into a large mass of black, inky liquid which sank in funeral fashion to the floor and flowed toward the doorway. But it did not open the door—it went out through the crack underneath. Tony was alone.

He looked at the cigarette lighter in his hand. He

touched his three separate pockets where phials of *lasf*—one almost empty, now—reposed. He reflected with savage satisfaction that it was not likely that he could be killed without some mangling, and that at least one of the bottles of *lasf* was practically sure to be smashed. And Tony's information on *lasf* was confined to about three sentences from Ghail, and one experience. And the picture of the leaf the Queen had drawn. That was all he knew. But he could extend his knowledge of a common phenomenon in the United States and guess that the Barkutian use of *lasf* was woefully inefficient. With a cigarette lighter he could do better.

The door opened again. The commander of the guard of honor was back. He saluted profoundly.

"Lord," he purred. "The king has made the proclamation you requested. He has appointed a place for the combat. He has given Es-Souk safe-conduct, and Es-Souk has appeared from hiding in the form of a rug on the audience-chamber floor and prepares himself for battle."

"Very well," snapped Tony, "I'll go there at once. If he isn't afraid, he'll follow immediately."

The *djinn* captain saluted again, with enormous formality, and withdrew for the second time.

Something stirred on the floor. A cockroach waggled its feelers imploringly, turned into an explosively expanding mistiness, and condensed again as Abdul.

"Lord!" said the stout *djinn* imploringly. "Hear me but a moment! The walls of this palace hear and report to the king! I asked to obey you. The king will know. If you do not accept me and protect me, I am lost!"

Tony shrugged.

"Unless," he said skeptically, "this is more of your king's conniving!"

"I swear by the beard of the Prophet!" panted Abdul. "Truly, lord, I can be most useful! Protect me, lord, and you will have the fleetest horse, the swiftest hound . . . I will carry you to the place of combat! I will bring you the fairest women! I will steal chickens—"

"Hm . . ." said Tony. "I suspect I did talk too fast. Where is this place of combat, anyhow?"

"I know, lord! I will take you there—"

"Then," said Tony, "let's get started."

"This way, lord!" panted Abdul. "I beg you, lord, protect me until we are free of the palace—and after. Indeed I spoke too soon. Here—the window, lord. . . ."

He raised the window. With an imploring gesture for Tony to follow, he jumped out. Tony walked to the window and looked out. There was no sign whatever of Abdul—but a wide stairway led to the ground from the windowsill. Tony swung up and tested it with his foot. It held. He went down. Instantly he touched the earth, the stairway collapsed into a cloud of dust which coalesced and was Abdul again. He wrung his hands.

"I should have waited," he said miserably. "Indeed, the king will call me a traitor. But if you are truly the most powerful—I am your steed, lord!"

He was. There was a rippling, a shifting, a bewildering alteration of plane surfaces and colors, and he was a highly suitable horse, fully saddled and caparisoned. The horse came trotting to Tony's side

and waited for him to mount. He put his foot on the
stirrup and heaved his leg over.

"Okay so far," he said grimly. "Full speed ahead."

The horse—Abdul—broke into a headlong run which
was convincingly like real panic. It headed away from
the palace at a pace even the *djinn* camels of the trip
across the desert could not have bettered.

And, as a matter of fact, the appearance of things
was enough to justify some apprehension. Word of the
approaching duel to the death had evidently spread.
Out of the gateway of the palace the *djinns* poured.
They wore every one of the eccentric shapes Tony had
noted in the line of courtiers welcoming him the night
before. There were still some wearing the shapes of
human women—those who had danced for him the
night before. And as they poured out of the palace, the
djinns whose shapes were adapted for speed retained
them, while others dissolved into forms capable of
more miles per hour. The whole assemblage looked
like a glorified zoo in flight toward one distant spot.
Even the palace began to come apart and join the
rush. Item after item of its structure vanished from
its place, swelled into a tall and somehow ghostlike
whirlwind, and swept away in eager competition for
good seats at the spectacle.

When the horse stopped, Tony swung out of the
saddle, and the short, fat *djinn* of the turban reappeared. He was utterly doleful.

"Lord," he said bitterly, "my life is in your hands!
If you do not win this battle, the king will surely
execute me in Es-Souk's stead! I beg you to conquer
in this battle!"

Tony wetted his finger to gauge the direction of the

wind. He made sure of his handkerchief. He stooped and picked up a pair of medium-sized stones and slipped them in his pocket. Then he waited.

He was in a huge, natural amphitheatre some four miles long by two wide. Its floor was practically desert sand. All about, on the mountainsides, were perched the *djinn*. The foremost rows were dots, but successive rearward rows were larger to get better views, until at the very back tall whirlwinds spun eagerly, reaching ever higher for full vision of what was to come.

The last arrivals settled into place. The entire *djinn* nation watched. Abdul despairingly shivered, and turned himself into a small stone, indistinguishable from any other. Tony waited in the center of the vast open space. And waited.

And waited.

Chapter 14

Tony's conscience said bitterly that since he was going to be killed anyhow, he might as well make a fight for it; but if he'd only listened at any single instant since Mr. Emurian offered him two thousand dollars for that ten-dirhim piece—

He swore softly. He felt singularly absurd, standing in the middle of a dusty, sandy plain with a cigarette lighter clutched in his hand, two small stones in his pocket, and with a multitude of lunatic shapes watching intently from the mountainsides about, and misty, ghost-like whirlwinds spinning expectantly beyond them.

For a long time, nothing happened.

"War of nerves," he muttered indignantly.

The small stone which was Abdul quivered, and seemed to inflate like a balloon. Abdul appeared in his customary shape, very much agitated.

"Lord! Do you see him?"

"Not yet," growled Tony. "I suppose he'll fly to contact as a mosquito and then materialize as a boa-constrictor at close quarters. Stand clear if he does."

"He cannot do it, lord," said Abdul, nervously. "He can take the shape of an insect, but as an insect he will be too heavy to fly. Our weight is the same regardless of our size, lord."

"Good!" said Tony, gratified. "Then in sand like this he can't crawl up as a centipede, either. He'd bog down." Abdul wrung his hands.

"I spoke too soon when I offered you my allegiance," he said bitterly. "It is my opinion, lord, that he will fly to a great height as a giant bird—he will need great wing-spread to fly—and then turn to a stone and drop upon you. That is an accepted form of combat."

"Hm . . . thanks," said Tony. "If anything else occurs to you, by all means mention it."

Abdul began to shrink. He wailed again:

"I spoke too soo—"

He was a stone once more. Tony could not possibly identify him among the other small stones scattered about. He began to search the sky, and remembered to wet his finger again and recheck the wind direction. There was very little movement of air, but he walked downwind from Abdul and snapped open his cigarette lighter. *Lasf*, as prepared in Barkut, had a distinct, slightly aromatic odor. Tony surrounded himself with a faint fragrance of the stuff. He could smash one of the phials of *lasf* yet remaining and make himself effectually unapproachable by Es-Souk. But he would certainly have to walk home if he did. And besides, Es-Souk could pick up stones and drop them, bomber-fashion, as easily as he could drop himself. Apparently, though, that was not an accepted form of combat. It appeared that *djinns* were so endowed that they could make anything they chose out of themselves, and therefore did not need to think of using inanimate things. It would not be good strategy to make Es-Souk so desperate that he might begin to have ideas.

And still nothing happened. There was what seemed to be a single dark bird in the sky, far away over the mountain tops. Tony wondered how far away. The larger a pair of wings might be, the more slowly they would tend to flap. Tony watched. The great bird's wings went downward only once in five seconds—it took five seconds for them to make their downward sweep, and recover, and begin another stroke. It looked as if it were flying in slow motion. Therefore the bird was very large, and very far away.

Tony nodded his head. At a guess, Es-Souk had adopted the outward form of a roc, and would gain an altitude of some ten or twelve thousand feet in that shape.

Then he might transform himself into a heavy small stone and try to brain Tony. But it wasn't likely that, as a stone, he could see where he was going or correct his line of fall once he was started. Even U.S. Army bombers, equipped with bombsights, suffered a certain amount of dispersion in their shots.

Inspiration struck Tony. He took off the camel's-hair, belted-in-the-back topcoat. When in human form, *djinns* wore clothes—when they remembered. Nasim was apt to be forgetful. But the clothes they created were a part of them, like their jewels and their weapons. They might know the theory of clothing, but in practice for Tony to take off his topcoat might confuse Es-Souk. He mightn't know whether to aim at the coat or at Tony himself. And besides, if that slowly flapping bird was a roc, and if the roc was Es-Souk, he probably couldn't see too clearly at the height he'd obtained. Tony draped his coat over a small, sparsely leaved bush that startlingly grew in the middle of this waste. He stood back. He was giving Es-Souk two targets to choose from, and the need for choice might be upsetting.

Apparently, it was. The great bird soared in circles for minutes. Then it dived lower, for a better look. Tony stood as still as his topcoat. He could see the shape of the huge flying thing. It was like a giant eagle, only vastly more terrifying. Its body would be seventy or eighty feet long. Its wings would have the spread of a four-motored bomber. Its claws would have the grip of half a dozen steam shovels in one. And its talons would be needle-sharp and more than three feet long. Decidedly, at close quarters, it wouldn't be anything to argue with

It vanished. Completely. Es-Souk had turned himself into a small round stone hurtling downward from the sky.

Tony counted:

"One—two—three—"

Give the stone time to pick up speed in free fall.

The time a parachuting flier waits before he opens his parachute.

"Eight—nine—ten—*Geronimo!*" said Tony.

He ran like the devil for fifty yards, stopped, and watched the spot where he had been. Then his jaw dropped open. His topcoat was running like the devil, too. The bush on which he had draped it was in full flight. As he stared, he saw the twinkling of pink legs under it. Then his topcoat stopped, and turned, and he saw Nasim in human form inside it. She waved gaily to him.

"Hello!" she called brightly. "I'm helping, too!"

WHOOOOOOSH!

Something smacked the desert a mighty blow. Dust arose as from a bomb explosion. A concussion wave spread out with such power that Tony felt a puff of wind, and the topcoat went sailing from around Nasim. She had been forgetful again. She went after the coat and picked it up, swinging it cheerily in one hand as she turned to watch.

Es-Souk arose from the crater which he had made as a stone. He had a new form. He was huge and— now—black and terrible to behold. He was a giant of ebony flesh with four-foot tusks and hands whose clawed fingertips were feet in length.

Tony ran toward him, blowing on the wick of the cigarette lighter.

The giant bellowed, but Tony sprinted even faster for hand-to-hand contact. And the *djinn* could not quite take it. Tony's challenge had included so furious an insult to the entire *djinn* nation that it could not possibly be a bluff—and now his confident rush to close in on Es-Souk was daunting.

Es-Souk spurted upward into a whirlwind half a mile high. He materialized as a roc at the top of the column of misty whirling air. The rest of the whirlwind flashed upward to be absorbed in the bird's body. It was an admirable technical solution of the problem of a quick take-off for so large a flying creature. Gigantic flappings of mighty pinions sent the roc soaring away. Es-Souk was uncertain. He did not quite know what to do. To cover his indecision, he suddenly swooped and made what looked like a dive-bomber plunge for Tony.

It was utterly horrible to watch. The monstrous creature, its incredibly curved beak gaping, plunged for him in ravening ferocity. Its claws were stretched to rend and tear. It was as perfectly calculated to inspire panic as any sight could possibly be.

Tony faced it. He had a phial of *lasf* in his handkerchief, now. In the handkerchief, too, were the small stones he'd pocketed. He held the cigarette lighter in his left hand. His right gripped that singularly innocuous bomb. At the last instant he'd squeeze, crush the phial between the stones, and hurl the dripping handkerchief—weighted by the stones—deep into the gaping throat. He didn't know how quickly it would work, but—

The roc zoomed just as Tony was sending the message to his fingers to tense and smash the *lasf*-phial. The great wings beat horrifically. Sand rose in clouds about Tony, blinding him. He found himself almost buried to his knees as the sand settled about him.

The roc was flapping into the sky again. Nasim ran up to Tony, beaming and offering him the coat.

"You're wonderful!" she said adoringly. "What are you going to do next? And what do you want me to do?" He said indignantly:

"You shouldn't mix into a private fight like this, Nasim!"

"Oh, do let me help!" she pleaded.

"Hell!" said Tony. "Put on something! Put on the coat! How do you expect me to keep my mind on fighting?"

The roc which was Es-Souk made a steep, banking turn. It power-dived at Tony again. And this time Es-Souk had a purpose, a new purpose. He'd seen Tony struggling up out of the sand. So Es-Souk came back only yards above the desert's surface, his monstrous wings beating almost straight back to give him the absolute maximum of speed. Then, only fifty feet from Tony, he swept his wings violently ahead, and not only checked his own speed and sent himself hurtling upward, but set up such a furious smother of swirling sand that Tony was buried breast-deep before he realized what was happening. Es-Souk had made a sizable sand dune with one stroke of his mighty roc's wings. It was sheer fortune that its deepest part did not overwhelm Tony.

He worked his way clear, Nasim pulling anxiously at him—with the topcoat lost again. Tony swore furiously. Something like a bubble appeared in the sand dune's flank. Abdul appeared and arose, with sand grains dripping from his turban. He sputtered and wailed:

"I know I spoke too soon! . . . Lord! Next time he will bury you, and you will smother, and then what will I do?"

Es-Souk whirled again, low down, and shot back toward Tony again. Nasim said firmly:

"Don't be so stupid, Abdul! Turn yourself into a griffin, with a saddle, and let him ride you to fight Es-Souk in the air!"

Abdul blinked and hastily drew a deep breath. He expanded, to a large round object with no identifiable features. He contracted to something that Tony could not identify, and which at the moment he did not examine. He saw wings and a saddle and a long, serpentine tail. He made a dash for the saddle, swung into it, and hung on.

Chapter 15

And he felt himself shooting skyward with breathtaking velocity! There was one instant when a huge, feathered body was directly below him—a body so huge that it gave him a queer sensation of being an insect chased by an infuriated hen. Then he was clear and rising. There were great, veined wings beating on either side, there was a scaly body below him, doubtlessly a serpentine tail behind him, and a long, snaky neck in front with a head he could not see clearly.

That neck twisted and a specifically indefinite face appeared—or rather, did not appear. It looked like mist, yet there were eyes in it, and Abdul's plaintive voice came to Tony above the beat of mighty wings.

"Lord," said Abdul miserably, "if you have some weapon to use against Es-Souk, if you tell me how you wish to use it, I will try to give you the opportunity. If you do not win this fight, lord, I am ruined!"

"I've got a weapon, all right," said Tony. "I'd intended to use it on the ground, away from you and Nasim. It's pretty deadly to any *djinn* anywhere near by."

Abdul make a moaning sound.

"But if anything happens to you," said Tony, "I'll have a nasty fall. So—hm . . . get us some height, and then if you can let Es-Souk dive at me from behind, I think I can use my weapon so you won't be affected."

The desert shrank as the unnamed creature into which Abdul had transformed himself strove desperately for height. Tony found a strap hitched to the saddle, intended to make the rider secure in his place. He fastened it and felt better. He saw the roc, far below, beginning to beat upward with furious strokes of its long pinions.

He tucked away his cigarette case and got out his two stones and the handkerchief and the full phial of *lasf*. He rearranged the stones and the phial in the handkerchief. He tied the whole together, tugging at the corners of the handkerchief with his teeth. The combination made a fairly handy if eccentric hand grenade. But of course it could not possibly explode.

Then he watched with an unnatural calm. Just as in an airplane one has no sensation of height, so on this peculiar mount he felt as if he were in some sensational illusory ride in an amusement park. He even examined the creature he rode, while the mountain tops grew level with him and then sank a thousand feet or more below.

"Abdul," he said. "What on earth are you, anyhow? I've never seen anything like this!"

Abdul said miserably:

"I had indigestion one night, lord, and dreamed this. So I practiced making myself into it. It has been much admired. The touch of having the creature possess no actual, visible face is considered very effective, and I—I thought at one time that Nasim was much impressed by it. But she became betrothed to Es-Souk. I think, lord, that the form I wear might be called a chimaera."

Tony said:

"Nasim liked it, eh? . . . here comes Es-Souk! Level off, Abdul, and let him get on our tail. When he comes diving in I'll do my stuff, and when I yell you put on the heat. Get away from there fast! Understand?"

"Aye, lord." And then Abdul wailed from that misty emptiness which was the chimaera's face, "If I ever get out of this, I will never speak so soon again! I will never offer allegiance to any other—"

The very mountains seemed like toadstools below them. Tony could see over uncountable square miles of desert and foothills. He even thought he saw a dark smudge against the horizon which might be the oasis and the city of Barkut—

Tony felt a shadow fall upon him—the shadow of the roc, a thousand feet above. It screamed at him.

"Get set now," said Tony, between his teeth. "Ready—let's go! He's diving, Abdul!"

The roc flattened its wings, partly folding them, and came rushing down in a deadly plunge. Actually, Es-Souk was still at least partly bluffed. Tony had been too confident, and Es-Souk was a cagey *djinn*.

He'd had one experience of hand-to-hand fighting with Tony, and he had sneezed so horribly that—knowing what he knew—he had been scared to the very last atom of his fissionable being. But since Tony was now some twelve thousand feet above ground-level, on chimaera-back, it would be possible to kill him even more surely than by tearing him limb from limb. A furious assault upon Abdul, in some tender member, should make the *djinn*-chimaera react in typical *djinn* fashion—by metamorphosis. Abdul could definitely be forced to change to something else. And if he failed of absolute presence of mind, he would forget to include Tony's saddle and safety belt in his new shape, and Tony would thump into the desert below in a completely conclusive finish to the duel.

So the roc plunged savagely—seemingly for Tony, but intending a last-second swerve and the chewing-up of one of Abdul's chimaera-wings. In sheer self-defense Abdul must repair the damage by changing form, and—

"Brakes, Abdul!" commanded Tony. "He's not gaining fast enough!"

Abdul slowed—and the roc gained. Closer—closer—its great beak gaping. It was almost time for the swerve and the slashing attack which would send Tony plunging some two miles and more to death

Tony shouted, "Now, Abdul! Brake hard! That'll make him overshoot—"

Abdul braked. Chimaeras are extraordinarily maneuverable creatures. Abdul seemed practically to stop short in mid-air. The roe almost crashed into him, its cavernous beak widening in awful menace.

Actually, the roc's beak was no more than twenty

feet away when Tony squeezed hard on his improvised bomb, felt the glass crunch—and heaved the
cloth-wrapped missile into the gaping throat. It was
an excellent shot. He saw the little object go flying
down the two-yard, open gullet to its maw.

"Roger!" roared Tony. "Step on it! Move!"

Then he felt as if his neck would snap off. Abdul
took evasive action. It began with an outside loop that
made the safety belt creak hideously, was followed
by a wing-over at the bottom, and then continued as
a power dive in which the wind went pouring into
Tony's open mouth until he felt as if he were being
forcibly inflated.

But even then he looked back.

The roc was motionless, as if paralyzed by some
awful shock. But the paralysis lasted only for seconds.
Suddenly the already huge form expanded still more.
It struggled convulsively. It sneezed. In its struggling
it had not stayed on an even keel. The sneeze had
all the propulsive effect of a high-temperature jet.
It kicked the suddenly shapeless object violently
higher. It writhed. It struggled again, very horribly.
It ceased to be a bird, it was impossible to say what
it was! Another convulsion even more violent than
the first. The almost amoeboid object shot higher—it
had pseudopods now, which appeared at random and
flailed aimlessly but with terrific force. A second
convulsive sneeze ejected so huge a volume of air
with such violence that the *djinn* was shot up a
good five thousand feet.

Es-Souk was maddened, now, with the knowledge
of his doom. He went into lunatic gyrations which
turned into flight straight upward. But he flew now

not by wings or any motion of any members, but by the lightning-swift protrusion of a threadlike pseudo-pod far ahead and the equally lightning-like flowing of all his substance up to and into it, and the instant repetition of the process.

Even huge as he now was, he rose so swiftly as to dwindle as Tony watched. At ten miles altitude there was a convulsive sidewise jerking of the climbing thing. Another sneeze. He continued to shoot franti-cally skyward. Twenty miles up . . . he was probably a quarter-mile across, but he became a speck which could barely be distinguished

Then he blew up. He must have been fifty miles high, at least. He was in the upper troposphere. And he must have weighed several hundred pounds. Perhaps not all his substance disintegrated. Even human atomic bombs do not detonate with one hundred percent conversion of their mass into free energy. Es-Souk's efficiency as a bomb was prob-ably less than that of purified U235 or plutonium. But the flare was colossal. There was a sensation of momentary, terrific heat. No sound, of course. The explosion took place where the air was too thin to carry sound. For the same reason there was no concussion wave. But the flash of Es-Souk's detona-tion was several times brighter than the sun and a dozen times the sun's diameter.

Minutes later, Abdul came rather heavily to a land-ing on the desert. Tony dismounted. Abdul seemed to dissolve suddenly and run together, without any intermediate state, to restore the *djinn* to his short, swart, human form, with the turban atop his head. He was trembling.

"Lord!" he said in a shaking voice. "I did not know how terrible was your weapon! I did not know that you were so much more powerful than the most powerful of *djinns*. Indeed, lord, I apologize for regretting that I offered my allegiance. I did not speak too soon, lord! I did not speak soon enough! And by the beard of the Prophet, I swear that you are my king and my ruler for always!"

Tony swallowed. That flare in the midday sky had been unnerving.

"All right, Abdul," he said. "We'll let it go at that. You've been worried about protection. As far as I can, I'll give it to you—"

"Protection, lord?" said Abdul, beaming. "It is I who will be begged for protection now! My friends who have seen Es-Souk destroyed will come to me begging me to intercede that you do not destroy them also! You will let me boast before them, lord? After all, I was the chimaera on which you rode when you destroyed Es-Souk in such a manner that no others of the *djinn* were harmed! I did help you, to the best of my poor ability!"

"Naturally—" began Tony. Then Nasim's voice came to him.

"You carried him, Abdul," said Nasim proudly, "which is what a *djinn* should do for his king. But I played the part of a proper *djinnee*, too! I held his coat!"

Tony turned to her. He accepted the belted-in-the-back camel's-hair coat. Then he said politely:

"That was very nice of you, Nasim. I appreciate it a lot. But won't you *please* put on some clothes?"

Chapter 16

The palace of the *djinn* king wasn't what it had been.
Not only the *djinn* officially off-duty, as it were, had
attended Tony's duel with Es-Souk; guardsmen also
had quietly transformed themselves from twelve-foot
military figures into gazelles, whirlwinds, lions, and
other swiftly moving creatures to attend the sporting
event. The court, generally, had poured out to see
the ruckus. And in addition, various *djinn* serving
as towers, pinnacles, rooms, articles of furniture and
virtu, rugs, hangings, plumbing fixtures and structural
elements had taken time off from supporting the state
and majesty of the king.

Some of them went back to their assigned positions in the structure after it was all over, but some
did not. In consequence, from the official lodging
of the Queen of Barkut, the all-encircling palace
looked ragged. Here an art gallery was exposed
to the blazing sunshine. There the more intimate
arrangements of the *djinn* monarch's seraglio were
in plain view. And the dusty, thinly grassed meadow
within the palace looked like a country fairground
on opening day. Some thousands of *djinn* milled
about, in all the diverse shapes and forms their
personal preferences dictated. Some talked. Some
argued. A few—even at such a moment—made such
romantic overtures to other members of the race
of opposite gender as might have been expected.
But on the whole, the several-thousand-odd *djinn*
gathered beyond the Queen's vegetable gardens were
there to see Tony.

He made his report to the Queen, drinking coffee in her cottage. Ghail moved about, ostensibly assisting the Queen in serving him, but actually listening avidly and looking at him from time to time with widely varying expressions.

"The devil of it is," said Tony querulously, "that instead of making me unpopular, killing Es-Souk seems to have made me something of a hero!"

The Queen nodded.

"They're like children," she said sagely. "Just like children—or apes. Much like horses, too. *Djinns* are great fun! They make lovely pets when you understand them!"

Tony's expression lacked something of full sympathy.

"Somehow," he admitted, "just personally, you understand, I can't imagine wanting to pet a quarter-ton of fissionable material, whether it was in the form of a chimaera or a cute little moth's egg hiding in a crack until the time was ripe for conversation."

"I still don't see," said the Queen, brightly, "just how you set him off—this Es-Souk, that is. Is it a secret of the royal family of your nation?"

Tony shrugged helplessly.

"I didn't intend to set him off," he admitted. "I did think I might pin his ears back, and with him, the king's, but I didn't anticipate an atomic explosion. But it does make sense, after a fashion. After all, when anything's put into an atomic pile it becomes radioactive, and a radioactive substance isn't immune to ordinary chemical effects. It works just like ordinary matter except for its radioactivity. So it's reasonable enough that perfectly normal, perfectly stable compounds like *lasf* would act chemically on *djinns*. The results, though—"

"Chemically?" queried the Queen. Ghail stood still, looking strangely at Tony.

"Of course," said Tony. "I had you draw me a picture of the *lasf*-leaf. Remember? And I recognized it. We have that plant in my country. We call it hogweed, or ragweed. It's a pest to some humans."

The Queen listened. Tony drank more coffee.

"Ragweed," he said. "Sneezing. You anoint your weapons with it. The *djinns* run away. Sometimes they sneeze. And I'd drunk some of the stuff the other day and that night Es-Souk tried to strangle me, and I coughed. And he sneezed. That's ragweed, all right! The pollen is worst of all. It hits some human people too. You see?"

The Queen said brightly: "I fear not, Lord Toni."

"Ragweed; sneezing; hay fever," explained Tony. "The *djinns* are subject to hay fever. It's an allergy. A racial trait. Ragweed, which doesn't bother most humans, is deadly poison to them. Like DDT to bugs. It's so strong a poison that merely its odor sets them crazy. You people have been wasting the stuff. You've swabbed guns and bullets with it. It dried, and by the time you got to where you were going to fight the *djinn*, most of it was gone. They ran away from the dried, dusty remains that by pure accident stuck to your weapons. You see? That night in my bedroom I had the stuff on my breath. When I coughed, Es-Souk got a whiff of it. And I figured that if so little of it would chase him, the real stuff tossed down his throat would really go to town. And it did!"

He looked hopefully at them. But he knew no Arabic

word for "allergy" or "hay fever" or "pollen," or for "radioactive" or "fissionable" or "atomic." Even the English word "ragweed" in an Arabic context did not seem to mean *lasf* to the Queen or Ghail. To the two of them, he seemed to be speaking quite sincerely about matters so erudite as to be beyond their understanding. And at that it would have taken him a week to clarify the word "allergy." They would never have understood DDT. The Queen dismissed the explanation.

"Doubtless it is clear to you, Lord Toni," she observed, "but we poor women find it too involved. You speak of the magics and arts of your own nation. What shall you do now?"

Tony blinked. Then he remembered his anger.

"I'm going to see the king," he said indignantly. "He arranged that business of Es-Souk's escape, dammit! He expected to get me killed, with himself in the clear! I'm going to give him the devil! And if he acts up," he added truculently, "I'll blow on my cigarette lighter! That will hardly set him off, but it'll scare him green!"

The Queen looked hard at Tony. Then she exchanged an astonished glance with Ghail.

"Have you looked out the door?" she asked softly.

Tony looked, and grew uncomfortable. "Do they have autograph hunters here, too?"

Ghail said firmly, "I do not know whether you are as stupid as you pretend, but certainly you had better go out and speak to those *djinns!* They are impressed enough now!"

"Impressed?"

Ghail said exasperatedly, "Get up! Go out! Let them

bow down to you! Then, if you wish, you can go to see the king!" But as he stood up with a bewildered expression, she said softly, "You are very wonderful!"

"What?" He looked incredulous, and then turned swiftly to the Queen. "Oh, yes! Ghail tells me, Majesty, that she is your personal slave and can't be sold or given without your consent. I'd—er—like to have a business conversation with you sooner or later."

Ghail stamped her foot. "Get—out!"

Tony looked incredulous again. He went reluctantly out of the door.

A bull elephant charged toward him from fifty feet away. Tony took one look and reached for his cigarette case. Then the elephant changed smoothly into some thousands of billiard balls in red, green, blue, black and pink, which swept onward in a clacking tide of bewildering intricate motions upon and against each other. The balls shrank as they rolled. Then, suddenly, they jerked to a halt and into the rotund, turbaned, swaggering form of Abdul in one instant.

"Majesty!" said Abdul, beaming. "Your people are gladdened by the sight of you! Will you deign to accept their allegiance now, or will you make a more formal ceremony?"

Tony said:

"Don't talk nonsense! Look here! I was invited to this place to see the king! He tried to get me killed! I'm not pleased with him! If I've got to have an interview with him, I want to get it over with! Then I'll go back to Barkut so the truce will be ended, and come back and start tearing things up. I've a sort of obligation—"

"Majesty!" protested Abdul. "You would endanger

your so-precious life by entering his presence? What would become of me if by treachery—"

Tony scowled. "I'd like to see him try something!" he said sourly. "How about showing me the way?"

He wasn't bluffing. The event of an hour or so ago, plus innumerable other oddities, had created in him a sort of fanatic disbelief in common sense. It suddenly occurred to him that his conscience hadn't said one word to him since the fight with Es-Souk. It did not seem possible that his maiden aunt's acid creation had ceased to exist—but still—

He winced.

His conscience was snarling bitingly that it was still on deck; but that his activities were so illimitably remote from sanity that they had no moral aspect at all. But, said his conscience—and it seemed to raise its voice—when it came to trying to make a business deal for the ownership of a poor slave girl whose morals were demonstrably so much superior to his own—

Tony straightened up. He felt better with his conscience nagging at him. More natural.

He marched toward the palace. Abdul scuttled around before him and swaggered, waving his arms imperiously for the clearing of a way. There was a swarming of *djinns* to be close to the point of his passage. It was a singular experience for Tony to walk through the mob in a lane cleared for him as if by magic, and to feel upon himself the respectful, avid starings of so many eyes. There were animals' faces and human faces and faces that were far from either. There were birds and reptiles and quaint assemblages of unrelated parts into forms which—like Abdul's chimaera—had probably been dreamed up by their wearers of the moment. There were also three *djinnees,* side by side, still in the same female human forms *they* had worn the night before. They were an odd illustration of the female fondness of fashion, because the night before their forms had included the gauzy draperies of Arab dancing girls. Now that was changed. Nasim's part in the victory over Es-Souk had been seen and noted. The three *djinnees* paid her tribute as a leader of fashion. Beaming at Tony as he passed, they displayed the new style Nasim had set among the lady *djinn:* They were, exclusively, pink skin.

Tony and Abdul walked through the palace. There were places where there was no longer a roof. The roof-members were out in the prison-meadow where they had waited for Tony to speak to them. There were places where there were no walls. There was one spot where even all flooring had vanished, and Tony saw with some astonishment that beneath the very fabric of the royal palace of the *djinn,* there was sparse grass and sandy soil, as if this particular part of the palace had not even been in existence for very many days.

Abdul made a dignified flourish before the chasm. He leaped agilely outward into emptiness in what might have been a graceful swan dive—and unfolded himself as a portable suspension bridge that neatly spanned the gap. Tony walked across. He did not quite turn in time to see the process by which Abdul returned to his more normal form.

"Majesty," said Abdul blandly, "have you made your plans as yet?"

"Eh? Plans? Hm—not yet," said Tony.

"I am the first of your servants and subjects, Majesty,"

Abdul told him piously. "I beg you to trust in me for a time—at least until you find a better!"

Tony said impatiently:

"All right. But why do you call me Maj—"

He stopped. As he spoke, he had passed through a doorway. It was but one of dozens he had allowed Abdul to lead him through. But this was different. He had come unannounced and unwittingly into the audience hall of the King of the *Djinns*. It was a colossal hall, some sixty feet high and perhaps six hundred feet long. Its walls blazed with all the phony grandeur the *djinn* assigned to wall-duty could imagine. It was very magnificent indeed.

The group of *djinns* at its far end was less magnificent. There were but half a dozen of them. They were gathered timorously about one of their number, who was patently their king. And he fumbled with what Tony suddenly realized was the only actual artifact he had seen in any *djinn's* hands. It was the only accessory he had noted which was not a part of the *djinn* who wore or carried it.

This object was distinctly non-*djinnian*. The ancient *djinn* who clutched it jealously was plainly bewildered by it. To judge by the crown on his head and various other royal insignia, he could be none but the *djinn* king in person. And he was the first and only *djinn* Tony had ever seen who really looked old. A *djinn* looked always as old as he thought, but the King of the *Djinns* was no longer even able to think of himself as young. He was very ancient indeed, and he was hideously ugly—Tony heard later that there was a trace of *efreet* blood in him—and he fumbled querulously with an object which surely no *djinn* had ever conceived or made.

It was a device of glass and corroded bronze and other metals. The glass part of it was remarkably familiar. It was exactly the shape of one of those fluorescent-ended tubes on whose larger, coated surface an image appears in a television set. The rest of it was completely cryptic to Tony. There were coils, and there was something that could be a condenser, and there were objects which could even be batteries, in age-blackened bronze cases. But the whole was old. Unspeakably old. And, of course, batteries could not be expected to hold a charge after as many centuries as the patina on the bronze implied.

"Greeting!" said Tony sternly. He had his cigarette lighter handy.

The *djinn* king looked up with an elderly start. Then he scowled portentously.

"Hah! The human Lord Toni," he rumbled. "You have betrayed my hospitality, human! It is well for you that I am merciful! But you are my guest! Therefore I take no vengeance on you in my own house. But your camel will return you to Barkut within the hour! The truce between me and Barkut ends! I shall destroy the city and the people. I shall blot out the memory of the nation! I shall—"

Tony found his eyes hot and angry.

"Interesting! You invited me here to have me murdered because you learned that my nation isn't troubled with *djinn!* You were afraid I might lead Barkut to security! But your planned murder backfired, so now you'll try the same thing openly!" Then he bluffed. "And how do you propose to destroy Barkut? You have seen what I can do!"

The *djinn* king glowered at Tony. With somehow the air of one changing costume to a more appropriate garb, he swelled to a greater size. Tusks appeared between his lips. His complexion became a ghastly blue. Horns showed on his head. The armor which appeared at the same time was tastefully decorated with human skulls. But he still looked old. And Tony felt that he was uneasy.

"Human!" he roared. "See you this thing in my hands? It is the great treasure of the *djinn* crown! With this have my *djinns* been kept subject! With this will I destroy Barkut and the sniveling traitors who bow to you! Know you what this is?"

Tony had a hunch amounting to conviction that the *djinn* king had been puzzling over the device when he entered. He had plainly no great knowledge either of machinery or electronics. Tony had not much more. But he simply could not believe that any device of such great age could still be in working order. He bluffed again.

"Of course I know what it is!" he said scornfully. "Every low drinking-place in my nation has one! You look in the large end of the tube!"

Speaking of the device as a television set, Tony spoke with strict truthfulness. But he felt the jerking tension in the *djinns* about the king grow suddenly less. The king himself relaxed visibly.

"Ho!" rumbled the king zestfully. "That was a matter I knew! I knew that! Ha! I but tested you to see if you truly know this device. Then you know that with it pointed at a rebellious *djinn* or a human city, at any distance I may create explosions beside which the destruction of Es-Souk is as the glow of a firefly!"

The other elderly *djinns* about him laughed uproariously. Their mirth was almost hysterically relieved. It sounded as if the *djinn* king had not known which was the business end of the gadget. He had been trying helplessly to figure out how to aim it. And Tony had told them.

"Go you back to Barkut," bellowed the king gleefully. "Tell the humans there that from my palace I shall destroy them all!"

Tony knitted his brows. He felt cold prickles up and down his spine. He couldn't believe the thing would work, as old as it was. But the *djinn* ought to know! So he said distastefully:

"From your palace? With its walls of *djinns*?" He remembered Abdul's weeping gratitude out on the sand, after the duel was over, because only Es-Souk had perished. "Remember what will happen if by accident you destroy a *djinn* nearby! I do not advise you to use that device. Besides, consider how much more deadly is mine!"

He snapped open the cigarette lighter. He blew gently on the wick. The faint fragrance of *lasf* . . .

There was instant, howling panic. Abdul flashed out the door by which he and Tony had entered. The king and his councilors fled in tumult. Even the floor of the audience hall heaved and melted away, and Tony tumbled some four or five feet to the ground. He was abruptly in the open air with the palace dissolving all about him and whirlwinds darting away in crazy flight in every direction.

Farthest, and fleeing fastest, seemed to be the king.

But the *djinn* king had not dropped his gadget.

Tony hunted anxiously all around. He didn't believe it could work, but still—

He worried about it as he walked gloomily back toward the mud cottage where the Queen and Ghail were quartered.

It shouldn't work. It positively was too old to work! But if it did—

Chapter 17

They started back for Barkut in a state wholly unlike the fashion of their arrival at the *djinn* palace. Abdul arranged the march. He seemed to delight in devising elaborate ceremonies. The parade began with dragons, sixty feet long and breathing fire. After them marched a troop of giants carrying very knobbly maces seemingly of iron, which should have weighed tons. Then a vast, long column of *djinn* camels, each camel the customary twenty feet tall and with an impressive pack load of unstable *djinn* riches, the whole draped with cloth-of-gold and similar stuff. Then *djinn* soldiers, looking remarkably ferocious. Tony and Ghail and the Queen rode in a colossal litter carried between two elephants. It was extremely luxurious, and the only incongruous note was that the Queen had packed a picnic lunch for the journey in crude earthen pots. They were covered over with seed-pearl brocades, however, and did not show.

Such ostentation had not been Tony's own idea. Abdul had presented himself fearfully at the Queen's cottage, almost half an hour after the use of *lasf* in the audience chamber.

"Majesty!" said Abdul reproachfully. "If you detonate me, who am the most abject of your subjects, how will the government go on?"

"Government?" Tony stared. "What government?"

"Of the *djinn*," said Abdul, more reproachfully still. "You are my king, Majesty. You are also king of these others who wait to swear allegiance. And there must be government!"

"Hold on!" Tony cried. "What's this? What have I got to do with government? How'd I get to be a king?"

"Majesty!" Abdul waved his hands. He had changed his costume, now, and appeared in garments which were exclusively seed pearls with ruby and emerald buttons. His turban emitted a slight and graceful plume of smoke, which looked incendiary but—he had explained—was quite safe under all ordinary conditions. "Majesty, it is simple! You, a human, defeated Es-Souk in single combat, hand-to-hand. This was in the night in Barkut. Such a thing has never before happened in the history of the *djinn*. Today you fought a duel with Es-Souk and detonated him so that no other of the *djinn* folk was even harmed. Only the King of the *Djinns* has even been able to destroy a *djinn*. It has been a thousand years since even our kings have had to resort to this measure, and on the last three occasions—going back more than two thousand years—in each case numerous other *djinns* died in the holocaust of the execution. And before my own eyes and many others you caused the former king and his councilors to flee and a part of his palace to dissolve. You are, therefore, more powerful than any *djinn*, you are more merciful than any king of the *djinn* in the past, and you are victor in a personal contest with the king we had this morning. Therefore you are the king!"

"The logic is elaborate," said Tony suspiciously, "but it isn't airtight."

"Majesty," repeated Abdul firmly, "you can destroy any of us, or you can spare any of us. Therefore we obey you. And therefore you are the king. It cannot be helped."

The Queen of Barkut looked at him, smiling.

"Obviously," she said brightly. "Abdul is quite right. And you can end my captivity if you wish. What rewards we poor humans of Barkut can offer you—"

Tony looked sharply at Ghail. She flushed hotly.

"All right," said Tony. "So I'm the king. Do we have a civil war, or is my authority unanimously accepted?"

"It is almost unanimous, Majesty," said Abdul, beaming. "It may be necessary to detonate the former king. That, however, is not yet certain. He has fled with a few of his councilors. They feel that you have a prejudice against them—"

"Intelligent of them," grunted Tony. "Very well, then! The first thing is to get Ghail and the Queen back to Barkut. Then we'll start fresh from there. Do you want to arrange matters?"

"For what else," asked Abdul blandly, "did your Majesty make me your grand vizier?"

He bowed to the ground and vanished. The parade formed almost immediately after. It set out across the desert with the celerity of *djinn* traffic. The elephant litter maintained a forty-mile speed principally because the elephants were nearly five stories tall. Whirlwinds went on before, spreading out as scouts on all sides, and overhead some dozens of rocs cruised at different altitudes for an air umbrella against possible attack by the former king and his half dozen malcontents. It was all quite preposterous. The elephant litter itself was the size of an eight-room house and actually contained two floors and different compartments on each floor. The Queen sat gracefully underneath the canopy on the sun deck on top. Ghail sat beside her, her lips tightly compressed. Despite the speed of their journeying, the litter was hot. Ghail, however, remained wrapped up in all the voluminous wrappings of a respectable woman during travel.

"Listen," said Tony, "aren't you hot?"

"I'll do," said Ghail composedly.

"As a slave," said Tony, "the Queen can give you permission to make yourself comfortable. Why not?"

Ghail regarded him ominously. But the Queen said:

"He's right, my dear. Why don't you slip out of that dreadfully hot cloak?"

"He," said Ghail in even tones, "is very fond of looking at legs. My legs, or anybody else's legs. And he hasn't any *djinnees* with him to sit around like the hussies they are—for instance, that *djinnee* who held his coat while he fought Es-Souk! So he is unhappy!" Then she flared out at Tony. "Why don't you get another litter for yourself? All you have to do is command it! Or we'll get out of this litter and ride on camels, and you can have as many *djinnees* around you as you want! You can—"

Tony scowled. "If you're thinking of Nasim . . . wait a minute!"

He stood up and went to the rail of the gently swaying sun deck. Alongside, a few hundred yards away, a smaller litter kept pace with this. That was the traveling carriage of Abdul, who had explained blandly that as grand vizier to Tony who was king of the *djinn* a certain amount of state for himself was desirable. But Abdul's litter was merely carried by two thirty-foot camels, and the litter slung between them was no larger than the cabin of an eight-passenger plane. It was suitably less stately than Tony's equipage. When Tony bellowed at it, its interior was completely hidden by silken draperies.

"Abdul!" roared Tony.

The thirty-foot camels intelligently swerved to bring Abdul's litter close. And even so soon, Abdul had attuned himself to react instantly to a call in Tony's voice. Instantly the drapes were torn aside. Abdul beamed across the space between litters.

But for half a breath Tony did not recognize him. Abdul swaggered, of course—but that was part of *his* personality. It was his form which was strangely unfamiliarly familiar. He was, in fact, a duplicate of Tony. He wore exact facsimiles of Tony's soft felt hat, his belted-in-the-back camel's-hair topcoat, and undoubtedly his feet were encased in duplicates of Tony's brown shoes. But the face was still the face of Abdul, and it beamed.

Behind him, in the litter, Nasim also beamed at Tony.

"Majesty!" cried Abdul happily. "What is your will?"

Tony stared—and inspiration struck.

"That is Nasim, isn't it?" he demanded.

"Yes, Majesty," called Nasim archly. She came and stood beside Abdul. "Look! Doesn't he look just like you? Isn't he wonderful?"

Tony said sternly:

"It was my thought that I had not yet rewarded Nasim for her aid in the fight with Es-Souk. I see that she has chosen her reward. It is my will that the two of you marry!"

Nasim giggled. Abdul bowed so low that he almost fell out of the litter.

"To hear is to obey, Majesty!"

"And it is also my will," said Tony severely, "that if at any time in the future Nasim comes into my presence, she must have some clothes on! After all, I'm human!"

"Aye, Majesty!" said Abdul. Nasim coyly pulled a drape about herself.

"That's all!" said Tony.

He turned his back. The camel litter swerved away. The Queen seemed to be trying to stifle laughter. Ghail looked utterly infuriated.

"Well?" said Tony.

"If the Queen," said Ghail furiously, "commands that I sacrifice my modesty to the King of the *Djinns* so that he can see if he wishes to purchase me—"

Tony said just as angrily:

"Hold on! I haven't talked business to the Queen yet! But I'll talk it now!" He turned to the much-amused Queen. "Majesty, I understand that I'm the King of the *Djinns*. Most of the riches I'm supposed to have are fake, as you know. But if there aren't any real riches, I'll make these *djinns* of mine work until there are! And I'll pay you any sum you care to name if you'll set Ghail free so she won't be a slave any longer."

His conscience spoke approvingly. Tony snarled at it. The Queen almost choked on her laughter. Ghail's face went blank. She stared incredulously at Tony.

"And—and then what?" asked the Queen.

"Then," said Tony doggedly, "I'll try to persuade her to marry me. It isn't that I'm too damned moral, but I don't think I'd like bought kisses, however legal the transaction might be in this country."

"And—and if she would not marry you?" asked the Queen.

Tony looked at Ghail. Her face was crimson, and though there was no perceptible softening in her expression, her eyes showed distinct satisfaction.

"If she wouldn't marry me," said Tony shrewdly, "then—I guess I'd have to take an interest in music. After all, I understand that Esir and Esim have pretty good voices."

The satisfaction vanished from Ghail's expression. Fury came back.

"I thought," she observed in detached scorn, "that you would not care for purchased kisses."

"But I didn't buy Esir and Esim," said Tony. "They were gifts. That's different!"

Then he ducked. A dark shadow flashed past overhead, so close that it seemed almost to touch the sun deck. It was the monstrous body of a roc, soaring swiftly downward from the sky. It touched ground almost directly before the leading elephant, shivered, and became a twelve-foot *djinn* in what was probably the *djinnian* air-force uniform. He raced toward the elephant litter.

"Majesty!" he bellowed. "Enemy *djinns* sighted twelve o'clock overhead! Closing fast!"

Tony reacted swiftly. He bellowed for Abdul and roared for a ladder. Instead, the gigantic trunk of the rear elephant swung around and held itself invitingly ready. Tony scrambled on board. Abdul bounced out of his litter in a wild leap, turned into something unusual on the way to the earth, and landed with a splashing of sand. He arose, himself again.

"Majesty!" he said, beaming. "The chimaera form for this conflict?"

"And make it snappy!" Tony rasped. "I don't think anything drastic can happen, but—"

Abdul puffed out into the snaky creation of his nightmare, with its face of mist. There was the saddle as before. Tony climbed into it and buckled the safety belt.

"Go ahead!" he commanded.

There was a sensation of almost unbearable acceleration and he rode upward into the blue.

At five thousand feet they passed the first flight of rocs. The great birds wheeled aside to make room for them and then craned their necks to watch. At ten thousand feet Abdul and Tony passed the second line of air defense. From this height Tony could distinctly see the oasis and the gleaming white walls of Barkut. Still the chimaera hurtled skyward. At fifteen thousand feet the ceiling squadron of rocs was left behind.

Abdul turned his temporarily snaky neck about and said triumphantly:

"Majesty! They flee! From us!"

Now Tony saw the *djinn* king and his few faithful councilors. They were not recognizable as such, of course. With the chimaera climbing vengefully toward them, they had adopted the emergency measures Es-Souk's *lasf* frenzies had led to: They were now mere shapeless objects which flew straight up with lightning-like amoeboid movements. They expanded as the air grew thinner and they needed to act upon greater surfaces for support. But they went up and up and up

Tony was relieved. He had only one full phial of *lasf*, and he was highly doubtful that he could duplicate his trick of the fight with Es-Souk. Certainly he couldn't handle half a dozen *djinns* with one improvised bomb, and if they attacked with any resolution at all . . .

The air grew thin as the chimaera climbed. Tony found himself panting for breath.

"Easy, Abdul!" he gasped. "No higher! This is enough!"

The chimaera leveled off. Tony's heart pounded horribly because of the lack of oxygen at this height. He felt dizzy. He sucked in great gulps of the unsatisfying thin stuff. Then he heard Abdul saying appreciatively:

"Pardon, Majesty! I had forgotten that even you will not wish to be too close to your enemies when they explode!"

Chapter 18

Tony could not answer. The way to live at great heights is not to exert yourself and to breathe fast and deep.

He busied himself with getting his breath. Presently he felt a little better. A little, not much. The horizon had broadened for hundreds of miles, it seemed. He saw the halted *djinn* caravan far below. It looked like a short length of string on a sand-colored blanket. But overhead, the climbing, writhing *djinns*—the ex-king and those who still obeyed him—were such tiny motes that, strain his eyes as he would, he lost them.

He understood. Not only was his own weapon mysterious to the *djinn*, so that even Abdul expected him to strike down the fugitives from afar, but there was an even more rational reason for this long climb. Es-Souk, exploding at a fifty-mile altitude, had dimmed the sun and given off a momentarily intolerable heat. If the former king believed that the human-made apparatus Tony had seen would detonate his rebellious subjects at a distance, he must expect a much more terrible cataclysm below. He would get as far away as possible, though he had still to remain in atmosphere for support.

The chimaera soared in huge, easy circles. Abdul said inquiringly:

"Majesty? They have not exploded."

"I—can't see them," said Tony absurdly.

He clung to his saddle, panting. Staying up here was a bluff, while he clung to two possible hopes. Perhaps the *djinn* king could not make the ancient weapon work—that was Tony's first hope. If nothing happened at all, he would go on down and explain that he had made the former king powerless, and now spared his life. The second hope was fainter. The instrument had bewildered its possessor. The king actually hadn't known which end was which. And Tony had told him quite truthfully, as far as television was concerned, that one looked in the large end of such tubes as the conical glass object he saw. Now, gasping for breath, he hoped very fervently that his advice would be taken, and that it would be bad. He recalled very vaguely that a television tube works because it shoots a beam of electrons from the small end against the large end. If the antique instrument worked in anything like the same fashion, whatever detonated *djinns* would come out of the large end, too. And if the *djinn* king happened to be looking into that end when he turned on the instrument . . .

Very high and far away, it seemed that the heavens burst. One splash of awful flame flashed into being, not directly overhead but near the horizon. The fugitives had not only put themselves as high as possible—a hundred miles perhaps—but had gone other hundreds of miles to one side so that as much sheer distance as they could manage would lie between them and the inferno they expected to create.

The first flash only dwindled when there was a second, and then two more, and then three. They went off soundlessly, but like firecrackers set off by the same fuse. And very high up indeed, in the icy chill of the heights, Tony found himself unbearably hot. Six or seven *djinns* breaking down in atomic explosions, even at two or three hundred miles distance, make for high-temperature effects. And Tony knew, then, that the apparatus which would destroy *djinns* had been blown to atoms along with the atoms it had blown up. The *djinn* king had, after all, been looking into the muzzle of an atomic gun when he pulled its trigger to destroy his subjects.

Abdul said happily:

"You found them, Majesty! Now none will question your right to reign!"

Without orders, he began a swift, slanting descent. In the thicker air, Tony's feelings of weakness ceased. But something else occurred to him. He reflected gloomily that nothing ever happens just right. No achievement is completely satisfying. Each one creates new worries and new troubles.

At five thousand feet, Abdul said:

"Majesty!"

"What?" asked Tony.

"You will marry the Queen of Barkut?" asked Abdul. "It seems the logical thing to do. May I begin to make plans for the wedding, Majesty?"

"Marry the Queen?" Tony shook his head. His new apprehensions hit him hard. "No! I'm not thinking of the Queen when I worry about what the gamma rays from those explosions may have done to me! Not a bit of it! I'm thinking of somebody else entirely!"

Chapter 19

The arrival of the *djinn* caravan created terror in Barkut. Practically the whole *djinn* nation—Tony learned that he had something over a hundred thousand subjects—came steaming out of the vastness which was the desert. The whirlwind scouts were sighted from the city walls. The aircraft curtain of rocs was sighted at the same time. When the caravan deployed before the city walls, fires of sulphurous material burned on the battlements, the city's last supply of *lasf* had been served out, and the people of Barkut were prepared to defend themselves to the last drop of ragweed solution.

There were the same people who only one day before had fired off cannon and danced in the streets to celebrate the defeat of a single *djinn* in Tony's bedroom. Now, prepared for destruction, when they learned that the *djinns* came not for conquest but as a guard of honor for the returned Queen of Barkut, that the Lord Toni who had gone away with only one slave girl for company had returned as King of the *Djinns*, there was no possible way to express their enthusiasm.

Abdul, bustling about, supervised the instant erection of a palace for Tony's lodging. It was simple enough, of course. He had merely to sketch the outline of a modest little overnight hut of some two hundred and forty rooms with floors of alternating gold and ivory squares, windows of sapphire and emerald and ruby, and a roof of jade and silver bearing fountains that sprayed milk, wine, honey, and diamond dust. Some three hundred *djinns* apportioned the structure among themselves, transformed themselves into the necessary sections and decorations, and the thing was done. It was waiting for Tony when he came back from his visit to the city of Barkut.

"Majesty!" said Abdul happily. "We were worried that you might not be adequately served in Barkut. You should at least have let a few hundred of your servants go before you with golden basins filled with jewels and the like."

"I am," said Tony, "a person of simple tastes. I came back mainly to give orders for tight discipline in the *djinn* camp tonight. I don't want anybody sneaking into the human town. No matter how innocently, no matter how inconspicuously! Nobody is to wander in as a little centipede. Nobody is to be a little beetle or a fly or a grease spot or a moth's egg. The human city is off-limits! Understand?"

"Yes, Majesty!" said Abdul. "And you will return—?"

"I sleep in Barkut," said Tony firmly. "There are some negotiations to be made. I'm quite safe. Hm . . . have you talked to Nasim about your marriage?"

"Yes, Majesty." Here Abdul wore the expression of a cat completely filled with cream and canaries. "We are quite agreed. Er . . . Majesty, you are not offended that I wore a costume and form resembling yours for—ah—courtship?"

"As long as you wear that form strictly in private," said Tony. "For the admiration of nobody but Nasim, and as long as you keep Nasim from bothering me, it's all right. Why don't you get married tonight?"

"To hear is to obey, Majesty!"

"You can use the palace I won't be sleeping in, for a honeymoon cottage," said Tony enthusiastically. "If you like, I'll bring the Queen and her court out for the wedding!"

"Your Majesty is too good!" protested Abdul ecstatically.

"Then it's settled—" Tony paused apprehensively. "You'll see that Nasim wears clothes while she's in human form?"

"Yes, Majesty," Abdul beamed. "May I ask about your Majesty's plans for this evening?"

"There's a banquet," said Tony, frowning, "and your wedding. And—the negotiations. If the negotiations are successful, I shall be engaged to be married and my plans are none of your business."

"It is unthinkable," Abdul assured him, "that your Majesty's desires should be opposed by any creature under the sky! But in such an impossible event—"

"Music—" said Tony glumly. "And in that case my plans are even less of your business! But remember, Barkut is off-limits for *djinns!*"

Abdul bowed to the ground.

Tony went back into the city. It was very pleasant to have all the people smile at him joyously. It was not too uncomfortable to have the men bow to him, at once respectfully and with the joy of human beings who feel a share in the feat of another human who has become King of the *Djinns*. It wasn't bad having large, lustrous eyes look warmly at him over traditional Moslem women's veils. And there was a melancholy satisfaction in going back to his old quarters in the palace—though he had occupied them only one night—to find Esir and Esim waiting for him in the most incredible excitement. They kissed him soundly.

"Indeed, lord—Your Majesty," said Esir, laughing, "you cannot protest, because by custom any slave may kiss her master when he performs a feat so that she gives thanks to Allah that she belongs to him and no other! King of the *Djinns*, no less! Tell me, are the *djinnees* beautiful?"

"Do you think you will prefer them to us?" asked Esim anxiously. "Indeed, lord—Your Majesty, we heard the news but an hour since, and we are fearful that you will not wish to keep us!"

Tony looked at them with a gloomy satisfaction.

"Things could be worse," he said. "For a little while I cannot tell you my plans, but whatever they turn out to be, I will bear you in mind. Oh, definitely I will bear you in mind! *Nil desperandum* will be my motto."

A tentative knock came at the door. They untangled themselves reluctantly from his embrace. It was a male slave.

"Majesty, the Queen of Barkut begs your attendance in the throne room."

"Coming up," said Tony with a sigh. To the two girls he said in comforting dejection, "I'm afraid I'll be right back."

He followed the slave to the great throne room he had seen once before, with the decrepit Council of Regency in session. The black marble floor was the same, and the brass zodiacal signs sunk into it. It occurred to Tony that life would be wearing in a house of which all interior and exterior features were subject to change without notice. There would be other disadvantages, too.

The great throne was occupied, now. The Queen sat on it. Soldiers in baggy trousers, wearing slippers and carrying flintlock guns, regarded Tony with the affection of men who have expected to fight a losing battle against the *djinns,* and now find that they can stay comfortably at home with their families. The courtiers of Barkut regarded him with no less approval. The Queen sat composed and non-committal on her throne.

"Majesty," said the Queen sedately, as Tony came to a stop before her, "we wish to offer you the thanks of the humans of Barkut for our liberation, and for the liberation of the nation from the fear of the *djinns*. We wish to express our admiration and our affection. We wish to ask if there is anything which it is in our power to do, which will add to your satisfaction or happiness."

Tony looked uneasily around. He did not see Ghail.

"I told you today, in the letter," he said awkwardly, "that if by any means I could secure the freedom of the slave girl Ghail, that I would wish to do that. If you will make her no longer a slave—"

The Queen nodded toward a side door. It opened. Two male slaves escorted Ghail to the dais before the throne. She was very pale. The Queen addressed her gently:

"His Majesty the King of the *Djinns* has asked your freedom as the price of his aid to us. He desires also to marry you."

Ghail's lips moved a little, but she did not look at Tony.

"Majesty," said the Queen, to him, "we can refuse you nothing. I make the slave girl Ghail free on one condition. If she does not marry you, she becomes again a slave. You would not impose that condition, but we can do no less!"

"But dammit—" began Tony indignantly.

"I—I can have no choice," said Ghail almost inaudibly. "I—I will marry him."

But she looked bitterly resigned. Tony bent over to her. She turned her face away. He whispered urgently:

"Damn it! Go through with it! I'll divorce you

before we leave this hall. As I understand it, all that's necessary is for me to say 'I divorce you' three times and the trick's done!"

She jerked her head about to look at him, her eyes wide. Then she flushed.

"Your hands?" said the Queen briskly. "The *cadi* is here. He will marry you now. At once. Immediately."

A venerable figure pushed his way forward. The ceremony began. Ghail was very quiet, but her voice was firm. The formula was strange to Tony, and he did not know when it was finished

But suddenly it was—and the Queen was laughing delightedly!

"Now, then! Majesty, the people of Barkut have been told only since my return that I am not their real queen! When I was kidnapped by the King of the *Djinns* he believed me the queen, and Ghail yonder was but a child. I am actually Ghail's aunt, and it seemed best to pose as the ruler of Barkut lest I be strangled and Ghail herself kidnapped and subjected to the *djinn* king's demands. A child might have been frightened into obedience. I—was otherwise.

"And so, while I posed as a captive Queen, Ghail remained among her people in disguise, learning the duties of queenship and also coming to know her people as few rulers do. The Council of Regency took its commands from her. And now that the King of the *Djinns* is also our friend and moreover a human being, it is right and fitting and proper that she return to her throne. And the kingdom of the *djinns* and the human kingdom of Barkut is now one nation, and there is now no reason for battle or anything but peace and joy."

Cannon began to boom outside. There was uproar. The audience hall itself filled with noise. And as Tony stood utterly stupefied, the erstwhile Queen stood up and beckoned to Ghail. And Ghail held Tony's hand fast and pulled him after her as she mounted to her throne. She pulled him firmly down beside her on it. It was a close fit, though not quite as close as the fit in the camel cabin, and it felt very pleasant.

The noise still continued. Presently Tony, still dazed, whispered into Ghail's ear:

"But—you didn't have to do it this way! If you were willing to marry me, why didn't you just tell me so?"

Ghail smiled composedly down at the cheering people in the throne room. She said fiercely under her breath:

"We'd have been engaged, and it might have been weeks before we got married! And do you think I'd trust you another night in any *djinn* palace with all those hussies trying to gain your favors since you're their king? Or do you think I'd trust you with Esir and Esim either?"

Tony said feebly:

"Oh-h-h . . ." and then he said, "I—I'll have to send them word I won't be home tonight."

Then he cheered up as the celebration began.

Chapter 20

It was late. The royal bridal party had graciously attended the *djinn* wedding of Nasim and Abdul in the palace outside the city walls. They had returned. Cannon still boomed. There were bonfires in the streets, and dancing, and joy was being expressed in all possible fashions, including the indecorous.

But in the royal palace of Barkut the last chamberlain bowed out, the last slave-in-waiting departed, and Tony closed the door firmly. He said:

"Er—Ghail, did I remember to send word to Esir and Esim that I wouldn't be home tonight?"

"Whether you did or not," Ghail told him, "I did!"

He took out his cigarette case. He snapped it open. He began to prowl about the bridal chamber, blowing on the wick. A faint but perceptible aroma of *lasf* became noticeable. Ghail watched him, uncomprehending and embarrassed.

"Why do you do that, Tony?" she asked.

"Oh, it's a sort of custom in my country," said Tony awkwardly. "We don't use *lasf*, of course. We use something else. It keeps away flies and mosquitoes. But I'm using this to keep away *djinns.*"

It was again night. Tony Gregg got out of a taxi-cab on lower East Broadway, in the Syrian quarter of New York, and paid off the driver. He helped a very pretty girl to the sidewalk and led her into a *shishkebab* restaurant.

The slick-haired proprietor grinned at him as he came to take his order.

"I remember you!" he said. "Mr. Emurian wanted to buy that gold piece you had! He offered you two thousan' bucks. Ain't that right?"

"That's right," said Tony. "Have you seen him lately?"

"Oh, sure," said the proprietor. "He comes in most every night . . . hey! Here he comes now!"

The girl with Tony had listened, frowning in attention to the difficult English words. She looked up sharply as the bald-headed man with the impeccably tailored clothes entered. He spoke pleasantly to the proprietor, glanced at Tony, and then came quickly to his table.

"Good evening!" he said warmly, twinkling through his eyeglasses. "I have hoped to find you again! I cabled my friend in Ispahan, and he is willing to pay you three thousand dollars for your coin!"

Tony reached in his pocket. He put down two gold pieces.

"Here are two of them," he said. "Send them to your friend as gifts. I had rather hoped to see you again, too." He slipped into the Arabic he had learned from Ghail. "This is my wife." To Ghail he explained, "This is Mr. Emurian. You have heard me speak of him."

"Oh, yes!" said Ghail. She smiled sweetly. "Tony is so grateful to you. And I also."

"Yes," said Tony. "I went to Barkut, you see. Met my wife there. In a sense, all due to you. And she wanted to see my world, so we came back here. I've a rather interesting business proposition for you. I'd like to have your friend make some contact with us in Barkut and establish a branch of his business there. It would be useful to have a regular commercial contact with this world and with the United States."

The bald-headed Mr. Emurian sat down slowly, his face a study.

"You say that you went to Barkut?"

"Oh, yes," said Tony briskly. "Hm . . . maybe I'd better sketch it out."

He gave the spectacled man a brief, hasty, and necessarily improbable account of what had happened to him since their last meeting in this same restaurant.

"The *djinns*," he concluded, "have some bad qualities, but their main trouble was that they could be anything they wanted, so they never learned how to make anything. I came back to get designs and pictures of all sorts of stuff. Not only statues and fashions and architecture—though I want those—but industrial products, and"—he paused—"the machines that make them. After all, a *djinn* can turn himself into a drill press as well as a beetle or a whirlwind, once he knows what a drill press is like. As a drill press he can turn out all sorts of stuff—including another drill press. And that manner of working would be congenial to them, too. They'll like being pieces of machinery and turning out things the humans can't make and are delighted to buy from them. Barkut ought to become a rather thriving industrial community before long."

Mr. Emurian simply stared, batting his eyes slowly from time to time.

"I'd like to have your friend set up a branch of his business in Barkut," said Tony earnestly. "And—well—I'd like a great deal to get an agent here in the United States, forwarding samples of new products, technical magazines, and above all pictures of everything under the sun. You could get them to Ispahan to be brought into Barkut by whatever route your friend discovers—if you'd take the agency. Could I interest you?"

Mr. Emurian said: "Yes. Indeed you interest me. Oh, indeed yes!"

"You work out the details," said Tony. "I'm staying at the Waldorf with my wife. I brought back quite a sum in gold, and can arrange for you to draw on it. You make your plans and get your friend to arrange to get in touch with me when he finds a way to Barkut. I'll have him watched for there, and he can locate me easily enough!"

"Indeed he can!" said Ghail proudly. "My husband is His Most Illustrious Majesty, the Great in Single Combat, the Destroyer of Evil, the Protector of the Poor, the Nobly Forgiving and Compassionate, the King of *Djinns* and Men, Tony Gregg."

"Yes," said Tony abstractedly, "he can find me."

Mr. Emurian turned over the two golden coins Tony had put on the table. And suddenly his fingers trembled a little. On one side was an inscription in conventionalized Arabic script. It said that the coin was a ten-dirhim piece of Barkut. The other side showed a rather elaborate throne. But it was not empty. It was occupied by two people. One—the girl—was in some native dress of considerable grandeur, and Mr. Emurian looked twice at her. The dark-eyed, proudly smiling girl beside Tony in the *shishkebab* restaurant had plainly been the model for that figure. But he looked three times, and four, and five, at the male figure on the coin. That half of the design was a young man in a soft hat and a belted-in-the-back topcoat, with undoubtedly highly polished brown shoes. It was, in fact, Tony Gregg.

"I—will be most happy to be your American agent," said Mr. Emurian. "Er—Your Majesty!"

It was later. Much later. Tony was in his pajamas in their hotel suite.

"It's funny," said Tony thoughtfully, as Ghail looked out a window at the lighted ways and skyscrapers of New York. "It's funny that my conscience doesn't seem to bother me any more. You remember I told you about it?"

He was sipping a final highball. Ghail stared almost affrightedly at the incredible panorama before her—a city ten miles long, with millions of bright lights, with mechanisms moving swiftly along its streets, with moving electric signs everywhere and even floating overhead to the sound of motors.

"I know, Tony," said Ghail, not turning around.

"Maybe it's dead," said Tony humorously. "It used to bother me a lot."

Then his conscience spoke. Startlingly. It said smugly that it was very well satisfied with Tony, and that he could be sure that his contentment was the result of its approval. He was very normally married, he was so far reasonably faithful to his wife—though he had turned around twice, today, to look at nylon-stockinged legs—and he had become a thriving young executive.

Tony denied it indignantly. But he was! said his conscience complacently. He was the executive head of the joint kingdom of *djinns* and men of Barkut, and he was arranging for the gradual introduction of an American standard of civilization. Eventually there would be electric refrigerators, nylon stockings, fertilizer, radio, and bubble gum in Barkut. It would be the result of Tony's executive action. And he was young. So he was a young executive. So his conscience was pleased with him, and he should feel the greatest happiness possible to man, because of his conscience's approval. "Not dead," said Tony grimly, "but merely sleeping."

Ghail turned from the window.

"Tony," she said, just a little bit unhappy, "I'm homesick! This world of yours is so big! So tremendous! There are so many people! I will stay here if you wish it—"

"I think," said Tony, "we can start back day after tomorrow. All right?"

She smiled at him, warmly. He put down his glass and stood up. He put his arms around her.

"But there's one thing," he observed comfortably, "that you can't beat this world for! Ten million people all around you may be daunting, but there's one thing we've got here that we can never be sure of in Barkut! Here, my dear, we've got privacy!"

He reached up and turned off the light.

THE DUPLICATORS

Chapter 1

It occurred to Link Denham, as a matter for mild regret, that he was about to wake up, and he'd had much too satisfactory a pre-slumber evening to want to do so. He lay between sleeping and awake, and he felt a splendid peacefulness, and the festive events in which he'd relaxed after six months on Glaeth ran pleasantly through his mind. He didn't want to think about Glaeth any more. He'd ventured forth for a large evening because he wanted to forget that man-killing world. Now, not fully asleep and very far from wide-awake, snatches of charming memory floated through his consciousness. There had been song, this past evening.

There had been conversation, man-talk upon matters

of great interest and no importance whatever. And things had gone on to a remarkably enjoyable climax.

He did not stir, but he remembered that one of his new-found intimate friends had been threatened with ejection from the place where Link and others relaxed. There were protests, in which Link joined. Then there was conflict, in which he took part. The intended ejectee was rescued before he was heaved into the darkness outside this particular spaceport joint. There was celebration of his rescue. Then the spaceport cops arrived, which was an insult to all the warm friends who now considered that they had been celebrating together.

Link drowsily and pleasurably recalled the uproar. There were many pleasing items it was delightful to review. Somebody'd defied fate and chance and spaceport cops from a pyramid of piled-up chairs and tables. Link himself, with many loyal comrades, had charged the cops who tried to pull him down. He recalled bottles spinning in the air, spouting their contents as they flew. Spaceport cops turned fire hoses on Link's new friends, and they and he heaved chairs at spaceport cops. Some friends fought cordially on the floor and others zestfully at other places, and all the tensions and all the tautness of nerves developed on Glaeth—where the death rate was ten per cent a month among carynth hunters—were relieved and smoothed out and totally erased. So Link now felt completely peaceful and beatifically content.

Somewhere, something mechanical clicked loudly. Something else made a subdued grunting noise which was also mechanical. These sounds were reality, intruding upon the blissful tranquility Link now enjoyed.

He remembered something. His eyes did not open, but his hand fumbled at his waist. He was reassured. His stake-belt was still there, and it still contained the gritty small objects for which he'd risked his life several times a day for some months in succession. Those pinkish crystals were at once the reason and the reward for his journey to Glaeth. He'd been lucky. But he'd become intolerably tense. He'd been unable to relax when the buy-boat picked him up with other carynth hunters, and he hadn't been able to loosen up his nerves at the planet to which the buy-boat took him. But here, on this remoter planet, Trent, he had relaxed at last. He was soothed. He was prepared to face reality with a cheerful confidence.

Remembering, he had become nearly awake. It occurred to him that the laws of the planet Trent were said to be severe. The cops were stern. It was highly probable that when he opened his eyes he would find himself in jail, with fines to be paid and a magistrate's lecture on proper behavior to be listened to. But he recalled unworriedly that he could pay his fines, and that he was ready to behave like an angel, now that he'd relaxed.

The loud clicking sound repeated. It was followed again by the grunting noise. Link opened his eyes.

Something that looked like a wall turned slowly around some six feet away from him. A moment later he found himself regarding a corner where three walls came together. He hadn't moved his head. The wall moved. Again, later, a square and more or less flat object with a billowing red cloth on it floated into view. He deduced that it was a table.

He was not standing on his feet, however. He

was not lying on a bunk. He floated, weightless, in mid-air in a cubicle perhaps ten feet by fifteen and seven feet high. The thing with the red cloth on it was truly a table, fastened to what ought to be a floor. There were chairs. There was a doorway with steps leading nowhere.

Link closed his eyes and counted ten, but the look of things remained the same when he reopened them. Before his relaxation of the night before, such a waking would have disturbed him. Now he contemplated his surroundings with calm. He was evidently not in jail. As evidently, he was not aground anywhere. The only possible explanation was unlikely to the point of insanity, but it had to be true. He was in a spaceship, and not a luxurious one. This particular compartment was definitely shabby. And on the evidence of no-gravity, the ship was in free fall. It was not exactly a normal state of things to wake up to.

There came again a loud clicking, followed by another subdued mechanical grunt. Link made a guess at the origin of the sounds. It was most likely a pressure reduction valve releasing air from a high-pressure tank to maintain a lower pressure somewhere else. If Link had taken thought, his hair would have stood on end immediately. But he didn't.

The cubicle, moving sedately around him, brought one of its walls within reach of his foot. He kicked. He floated away from the ceiling to a gentle impact on the floor. He held on, more or less, by using the palms of his hands as suction-cups—a most unsatisfactory system—and got within reach of a table leg. He swung himself about and shoved for the doorway. He floated to it in slow motion, caught hold of a stair tread, got a grip on the door frame, and oriented himself with respect to the room.

He was in the mess room of a certainly ancient and obviously small ship of space. All was shabbiness. Where paint had not peeled off, it stayed on in blisters. The flooring was worn through to the metal plates beneath. There were other signs of neglect. There had been no tidying of this mess room for a long time.

He heard a faint, new, rumbling sound. It stopped, and came again. It was overhead, in the direction the stairway led to. The rumbling came once more. It was rhythmic.

Link grasped a handrail and heaved himself gently upward. He arrived at a landing, and the rumbling noise was louder. This level of the ship contained cabins for the crew. The rumbling came from a higher level still. He went up more steps, floating as before.

He arrived at a control room which was antiquated and grubby and of very doubtful efficiency. There were ports, which were covered with frost.

Somebody snored above his head. That was the rumbling sound. Link lifted his eyes and saw the snorer. A small, whiskery man scowled portentiously even in his sleep. He floated in mid-air as Link had floated, but with his knees drawn up and his two hands beside his cheek as if resting on an imaginary pillow. And he snored.

Link reflected, and then said genially,

"Hello!"

The whiskery man snored again. Link saw something familiar about him. Yes. He'd been involved in the festivity of the night before. Link remembered having seen him scowling ferociously from the sidelines while tumult raged and firehoses played.

"Ship ahoy!" said Link loudly.

The small man jumped, in the very middle of a snore. He choked and blinked and made astonished movements, and of course began to turn eccentric half-circles in mid-air. In one of his turnings he saw Link. He said peevishly,

"Dammit, don't stand there starin'! Get me down! But don't turn on the gravity! Want me to break my neck?"

Link reached up and caught a foot. He brought the little man down to solidity and released him.

"Huh!" said the little man waspishly. "You're awake."

"Apparently," admitted Link. "Are you?"

The little man snorted. He aligned himself and gave a shove. He floated through the air to the control board. He caught its corner. He looked it over and pushed a button. Ship gravity came on. There was a sudden slight jolt, and then a series of lesser jolts, and then the fine normal feeling of gravity and weight and up and down. Things abruptly looked more sensible. They weren't, but they looked that way.

"I'm curious," said Link. "Have you any idea where we are?"

The whiskery man said scornfully, "Where we are? How'd I know? That's your business!" His air grew truculent as Link didn't grasp the idea.

"My business?"

"You're the astrogator, ain't you? You signed on last night; I had to help you hold the pen, but you signed on! Astrogator, third officer's ticket, and you

said you could astrogate a wash bucket from Sirius
Three to the Rim with nothin' but a root-rule and a
logarithm table. That's what you said! You said you'd
astrogated a Norse spaceliner six hundred lightyears
tail-first to port after her overdrive unit switched
poles. You said—"

Link held up his hand.

"I . . . er . . . I recognize the imaginative style,"
he said painfully. "It's mine, in my more exuberant
moments. But how did that land me . . . wherever I
am?"

"You made a deal with me," said the little man,
truculently. "Thistlethwaite's the name. You signed on
this ship, the *Glamorgan,* an' you said you were an
astrogator and I made the deal on that representation.
It's four years in jail, on Trent, to sign on or act as
a astrogator unless you're duly licensed."

"Morbid people, the lawmakers of Trent," said
Link. "What else?"

"You don't draw wages," said the whiskery man, as
truculently as before. "You're a junior partner in the
business I'm startin'. You agreed to leave all matters
but astrogation to me, on penalty of forfeitin' all mon-
eys due or accrued or to accrue. It's a tight contract.
I wrote it myself."

"I am lost in admiration," said Link politely.
"But—"

"We're goin'," said Thistlethwaite sternly, "to a planet
I know. Another fella and me, we landed there in a
spaceboat after the ship we was in got wrecked. We
made a deal with the . . . uh . . . authorities. We took
off again in the spaceboat. It was loaded down with
plenty valuable cargo! We was to go back, but my

partner—he was the astrogator of the spaceboat—he took his share of the money and started celebratin'. Two weeks later he jumped out a window because he thought pink gryphs was coming out of the wall after him. That left me sole owner of the business, but strapped for cash. I'd been celebratin' too. So I bought the *Glamorgan* with what I had, an' bought a cargo for her."

"A very fine ship, the *Glamorgan*," said Link, politely. "But I'm a little dense this morning, or evening, or whatever it may be. How do I fit into the picture of commercial enterprise aboard this splendid ship the *Glamorgan*?"

The whiskery man spat, venomously.

"The ship's junk," he snapped. "I couldn't get papers for her to go anywhere but to a junk yard on Bellaire to be scrapped. I hadda astrogator and a fella to spell me in the engine room. They believed we was going to the junkyard, but we had some trouble with the engines layin' down, and she leaked air. Plenty! So when we got to Trent those two run off. They're liable to two years in jail for runnin' out on a contract concernin' personal services. Hell! They didn't think we'd make Trent! They wanted to take to the spaceboat and abandon ship halfway there! And me with all my capital tied up in it!"

Link regarded his companion uncomfortably. Thistlethwaite snapped, "So I was stuck on Trent with no astrogator an' port-dues pilin' up. Until you came along."

"Ah!" said Link. "I came along! Riding a white horse, no doubt, and kissing my hand to the ladies. Then what?"

"I asked you if you was a astrogator, and you told me yes."

"I hate to disappoint people," said Link regretfully. "I probably wanted to brighten up your day, or evening. I tried."

"Then," said Thistlethwaite portentously, "I told you enough about what I'm goin' after so you said it was a splendid venture, befittin' such men as you and me. You'd join me, you said. But you wanted to fight some more policemen before liftin' off. I'd already drug you out of a fight where the spaceport cops was usin' fire-hoses on both sides. I told you fightin' policemen carries six months in jail, on Trent. But you wouldn't listen. Even after I told you why we had to take off quick."

"And that reason was—"

"Spaceport dues," snapped the little man. "On the *Glamorgan*. Landin'-grid fees. On the *Glamorgan*. I run out of money! Besides, there was grub and some parts for the engines that'd been givin' trouble. I bought 'em and charged 'em, like a business man does, expectin' to come back some day and pay for 'em. But the spaceport people got suspicious. They were goin' to seize the ship tomorrow—today—and sell her if they could for the port bills and grub bills and parts bills."

"I see," said Link. "And I probably sympathized with you."

"You said," said the little man grimly, "that it was a conspiracy against brave an' valiant souls like us two, an' you'd only fight two more policemen—six months more on top of what you was already liable to—and then we'd defy such crass and commercial individuals and take off into the wild blue yonder."

Link reflected. He shook his head in mild disapproval. "So what happened?"

"You fought four policemen," said his companion succinctly. "In two separate scraps, addin' a year in jail to what you'd piled up before."

"It begins to look," said Link, "as if I may have made myself unpopular on Trent. Is there anything else I ought to know?"

"They started to use tear gas on you," the whiskery man told him, "so you set fire to a police truck. To let the flames lift up the gas, you said. That would be some more years in jail. But I got you in the *Glamorgan*—"

"And got the grid to lift us off?" When the little man shook his head, Link asked hopefully. "I got the grid to lift us off? We persuaded—"

"Nope," said Thistlethwaite. "You just took off. On emergency rockets. Off the spaceport tarmac. With no clearance. Leavin' the oiled tarmac on fire." Link winced. The little man went on inexorably, "We hit for space at six gees acceleration and near as I can make out you kept goin' at that till the first rockets burned out. And then you went down into the mess room."

"I suppose," said Link unhappily, "that I'd worked up an appetite. Or was there some way I could pile up a few more years to spend in jail?"

"You went to sleep," said the little man. "And I wasn't goin' to bother you!"

Link thought it over.

"No," he agreed. "I can see that you mightn't have wanted to bother me. Do you intend to turn around and go back to Trent?"

"What for?" demanded the little man bitterly. "For jail? An' for them to sell off the *Glamorgan* for port dues and such?"

"There's that, of course," acknowledged Link. "But I'd rather believe you wouldn't leave a friend in distress, or jail. All right. I don't want to go back to Trent either. I'm an outdoorsy sort of character and I wouldn't like to spend the next eighteen years in jail."

"Twenty-two," said Thistlethwaite. "And six months."

"So," finished Link, "I'll play along. Since I'm the astrogator I'll try to find out where we are. Then you'll tell me where you want to go. And after that, some evening when there's nothing special to do, you'll tell me why. Right?"

"The why," snapped the whiskery man, "is I promised to make you so rich y'couldn't spend the interest on y'money! And you a junior partner!"

"Carynths?" suggested Link.

Carynths were the galaxy's latest and most fabulous status gems. They couldn't be synthesized—they were said to be the result of meteoric impacts on a special peach-colored ore—and they were as beautiful as they were rare. So far they'd only been found on Glaeth. But if a woman had a carynth ring, she was somebody. If she had a carynth bracelet, she was Somebody. And if she had a carynth necklace, she ruled society on the planet on which she was pleased to reside. But—

"Carynths are garbage," said Thistlethwaite contemptuously, "alongside of what's waitin' for us! For each one of what I'm tradin' for, to bring it away from where we're goin', I'll get a hundred million credits an' half the profits after that! An' I'll have a shipload of 'em! And it's all set! Now you do your stuff and I'll check over the engines."

He headed down the stairwell. He reached the first landing below. The second. Link heard a faint click and then a mechanical grunting noise. At the sound, the little man howled enragedly. Link jumped.

"What's the matter?" he asked anxiously.

"We're leakin' air!" roared the little man. "Bleedin' it! You musta started some places, takin' off at six gees! All the air's pourin' out!"

His words became unintelligible, but they were definitely profane. Doors clanged shut, cutting off his voice. He was sealing all compartments.

Link surveyed the control room of the ship. In his younger days he'd aspired to be a spaceman. He'd been a cadet in the Merchant Space Academy on Malibu for two complete terms. Then the faculty let him go. He liked novelty and excitement and on occasion, tumult. The faculty didn't. His grades were all right but they heaved him out. So he knew a certain amount about astrogation. Not much, but enough to keep from having to go back to Trent.

A door closed below. The little man's voice could be heard, swearing sulfurously. He got something from somewhere and the door clanged behind him again, cutting off his voice once more.

Link resumed his survey. There was the control board, reasonably easy to understand. There was the computer, simple enough for him to operate. There were reference books. A *Galactic Directory* for this sector. Alditch's *Practical Astrogator.* A luridly bound volume of *Space-Commerce Regulations.* The *Directory* was brand new. The others were old and tattered volumes.

Link went carefully over the ship's log, which contained every course steered, time elapsed, and therefore distance run in parsecs and fractions of them. He could take the *Glamorgan* back to the last three ports she'd visited by reversing the recorded maneuvers. But that didn't seem enterprising.

He skimmed through the *Astrogator.* He'd be somewhere not too many millions of miles from the sun of the planet Trent. He'd take a look at the Trent listing in the *Directory,* copy out its coordinates and proper motion, check the galactic poles and zero galactic longitude by observation out the ports, and then get at the really tricky stuff when he learned the ship's destination.

He threw on the heater switch so he could see out the ports and observe the sun which shone on Trent. Instantly an infuriated bellow came up from below.

"Turn off the heat!" raged Thistlethwaite from below. "Turn it off!"

"But the ports are frosted," Link called back. "I need to see out! We need the heaters!"

"I was sittin' on one! Turn 'em off!"

A door clanged below. Link shrugged. If Thistle-thwaite had to sit on a heater, the heater shouldn't be on. Delay was indicated.

He wasn't worried. The mood of tranquility and repose he'd waked with still stayed with him. Naturally! His current situation might have seemed disturbing to somebody else, but to a man who'd just left the planet Glaeth, with its strictly murderous fauna and flora and climatic conditions, to be aboard a merely leaking spaceship of creaking antiquity was restful. That it was only licensed to travel to a junkyard for scrapping seemed no cause for worry. That it was bound on a mysterious errand instead seemed interesting. With no cares whatever, Link was charmed to find himself in a situation where practically anything was more than likely to happen.

He thought restfully of not being on Glaeth. There were animals there which looked like rocks and acted like stones until one got within reach of remarkably extensible hooked claws. There were trees which dripped a corrosive fluid on any moving creature that disturbed them. There were gigantic flying things against which the only defense was concealment, and things which tunneled underground and made traps into which anything heavier than a rabbit would drop as the ground gave way beneath it. And there was the climate. In the area in which the best finds of carynths had been made, there was no record of rain having ever fallen, and noon temperature in the most favorable season hovered around a hundred forty in the shade. But it was the only world on which carynths were to be found. The carynth prospectors who landed there, during the most favorable season, of course, sometimes got rich. Much more often they didn't. Only forty per cent of those set aground at the beginning of the prospecting season met the buy-boat which came for them at its close. Link had been one of that lucky minority. Naturally he did not feel alarm on the *Glamorgan*. He'd almost gotten used to Glaeth! So he waited peacefully until Thistlethwaite said it was all right to turn on the heaters and melt the frost off the ports.

He began to set up for astrogation. The coordinates for Trent would go into the computer, and then the coordinates for the ship's destination. The computer would figure the course between them and its length in parsecs and fractions of parsecs. One would drive on that course. One could, if it was desirable, look for possible ports of call on the way. Link took down the *Directory* to set up the first figures.

He happened to notice a certain consequence of the *Directory's* newness. It was the only un-shabby, un-worn object on the ship. But even it showed a grayish, well-thumbed line on the edge of certain pages which had been often referred to. The grayishness should be a guide to the information about Trent, as the *Glamorgan's* latest port of call. Link opened the grayest page, pleased with himself for his acuteness.

But Trent wasn't listed on that page. Trent wasn't even in that part of the book. The heading of this particular chapter of listings was, *"Non-Cluster Planets Between Huyla and Claire."* It described the maverick solar systems not on regular trade routes and requiring long voyages from commercial spaceports if anybody was to reach them. People rarely wanted to.

Link stared. He found signs that this had been repeatedly referred to by somebody with engine oil on his fingers. One page had plainly been read and re-read and re-read. The margin was darkened as if an oily thumb had held a place there while the item was gloated over.

From any normal standpoint it was not easy to understand.

"SORD," said the *Directory*. There followed the galactic coordinates to three places of decimals. *"Yel.*

sol-type approx. 1.4 sols mass, mny faculae all times, spectrum—"

The spectrum symbols could be skipped. If one wanted to be sure that a particular sun was such-and-such, one would take a spectro-photo and compare it with the *Directory*. Otherwise the spectrum was for the birds. Link labored over the abbreviations that compilers of reference books use to make things difficult.

"3rd. pl. blved. hab. ox atm. 2/3 sea nml brine, usual ice-caps cloud-systems hab. est. 1."

Then came the interesting part. In the clear language that informative books use with such reluctance, he read:

"This planet is said to have been colonized from Surheil 11 some centuries since, and may be inhabited, but no spaceport is known to exist. The last report on this planet was from a spaceyacht some two centuries ago. The yacht called down asking permission to land and was threatened with destruction if it did. The yacht took pictures from space showing specks that could be villages or the ruins of same, but this is doubtful. No other landings or communications are known. Any records which might have existed on Surheil 11 were destroyed in the Economic Wars on that planet."

In the *Glamorgan*'s control room, Link was intrigued. He went back to the abbreviations and deciphered them. Sord was a yellow sol-type sun with a mass of 1.4 sols and many faculae. Its third planet was believed habitable. It had an oxygen atmosphere, two-thirds of its surface was sea, the sea was normal brine and there were the usual ice caps and cloud systems of a planet whose habitability was estimated at one.

And two centuries ago its inhabitants had threatened to smash a spaceyacht which wanted to land on it.

According to Thistlethwaite, the bill for last evening's relaxation, for Link, amounted to twenty-some years to be served in jail. Even with some sentences running concurrently, it was preferable not to return to Trent. On the other hand—

But it didn't really need to be thought about. Thistlethwaite plainly intended to go to Sord Three, whose inhabitants strongly preferred to be left alone. But they seemed to have made an exception in his favor. He was so anxious to get there and so confident of a welcome that he'd bought the *Glamorgan* and loaded her up with freight, and he'd taken an unholy chance in his choice of a ship. He'd taken another in depending on Link as an astrogator. But it would be a pity to disappoint him!

So Link carefully copied down in the log the three coordinates of Sord Three, and hunted up its proper solar motion, and put that in the log, and then put the figures for Trent in the computer and copied the answer in the log, too. It seemed the professional thing to do. Then he scraped away frost from the ports and got observations of the *Glamorgan*'s current heading, and went back to the board and adjusted that. He was just entering the last item in the log when Thistlethwaite came in. His hands were black from the work he'd done, and somehow he gave the impression of a man who had used up all his store of naughty words and still was unrelieved.

"Well?" asked Link pleasantly.

"We're leakin' air," said the whiskered man bitterly. "It's whistlin' out! Playin' tunes as it goes! I had to

seal off the spaceboat blister. If we need that spaceboat we'll be in a fix! When my business gets goin',
I'll never use another junk ship like this! You raised
hell in that take-off!"

"It's very bad?" asked Link.

"I shut off all the compartments I couldn't seal
tight," said Thistlethwaite bitterly. "And there's still
some leakage in the engine room, but I can't find it.
I ain't found it so far, anyways."

Link said, "How's the air supply?"

"I pumped up on Trent," said the little man. "If
they'd known, they'd ha' charged me for that, too!"

"Can we make out for two weeks?" asked Link.

"We can make out for ten!" snapped the whiskery
one. "There's only two of us an' we can seal off everything but the control room an' the engine room an'
a way between 'em. We can go ten weeks."

"Then," said Link relievedly, "we're all right." He
made final adjustments. "The engines are all right?"

He looked up pleasantly, his hand on a switch.

"With coddlin'," said Thistlethwaite. "What're you
doin'?" he demanded suspiciously. "I ain't give you—"

Link threw the circuit completing switch. The
universe seemed to reel. Everything appeared to turn
inside out, including Link's stomach. He had the feeling of panicky fall in a contracting spiral. The lights
in the control room dimmed almost to extinction. The
whiskery man uttered a strangled howl. This was the
normal experience when going into overdrive travel
at a number of times the speed of light.

Then, abruptly, everything was all right again. The
vision ports were dark, but the lights came back to full
brightness. The *Glamorgan* was in overdrive, hurtling

through emptiness very, very much faster than theory permitted in the normal universe. But the universe immediately around the *Glamorgan* was not normal. The ship was in an overdrive field, which does not occur normally, at all.

"What the hell've you done?" raged Thistlethwaite. "Where you headed for? I didn't tell you—"

"I'm driving the ship," said Link pleasantly, "for a place called Sord Three. There ought to be some good business prospects there. Isn't that where you want to go?"

The little man's face turned purple. He glared.

"How'd you find that out?" he demanded ferociously.

"Well, I've got friends there," said Link untruthfully. The little man leaped for him, uttering howls of fury.

Link turned off the ship's gravity. Thistlethwaite wound up bouncing against the ceiling. He clung there, swearing. Link kept his hand on the gravity button. At any instant he could throw the gravity back on, and as immediately off again.

"Tut, tut!" said Link reproachfully. "Such naughty words. And I thought you'd be pleased to find your junior partner displaying energy and enthusiasm and using his brains loyally to further the magnificent business enterprise we've started!"

Chapter 2

The *Glamorgan* bored on through space. Not normal space, of course. In the ordinary sort of space between

suns and planets and solar systems generally, a ship
is strictly limited to ninety-eight-point-something per
cent of the speed of light, because mass increases
with speed, and inertia increases with mass. But in
an overdrive field the properties of space are modified. The effect of a magnet on iron is changed past
recognition. The effect of electrostatic stress upon
dielectrics is wholly abnormal. And inertia, instead
of multiplying itself with high velocity, becomes as
undetectable as at zero velocity. In fact, theory says
that a ship has no velocity on an overdrive field. The
speed is of the field itself. The ship is carried. It goes
along for the ride.

But there was no thinking about such abstractions
on the *Glamorgan.* The effect of overdrive was the
same as if the ship did pierce space at many times
the speed of light. Obviously, light from ahead was
transposed a great many octaves upward, into something
as different from light as long wave radiation is from
heat. This radiation was refracted outward from the
ship by the overdrive field, and was therefore without
effect upon instruments or persons. Light from behind
was left there. Light from the sides was also refracted
outward and away. The *Glamorgan* floated at ease in
a hurtling, unsubstantial space-stress center, and to
try to understand it might produce a headache, but
hardly anything more useful.

But though the *Glamorgan* in overdrive attained
the end of speed without the need for velocity, the
human relationship between Link and Thistlethwaite
was less simple. The whiskery little man was impas-
sioned about his enterprise. Link had guessed his highly
secret destination, and Thistlethwaite was outraged

by the achievement. Even when Link showed him how Sord Three had been revealed as the objective of the voyage, Thistlethwaite wasn't mollified. He clamped his lips shut tightly. He refused to give any further intimation about what he proposed to do when he arrived at Sord Three. Link knew only that he'd touched ground there in a spaceboat with one companion and they'd left with a valuable cargo, and now Thistlethwaite was bound back there again, if Link could get him there.

There were times when it seemed doubtful. Then Link blamed himself for trying it. Still, Thistlethwaite had chosen the *Glamorgan* on his own and had gotten as far as Trent in her. But there were times when it didn't appear that the ship would ever get anywhere else. The log book had a plenitude of emergencies written in its pages as the *Glamorgan* went onward.

She leaked air. They didn't try to keep the inside pressure up to the standard 14.7 pounds. They compromised on eleven, because they'd lose less air at the lower pressure. Even so, the fact that the *Glamorgan* leaked was only one of her oddities. She also smelled. Her air system was patched and her generators were cobbled, and at odd moments she made unrefined noises for no reason that anybody could find out. The water pressure system sometimes worked and sometimes did not. The refrigeration unit occasionally turned on when it shouldn't and sometimes didn't when it should. It was wise to tap the thermostat several times a day to keep frozen stores from thawing.

The overdrive field generator was also a subject for nightmares. Link didn't understand overdrive, but he did know that a field shouldn't be kept in existence by hand-wound outer layers on some of the coils, with wedges driven in to keep contacts tight which ought to be free to cut off in case of emergency. But it could be said that everything about the ship was an emergency. Link would have come to have a very great respect for Thistlethwaite because he kept such tinkered wreckage working. But he was appalled at the idea of anybody deliberately trusting his life to it.

The thing was, he realized ultimately, that Thistlethwaite was an eccentric. The galaxy is full of crackpots, each of whom has mysterious secret information about illimitable wealth to be found on the nonexistent outer planets of rarely visited suns, or in the depths of the watery satellites of Cepheids. But crackpots only talk. Their ambition is to be admired as men of mystery and vast secret knowledge. They will never try actually to find the treasures they claim to know about. If you offer to provide a ship and crew to pick up the riches they describe in such detail, they'll impose impossible conditions. They don't want to risk their dreams by trying to make them come true.

But Thistlethwaite wasn't that way. He wasn't a crackpot. In his description of the wealth awaiting him, Link considered that he must be off the beam. There was no such treasure in the galaxy. But he'd been on Sord Three, and he'd had some money—enough to buy the *Glamorgan* and her cargo—and he was trying to get back. He'd cut Link in out of necessity, because the *Glamorgan* had to get off Trent when she did, or not get off at all. So Thistlethwaite was not a crackpot. But an eccentric, that he was!

Fuming but resolute, the little man tried valiantly to make the ship hold together until his project was completed. From the beginning, four compartments besides the spaceboat blister were sealed off because they couldn't be made airtight. A fifth compartment lost half a pound of air every hour on the hour. Thistlethwaite labored over it, daubing extinguisher foam on joints and cracks until he found where the foam vanished first. Then he lavishly applied sealing compound. This was not the act of a crackpot who only wants to be admired. It was consistent with a far-out mentality which would run the wildest of risks to carry out a purpose. Moreover, when after days of labor he still couldn't bring the air loss down below half a pound a day, he sealed off that compartment too. The *Glamorgan* had been a tub to begin with. Now she displayed characteristics to make a reasonably patient man break down and cry.

Link offered to help in the sealing-off process. Thistlethwaite snapped at him.

"You tend to your knitting and I'll tend to mine," he said acidly. "You're so smart at workin' out things I want to keep to myself."

"I only found out where we're going," said Link. "I didn't find out why."

"To get rich," snapped Thistlethwaite. "That's why! I want to get rich! I spent my life bein' poor. Now I want to get kowtowed to! My first partner got money and he couldn't wait to enjoy it. I've waited. I'm not telling anybody anything! I know what I'm goin' to do. I got a talent for business. I never had a chance to use it. No capital. Now I'm going to get rich and do things like I always wanted to do."

Link asked more questions and the little man turned waspishly upon him.

"That's my business, like runnin' this ship to where we're goin' is yours! You leave me be! I'm not riskin' you knowin' what I know. I'm not takin' the chance of you figurin' you'll do better cheating me than playin' fair."

This was shrewdness, after a fashion. There are plenty of men who quite simply and naturally believe that the way to profit in any enterprise is to double-cross their associates. The whiskery man had evidently met them. He wasn't sure Link wasn't one of them. He kept his mouth shut.

"Eventually," said Link, "I'm going to have to come out of overdrive to check my course. Is that all right with you?"

"That's your business!" rasped Thistlethwaite. "You tend to your business and I'll tend to mine!"

He disappeared, prowling around the ship, checking the air pressure, spending long periods in the engine room and not infrequently coming silently and secretly up the stairway to the control room to regard Link with inveterate suspicion.

It annoyed Link. So when he determined that he should break out of overdrive to verify his position—a dubious business considering the limits of his knowledge—he did not notify Thistlethwaite. He simply broke out of overdrive.

There should have been merely an instant of intolerable vertigo and of intense nausea, and then the sensation of a spiral fall toward infinity, but nothing more. Those sensations occurred. But as they began there was also a wild, rasping roar in the engine room. Lights dimmed. Thistlethwaite howled with fury and flung himself down into an inferno of blue arcs and stinking scorched insulation. In that incredible nightmare-like atmosphere he hit something with a stick. He pulled violently on a rope. He spun a wheel rapidly. And the arcs died. The ship's ancient air system began to struggle with the smoke and smells.

It took him two days to make repairs, during which he did not address one syllable to Link. But Link was busy anyhow. He was taking observations and checking the process with the *Practical Astrogator* as he went along. Then he used the computer to make his observations mean something. He faithfully wrote all these exercises in the ship's log. It helped to pass the time. But when determination of the ship's position by three different methods gave the same result, he arrived at the astonishing conclusion that the *Glamorgan* was actually on course.

He was composing a tribute to himself for the feat when Thistlethwaite came bristling into the control room.

"I fixed what you messed up," he said bitterly. "We can go on now. But next time you do something, don't do it till you ask me, and I'll fix it so you can. You could've wrecked us."

Link opened his mouth to ask what could be a more complete wreck than the *Glamorgan* right now, but he refrained. He arranged for Thistlethwaite to go down into the engine room. He shouted down the stairways. Thistlethwaite bellowed a reply. Link checked the ship's heading again, glanced at the ship's chronometer, and threw the overdrive on.

Nothing happened except vertigo and nausea and the feeling of falling in a spiral fashion toward nowhere at all. The *Glamorgan* was again in overdrive. The little man came in, brushing off his hands.

"That's the way," he said truculently, "to handle this ship!" Link scribbled a memo of the instant the *Glamorgan* had gone into overdrive.

"In two days, four hours, thirty-three minutes and twenty seconds," he observed, "we'll want to break out again. We ought to be somewhere near Sord, then."

"If," said Thistlethwaite suspiciously, "if you're not tryin' to put something over on me!"

Link shrugged. He'd begun to wonder, lately, why he'd come on this highly mysterious journey. In one sense he'd had good reason. Jail. But now he began to be restless. He wore a stake-belt next to his skin, and in it he had certain small crystals. There were people who would murder him enthusiastically for those crystals. There were others who would pay him very large sums for them. The trouble was that he had no specific idea of what he wanted to do with a large sum. Small sums, yes. He could relax with them. But large ones— He felt a need for the pleasingly unexpected. Even the exciting.

One day passed and he was definitely impatient. He was bored. He couldn't even think of anything to write in the log book. There'd been a girl about whom he'd felt romantic, not so long ago. He tried to think sentimentally about her. He failed. He hadn't seen her in months and she was probably married to somebody else now. The thought didn't bother him. It was annoying that it didn't. He craved excitement and interesting happenings, and he was merely heading for a planet that hadn't made authenticated contact with the rest of the galaxy in two hundred years, and then had promised to shoot anybody who landed. He was only in a leaky ship whose machinery broke down frequently and might at any time burn out.

He was, in a word, bored.

The second day passed. Four hours, thirty-three minutes remained. He tried to hope for interesting events. He knew of no reason to anticipate them. If Thistlethwaite were right, there would be only business dealings aground, and presently an attempt to get to somewhere else in the *Glamorgan*, and after that—

The whiskery man went down into the engine room and bellowed that everything was set. Link sat by the control board, leaning on his elbows, in a mood of deep skepticism. He didn't believe anything in particular was likely to happen. Especially he didn't believe in Thistlethwaite's story of fabulous wealth. There was nothing as valuable as Thistlethwaite described. Such things simply didn't exist. But since he'd come this far—

Two minutes to go. One minute twenty seconds. Twenty seconds. Ten . . . five . . . four . . . three . . . two . . . one!

He flipped the overdrive switch to off. There were the customary sensations of dizzy fall and vertigo and nausea. Then the *Glamorgan* floated in normal space, and there was a sun not unreasonably far away, and all the sky was stars. Link was even pessimistic about the identity of the sun, but a spectro-photo identified it. It was truly Sord. There were planets. One. Two. Three. Three had ice-caps; it looked as if two-thirds of its surface was sea, and in general it matched the *Directory's* description. It might . . . just possibly . . . be inhabited.

A tediously long time later the *Glamorgan* floated

in orbit around the third planet out from its sun. Mottled land masses whipped by below. There were seas, and more land masses.

Thistlethwaite watched in silence. There could be no communication with the ground, even if the ground was prepared to communicate. The *Glamorgan*'s communication system didn't work. Link waited for the little man to identify his destination. When it was named there would probably be trouble.

"No maps," said Thistlethwaite bitterly, on the second time around. "I asked Old Man Addison for a map but he hardly knew what I meant. They never bothered to make 'em! But Old Man Addison's Household is near a sea. Near a bay, with mountains not too far off."

Link was not relieved. It isn't easy to find a landmark of limited size on a large world from a ship in space that has no maps or even a working communicator. But on the fourth orbital circuit, clouds that had formerly hidden a certain place had moved away. Thistlethwaite pointed.

"That's it!" he said, scowling as if to cover his own doubts. "That's it! Get her down yonder!"

Link took a deep breath. Standard spaceport procedure is for a ship to call down by communicator, have coordinates supplied from the ground, get into position, and wait. Then the landing grid reaches out its force fields and lets the ship down. It is neat, and comfortable, and safe. But there was no landing grid here. There was no information. And Link had no experience, either.

He made one extra orbit to fix the indicated landing point in his mind and to try to guess at the relative speed of ship and planetary surface. On the seventh circling of the planet, he swung the ship so it traveled stern-first and its emergency rockets could be used as retros. The drive engine would be useless here. Thistlethwaite stayed in the control room to watch. He chewed agitatedly on wisps of whisker.

The ship hit atmosphere. There was a keening, howling sound, as if the ancient hull were protesting its own destruction. There were thumpings and bumpings. Loose plates rattled at their rivets and remaining welds.

Something came free and battered thunderously at other hull plates before it went crazily off to nowhere. Vibration began. It became a thoroughly ominous quivering of all the ship. Link threw over the rocket lever, and the vibration ceased to increase as the emergencies bellowed below. He gave them more power, and more, until the deceleration made it difficult to stand. Then, at very long last, the vibration seemed to lessen a very little.

The ship descended into a hurricane of wind from its own motion. Unbelievable noises sounded here and there. The hole where a plate had torn away developed an organ tone with the volume of a baby earthquake's roar.

The ship hurtled on. Far ahead there was blue sea. Nearer, there were mountains. There was a sandy look to the surface of the soil. Clouds enveloped the ship, and she came out below them, bellowing, and Link gave the rockets more braking power. But the ground still seemed to race past at an intolerable speed. He tilted the ship until her rockets did not support her at all, but only served as brakes.

Then she really went down, wallowing. He fought her, learning how to land by doing it, but without even a close idea of what it should feel like. Twice he attempted to check his descent at the cost of not checking motion toward the now-not-so-distant shore-line. He began to hope. He concentrated on matching speed with the flowing landscape.

He made it. The ship moved almost impercepti-bly with respect to such landmarks as he could see. Something vaguely resembling a village appeared, far below, but he could not attend to it. The ship sud-denly hovered, no more than five thousand feet high. Then Link, sweating, started to ease down.

Thistlethwaite protested agitatedly,

"I saw a village! Get her down! Get her down!'

Link cut the rockets entirely; the ship began to drop like a stone, and he cut them in again and out and in.

The *Glamorgan* landed with a tremendous crash. It teetered back and forth, making loud grinding noises. It steadied. It stopped.

Link mopped his forehead. Thistlethwaite said accus-ingly,

"But this ain't where we shoulda landed! We shoulda stopped by that village! And even that ain't the one I want!"

"This is where we did land," said Link, "and lucky we made it! You don't know how lucky!"

He went to a port to look out. The ship had landed in a sort of hollow, liberally sprinkled with boulders of various shapes and sizes. Sandy hillocks with sparse vegetation on their slopes appeared on every hand. Despite the ship's upright position, Link could not see over the hills to a true horizon.

"I'll go over to that village we saw comin' down," said Thistlethwaite importantly, "an' arrange to send a message to my friends. Then we'll get down to business. And there's never been a business like this one before in all the time since us men stopped swappin' arrowheads! You stay here an' keep ship."

He swung the ship's one weapon, a stun gun, over his shoulder. It gave him a rakish air. He put on a hat.

"Yep. You keep ship till I come back!"

He went down the stairs. Link heard him go down all the levels until he came to the exit port in one of the ship's landing fins. From the control room he saw Thistlethwaite stride grandly to the top of the nearest hill, look exhaustively from there, and then march away with an air of great and confident composure. He went out of sight beyond the hillcrest.

Link went down to the exit port himself. The air in the opening was fresh and markedly pleasant to breathe. He felt that it was about time that something interesting happened. This wasn't it. Here was only commonplace landscape, commonplace sky, and commonplace tedium. He sat on the sill of the open exit port and waited without expectation for something interesting to happen.

Presently he heard tiny clickings. Two small animals, very much like pigs in size and appearance, came trotting hurriedly into view. Their hoofs had made the clicking sounds. They saw the ship and stopped short, staring at it. They didn't look dangerous.

"Hi, there," said Link companionably.

The small creatures vanished instantly. They plunged behind boulders. Link shrugged. He gazed about him.

After a little, he saw an eye peering at him around a boulder. It was the eye of one of the pig-like animals. Link moved abruptly and the eye vanished.

A voice spoke, apparently from nowhere. It was scornful. "Jumpy, huh? Scared?"

"I was startled," said Link mildly, "but I wouldn't say I was scared. Should I be?"

The voice said sardonically, "Huh!"

There was silence again. There was stillness. A very sparse vegetation appeared to have existed where the *Glamorgan* came down on her rockets. Those scattered bits of growing stuff had been burned to ash by the rocket flames, but at the edge of the burned area some few small smoldering fragments sent threads of smoke skyward to be dissipated by wind that came over the hilltops. On a hillcrest itself a tiny sand-devil whirled for a moment and then vanished.

The voice said abruptly and scornfully, "You in the door there! Where'd you come from?"

Link said agreeably, "From Trent."

"What's that?" demanded the voice, disparagingly.

"A planet—a world like this," explained Link.

The voice said, "Huh!" There was a long pause. It said, "Why?"

Link had no idea what or who his unseen questioner might be, but the tone of the questioning was scornful. He felt that a certain impressiveness on his own part was in order. He said, "That is something to be disclosed only to proper authority. The purpose of my companion and myself, however, is entirely admirable. I may say that in time to come it is probable that the anniversary of our landing will be celebrated over the entire planet."

Having made the statement, he rather admired it. Almost anything could be deduced from it, yet it did not mean a thing.

There was again a silence. Then the voice said cagily, "Celebrated by uffts?"

Here Link made a slight but natural error. The word "uffts," which was unfamiliar, sounded very much like "us," and he took it for the latter. He said profoundly, "I would say that that is a reasonable assumption."

Dead silence once more. It lasted for a long time. Then the same voice said sharply, "Somebody's coming."

There came a scurrying behind the boulders. Little clickings sounded. There were flashes of pinkish-white hide. Then the two pig-like creatures darted back into view, galloping madly for the hillcrest over which they'd come. They vanished beyond it. Link spoke again, but there was no reply.

For a long time silence lay over the hollow in which the *Glamorgan* had come to rest. Link spoke repeatedly—chattily, seriously. The silence seemed almost ominous. He began to realize that Thistlethwaite had been gone for a long time. It was well over an hour, now. He ought to be getting back.

He didn't come. Link was genuinely concerned when, at least another half-hour later, a remarkably improbable cavalcade came leisurely over the hillcrest, crossed by Thistlethwaite to begin with, and the pig-like animals later. The members of the cavalcade regarded the ship interestedly, and came on at a deliberate and unhurried pace. There were half a dozen men, mounted on large, splay-footed animals which had to be called unicorns, because from the middle of their foreheads drooped flexible, flabby, horn-shaped appendages. The appendages looked discouraged. The facial expression of the animals who wore them was of complete, inquiring idiocy.

That was the first impression. The second was less pleasing. The leader of the riders wore Thistlethwaite's hat—it was too small for him—and had Thistlethwaite's stun gun slung over his shoulder. Another rider wore Thistlethwaite's shirt and a third wore the whiskery man's pants. A fourth had his shoes dangling as an ornament from his saddle. But of Thistlethwaite himself there was no sign.

All the newcomers carried long spears, lances, and wore at their belts large knives in decorated scabbards half the length of a sword.

The cavalcade came comfortably but ominously toward the *Glamorgan*. It came to a halt, its members regarding Link with expressions whose exact meaning it was not easy to decide. But Thistlethwaite had marched away from the ship with the only weapon on board, a stun rifle. The leader of this group carried it, but without any sign of familiarity with it. Link considered that he could probably get inside the ship with the port door closed before anything drastic could happen to him. He should, too, find out what had happened to Thistlethwaite.

So he said, "How do you do? Nice weather, isn't it?"

Chapter 3

There was a movement among the members of the cavalcade. The leader, wearing Thistlethwaite's hat and carrying his stun rifle, looked significantly at his followers. Then he turned to Link and spoke with a certain painful politeness. There was no irony in it. It was manners. It was the most courteous of greetings.

"I'm pretty good, thank you, suh. And the weather's pretty good too, only we could do with a mite of rain." He paused, and said with an elaborate stateliness, "I'm the Householder of the Household over yonder. We heard your ship come down and we wondered about it. An' then . . . uh . . . somethin' happened and we come to look it over. We never seen a ship like this before, only o'course there's the tales from old times about 'em."

His manner was one of vast dignity. He wore Thistlethwaite's hat, and his companions or followers wore everything else that Thistlethwaite had had on in the *Glamorgan*. But he ignored the fact. It appeared that he obeyed strict rules of etiquette. And of course, people who follow etiquette are bound by it even in the preliminaries to homicide. Which is important if violence is in the air. Link took advantage of the known fact.

"It's not much of a ship," he said deprecatingly, "but such as it is I'm glad to have you see it."

The leader of the cavalcade was visibly pleased. He frowned, but he said with the same elaborate courtesy,

"My name's Harl, suh. Would you care to give me

a name to call you by? I wouldn't presume for more than that."

Out of the corner of his eye Link saw that two pig-like animals had appeared not far away. They might be the same two he'd seen before. They squatted on their haunches and watched curiously, what went on as between men. He said,

"My name's Link. Link Denham, in fact. Pleased to meet you."

"The same, suh! The same!" The leader's tone became warm while remaining stately. "I take that very kindly, Link, tellin' me your last name, too. And right off Denham . . . Denham . . . I never met none of your Household before, but I'll remember it's a mannerly group. Would you . . . uh . . . have anything else to say?"

Link thought it over.

"I've come a long way," he observed. "I'm not sure what to say that would be most welcome."

"Welcome!" said the man who called himself Harl. He beamed. "Now, that's right nice! Boys, we been welcomed by this here Link and he's told us his last name and that's manners! This here gentleman ain't like that other fella! We're guestin'."

He slipped from his saddle, hung Thistlethwaite's stun gun on his saddle horn, and leaned his spear against the *Glamorgan*. He held out his hand cordially to Link. Link shook it. Harl's followers similarly divested themselves of weapons. They solemnly shook hands with Link. Harl rapped on one of the *Glamorgan*'s hull plates and said admiringly,

"This here ship's iron, ain't it? M-m-m-h! I never saw so much iron to one place in all my lifetime!"

A scornful voice from somewhere said indignantly, "We saw it first! It's ours!"

"Shut up," said Harl to the landscape at large. "And stay shut up." He turned, "Now, Link—"

"We saw it first!" insisted the voice furiously. "We saw it first! It's ours!"

"This gentleman," said Harl firmly, and again to the landscape, "is maybe thinkin' of settin' up a Household here! You uffts clear out!"

Two voices, now, insisted stridently,

"It's ours! We saw it first! It's ours!"

Harl said apologetically,

"I'm real sorry, Link, but you know how it is with uffts! Uh . . . I'd like to ask you something private."

"Come inside," said Link. He rose.

Harl and his companions—Link thought of the word "retainers" for no special reason—came trooping into the port. Link was very alertly interested. He didn't understand this state of things at all, but men with inhospitable intentions do not disarm themselves. These men had. Men with unpleasant purposes tend to cast furtive glances from one to another. These men didn't. If one ignored the presence of Thistlethwaite's garments, and the absence of Thistlethwaite himself, the atmosphere was almost insanely cordial and friendly and uncalculating. It verified past question that this planet had very little contact with other worlds. People of brisk and progressive cultures feel a deep suspicion of strangers and of each other. With reason. Yet Thistlethwaite—

Link let the small group precede him up the steps inside the landing fin. He could get down and outside before any of them, and very probably lock them in. Then he'd be armed and mounted, which in case of unfriendliness might be an advantage. But in spite of whatever had happened to Thistlethwaite, the feel of things was in no sense ominous. The visitors to the ship were openly curious and openly astonished at what they saw.

They commented almost incredulously that the long flight of steps was made of iron. Link tactfully did not refer to the sealed-off cargo compartments—the lifeboat was sealed off, too—nor to Thistlethwaite's garments worn so matter-of-factly by his guests. They passed the engine room without recognizing the door to it as what it was. They marveled to each other that iron showed through the worn floor-covering of the mess room. They were astounded by the cabins. But the control room left them entirely uninterested except for small metal objects—instruments—fastened to the control board and fitted into the walls.

The man wearing Thistlethwaite's pants took a deep breath. He caught Link's eye and said wistfully,

"Mistuh Link, that's a right pretty little thing!"

He pointed to the ship's chronometer. Harl said angrily:

"You shut up! What kinds guest-gift have *you* brought? I beg y'pardon, Link, for this fella!" He glared at his following. "Sput! You fellas go downstairs an' wait outside, so's you won't shame me again! I got to talk confidential to Mistuh Link, anyway."

His followers, still flaunting Thistlethwaite's garments, went trooping down and out. Silence fell, below. Then Harl said,

"Link, I'm right sorry about that fella! Admirin' something of yours to get it, without givin' you a gift first! I'd ought to chase him outa my Household for bad manners! I hope you'll excuse me for him!"

"No harm done," said Link. "He just forgot." It was evident that etiquette played a great part in the lives of the people of Sord Three. It looked promising. "I'd like to ask—"

Harl said confidentially, "Let's talk private, Link. Do you know a little fella with whiskers that cusses dreadful an' insults people right an' left an' says—" his voice dropped to a shocked tone—"an' says he's a friend of Old Man Addison? A fella like that come to my Household and—you maybe won't believe this, Link, but it's so—he offered to pay me for sendin' a message to Old Man Addison! He . . . offered to . . . pay me! Like I was an ufft! I'm beggin' your pardon for askin' such a thing, but we're talkin' private. Do you know a fella like that?"

"He ran the engines of this ship," said Link. "His name's Thistlethwaite. I don't know what he has to do with Old Man Addison."

"Natural!" said Harl hastily. "I wouldn't suspect you of anything like that! But . . . uh . . . the womenfolks said his clothes wasn't duplied. Is that a fact, Link? They went crazy fingerin' the cloth he was wearin'. Was it unduplied, Link?"

"I wouldn't know anything about his clothes," said Link. "I did notice your men were wearing them. I wondered."

"But you didn't say a word," said Harl, warmly. "Yes, suh! You got manners! But did you ever hear anything like what I just told you? Offerin' to pay me—and me a Householder—for sendin' a message to Old Man Addison! Did you ever, Link?"

"It's bad?" asked Link, blinking.

"I left word," said Harl indignantly, "to hang him as soon as enough folks got together to enjoy it. What else could I do? But I'd heard the noise when this ship came down, and it was you, landin' here! It's a great thing havin' you land here, Link! And think of havin' clothes that ain't duplied! If you set up a Household—"

Link stared. He'd always believed that he craved the new and the unpredictable. But this talk left him way behind. He felt that it would be a good idea to go off by himself and hold his head for a while. Yet Thistlethwaite—

"Sput!" said Harl, frowning to himself. "Here I am, guestin' with you, an' no guest-gift! But in a way you're guestin' with me, being this is on my Household land. And I ain't been hospitable! Look, Link! I'll send a ufft over with a message to hold up the hangin' till we get there and we'll go watch with the rest. What say?"

For perhaps the first time in his life, Link felt that things were a good deal more unexpected than he entirely enjoyed. There was only one way to stay ahead of developments until he could sort things out.

"That suggestion," he said profoundly, "is highly consistent with the emergency measures I feel should be substituted for apparently standard operational procedures with reference to discourteous space travelers." He saw that Harl looked at once blank and admiring, which was what he'd hoped. "In other words," said Link, "yes."

"Then let's get started," said Harl in a pleased tone.

"Y'know, Link, you not only got manners, you got words! I got to introduce you to my sister!"

He descended the stairs, Link following. The situation was probably serious. It could be appalling. But Link had been restless for days, now, from a lack of things to interest his normally active brain. He felt himself challenged. It appeared that Sord Three might turn out to be a very interesting place.

When they reached the open-air, the two pig-like animals had joined the party of waiting unicorns and men. They moved about underfoot with the accustomed air of dogs with a hunting party of men. But they did not wear dogs' amiable expressions. They looked distinctly peevish.

"I want somebody to take a message," said Harl briskly. "It's worth two beers."

A pig-like animal looked at him scornfully. Link heard a voice remarkably resembling that of the invisible conversationalist he'd talked to before these men arrived.

"This is our ship!" said the voice stridently. "We saw it first!"

"You didn't tell us," said Harl firmly. "And we found it without you. Besides, it belongs to this gentleman. You want two beers?"

"Tyrant!" snapped the voice. "Robber! Grinding down the poor! Robbing—"

"Hush up!" said Harl. "Do you take the message or not?"

A second voice said defiantly,

"For four beers! It's worth ten!"

"All right, four beers it is," agreed Harl. "The message is not to hang that whiskery fella till we get there. We'll be right along."

The first scornful voice snapped,

"Who gets the message?"

"Tell my sister," said Harl impatiently. "Shoo!"

The two pig-like animals broke into a gallop together and went streaking over the nearest hill crest. As they went, squabbling voices accused each other, the one because the bargain was for only two beers apiece, and the other for having gotten himself included in the bargain out of all reason. Link stared after them, his jaw dropped open. The voices dwindled, disputing, and ended as the piggish creatures disappeared.

Link swallowed and blinked. Harl appointed one of his followers to remain in the *Glamorgan* as caretaker. That left a splay-footed animal with a drooping nose-horn as a mount for Link. Bemused and almost incredulous, he climbed into the saddle on a signal from Harl. The completely improbable cavalcade moved briskly away from the landed spaceship. It was not an indiscretion on Link's part. A care-taker remained with the ship, and Thistlethwaite was in trouble. Link went to try to get him out. Also, it appeared to be definite that Link had somehow made himself a guest in Harl's Household—whatever that might be—and etiquette protected him from ordinary peril so long as he did nothing equivalent to offering to pay to have a message delivered, or rather, so long as he did nothing equivalent to offering to pay Harl for having a message delivered. It was approvable to offer to pay small animals like pigs who—

"My fella back there," said Harl reassuringly as they mounted a hillock and from its top saw other hillocks stretching away indefinitely, "my fella, he'll take good care of your ship, Link. I warned him not to touch a thing but just keep uffts out and if any human come by to say you're guestin' with me."

"Thanks," said Link. Then he said painfully, "Those small fat animals—"

"Uffts?" said Harl. "Don't you have 'em where you come from?"

"No," said Link. "We don't. It seems that . . . they talk!"

"Natural," Harl agreed. "They talk too much, if you ask me. Those two will stop on the way an' tell all the other uffts all about the message, and about you, an' everything. But they were on this world when the old-timers came an' settled' here. They were the smartest critters on the planet. Plenty smart! But they're awful proud. They got brains, but they've got hoofs instead of hands, so all they can do is talk. They have big gatherin's and drink beer and make speeches to each other about how superior they are to human bein's because they ain't got paws like us."

The motion of the splay-footed unicorns was unpleasant. The one Link rode put down each foot separately, and the result was a series of swayings in various directions which had a tendency to make a rider sea-sick. Link struggled with that sensation. Harl appeared to be thinking deeply, and sadly. The unicorns were not hoofed animals so there was no sound of hoofbeats. There was only the creaking of saddle leather and very occasionally the clatter of a spear or some other object against something else.

"Y'know," said Harl presently, "I'd like to believe that you comin' here, Link, is meant, or something. I've been getting pretty discouraged, with things seemin' to get worse all the time. Time was, the old

folks say, when uffts was polite and respectful and
did what they was told and took thank-you gifts and
was glad to've done a human a favor. But nowadays
they won't work for anybody without a agreement
of just how much beer they're goin' to get for doin'
it. And the old folks say there used to be unduplied
cloth an' stuff that was better than we got now. And
knives was better, an' tools was better, and there was
lectric and machines and folks lived real comfortable.
But lately it's been gettin' harder an' harder to get
uffts to bring in greenstuff, an' they want more an'
more beer for it. I tell you, it ain't simple, bein' a
Householder these days! You got people to feed an'
clothe, and the women fuss and the men get sour
and the uffts set back and laugh, and make speeches
to each other about how much smarter they are than
us. I tell you, Link, it's time for something to happen, or things are goin' to get just so bad we can't
stand them!"

The cavalcade went on, and Harl's voice continued.
The thing he deplored came out properly marshaled,
and it was evident that responsibilities in an imper-
fect universe had caused him much grief, of which
he was conscious.

Link caught an idea now and then, but most of
Harl's melancholy referred to conditions Harl took as
a matter of course and Link knew nothing about. For
example, there was the idea that it was disgraceful
to pay or be paid for anything that was done, except
by uffts. On no other planet Link had heard of was
commerce considered disreputable. He knew of none
on which work was not supposed to be performed
in exchange for wages. And there was, irrelevantly,

the matter of Thistlethwaite's clothing. It was not "duplied." What was "duplied"? Everywhere, of course, the good old days are praised by those who managed to live through them. But when cloth was duplied it was inferior, and tools were inferior, and there was no more lectric—that would be electricity—and there were no more engines.

Link almost asked a question, then. The ancestors of Harl and his followers had colonized this planet from space. By spaceship. It was unthinkable that they hadn't had electricity and engines or motors. And when the way to make things is known and they are wanted, they are made! The way to make them is not forgotten! It simply isn't! But according to Harl they'd had those things and lost them. Why?

Harl murmured on, with a sort of resigned unhappiness. The state of things on Sord Three was bad. He hoped Link's arrival might help, but it didn't seem really likely. He named ways in which times had formerly been better. He named matters in which deterioration had plainly gone a long way. But he gave no clue to what made them worse, except that everything that was duplied was inferior, and everything was duplied. But what duplying was—

They passed over the top of a rolling hill. Below them the ground was disturbed. An illimitable number of burrows broke its surface, with piles of dirt and stones as evidence of excavations below ground. An incredible number of pink-skinned, pig-like creatures appeared to live here.

"This," said Harl uncomfortably, "this is an ufft town. It's shortest to get back to the Household if we ride through it. They fuss a lot, but they don't ever actual do more than yell at humans goin' through. Bein' uffts, though, and knowing from those two I sent ahead that you're a stranger, they may be extra noisy just to show off."

Link shrugged.

"You fellas," said Harl sternly to his following, "don't you pay any attention to what they say! Hear me? Ignore 'em!"

The cavalcade rode down the farther hillside and entered the ufft metropolis. The splay-footed unicorns walked daintily, avoiding the innumerable holes which were exactly large enough to let full-grown uffts pop in and out with great rapidity. Had Link known prairie-dogs, he would have said that it was much like a much-enlarged prairie-dog town. The burrows were arranged absolutely without pattern, here and there and everywhere. Uffts sat in their doorways, so to speak, and regarded the animals and men with scornful disapproval. It seemed to Link that they eyed him with special attention, and not too much of cordiality.

A voice from somewhere among the burrows snapped,

"Humans! Huh! And here's a new one. Pth-th-th-thl!" It was a Bronx cheer. Another voice said icily, "Thieves! Robbers! Humans!" A third voice cried shrilly, "Oppressors! Tyrants! Scoundrels!"

The six riders, including Link, gazed fixedly at the distance. They let their mounts pick their way. The scornful voices increased their clamor. Uffts—they did look astonishingly like pigs—popped out of burrows practically under the feet of the unicorns and cried out enragedly,

"That's right! That's right! Tread on us! Show the stranger! Tread on us!"

Uffts seemed to boil around the clump of unicorns. They dived out of sight as the large splay feet of the riding-animals neared them, and then popped up immediately behind them with cries of rage, "Tyrants! Oppressors! Stranger, tell the galaxy what you see!" Then other confused shoutings, "Go ahead! Crush us! Are you ashamed to let the stranger see? It's what you want to do!"

There was a chorus of yapping ufft voices a little distance away. One of them, squatted upright, waved a fore-paw to give the cadence for choral shouts of, "Men, go home! Men, go home! Men, go home!"

Harl looked unhappily at Link.

"They never had manners, Link. But this is worse than I've seen before. Some of it's to make you think bad of us, you bein' a stranger. I'm right sorry, Link."

"Humans seem pretty unpopular," said Link. "They aren't afraid of you, though."

"I can't afford to be hard on 'em," admitted Harl. "I need 'em to bring in greenstuff. They know it. They work when they feel like they want some beer. They get enough beer for a party an' then they make speeches to each other about how grand they are an' how stupid us humans are. If I was to try to make 'em act respectful, they'd go get their beer from another Household, an' we wouldn't have any greenstuff brought in. An' they know I know it. So they get plenty fresh!"

"Yah!" rasped a voice almost underfoot. "Humans! Humans have paws! Humans have hands! Shame! Shame! Shame!"

The unicorns plodded on, their flaccid upside-down horns drooping and wobbling. They climbed over mounds of dirt and stones, and down to level ground between burrows, and then over other mounds. Their gait was incredibly ungainly. The clamor of ufft voices increased. The nearby tumult was loud enough, but the ufft city stretched for a long way. It seemed that for miles to right and left there were shrilling, pink-skinned uffts galloping on their stubby legs to join in the abuse of the human party.

"Yah! Yah! Humans! Men, go home! Hide your paws, Humans!" A small group yelled in chorus, "The uffts will rise again! The uffts will rise again!" Yet another party roared, although some of the voices were squeaky, "Down with Households! Down with tyrants! Down with Humans! Up with uffts!"

The cavalcade was the center of a moving uproar. At the beginning there'd been some clear space around the feet of the unicorns. But uffts came from all directions, shrilling abuse. Swarms of rotund bodies scuttled up and over the heaps of dug-out dirt and stones, and they ran into other swarms, and they crowded each other closer to the mounted men. Some were unable to dart aside, and dived down into burrows to escape trampling. They popped out behind the unicorns to yap fresh insults. Then one popped out directly underneath a unicorn, and the unicorn's pillowy foot sent him rolling, and squealing, but unhurt, and then there was an uproar.

"Dirty humans! Tyrants! Now you kill us."

"Hold fast to your saddle, Link," said Harl bitterly. 'They'll be bitin' the unicorns' feet in a minute. That'll be the devil! They'll run away and y'don't want to get thrown! Not down among them!"

Link reined aside and held up his hand for attention. He was a stranger and part of this demonstration was for him. He knew something about demonstrators. For one thing, they are always attracted, almost irresistibly, to new audiences. But there is another and profound weakness in the psychology of a mob. When it is farthest from sane behavior, it likes to be told how intelligent it is.

"My friends!" boomed Link, in a fine and oratorical carrying voice. "My friends, back at the ship I had a conversation with two of your cultured and brilliant race, which filled me with even increased respect for your known intellectuality!" There was a slight lessening of the tumult nearby. Some uffts had heard pleasing words. They listened.

"But that conversation was not necessary," Link announced splendidly, "to inform me of your brilliance. On my home planet the intellect of the uffts of Sord Three has already become a byword! When a knotty problem arises, someone is sure to say, 'If we could ask the uffts of Sord Three about this, they'd settle it!'"

The nearer uffts were definitely quieter. They shushed those just behind them. Then they shouted to Link to go on. There was still babbling and abuse, but it came from farther away.

"So I came here," Link announced in ringing tones, "to carry out a purpose which, if accomplished, will make it probable that the anniversary of my arrival will be celebrated over the entire surface of at least one planet! My friends, I call upon you to bring this about! I call upon you to cause such rejoicing as indubitably will modify the future of all intellectual activities! Which will bring about a permanent orientation ufftward of the more abstruse ratiocination of the intellectuals of the galaxy! I call upon you, my friends, to give to other worlds the benefit of your brains!"

He paused. He knew that Harl listened with startled incomprehension. He could see out of the corner of his eyes that the other halted men were bemused and uneasy, but the uffts within hearing cheered. Those too far away to hear clearly were trying to silence those behind them. They cheered to make the balance listen. Link bowed to the applause.

"I bring you," he boomed with a fine gesture, "I bring you a philosophical problem, which is also a problem in sophistic logic, that the greatest minds of my home planet have not been able to solve! I have come to ask the uffts of Sord Three to use their superlative intellects upon this baffling intellectual question! There must be an answer! But it has eluded the greatest brains of my home system. So I ask the uffts of Sord Three to become the pedagogues of my world. You are our only hope! But I do not feel only hope! I feel confidence! I am sure that ufftian intellect will find the answer which will initiate a new era in intellectual processes!"

He paused again. There were more cheers. Much of the cheering came from uffts who cheered because other uffts were cheering.

"The problem," said Link impressively, and with ample volume, "the problem is this! You know what whiskers are. You know what shaving is. You know that a barber is a man who shaves off the whiskers of other men. Now, there is a Household in which there is a barber. He shaves everybody in the Household who does not shave himself. He does not shave anybody who does shave himself. The ineluctable problem is, who shaves the barber?"

He stopped. He looked earnestly at all parts of his audience.

"Who shaves the barber?" he repeated dramatically. "Consider this, my friends! Discuss it! It has baffled the philosophers and logicians of my home world! I have brought it to you in complete confidence that, without haste and after examining every aspect of the situation, you will penetrate its intricacies and find the one true solution! When this is done I shall return to my home world bearing the triumphant result of your cerebration and a new field of intellectual research will be opened for the minds of all future generations!"

He made a gesture of finality. There was really loud cheering now. Link was a stranger. He had flattered the uffts and those near him were charmed by his tribute, and those farther away cheered because those near him had cheered, and those still farther away—

"Let's get going," said Link briefly.

The cavalcade took up its march again. But now there were groups of uffts running alongside Link's unicorn, cheering him from time to time and in between beginning to argue vociferously among themselves that the barber did or didn't shave himself because if he didn't, or if he did, why? And if he wore whiskers he would not shave himself and therefore would have to shave himself and therefore couldn't have whiskers.

The angular, ungainly unicorns moved in their slab-sided fashion across the remaining dirt piles and burrows of the ufft city. Behind them, a buzz of argument began and rose to the sky. Uffts by thousands zestfully discussed the problem of the barber. He shaved everybody who didn't shave himself. He didn't shave anybody who did shave himself. Therefore—

Harl rode in something like a brown study for a long way after the ufft metropolis was left behind. Then he said heavily,

"Uh . . . Link, did you sure enough come here to ask the uffts that there question?"

"No," admitted Link. "But it seemed like a good idea to ask it."

Harl considered for a long time. Then he said,

"What did you come here for, Link?"

Link considered in his turn. Viewing the matter dispassionately, he didn't seem to have had any clear cut reason. One thing had led to another, and here he was. But a serious minded character like Harl might find the truth difficult to understand. So Link said with a fine air of regret,

"I'll tell you, Harl. There was a girl named Imogene—"

"Uh-uh," said Harl regretfully. "I'm gettin' kind of troubled about you, Link. You're guestin' with me, an' all that, but that whiskery fella that cussed so bad an' insulted me, he came on the spaceship with you. And that speech you made to those uffts—I don't understand it, Link. I just don't understand it! You seem like a right nice fella to me, but I'm a Householder and I got responsibilities. And I'm gettin' to think that with times like they are, and the uffts cheering you like they did, an' all my other troubles—"

"What?" asked Link.

"I hate to say it, Link," said Harl apologetically, "an' it may not seem mannerly of me, but honest I think I'd better get you hung along with that whiskery fella that wanted to send a message to Old Man Addison. I won't like doin' it, Link, and I hope you won't take it unkindly, but it does look like I better hang you both to avoid trouble."

Harl's followers rearranged themselves, closing Link in so there was no possibility of his escape.

Chapter 4

They reached the village which Harl pointed to with the comment that it was his Household. They rode into it, and there were a good many women and girls in sight. They were elaborately clothed in garments at once incredibly brilliant and sometimes patched. But only a few men were visible. There were no dogs, such as properly belong in a small human settlement, but there were uffts in the streets sauntering about entirely at their ease. Once the cavalcade passed two of them, squatted on their haunches in the position of quadrupeds sitting down, apparently deep in satisfying conversation. It overtook a small cart loaded with a remarkable mixture of leaves, weeds, roots, grass, and all manner of similar debris. It looked like the trash from a gardening job, headed either for a compost heap or for a place where it would be burned to be gotten rid of. But there were four uffts pulling it by leather thongs they held in their teeth. It had somehow the look of a personal enterprise of the uffts, personally carried out.

A little way on there was a similar cart backed up to a wide door in the largest building of the village. That cart was empty, but a man in strikingly colored, but patched, clothing was putting plastic bottles into it. The contents looked like beer. An ufft supervised the placing, counting aloud in a sardonic voice as if ostentatiously guarding against being cheated. Three other uffts waited for the tally to be complete.

The cavalcade drew rein at a grand entrance to this largest building. Harl dismounted and said heavily,

"Here's where I live. I don't see anything else to do but hang you, Link, but there's no need to lock you up. Come along with me. My fellas will be watchin' all the doors an' windows. You can't get away, though I mighty near wish you could."

The four other riders dismounted. There'd been no obvious sign of Link's change of status, from warmly approved guest to somebody it seemed regrettably necessary to hang, but after Harl's decision his followers had matter-of-factly taken measures to prevent his escape. There was no hope of a successful dash now, nor was there any place to dash to.

Link climbed down to the ground. During all his life, up to now, he'd craved the novel and the unexpected. But it hadn't happened that the prospect of being hanged had ever been a part of his life. In a way, without realizing it, he'd taken the state of not being hanged for granted. He'd never felt that he needed to work out solid reasons against his hanging as a project. But Harl appeared to be wholly in earnest. His air of regret about the necessity seemed sincere, and Link rather startledly believed that he needed some good arguments. He needed them both good and quick.

"Come inside," said Harl gloomily. "I never had anything bother me so much, Link! I don't even know what it's mannerly to do about your ship. You ain't given it to me, and you welcomed me in it, so it would be disgraceful to take it. But it's the most iron I ever did see! And things are pretty bad for iron, like most other things. I got to think things out."

Link followed him through huge, wide doors. It looked like a ceremonial entranceway. Inside there was a splendid hall hung with draperies that at some time had been impressive. They were a mass of embroidery from top to bottom and the original effect must have been one of genuine splendor. But they were ancient, now, and they showed it. At the end of the hall there was a grandiose, stately, canopied chair upon a raised dais. It looked like a chair of state. The entire effect was one of badly faded grandeur. The present effect was badly marred by electric panels which obviously didn't light, and by three uffts sprawled out and sleeping comfortably on the floor.

"Most of my fellas are away," said Harl worriedly. "An ufft came in yesterday with some bog-iron and said he'd found the biggest deposit of it that ever was found. But y'can't trust uffts! He wanted a thousand bottles of beer for showin' us where it was, and five bottles for every load we took away. So I got most of my fellas out huntin' for it themselves. The ufft'd think it was a smart trick to get a thousand bottles of beer out of me for nothing, and then laugh!"

One of the seemingly dozing uffts yawned elaborately. It was not exactly derisive, but it was not respectful, either.

Harl scowled. He led the way past the ceremonial chair and out a small sized door just beyond. Here, abruptly, there was open air again. And here, in a space some fifty by fifty feet, there was an absolutely startling garden. It struck Link forcibly because it made him realize that at no time on the journey from the landed *Glamorgan* to the village had he seen a sign of cultivated land. There was very little vegetation of any sort. Isolated threads of green appeared here and there, perhaps, but nothing else. There'd been no fields, no crops, no growing things of any sort. There was literally no food being grown outside the village for the feeding of its inhabitants. But here, in a space less than twenty yards across, there was a ten-foot patch of wheat, and a five-foot patch of barley, and a row of root-plants which were almost certainly turnips. Every square inch was cultivated. There were rows of plants not yet identifiable. There was a rather straggly row of lettuce. It was strictly a kitchen garden, growing foodstuffs, but on so small a scale that it wouldn't markedly improve the diet of a single small family. In one corner there was an apple tree showing some small and probably wormy apples on its branches. There was another tree not yet of an age to bear fruit, but Link did not know what it was.

And there was a girl with a watering can, carefully giving water to a row of radishes.

"Thana," said Harl, troubled. "This's Link Denham.

He came down in that noise we heard a while ago. It was a spaceship. That whiskery fella came in it too. I'm goin' to have to hang Link along with him—I hate to do it, because he seems a nice fella—but I thought I'd have you talk to him beforehand. Coming from far off, he might be able to tell you some of those things you're always wishin' you knew."

To Link he added, "This's my sister Thana. She runs this growin' place and not many Households eat as fancy as mine does! See that apple tree?"

Link said, "Very pretty" and looked carefully at the girl. At this stage in his affairs he wasn't overlooking any bets. She'd be a pretty girl if she had a less troubled expression. But she did not smile when she looked at him.

"You'd better talk to that whiskery man," she said severely to her brother. "I had to have him put in a cage."

"Why not just have a fella watch him?" demanded Harl. 'Even if a man is goin' to be hung, it ain't manners not to make him comfortable."

The girl looked at Link. She was embarrassed. She moved a little distance away. Harl went to her and she reported something in a low tone. Harl said vexedly, "Sput! I never heard of such a thing! I . . . never . . . heard of such a thing! Link, I'm goin' to ask you to do me a favor."

Link was in a state of very considerable confusion. It seemed settled that he faced a very undesirable experience. Hanging. But he was not treated as a criminal. Harl, in fact, seemed to feel rather apologetic about it and to wish Link well in everything but continued existence. But now he returned to Link, very angry.

"I'm going to ask you, Link," he said indignantly, "to go see that whiskery fella and tell him there's an end to my patience! He insulted me, an' that's all right. He'll get hung for it and that's the end of it. But you tell him he's got to behave himself until he does get hung! When it comes to tryin' to send a message to my sister—my *sister*, Link offerin' to *pay her* for sendin' a message to Old Man Addison, I'm not goin' to stand for it! He's gettin' hung for sayin' that to me! What more does he want?"

Link opened his mouth to suggest that perhaps Thistlethwaite wanted to get a message to Old Man Addison. But it did not seem tactful.

"You see him," said Harl wrathfully. "If I was to go I'd prob'ly have him hung right off, and all my fellas that didn't see it would think it was unmannerly of me not to wait. So you talk to him, will you?"

Link swallowed. Then he asked,

"How will I find him?"

"Go in yonder," said Harl, pointing, "and ask an ufft to show you. There'll be some house-uffts around. Ask any one of 'em."

He turned back to his sister. Link headed for the pointed-out door. He heard Harl, behind him, saying angrily,

"If he don't behave himself, sput! Hangin's too good for him!"

But then Link passed through the door and heard no more. Uffts in their own village were openly derisive of Harl. But they sauntered about his house and slept on his floors and he certainly tolerated it. He found himself in a hallway with doors on either side and an unusually heavy door at the end. It occurred to him that he was nearly in the same fix as Thistle-thwaite, though Thistlethwaite had wanted to send a message, while he'd only made a speech to the uffts. He groped for something that would make sense out of the situation.

An ufft slept tranquilly in the hall. It was very pig-like indeed. It looked like about a hundred-pound shote, with pinkish hide under a sparse coating of hair. Link stirred the creature with his foot. The ufft waked with a convulsive, frightened scramble of small hoofs.

"Where's the jail?" asked Link. He'd just realized that he couldn't make plans for himself alone, since Thistlethwaite was in the same fix. It made things look more difficult.

The ufft said sulkily, "What's a jail?"

"In this case, the room where that man who's to be hung is locked up," said Link. "Where is it?"

"There isn't any," said the ufft, more sulkily than before. "And he's not locked up in a room. He's in a cage."

"Then where's the cage?"

"Around him," said the ufft with an air of extreme fretfulness. "Just because you humans have paws isn't any reason to wake people up when they're resting."

"You!" snapped Link. "Where's that cage?

The ufft backed away affrightedly.

"Don't do that!" it protested nervously. "Don't threaten me! Don't get me upset!"

It began to back away again. Link advanced upon the ufft. "Then tell me what I want to know!"

The ufft summoned courage. It bolted. Some

distance away it halted at a branching passage to stare at Link in the same extreme unease.

"He's in the cellar," said the ufft. "Down there!"

It pointed with a fore-hoof.

"Thanks," said Link, with irony.

The ufft protested, complainingly,

"It's all very well for you to say thanks after you've scared a person."

Link moved forward, and the ufft fled. But Link's intentions were not offensive. He was simply following instructions. He moved doggedly down the hallway. It was carpeted. But the carpet was worn and frayed, though once it had been luxurious. He noted that the plastering was the work of a less than skilled workman.

He came to a corner in the hallway wall. A flight of steps went downward, to the left. He went down them. He heard voices. One of them had the quality of an ufft's speech.

"Now, we can do it. The fee will be five thousand beers."

Thistlethwaite sounded enraged.

"Outrageous! Robbery! One thousand bottles!"

"Business is business," said the other voice. "Four. After all, you're a human!"

Link's foot made a scraping sound on the floor. There was an instant scuffling and low-voiced whispers and mutterings of alarm. Link went toward the sound and came to a place where a wick burned in a dish of oil. The light played upon an oversized cage of four-by-four timbers elaborately lashed together with rope. Inside the cage, Thistlethwaite glared toward the sound of the interruption.

Beyond the cage there was a very neat pile of vision-receivers, all seemingly new and every one dusty. The combination of unused vision-receivers and a wick floating in a disk of oil for light was startling. The light was primitive and smoky. The vision-sets were not. But the light worked and the vision-sets didn't. Evidently. There were electric-light panels. But they wouldn't work either, or the oil lamp would not exist. Thistlethwaite didn't see Link, as yet.

"You'd better tell your boss," rasped Thistlethwaite to the sound that was Link, "that if he ever expects to do any business with Old Man Addison he'd better let me loose and give me back my clothes and—"

He stopped short. He and Link could see each other now. Thistlethwaite was bare and hairy and caged. At sight of Link he uttered a bellow of rage through the heavy wooden bars.

"You!" he roared. "What' you doin' here? I told you to keep ship! You go back there! You want the ship to be claimed as jetsam, an abandoned ship with no representative of the owner on board? You get there! Lock y'self in! You stay on board till I finish my business dealin' and come an' tell you what to do next!"

"There's someone in charge," said Link mildly. "One of Harl's retainers is acting as watchman. For me. There've been developments since then, but that's that about the ship. I've got a message for you from Harl."

Thistlethwaite sputtered naughty words in naughtier combinations.

"It seems," said Link, "that to offer to pay a House-holder for something is insult amounting to a crime.

That's what you're to be hung for. Offering to pay a Householder's sister for something is a worse crime. It appears that doing business, except with uffts, is considered disgraceful. I don't see how they make it work, but there you are. If you'll apologize, I think there's a chance."

Thistlethwaite cried out, furiously, "How can you do business without doin' business? You go tell him—"

"I'd like to get you off," said Link mildly. "I'm supposed to be hanged, too. But if I get you a pardon I might get one for myself as a *particept noncriminus*. So—"

He heard faint sounds. He said, "If you've a better way of getting out of being hanged than apologizing, I'd like to join you. I have an idea that there are persons of larger views than . . . ah . . . the humans on Sord Three. I refer to that brilliantly intellectual race, the uffts. With their cooperation—"

He definitely heard faint sounds. There had been voices before he arrived at Thistlethwaite's cage. He waited hopefully.

"Look here!" snapped Thistlethwaite, "I'm the senior partner in this business! You signed a contract leavin' all decisions to me an' you doin' only astrogatin'! You leave this kinda business to me! I'll tend to it!"

There was a slight scraping noise. An ufft came out from behind the pile of vision-sets. Other uffts appeared from other places. The first ufft said, "You said you are to be hanged. Would you be interested in a deal with us? We can do all sorts of jail deliveries, strikes, sabotage, spying and intelligence work, and we specialize in political demonstrations." The ufft grew enthusiastic. "How about a public demonstration against hanging visitors from other worlds? Mobs shouting in the streets! Pickets around the Householder's home! Chanted slogans! Marching students! And demonstrators lying on the ground and daring men to ride unicorns over them! We can—"

"Can you guarantee results?" asked Link politely.

"It'll be known all over the planet!" said the ufft proudly. "Public opinion will be mobilized! There'll probably be sympathetic demonstrations at other Households. There'll be indignation, meetings! There'll be petitions! There'll be—"

"But what," asked Link as politely as before, "just what will be the actual physical result? Will Thistlethwaite be released? And I'm supposed to be hanged too. Will I be pardoned? What will Harl actually do in response to all these demonstrations?"

"His name will go down in history as among the most despicable of all tyrants who tried to keep us uffts in bondage!"

"Not in human histories," said Link. "Not in histories written by men! Actually, Harl will go his placid way and hang Thistlethwaite and me. And I hate to say it, but our ghosts won't get the least bit of comfort out of even the most violent of public reactions after the event."

The ufft made no reply.

"I have a thought," said Link. "Everybody has a weakness. You have yours, Harl has his, I have mine. Hart's is that he is hell on manners. Fix things so he'll be unmannerly if he doesn't pardon both of us, and he'll be like putty. If Thistlethwaite apologizes elaborately enough, pleading ignorance of the local customs—"

Thistlethwaite protested bitterly, "Apologize for a straight business proposal? A sound business transaction? I offered to pay him liberal—"

"Exactly the point," said Link. "Exactly!"

"Mobs in the streets, shouting to shame him," said the first ufft, enthusiastically. "Pickets around his house, chanting slogans! Uffts lying in the streets, daring men to ride over them."

"No," said Link patiently. "Thistlethwaite apologizes. He didn't know the local customs. He asks Harl to forgive him and permit him to make a guest-gift of the clothes and the stun rifle Harl has already taken. No expense there! Then he asks Harl to instruct me in local etiquette so he can observe it in future contacts with Harl, whom he hopes to make his guide, mentor, friend, and most intimate companion when he has made himself worthy of Harl's friendship."

"I won't do it!" raged Thistlethwaite ferociously. "I won't do it! I'm goin' to run this in a businesslike way! That ain't business!"

"It's sense," observed Link.

"You're fired!" bellowed Thistlethwaite. "You're fired! You ain't a junior partner any more! Your contract with me says I can heave you out any time I want! You're heaved! I'm runnin' this my way!"

Link looked at him earnestly, but the little man glared furiously at him. Link shrugged and went away. He returned to the garden, where Harl paced up and down and up and down, and where his sister again watered a row of not over-prosperous plants.

"Thistlethwaite," said Link untruthfully, "had an unhappy childhood, practically surrounded by people with the manners, morals, and many of the customs of uffts. It warped his whole personality. He is aware that he ought to apologize for having insulted you. But he's ashamed. He feels that he should be punished. Also he feels that he should make reparation. At the moment he is struggling between a death-wish and an inferiority complex. He will offer no more insults unless the struggle goes the wrong way."

Harl scowled.

"But there is a reasonable probability," added Link, "that he will end up by making the spaceship and its cargo his guest-gift to you. That would get you out of an unpleasant dilemma. It would be very mannerly to accept it. You'd have the ship and your manners in getting it would be above reproach."

Harl said suspiciously, "How much time is he likely to take?"

"When were you planning to hang us?" asked Link.

"After the fellas get back," said Harl. "They may be a while having their suppers. Then I was figurin' we'd have the hangin' by torch-light. It'll make a right interestin' spectacle, flamin' torches an' such and a hangin' by their light. My fellas will talk about it for years!"

"Just take it easy," advised Link. "Don't hurry things. He'll come around before anybody gets too sleepy to appreciate his hanging!"

He hoped it was true. It ought to be. But Harl paced up and down.

"I wouldn't want to do anything unmannerly," he said grudgingly. "All right. I'll give him until hangin' time." Then he seemed to rouse himself. "Thana, you pick the stuff for supper and I'll get it duplied while you ask Link questions about the things you want to know."

The girl plucked half a dozen lettuce plants. A handful of peas. She examined the apples on the tree and picked one. It was a small and scrawny apple. Link saw a worm-hole near its stem. She handed the vegetation to her brother. Then she said to Link,

"I'll show you."

He followed her. She went into the building, and they were in the great hall with the canopied chair. She led the way across the hall and into a smaller room. It was lined with shelves, and ranged upon them were all the objects a Householder could desire or feel called on to supply to his retainers. There were shelves of tools, but only one of each. There were shelves of cloth. Much of it was incredibly beautiful embroidery, but it was age-yellowed and old. There were knives of various shapes and sizes, plates, dishes, and glassware, bits of small hardware, and sandals, purses, and neckerchiefs, although these last categories were in poor condition indeed. In general, there was every artifact of a culture which had made vision-sets and now was used floating wicks in oil for illumination.

Link suddenly knew that this was in a sense the treasury of the Household. But there was only one of each object on display.

Thana pulled out a drawer and showed Link an assortment of rocks and stones of every imaginable variety. She searched his expression and said, "When you make a stew, you put in meat and flour and what vegetables you have. That's right, isn't it?"

"I suppose so," agreed Link. He was baffled again

by his surroundings and, of all possible openings for a conversation, the subject she'd just mentioned.

"But," said Thana uncomfortably, "it doesn't taste very good unless you put in salt and herbs. That's right too, isn't it?"

"I'm sure it is," said Link. "But—"

"Here's a knife." It was in the drawer with the rocks. She handed it to him. It was a perfectly ordinary knife; good steel, of a more or less antique shape, with a mended handle. It had probably had a handle of bone or plastic which by some accident had been destroyed, so someone had painstakingly fitted a new one of wood. She reached to a shelf and picked up another knife. She handed it to Link, too.

He looked at the pair of them, at first puzzled and then incredulous. They were identical. They were really identical! They were identical as Link had never seen two objects before. There was a scratch on the handle of each. The scratches were identical. There was a partly broken rivet in one, and the same rivet was partly broken in precisely the same fashion in the other. The resemblance was microscopically exact! Link went to a window to examine them again, and the grain of the wooden handles had the same pattern, the same sequence of growth-rings, and there was a jagged nick in one blade, and a precise duplicate of that nick in the other. Perhaps it was the wood that most bewildered Link. No two pieces of wood are ever exactly alike. It can't happen. But here it had.

"This knife is duplied from that," said Thana. "This one is duplied. That one isn't. The unduplied one is better. It's sharper and stays sharper. Its edge doesn't turn. I . . ." She hesitated a moment. "I've been wondering if it isn't something like a stew. Maybe the unduplied knife has something in it like salt, that's been left out of the duplied one. Maybe we didn't give it something it needs, like salt. Could that be so?"

Link gaped at her. She didn't looked troubled now. She looked appealing and anxious and—when she didn't look troubled she was a very pretty girl. He noticed that even in this moment of astonishment. Because he began to make a very wild guess at what might explain human society on Sord Three.

His limited experience with it was baffling. From the moment when he sat on the exit port threshold of the *Glamorgan* and chatted with an invisible conversationalist, to the moment he'd been told regretfully by Harl that he'd have to be hanged because of a speech he'd made about a barber, every single happening had confused him. It seemed that beer was currency. It seemed that a fifty-foot-square garden somehow supplied food for an entire village, though its plants seemed quite ordinary. Right now, dazedly surveying the whole experience, he recalled that there was no highway leading to the village. No road. It was not irrelevant. It fitted into the preposterous entire pattern.

"Wait a minute!" said Link, astounded and still unbelieving. "When you duply something you . . . furnish a sample and the material for it to something and it . . . duplicates the sample?"

"Of course," said Thana. Her forehead wrinkled a little as she watched his expression. "I want to know if the reason some duplied things aren't as good as unduplied ones is that we leave something out of the material we give the duplier to duply unduplied things with."

His expression did not satisfy her.

"Of course if the sample is poor, the duplied thing will be poor quality too. That's why our cloth is so weak. The samples are all old and brittle and weak. So duplied cloth is brittle and weak too. But," she asked unbelievingly, "don't you have dupliers where you come from?"

Link swallowed. If what Thana said was true—if it was true—an enormous number of things fell into place, including Thistlethwaite's scornful conviction that wealth in carynths was garbage compared with the wealth that could be had from one trading voyage to Sord Three. If what Thana said was true, that was true, too. But there were other consequences. If dupliers were exported from Sord Three, the civilization of the galaxy could collapse. There was no commerce, no business on Sord Three. Naturally! Why should anybody manufacture or grow anything if raw material could be supplied and an existent specimen exactly reproduced. What price riches, manufactures, crops, . . . civilization itself? What price anything?

Here, the price was manners. If someone admired something you owned, you gave it to him, it or a duplied, microscopically accurate replica. Or maybe you kept the replica and gave him the original. It didn't matter. They'd be the same! But the rest of the galaxy wouldn't find it easy to practice manners, after scores of thousands of years of rude and uncouth habits.

"Don't they have dupliers where you come from?" repeated Thana. She was astonished at the very idea.

"N-no," said Link, dry-throated. "N-no, we d-don't."

"But you poor things!" said Thana commiseratingly. "How do you live?"

For the first time in his life, Link was actually terrified. He said the first thing that came into his mind.

"We don't," he said thinly. "At least, we won't live long after we get dupliers!"

Chapter 5

There was movement in the great hall next door, but Thana paid no attention. She put one knife back on the shelf from which she'd taken it. She began to show Link the collection of small rocks and stones she'd accumulated.

"Here's a piece of rock we call bog-iron," she said absorbedly. "It has iron in it. Put this rock, with some wood, in the duplier, and a sample knife for it to duply, and the duplier takes iron out of the bog-iron and wood out of the wood and makes another knife. Of course the rock crumbles because part of it has been taken away. So does the wood, for the same reason. But then we have another knife. Only it's only so good. So I thought that if an unduplied knife has something besides iron in it, like a stew has salt, maybe if I found the right kind of rock the duplier would take something out of it, and if it was the right kind of . . . of whatever-it-is, the duplied knife would be as good as the original because it had everything in it the original knife had."

"Yes," said Link, still dizzy. "It would. It should. If you get the right kind of rock."

"Do you know what kind that would be?" asked Thana eagerly. "Can you show me the right kind?"

Link shook his head.

"Not I," he said wryly. "It's a special profession to know what rocks are ores and which aren't. Some of these rocks I do recognize. That blue one may have copper in it. I've seen it but I'm not sure. This pink one I know. I spent months digging it out in mountain-size masses, looking for a place where a meteor might have struck it on a world where they used to have severe meteor-showers. But the rest, no."

She looked distressed.

"Then there's not much use in having guessed something right, is there? When you go away in your spaceship could you send somebody back who does know about rocks? We might even have lectric again!"

"I'm supposed to be hung," said Link more wryly still. "And even if I could, I don't think I'd do it. Because he'd go away again and tell the outside worlds that you have dupliers on Sord Three. And men would come here to take them away from you. They'd rob you at least, more likely murder you to get your dupliers and then they'd take them and destroy themselves."

He made a rather absurd gesture. When one had been raised in a galaxy where every world has its own government, but they are so far apart that they can't fight each other, patriotism as loyalty to a given place

or planet tends to die out. It has no function. It serves
no purpose. But Link knew now that when men no
longer cherished small nations, whether they knew
it or not they were loyal to mankind. And dupliers
released to mankind would amount to treason.

If there can be a device which performs every sort
of work a world wants done, then those who first
have that instrument are rich beyond the dreams of
anything but pride. But pride will make riches a drug
upon the market. Men will no longer work, because
there is no need for their work. Men will starve
because there is no longer any need to provide them
with food. There will be no way to earn necessities.
One can only take them. And presently nobody will
attempt to provide them to be taken.

Thana said interestedly, "There are stories about the
fighting back on Surheil Two before our ancestors ran
away. Everybody was trying to kill them because they
had dupliers. They had to flee. It seems ridiculous, but
they did run away, in spaceships, and they came here.
There were only a few hundreds of them. The uffts
made quite a fuss about their setting up Households,
but the men had beer and the uffts couldn't make it.
They had no hands. So things got straightened out in
time. But for a long, long while it was believed that
nobody from any other world must ever be allowed
to land here. I'm glad you landed, though."

"To be hanged," said Link.

But he understood the history of Sord Three better
than she did. He could imagine the Economic Wars
on Surheil Two, after the ancestors of Thana had
fled. There were dupliers that weren't taken away
by the fugitives. A few. So men fought to possess

them, and other men fought to take them away, and ultimately they'd be destroyed by men who couldn't defend them. And then there'd be wholesale murder for food, and brigandage for what scraps were left. And at last civilization would have to start all over again with starving people and unplanted fields for a beginning. But no dupliers.

Here the disaster had taken a different form. While dupliers worked there was no need to learn useful things, such as the mechanical arts, and chemistry, and mineralogy. So such knowledge was forgotten. The art of weaving would vanish, too, when dupliers could make cloth to any demand. The composition of alloys. Electrical apparatus could not work without rare metals nobody knew how to find for the dupliers. So when the original units wore out there was no more electricity. And all cloth grows old and yellow and brittle, so old cloth, duplied, merely meant more old cloth, and alloy steel objects could not be reproduced, but only duplied, without the alloying materials, so there were only soft-iron knives and patched garments. And since the smallest of gardens, with any kind of vegetable matter for raw material, could have its produce duplied without limit, only the smallest of gardens were cultivated. Wherefore Harl's Household was hung with rich drapery which was falling apart, the carpets on its floors were threadbare, and he was proud that his Household had one scrawny apple tree with wormy fruit on it. Because on Sord Three men were not needed to make things or grow things or do things. And Harl's Household was ready to break apart.

"I begin," said Link unhappily, "to agree with Harl.

Since Thistlethwaite can't hope to astrogate his ship if I'm hanged, he can't report the state of things without me. So it's probably wise to hang me. On the other hand I couldn't run the ship's engines, so I couldn't take the news if he were hanged. But one or the other of us should be disposed of."

Thana said sympathetically, "You feel terrible, don't you? Let's go see Harl. Maybe you'll feel better. No, wait!" An idea had occurred to her. She surveyed a shelf of elaborately embroidered garments. She picked out one. "Do you think this is pretty?"

"Very," said Link forlornly. There hadn't been too many things he'd taken seriously, in his lifetime, but he did know that if dupliers got loose in the galaxy, there'd be no man certain of his life if he hadn't a duplier, nor any man whose life was worth a pebble if he did.

"Fine!" said Thana brightly. "Come along!"

She picked up a bundle of what looked like ancient, yellowed, cloth scraps, plus a lump of bog-iron. She led the way into the great hall.

Her brother Harl was there, wearing an expression of patient gloom. There were two retainers, working at something which gradually became clear. A third man rolled in a large wheeled box from somewhere. It was filled to the brim with a confused mass of leaves and roots and branches and weeds. It was the mixture uffts had been dragging into the village in a wheeled cart some little while ago. As a mixture, it belonged on a compost heap or on a brush pile to be burned. But instead it was brought into the hall with the incredible, falling-apart, floor-to-ceiling draperies.

There was a stirring. The dais and the canopied

chair moved. Together, chair and dais rose ceilingward. A deep pit was revealed where they had stood. And something rose in the pit, like a freight-elevator. It came plainly into view, and it was a complex metal contrivance with three hoppers on top which were plainly meant to hold things. One of the hoppers contained a damp mass of greenish powder in a highly irregular mound. One of Harl's retainers began to brush that out into a box for waste. The middle hopper contained a pile of apples, all small, all scrawny, and each with a wormhole next its stem. It contained a bushel or more of lettuce heaped up with the apples. The rest of the hopper was filled with peas.

The third of the hoppers contained an exact duplicate of the contents of the middle hopper. Each leaf of lettuce in the third hopper was a duplicate of one in the middle hopper. Each apple was a duplicate of an apple in the middle hopper. Each pea—

"Pyramid it once more," said Harl, "and it'll be enough."

His retainers piled the contents of the third hopper into the second. They piled the first one high with the contents of the box of vegetable debris. Link knew the theory now. The trash was vegetation. There were the same elements and same compounds in the trash as in apples, lettuce leaves, and peas. The proportions would be different, but the substance would be there. The duplier would take from the trash the materials needed to duplicate the sample edibles.

The same thing could more or less be done with roasts and steaks. Or elaborate embroidery, provided one had a sample for the duplier to work from. There would be left-over raw materials, of course, but a duplier could duplicate anything. Including a duplier.

And that was the thought which was frightening.

Harl said, "All right."

The men moved back. The contrivance descended into the pit. The chair of state descended until its dais rested on the floor, covering the pit. Harl said casually,

"How'd you make out, Thana? Does Link know some of the things you were wonderin' about?"

"Most of them," said Thana confidently. "Nearly all!"

It was less than an accurate statement, and Link wondered morosely why she made it. But then Harl pressed the button. The chair of state rose. The deep pit was revealed. The metal contrivance rose to floor-level. The pile of assorted fragments in the first hopper had practically vanished. The fruit and lettuce and peas in the second hopper were unchanged. The third hopper was full of an exact duplicate of the assortment of edibles in the middle one.

"We don't need any more," observed Harl. "Just clean up and—"

"Wait!" said Thana. "I was showing Link things, and he admired this shirt."

She unfolded the garment she'd asked Link's opinion on. It was a shirt. It was lavishly embroidered. Link opened his mouth, but Harl said indulgently, "All right."

Thana put the shirt in the middle—sample—hopper. Then she said,

"He told me the knife you've got is the prettiest he's seen, too!"

Harl said, "Sput!" His tone was not entirely pleased. Then he said, "I got to have manners, huh?"

"Of course," said Thana.

With a grimace, Harl unbuckled his belt and handed the belt and knife to Thana. She put them into the middle hopper. Then she put bog-iron, wood, and the scraps of cloth from the treasury room into the raw materials place. She nodded confidently to her brother.

He pressed something, the chair of state sank down, following the duplier mechanism, the room looked normal for a moment, and then the chair of state rose up, the pit appeared, and then the duplier.

There was much less bog-iron in the materials hopper. There was some sand on the hopper bottom. The embroidered shirt and the knife and belt were, as they'd been before, in the middle hopper. Exact duplicates of both knife and shirt were in the third hopper.

Thana handed her brother his knife. She took out and put aside the sample garment. She spread out its duplicate and said to Link, "Do put it on! Please!"

Harl watched impatiently, as Link took off his own shirt and donned the embroidered one. He was embarrassed by his own decorative appearance in the new apparel. Thana picked up the shirt he'd taken off.

"Look! This is unduplied, Harl!" she said with extravagant admiration. "Have you ever seen anything so wonderful?"

"Sput!" said Harl angrily. "What you tryin' to do?"

"I'm saying that this is a wonderful shirt," said Thana, beaming. "It isn't duplied. It's the nicest, newest shirt

I've ever seen. Don't you think so? I dare you to lie and still pretend you've manners!"

Harl said, "Sput!" again, and then, "All right," he admitted peevishly. "It's true. I never saw a new, unduplied shirt before. It's a nice shirt."

Thana turned triumphantly to Link. He didn't see any reason for triumph. But she waited, and waited. Harl glared at him. Suddenly, Link understood. He might be scheduled to hang, but he was expected to be mannerly.

"The shirt is yours," he said dourly to Harl. "It's a gift."

Harl hesitated for what seemed a long time. Then, "Thanks," he said reluctantly. "It's a right nice guest-gift. I appreciate it."

Thana looked radiant. She sent one of the retainers, standing by, for all the cloth on the treasury room shelves. She fairly glowed with enthusiasm. She put Link's former shirt in the sample hopper and filled another with scraps, and sent the duplier down. It came up and there were two shirts. It went down again with two shirts in the sample hopper. When it came up there were four. The chair of state and the duplier went down and up and down and up and down and up. When the last morsel of raw material was exhausted, there were one hundred twenty-seven duplicates of Link's own shirt, besides the original shirt itself.

"I guess that'll do," said Harl, ungraciously. "I'll be sendin' gifts to all my friends, and all my own fellas will have new shirts, an' their wives'll be takin' 'em apart to make dresses and sheets and stuff." He nodded to Link. "I appreciate that shirt a lot, Link. Thanks."

He went away, and Link stirred stiffly. He'd watched the entire process. Objects could be duplicated without labor or skill or industry. He'd observed what his mind told him was the doom of human civilization unless he or Thistlethwaite were hanged. Or both. But now he saw something more. Even that would not preserve the galaxy from destroying itself by riches out of dupliers. Eventually, certainly, another ship must land on Sord Three. It might be by accident. But some day another ship would come. And then this same intolerable situation would exist again.

"I'll see about dinner now," said Thana. She turned warm, grateful, admiring eyes upon Link, and vanished.

Harl shook his head as she disappeared.

"Smart girl, that! I wouldn't ha' thought of usin' manners to get your shirt off your back so's I could admire it and have the first new cloth since the old days! Mighty smart girl, Link!"

Link said stiffly, "If you're through with taking my shirt in vain, what now?"

Harl looked surprised. "Oh, you go off somewheres and set down and rest yourself, Link," he said kindly. "I got things to do. Excuse me!"

He departed. Link was left alone in the great hall, morbidly weighing the alternatives, himself or Thistlethwaite or both of them hanged against the collapse of all the economy of all the galaxy, with wars, murders, lootings and rapine as a necessary consequence. He didn't have to ask what Thistlethwaite had planned to trade for, on Sord Three. It was dupliers. And dupliers could obviously duplicate each other as well as more commonplace objects. Thistlethwaite wanted to make contact with Old Man Addison to trade unduplied objects for dupliers. Old Man Addison was evidently so disreputable a Householder that he would do business, if tempted. He'd provide a shipload of dupliers, especially duplied for the off-planet trade, in exchange for objects that dupliers couldn't duplicate on Sord Three. It would seem to him an excellent bargain.

It would seem an excellent bargain to business men elsewhere, too, to pay a hundred million credits and half the profits for a duplier. Thistlethwaite was right. Carynths were garbage in comparative value. A business man could begin with the luxury trade and undersell all other supplies, dispensing duplied luxury items. Then he could undersell any manufacturer of any other line of goods. He could undersell normally grown foodstuffs. Any supplier of meat products. Any supplier of anything else men needed or desired. All factories would become unprofitable. They'd close. All working men would become unemployed. All wages would cease to move except into a duplier-owner's pockets. And then there would be disaster, calamity, collapse, destruction, and hell to pay generally.

And Thistlethwaite couldn't foresee it. He was incapable of looking beyond an immediate, enormously profitable deal.

Link scowled. He alone could envision the coming disaster. He alone could think of measures to prevent it. And he was supposed to be hanged presently for a speech about an imaginary barber! It was wrong! It was monstrous! He had to stay alive to save the galaxy from the otherwise inevitable!

There was an ufft seemingly asleep in the far corner

of the hall. As Link approached, the ufft opened its eyes.

"Why didn't you tell Harl you admired Thana when he said she was a smart girl?"

The ufft had evidently been eavesdropping. It occurred to Link that there probably weren't many human secrets unknown to the uffts. They lounged about the village streets and they casually napped or seemed to doze in the Householder's home itself.

"Why should I say that?" asked Link irritably.

"If you want to marry her," said the ufft, "that's the start of it."

"But I just met her!" said Link.

The ufft stirred, in a manner suggesting a shrug by a four-footed animal lying prone on the floor.

"And what are you going to do about Thistlethwaite?" the ufft demanded. "He's going to escape. It's all arranged. Three thousand bottles of beer, payable by written contract when he gets to Old Man Addison's. But he's mad with you. He says you're not part of his organization anymore. You're fired for disobeying orders to stay in the ship. He says he got you for an astrogator—what's an astrogator?—because he couldn't get anybody better. He says he can astrogate the ship to where he wants to go by doing everything you did, backwards." Link thought sulfurous thoughts. The ufft went on, "He says he and Old Man Addison will make history on Sord Three. Why is Sord Three Sord Three? Why not just Sord?"

"Sord's the sun," said Link grimly, thinking of something else. "This is the third world from it."

"That's silly!" said the ufft. "What did you come here for, anyway? What did you expect to get out of it?"

"In spite," said Link, "of the remarkable similarity between your interrogation and those of other individuals with equally dubious justification, I merely observe that my motivation is only to be revealed to properly constituted authorities, and refrain from telling you to go fly a kite."

"What's a kite?" asked the ufft.

Link said, "Look! I'm supposed to be hung presently. I disapprove of the idea. How about arranging for me to escape along with Thistlethwaite?"

The ufft said, "Five thousand beers?"

"I haven't got them," admitted Link.

"Three? Will Old Man Addison pay them for you?"

"I've never met him," said Link.

"What else have you to offer, then?" asked the ufft in a businesslike tone. "I have to get a commission, of course."

"I made a speech in the ufft city," said Link hopefully, "on the way here from the ship. It was very well received. I may have some . . . hm . . . friends among my listeners who would think it unfortunate if I were hanged."

The ufft got to its four feet. It stretched itself. It yawned. Then it said, "Too bad!"

It trotted out of the hall.

Link found himself angry. In fact, he raged. Thistlethwaite, if he escaped, might actually try to astrogate the *Glamorgan* back to Trent by the careful notes Link had made in the ship's log. It wasn't too likely he'd manage it, but it was possible. If he did, then Link would have died in vain. He went storming about the building. He hadn't realized it, but it was now near sunset and what of the sky could be seen through windows was a flaming, crimson red. He came upon an ufft sauntering at ease from one room to another, and a second settling down for a tranquil nap. But he saw no human until he blundered into what must be a kitchen. There Thana bustled about in what must once have been a completely electrified kitchen, now with lamps which were simply floating wicks for illumination. There were two retainer girls assisting her. They used the former equipment as tables, and the cooking was done over a fire of dried-out leaves and twigs.

"Oh," said Thana cordially. "Hello."

"Listen!" said Link, "I want to make a protest!"

"I'm terribly busy," said Thana pleasantly, "and anyhow Harl's the one to tell about anything that's missing in the treatment of a guest. Would you excuse me?"

Link changed his approach.

"I've got an idea," he said rather desperately. "I think I know how to identify the kind of . . . of salt you want to add to bog-iron to make good knives from your unduplied sample."

"For that," said Thana warmly, "I'll stop cooking! What is it, Link?"

"When you put bog-iron in the duplier," said Link harassedly, "and the duplier makes a knife, the bog-iron crumbles because the iron's been taken away." Link was irritated, now. "The idea is to make a series of knives, adding different rock samples to each one, until you get a good knife. Then the rock that contained the alloy-metal you wanted will be crumbled like the iron. See?"

"Wonderful!" said Thana, pleased. "I should have thought of it! I'll try it tomorrow!"

There was a faint noise outside. It was a shrill, ululating sound. Link paid no attention. Instead, he said urgently,

"And I think I can work out some ways that might get electricity back!"

"That would be marvelous," said Thana. "You must tell Harl what they are! At dinner, Link. Tell him about them at dinner. He's busy now, arranging about the torchlight for the hanging. But I thank you very kindly for telling me the trick to make better knives. I'm sure it will work! But I really do have to get dinner ready!"

The noise outside grew louder. There were shouts. It sounded like a first-class riot beginning. Thana tilted her head on one side, listening.

"The uffts are putting on a demonstration," she said without particular interest. "Why don't you go watch it, Link? You can tell Harl all your new ideas when we have dinner! I think it's wonderful of you to think of things like this! You've no idea how important it will be! Excuse me now?"

She bustled away. Link ground his teeth. If Thistlethwaite escaped, he must, too. Thistlethwaite might carry out the bargain with Old Man Addison and try to astrogate back to Trent. The emergency wasn't that he might not make it, but that he might.

Link made his way in the general direction of the tumult. It was dark inside the big building, now. Once away from the feeble oil-wick lamps, he seemed merely to run into walls and partly-opened doors and heavy, misplaced furniture. Once he heard a heavy clattering of small hoofs indoors, somewhere inside the building. A remarkable number of uffts seemed to be racing madly up stairs and down a hallway to the open air. The sound of their hoofs changed as they went out-of-doors. The noises from outside changed as they left the door open behind them. Link had heard only the background noise, a continual shrill yapping, but now he heard individual voices.

"Down with humans! Down With the Murderers of Interstellar Travelers! Uffts forever! Men go home!" There was a particularly loud outburst. *"We want freedom! We want freedom!"* Then a squealing from a myriad voices from small pig-like throats. *"Yah! Yah! Yah! Men have hands! Yah! Yah! Yah!"*

Link reached the open door. Darkness had fallen with the suddenness only observable in the tropics of some ten thousand planets. It occurred to him that the troop of uffts he'd heard in the building was probably Thistlethwaite's special rescue squad. If they'd had to rush past or through a human guard at the doorway, such a guard would now be in poor condition to resist his own exit. And it was dark and there was enough confusion to cover one man, even a man supposed to be hanged, while he left the householder's residence.

He was right. Starlight showed hundreds of small, rotund bodies galloping madly up and down the street, shrilling squealed insults at the human race in general and Harl in particular. There was one especial focus of tumult. Three men on unicorns were its center. They were apparently Harl's retainers returning from a hunt for an alleged new deposit of bog-iron. They'd been caught in the village street by the suddenly erupting disorder. They were surrounded by uffts, running around them like a merry-go-round, squealing denunciations at the tops of their voices.

"Men have hands. Shame! Shame! Shame! Down with murderers of interstellar travelers! Uffts forever! Down with men! Down—"

The retainers' ungainly mounts tried to find a way through the squealing mob of uffts. But they were timorous. They lifted their large splay feet with a certain fearful suddenness and put them down with an attempt at delicacy. They managed to make their way along the ufft-covered street until they were almost opposite the doorway in which Link waited for a chance to leave without being instantly bowled over.

Then a unicorn made a misstep. A foot came down on an ufft. The galloping small animal squealed, *"He tramped on me!"* and ran away shrieking its complaint.

The sound of uproar doubled. Link went out into the darkness, to escape. He saw torches burning where men were at work building something which was plainly a gallows. Until this instant they had taken the noise and galloping calmly. They'd continued to work, though from time to time they looked with mild interest at the milling, racing small creatures which raced up and down the street, making all the noise they possibly could.

But the stepped-on shrieking ufft, complaining to high heaven of the indignity put upon him, which did not lessen his speed or his voice, changed everything. Uffts came swarming more thickly than ever about the mounted men. They seemed to climb over each other to get closer to the unicorns and squeal more ferociously than before.

And the unicorns panicked. Link saw a huge, pillowy forefoot lift with an ufft clinging to it, biting viciously. The ufft let go and bounced off its fellows on the ground. Other uffts bit at the unicorns' feet. One of them went down to its knees and its rider toppled off. The three awkward animals bolted. All three fled crazily from the village with gigantic, splay-footed strides. The man who'd been thrown was buried under squealing uffts, while the greater number of the demonstrators went galloping after the runaway unicorns. The riders of two unicorns tried frantically to control them, but the saddle of the third was empty.

Link heard the covered-up man swearing blood-curdlingly.

He found himself plunging toward his fellow human. Quite automatically, his hands grasped two ufftian hind-legs and threw two uffts away over the heads of their fellows. Two more. Two more. Squealings from the thrown uffts seemed suddenly to terrify those who had been most valiant and most vocal in the attack.

Link again threw away two more and two more still, and suddenly the creatures were running insanely in all directions. Some ran between his legs in wild, shrill terror. They jammed that opening and Link went down with a crash, still hanging on to a kicking hind-leg. The man he'd come to rescue continued to swear, now without uffts to muffle his words, which were remarkable. And there were men running to the scene with torches.

Link let go of the ufft he held captive. He had to, to get up. The ufft went streaking for the far horizon at the top of his voice. Harl came out of the Household, fuming.

"Sput!" he fumed. "Those uffts! They bit through the lashin's of that whiskery man's cage an' let him loose! All this fuss was gettin' him escaped! Sput! I was figurin' on havin' a real spectacular hangin'! An' he's got away!"

The man to whose rescue Link had gone now got to his feet. He spoke, with a depth of feeling and aptness of expression that put Harl's indignation in the shade. His garments were shreds. He'd been nipped at until he was practically nude. The arriving torches even showed places where blood flowed from deeper nips than usual.

"And it was goin' to be a swell hangin'," mourned Harl indignantly. "Torchlight an' stuff! I was just waitin' for all the fellas to get back, and the fella had to escape! But there's—"

He stared.

"Link!"

Chapter 6

"This," said Link, at once with dignity and with passion, "this is no time to be fooling around with hangings!"

Harl blinked at him in the starlight.

"What's the matter, Link? What' you doin' outside the house? That fella got away, but there's—"

"Me, yes!" snapped Link. "But we can't spare the time for that now! Get some men mounted! We've got to catch Thistlethwaite!"

"We don't know where he went," objected Harl.

"I do!" Link snapped at him. "He went to the ship! If for nothing else, to get some pants! Then he'll go to Old Man Addison's. The uffts'll take him. He'll make a business deal with him! A trade! A bargain!"

It was an absurd time and place for an argument. Men with torches lighted one small part of the street. They'd come to help a fellow human momentarily buried under swarming, squealing uffts. Link had gotten there first. Then Harl. Now Link, with clenched fists, faced Harl in a sort of passionate frustration.

"Don't you see?" he demanded fiercely. "He was on Sord Three last year! He made a deal with Old Man Addison then! He's brought a shipload of undupiled stuff to trade with Old Man Addison for dupliers! Don't you see?"

Harl wrinkled his forehead.

"But that'd be . . . that wouldn't be mannerly!" he objected. "That'd be—sput, Link! That'd be . . . business!"

He used the term as if it were one only to be used in strictly private consultation with a physician, as if it were a euphemism for something unspeakable.

"That's exactly what it is!" rasped Link. "Business! And bad business at that! He'll sell the contents of his ship to Old Man Addison and be paid in dupliers! And with the dupliers—"

"Sput!" Harl waved his hands. He bellowed, "Everybody out! Big trouble! Everybody out! Bring y'spears!"

Men came out of houses. Some of them wore shirts such as Link wore no longer. They were pleased with them. Since the article duplicated was relatively new, the replicas of it had all the properties of new shirts, though the raw stuff of the thread involved had previously had the properties of the centuries-old sample from which it had been duplied, and which hadn't been new since before the art of weaving was forgotten. New-shirted retainers came out of houses to hear Link's commands.

"Get mounted!" roared Harl. "We' ridin' to that ship that come down today. What's in it's goin' to Old Man Addison if we don't get there first! Take y'spears! Get movin'! The uffts are goin' too far!"

There was confusion. More men appeared and ran out of sight. Some of them came back riding unicorns. Some led them. The three animals that had been ringed in and whose tender feet had been bitten by the uffts now came limping back into the village. The two riders had somehow managed to subdue their own beasts, and then had overtaken and caught the riderless animal.

"A unicorn for Link!" roared Harl, in what he evidently considered a military manner. "Get him a spear!"

"Hold it!" said Link grimly. "That stun gun you took from Thistlethwaite! You were carrying it. I'll take that, Harl! I know how to use it!"

"I ain't had time to figure it out," said Harl, agreeing.

He roared. "Get that funny dinkus the whiskery man was carryin' this mornin'! Give it to Link!"

Confusion developed further. Since his first sight of Harl, riding up to the ship with five unicorn mounted men at his back, Link had made innumerable guesses about the social and economic system of Sord Three.

Most of them had been wrong. He'd been sure, though, that the organization into Households was a revival or reinvention of a feudal system, in which a Householder was responsible for the feeding and clothing of his retainers, and in return had an indefinite amount of power. Harl had the power, certainly, to order strangers hanged.

But it became clear that whether it was feudal or not, the system was not designed for warfare. Harl was in command, but nobody else had secondary rank. There were no under-officers or non-commissioned ones. Harl's howled and bellowed orders got a troop of mounted men assembled. Confusedly and raggedly, they grouped themselves. They carried spears and wore large knives. Harl bellowed additional orders and whoever heard them obeyed them more or less. With great confusion, the group of armed and mounted men got ready to start out in the moonlight.

Just as he was about to give the order to march, Thana's voice came from the building which was the Householder's residence.

"Harl! Harl! If you go off now, dinner will get cold!"

"Let it!" snapped Harl. "We got to catch that whiskery fella!"

He roared for his followers to march, and march they did in a straggling column behind him. Somebody confusedly searched for and found Link, riding next to Harl, to give him the stun gun which was the only weapon that had been aboard the *Glamorgan*. He felt it over in the darkness.

"It seems to be in working order," he told Harl. "Thanks."

"What—" Then Harl saw the stun gun. The starlight was moderately bright, but it was not possible to see the details of anything, whether of the armed party or the landscape. "Oh. You got that thing. I was layin' off to figure out what it was, but I didn't have time. What's it do, Link?"

"It knocks a man or an animal out," said Link curtly. "It shoots an electric charge. But you can set the charge not to stun him, but only sting him up more or less."

"'Lectric? asked Harl. "That's interestin'! How far does it throw?"

"That depends," said Link.

"Mmmmm. Uh, Link, how did you find out that that whiskery fella is makin' a deal with Old Man Addison?"

"Uffts told me," said Link grimly. "Old Man Addison is going to pay three thousand bottles of beer for Thistlethwaite's delivery to him. It's a written contract. Thistlethwaite wouldn't promise anything like that if he didn't know his value to Old Man Addison!"

Harl shook his head.

"You spoiled a good hangin' by not tellin' me!" he said reproachfully. "He got away. But how d'you know he's headin' for the ship?"

"I told you!" said Link. "He wants pants. He wants a shirt. He wants clothes. He wants to be dressed like a business man when he does business with Old Man Addison!"

Harl considered.

"It looks reasonable," he admitted. "Right reasonable!"

"I was offered a deal to escape, too," said Link

sourly. "The uffts wanted five thousand bottles of beer to take me to Old Man Addison's Household."

"You wouldn't like him," said Harl sagely. "He's hardly got any more manners than an ufft. Anybody who's mannerly like you are couldn't get along with him, Link. You showed sense in stayin' with me."

"To be hanged!" said Link bitterly. "But—"

"Hold on!" said Harl in astonishment. "Didn't I admire that shirt o' yours? An' didn't I accept it as a gift? I could make a gift to a man I was goin' to hang, Link. That'd be just manners! But I couldn't accept a gift an' then hang him! That'd be disgraceful!" He paused and said in an injured tone, "I've heard of Old Man Addison doin' things like that, but I never thought anybody'd suspect it of me!"

Link waved his hand impatiently. It was remarkable that the discovery that plans for his hanging were changed should make so little difference in this thinking. But right now he was concerned with the prevention of a disaster vastly more important than any concern of his own.

"I doubt," he said, "that we'd better go through the ufft city. We'd better circle it. We'd be delayed at best, and Thistlethwaite is in a hurry to settle his bargain with Old Man Addison. He'll hurry."

Harl cleared his throat and bellowed toward the skies. The trailing cavalcade of ungainly unicorns changed direction to follow him.

The mounted party was probably fifty men and animals strong. In the dimness of starlight alone, it was an extraordinary sight. The men rode in clumps of two or three or half a dozen, on steeds whose gait was camel-like and awkward. The unicorns wobbled as they strode. Their limp and fleshy horns swayed and swung. Link, looking back and observing the total tack of discipline, felt an enormous exasperation.

He didn't like the situation he was in, even when immediate hanging was no longer included. In all his life before he'd been carefree and zestfully concerned only with doing things because they were novel or exciting, and on occasion because they involved some tumult. In anybody his age, that was a completely normal trait. But now he had a responsibility of intolerable importance. The future of *very* many millions of human beings would depend on what he did, but he'd get no thanks for his trouble. It went against the grain of Link's entire nature to dedicate himself to a tedious and exacting task like this. If he were successful it would never be known. In fact, it was a condition of success that it must never be known anywhere off of Sord Three. And it mustn't be understood there!

At least an hour after their starting out a high, shrill clamor set up, very far away.

"That's uffts," said Harl. "Somethin's happened an' they feel all happy an' excited."

"It's Thistlethwaite," said Link. "He got to the ship. He probably passed out some gifts to the uffts."

The cavalcade went on. The faint shrill clamor continued.

"Uh, Link," said Harl, in a tone at once apologetic and depressed, "I thought of somethin' that might make the uffts feel good. If like you said he gave presents to the uffts, maybe it was unduplied things. They couldn't use 'em, havin' hoofs instead of hands. But they'd know us humans 'ud have to buy 'em.

They like to bargain. They enjoy makin' humans pay too much. It makes 'em feel smart and superior. He could ha' made a lot of trouble for us humans! A lot o' trouble!"

The long, somehow lumpy line of men and animals went on through the darkness. Harl said unhappily,

"The uffts were tryin' to make me pay 'em for news of where there was a lot of bog-iron. You figure what they'd make me pay for somethin' unduplied! If that fella's passin' out that kinda gifts, the uffts feel swell. They feel happy. But I don't!"

Link said nothing. It would be reasonable for Thistlethwaite to feel that he had to get samples of his cargo aground to ensure his deal with Old Man Addison, and then to have a train of armed men and animals come to unload the *Glamorgan* and carry its specially purchased cargo away. If he opened a cargo compartment to get samples, the uffts could well have demanded samples for themselves. Or they could simply take them.

"And," Harl fumed, "when they got something they'll ask fifty bottles of beer for, they won't bother bringin' in greenstuff, and how'll I get the beer to pay 'em? They'll bring in knives an' cloth and demand beer! And if I don't have the beer, they'll take the stuff to another Household."

"Then you'll probably have to pay it."

"Without greenstuff, I can't," said Harl bitterly.

There was an addition to the faint, joyous clamor beyond the horizon. Link began to discount any chance of success in this expedition. If Harl was right, Thistlethwaite had gotten to the ship, had gotten more clothing, and had very probably passed out in lieu of cash or beer, such objects of virtue as mirrors, cosmetics, cooking pots made of other metals than iron, crockery, small electric appliances like flashlights, pens, pencils, and synthetic fabrics. None of these things could be duplied on Sord Three, because the minerals required as raw materials had been forgotten if they were ever known.

And all this would put Harl in a bad situation, no doubt. Every Householder would need to deal with Old Man Addison for such trinkets, which he must supply to his retainers or seem less than a desirable feudal superior. But to Link the grim fact was that Thistlethwaite must have gotten to the ship before the mounted party. If he suspected pursuit he'd waste no time. He'd go on. And if he had gone on—

Dead ahead, now, there were peculiar small sounds. It took Link seconds to realize that it was the hoofs of uffts on metal stair treads and metal floors, the sound coming out of an opened exit port.

"Harl," said Link in a low tone, "Thistlethwaite may still be in the ship. There are certainly plenty of uffts rummaging around in there! Can you get your men—"

But Harl did not wait for such advice as a self-appointed chief of staff might give to his commander-in-chief on the eve of battle. He raised his voice.

"There they are, boys!" he bellowed. "Come along an' get 'em! Get the whiskery fella! If we don't get him there'll be no hangin' tonight!"

Roaring impressively, he urged his awkward mount forward. He was followed by all his undisciplined troop. It was a wild and furious and completely confused charge. Link and Harl led it, of course. They topped a natural rise in the ground and saw the tall shape of the *Glamorgan* against the stars.

There was a wild stirring of what seemed to be hordes of uffts, clustered about the exit port and swarming in and swarming out again. A light inside the port cast an inadequate glow outside and in that dim light, rotund, pig-like shapes could be seen squirming and struggling to get into the ship, if they were outside, or to get out if they happened to be in. Link saw the glitter of that light upon metal. Evidently the uffts were making free with at least the contents of one cargo compartment. They were bringing out what small objects they could carry.

Harl bellowed again, and his followers dutifully yelled behind him, and the whole pack of them went sweeping over the hillcrest and down upon the aggregation of uffts. The unicorns were apparently blessed with good night vision, because none of them fell among the boulders that strewed the hillside.

The charge was discovered. Squeals and squeaks of alarm came from the uffts. It was not as much of a tumult as so many small creatures should make, however. Those with aluminum pots and pans, or kitchen appliances, or small tools or other booty, those of them with objects carried in their mouths simply bolted off into the dark, making no outcry because it would have made them drop their loot. Link saw one of them with an especially large pot dive into it and roll over, and pick it up again and run ten paces and then trip and dive into it again before it found a way to hold the pot safely and go galloping madly away.

The other uffts scattered. But there were boulders here. They shrilled defiant slogans from behind them. *"Down with men! Uffts forever!"* they yapped at the men on their unicorns. So far as combat was concerned, however, the charge on the spaceship was anticlimactic. The uffts outside either fled with whatever they'd picked up in their teeth, or scattered to abuse the men from lurking-places among the boulders all round about. But there were very many more inside the ship. They came streaming out in a struggling, squabbling flood. The riders did not try to stop them. They seemed satisfied and even pleased with themselves over the panicky flight of the uffts. They clustered about the exit port, but they allowed the uffts through as they fled.

"What'll we do now?" asked Harl.

"See if Thistlethwaite's inside," said Link curtly.

He got the stun gun ready. There'd been no effort by any of the riders to use their spears on the uffts. Link could understand it. Uffts talked. And a man can kill a dangerous animal, or even a merely annoying one, but it would seem like murder to use a deadly weapon on a creature which was apparently incapable of anything more dangerous than nipping at a unicorn's foot or tearing the clothes of a man buried under a squealing heap of them. A man simply wouldn't think of killing a talking animal which couldn't harm him save by abuse.

Harl swung from his saddle and strode inside the ship. Link heard him climb the metal stairs inside. There was a wild squealing sound, and something came falling down the steps with a clatter as of tinware. An ufft rolled out of the door and streaked for the horizon, squealing.

There were more yellings.

"Down with murderers of interstellar travelers!" squeaked an invisible ufft somewhere nearby. *"Men have hands!*

"Shame! Shame! Shame!" yapped another. Then a chorus set up, *"Men go home! Men go home! Men go home!"*

The men on the unicorns seemed to grow uneasy. They were bunched around the exit port of the ship. There were very many uffts concealed nearby. They made a racket of abuse. Sometimes they shouted whatever of competing outcries caught their fancy, as in the rhythmic, "Men go home!" effort. Then there was merely a wild clamor until some especially strident voice began a more attractive phrase of insulting content.

There were thumpings inside the ship. Harl bellowed somewhere. More thumpings. The yellings of abuse grew louder and louder. Apparently the burdenless uffts had ceased to flee when they found themselves not pursued. The torrent of insult became deafening. At the very farthest limit of the light from the port, round bodies could be seen, running among the boulders as they yelled epithets.

The riders stirred apprehensively. The military tactics of the uffts, it could be said, consisted of derogatory outcries for moral effect and the biting of unicorns' feet as direct attack. Agitated running in circles had prefaced the attack on three unicorns, most tender parts in the village street. The riders in the starlight, here, were held immobile because Harl was inside the ship. But they showed disturbance at the prospect of another such attack on their mounts. More, there came encouraging, bloodthirsty cries from across the hilltop as if a war party from the ufft city were on the way to reinforce the uffts making a tumult about the ship.

Footsteps. Two pairs of them. Harl came out the exit port, very angry, with a woebegone retainer following him.

"This fella," said Harl, fuming, "is the one I left to watch the ship for you, Link. The whiskery fella came here with a crowd of uffts. He hadn't any clothes on and he told this fella he'd got in trouble and needed to get his clothes. The fella thought it was only mannerly to let a man have his own clothes, so he let him in. An' then the whiskery fella hit him from behind with somethin', an' locked him in a cabin an' let the uffts in."

Link said curtly, "Too bad, but—"

"We'd better get movin'," said Harl angrily. "We missed him. He musta got away before we found it out. He opened up a door somewheres, this fella says, and he heard him cussin' the uffts like they were just takin' anything they could close their teeth on. Then he heard some noise."

An ufft leaped a boulder and darted at the uneasily stamping unicorns. He hadn't quite the nerve to make it all the way. He swerved back. But other uffts made similar short rushes. Presently there'd be one underfoot, nipping at the animals' feet, and they'd stampede.

"We'd better get movin'," said Harl. "They're gettin' nervy."

"No," said Link, grimly. "Wait a minute!"

He swung the stun gun around. He opened the cone-of-fire aperture. He adjusted the intensity-of-shock stud. He raised it. The yells were truly deafening. "Scoundrels! Villains!" yapped the racing, jumping small creatures.

Link pulled the trigger. The stun gun made a burping noise. Electric charges sped out of it, scattering. The gun would carry nearly a hundred yards at widest dispersion of its fire. Within the cone-shaped space it affected, any flesh unshielded by metal would receive a sharp and painful but totally uninjurious electric shock. To men who knew nothing of electricity it would have been startling. To uffts it would be unparalleled and utterly horrifying. They squealed.

Link fired it again, at another area in the darkness. Shrieks of ufftian terror rose to the stars.

"Murderers!" cried ufft voices. "Murderers! You're killing us!"

Link aimed at the voices and fired again. Twice.

The uffts around the spaceship went away from there, making an hysterical outcry in which complaints that the complainer had been killed were only drowned out by louder squealings to the effect that the squealers were dead.

"Sput!" said Harl, astounded. "What're you doin', Link? You ain't killin' 'em, are you? I need 'em to bring in greenstuff!"

"They'll live," said Link. "Wait here. I want to see what Thistlethwaite did. Anyhow, he didn't try to lift the ship off to Old Man Addison's Household!"

He went in. He climbed the stairway. He saw a cargo compartment door. It had been sealed. It was now welded shut. Thistlethwaite had used an oxygen torch on it. A second cargo door. Welded shut. The third door was open. It was apparently the compartment

from which the loot of the uffts had come. It appeared
to be empty. The engine room door was welded shut,
and the spaceboat blister. The control room was sealed
off from any entry by anybody without at least a cold
chisel, but preferably a torch. And the oxygen torch
was gone.

Link went down the stairs again, muttering. Thistlethwaite had made the *Glamorgan* useless to anybody
possessing neither a cold chisel nor an oxygen torch.
Harl couldn't seize the materials Thistlethwaite planned
to trade for dupliers. Old Man Addison might—

In the one gutted cargo space—he looked into it
again with no hope at all—he found a plastic can of
beans, toppled on the floor. He picked it up. It was
too large for the jaws of uffts to grasp.

He went down to the exit port again, piously turning out the electric lights that Thistlethwaite had left
burning. He was deeply and savagely disappointed.
He was almost at the exit port when an idea came
to him. He climbed back up and touched the bot-
tommost weld. It scorched his fingers.

Thistlethwaite hadn't done it long ago. He couldn't
be far off.

Link turned on the lights again and searched. The
only loose object left anywhere was an open can of
seal-off compound, for stopping air leaks such as the
Glamorgan had a habit of developing. It was black and
tarry and even an ufft would not want it. Link did.

He reached the open air again. He said briefly,
"Hold this, Harl."

He handed over the container of beans and worked
on the landing fin in which the exit port existed. He
had only the narrow bristle brush used to apply the

seal-off compound, and only the compound to apply. The light was starlight alone. But when he'd finished he read the straggling letters of the message with some satisfaction. The message read:

> THISTLETHWAITE,
>   HOUSEHOLDERS DELIGHTED WITH TEST OF WEAPONS TO MAKE UFFTS WORK WITHOUT PAY. LEAD YOUR GANG INTO AMBUSH AS PLANNED FOR LARGE SCALE USE OF WEAPON. WATCH OUT FOR LINK. HE IS PRO-UFFT AND SECRETLY AN UFFT SYM-PATHIZER.

"What'd you do, Link?" demanded Harl. "The uffts've all run away, squealing. What'd you do? And what's that writing for?"

"That writing," said Link, "is to end the Thistle-thwaite problem on Sord Three. You may not realize that there is such a problem, Harl, but that's to take care of it. And what I did was use a stun gun at maximum dispersion and minimum power. And I'm going to ask you, Harl, to go back to the Household straight through the ufft city. If they try to object I'll give them more of what they've had. I think the psychological effect will be salutary."

Harl thought it over. His followers did not look very military in the starlight.

"Wel-l-l-l," said Harl, "I'm not sure what those words mean, Link, but I was thinkin' we'd have a tough time gettin' home, with uffts bitin' the unicorns' feet all the way. But you say we won't. Or do you?"

"Yes," said Link. "I say we won't. I guarantee it."

"Then we'll try it," said Harl heavily. "Uh . . . what's this you gave me to hold?"

"It's a guest-gift for Thana," said Link.

Harl bellowed.

"Come on, fellas! Back to home! We're ridin' through the ufft city! There's a dinkus with maximum dispersion an' minimum power that drove off the uffts just now, an' we want to use it on them some more."

The cavalcade set out upon another long, shambling journey underneath the stars. It was some time before the unicorns reached the ufft city. It was not silent, even though all was darkness. There were shrill babblings everywhere. The agitated stories of uffts who'd experienced stun gun stings were being discussed by uffts who hadn't experienced them. Those who'd felt the shocks couldn't describe them, and those who hadn't couldn't believe them. The discussions tended to grow acrimonious. Then there were squealings that men were about to pass through the city. Those who hadn't been shocked went valiantly to oppose the passage, or at least make it as unpleasant as possible by abuse.

Link let the congregation of zestfully vituperative uffts grow very large and get very near. *"Murderers!"* and *"Massacrers!"* were the least of the epithets thrown at the men. *"The world will hear of this massacre!"* shouted an ufft. Another took it up, *"They'll know how many of our comrades you murdered tonight!"* The unicorns picked their way onward in their loose-jointed, wobbling fashion. Voices found an easier word. *"Killers!"* they shouted from the darkness. *"Killers! Killers!"* Actually, and Link knew it, no ufft in all the city would be able to find so much as a spot on his hide that was pinker than the rest, come tomorrow morning.

But now— Presently there was a huge, milling, madly galloping and wildly yelling barrier of uffts before the cavalcade. If the animals went into it, their feet would suffer. They'd be bitten. If they turned back, the uffts would be encouraged to follow and close in on them and again bite large splay feet.

Harl bellowed a halt. The cavalcade came to a standstill. Link gave the running, tumbling aggregation of abusive creatures two more shots from the stun gun. Individuals suffered the equivalent of bee stings for the fraction of a second. They shrieked and ran away.

The rest of the travel through the city was without incident, save that very occasionally very brave uffts squealed insults from not less than half a mile away, and then fled still farther from the shambling line of mounts and men.

Then there were the undulating miles beyond, to where very faint and feeble lights showed through the darkness. And then eventually the houses of the village loomed up on either side.

Thana welcomed Harl and Link, but she was inclined to be distressed that their dinner now had to be warmed over and was inferior in quality for that reason. They dined. Link presented Thana with the plastic can of beans. Harl asked what they were. When Link told him, he said absorbedly,

"I've heard that there's a Household over past Old Man Addison that has beans. But I never tasted 'em myself. We'll duply some an' have 'em for breakfast. Right?"

And Link was ushered into a guest room, with a light consisting of a wick floating in a dish of oil. He slept soundly, until an hour after sunrise. Then he was waked by the sound of shoutings. He could see nothing from his window, so he dressed and went leisurely to see from the street.

There were many villagers out-of-doors, staring at the distance. From time to time they shouted encouragement. Link saw what they shouted at.

A small, hairy figure, chastely clad in a red-checked tablecloth around his middle, ran madly toward the Household. The figure was Thistlethwaite. The red-checked cloth had once been draped over a table in the *Glamorgan's* mess room. Thistlethwaite ran like a deer and behind him came uffts yapping insults and trying to nip his heels.

He reached safety and the uffts drew off, shouting *"Traitor!"* and *"Murderer!"* as the mildest of accusations. But now and then one roared shrilly at him, *"Agent provocateur!"*

Chapter 7

The situation developed in a strictly logical fashion. The uffts remained at a distance, shouting insults and abuse at all the humans in the village which was Harl's Household. Hours passed. No small, ufft-drawn carts came in bringing loads of roots, barks, herbs, berries, blossoms and flowers. Normally they were brought in for the duplier to convert in part to beer, with added moisture, and in part into such items as slightly wormy apples, legumes like peas, and discouraged succulents like lettuce. There were all sorts of foodstuffs duplied with the same ufft-cart loads of material, of course. Wheat, and even flour, could be synthesized by the duplier from the assorted compounds in the vegetation the carts contained. Radishes could be multiplied. Every product of Thana's garden could be increased indefinitely. But this morning no raw material for beer or victuals appeared. The uffts remained at a distance, shrilling insults.

Thistlethwaite revealed the background events behind this development. He'd escaped from the Household, surrounded by a scurrying guard of uffts, while the political demonstration in the street was at its height. That tumult continued while he was hurried to the ufft city. There he was feted, but not fed. The uffts did not make use of human food. They were herbivorous and had no provisions for him. But they did make speeches about his escape.

He stood it so long, but he was a business man. He wanted food and he wanted clothing and he wanted to get to Old Man Addison's Household to proceed with his business deal to end all business deals. He did not think of it in such accurate terms. But he insisted on being taken first to the *Glamorgan* for food and clothing. He spoke with pride of his talent for business. The uffts mentioned, as business men, that the contract for his rescue and escort did not include food, clothing, or a trip west of the ufft city. There would be a slight extra charge. He was indignant, but he agreed.

He'd been taken to the ship. The watchman left by

Harl admitted him. He overpowered that watchman
and put him in a cabin for crew members. He stuffed
himself, because food was more urgent than clothing.
He admitted uffts, because they were clamoring below.
They wanted the extra fees they'd charged him. They
announced that they were not interested in human
artifacts. They wanted the usual currency, beer. The
whiskery man didn't have it. They suggested that
they would accept cargo at a proper discount. The
discount was for the fact that they'd have to trade
human goods to humans for the beer they preferred.
The discount would be great.

Thistlethwaite had to yield, though he raged. He
opened a cargo compartment and the uffts began to
empty it. Thistlethwaite wept with fury because circumstances had put him at the mercy of the uffts. In
business matters they were businesslike. They didn't
have any mercy. He was expressing his indignation at
their attitude when they spoke of demurrage to be
paid for the delay he was causing. Strangling upon
his wrath, he took measures. He was still taking
measures when the expedition of men and unicorns
charged down into the hollow where the *Glamorgan*
rested. Thistlethwaite got out among the first, and
was well away before the stun gun was put into use.
And then, back in the ufft city, the uffts demanded
compensation for the injury of an exaggerated number
of their fellows in his employ.

Telling about it later, even returned to Harl's Household and presumably the prospect of being hanged,
even later Thistlethwaite purpled with fury over the
ufft demands. They'd have stripped him of all the
Glamorgan's cargo if not the ship itself, and he'd

have reached Old Man Addison without a smidgen of trade goods with which to deal. His entire journey would have been in vain. It was even unlikely that Old Man Addison would pay for his delivery, when he had nothing to offer that feudal chieftain in the way of trade.

Listening to the account, Harl said safely,

"Uffts haven't got any manners. You shoulda known better then to deal with them! You did right to come back." Then something occurred to him. "Why'd they chase you?"

Thistlethwaite turned burning, bloodshot eyes upon Link.

"Somebody," he said balefully, "somebody painted a note on the *Glamorgan*'s fin. It was addressed to me! So the uffts read it an' it said I'd brought guns for Householders to use on uffts to make 'em work for free! And the note said for me to lead the uffts into a ambush as previous arranged so's they'd get shot up! So they decided that me gettin' put in a cage an' gettin' them to escape me was a trick so's you'd get a chance to try out that stun gun on 'em last night!"

Link said mildly, "Now, I wonder who could have done such a thing!"

Thistlethwaite strangled on his fury. He was speechless.

"It begins to look," said Link with the same mildness, "like the uffts are really wrought up. I doubt that they're hanging around the Household just for the pleasure of calling us names. What do you think they want, Harl?"

"Plenty!" said Harl gloomily. "Plenty!"

"I suggest," said Link, "that you find out."

"'Might as well," said Harl, more gloomily still. "If they don't bring in greenstuff, we don't eat. You can't duply what Thana grows unless you've got something to duply it with!"

He rose and went morosely out of the room where the conference had taken place. Thistlethwaite said bitterly,

"I'd ha' done better if I'd astrogated here myself!"

"Question," said Link. "You say the uffts believe you brought guns for them to be enslaved with. Did you?"

"No!" snapped Thistlethwaite.

"Did the uffts mention me?" asked Link.

Thistlethwaite practically foamed at the mouth.

"They said y'were their friend!" he raged. "They said—"

"I made them a speech," said Link modestly. "It was about a barber who shaved everybody in his village who didn't shave himself, and didn't shave anybody who did shave himself. There's been some trouble deciding who shaved the barber. They may like me for that."

Thistlethwaite made incoherent noises.

"Tut tut!" said Link. "There's one more question, but you haven't got the answer to it. I'll get Thana to help me find it out. I don't think you'll run away to the uffts again, and I don't *think* they'll hang you before I have a chance to protest. I shall hope not, anyhow."

He went in search of Thana. He found her ruefully regarding the plants in her kitchen garden.

"There's not been an ufft-cart of greenstuff come in today," she told Link unhappily, "and the uffts are shouting such bad language I don't know when they'll start bringing carts in again!"

"You've got food stored ahead?" asked Link.

"Not much," admitted Thana. "The uffts always bring in greenstuff, so there's been no need to store food."

Link shook his head.

"It looks bad," he observed. "Will you duply that gun I used last night and see if it works? It might be a solution to the problem. An unwelcome solution, but still a solution."

"Of course!" said Thana.

She led the way. To the great hall and across it, and into the room with innumerable shelves that served the purpose of a treasury. She lifted down the stun gun from a high shelf, which Link realized no uffts with hoofs instead of hands could ever climb to. She gave Link some large lumps of bog-iron. She brought out a ready-cut billet of wood.

Into the great hall again. She pressed a button and the chair of state and its dais rose ceilingward. The contrivance which was the duplier came up out of the pit the chair and dais ordinarily covered. Thana put the bog-iron and the wood in the raw material hopper. She put the stun gun in the hopper holding the object to be duplicated. She left the third hopper empty. The duplicate to be produced should appear there.

She pressed the button. The duplier descended. The chair of state came down. She pressed the button again. The chair of state went up and the duplier arose, at a different rate of rising. The bog-iron in the first hopper was visibly diminished and there was much sand on the hopper bottom. The sample, authentic, original stun gun remained where it had been placed, in the middle hopper. But a seemingly exact duplicate remained in the last hopper.

Link took the duplied object. He examined it. He aimed it skyward and pulled the trigger. Nothing happened, not even the slight hiccough which accompanies a stun gun's operation.

He twisted the disassembly screw and the gun opened up for inspection. Link looked, and shook his head.

"No transistors," he reported regretfully. "They're made of germanium and stuff, rare metals at the best of times. We haven't any. So the gun is incomplete. A duplied stun gun needs germanium and without it it's no good, just like a duplied knife. No dice. I'm very glad of it."

Harl came in, indignant.

"Link!" he said in a tone expressing something like shock at something appalling and outrage at something crushing, "I sent a coupla fellas to find out what the uffts wanted, and the uffts chased 'em back!"

"Did they mention their reason?" asked Link.

"They yelled I was a conspirator. They yelled that the whiskery man was goin' to lead 'em into a ambush last night to be massacred. They yelled I was goin' to try to make 'em work all the time without payin' 'em beer! They yelled down with me. Me!" said Harl incredulously. "They said they were makin' a general strike against me! No greenstuff! No carrying messages from me to anywhere! No anything! I got to get rid of the thing they say killed 'em by hundreds last night. Did it kill 'em, Link?"

"Not a one," said Link. "They got stung a bit, but that's all. Nothing worse than a sting for the fraction of a second."

"They say," finished Harl astonishedly, "that the strike keeps up till I hang the whiskery fella and get rid of the gun that was used on 'em, an' let uffts search the whole Household to see if there are any more, an' repeat that search any time they please! They got to read all messages to me from anybody else, and from me to anybody! And I got to give 'em four more bottles of beer for each cartload of greenstuff they bring in from now on!"

Link considered for a moment. Then he said, "What have you decided?"

"I couldn't if I wanted to!" said Harl. "Sput, Link! If I hung that whiskery fella because the uffts wanted it, I'd be disgraced! Not a fella in the Household would stay here! If I let the uffts search anybody's house any time they wanted, not a woman would let her husband stay! If I agreed to that, Link, there wouldn't be a livin' soul here by sundown!"

Link somehow felt relieved. The human economy here on Sord Three had defects, even to his tolerant eyes. The humans were utterly dependent upon the uffts for the food they ate and the clothes they wore, in the sense that they depended on ufft-cart loads of raw material. At any time the uffts could shut down and starve out a human household. It was a relief to discover that humans would not submit.

'What'll you do?"

"Send a messenger to my next neighbor," said Harl

angrily. "I'll say I'm comin' guestin'. I'll take half a dozen men an' forty or fifty unicorns. I'll go to his household. I'll make him a guest-gift of a duplied new shirt and a duplied can of beans. Then he can have all the shirts an' beans he wants from now on. That's a right grand gift, Link! So he'll be anxious to make a mannerly host-gift to me. So I'll admire how much ready-duplied food he has stored away. So he'll duply enough food to load up my train of unicorns and I'll bring it back here!"

"And then what? Suppose the uffts stage a political demonstration in the street while you're gone?"

Harl scowled.

"They better not!" he said darkly. "They . . . uh . . . they'd better not! I'll go send my messenger."

He hurried away.

Thana said, "You don't think that's going to work out."

"It might," said Link. "But it needn't."

Thana said in a practical tone of voice, "Let's see what we can do with that unduplied knife, Link."

She went into the room Link considered the Household treasury. She came back with the alloy steel knife, of which duplied copies so far had been only soft iron. She had her collection of variegated rocks.

She duplied the knife with bog-iron alone in the raw materials hopper. The contrivance went down in the pit, the canopied chair descended and covered the pit, then rose again and the contrivance came up once more. There was a second knife in the products hopper. She handed it to Link. He tested its edge. It turned immediately. It was soft iron. He handed it back. She cleaned out the materials hopper of sand and bog-iron, and put the just-duplied, soft-iron knife in for raw material. She added a dozen of the stones and pebbles of which some might be ores.

The duplier descended and rose. The knife had again been duplied. Its edge was still useless. The duplier had not been able to extract from the rock samples the alloying elements the original knife contained in addition to iron, and which a true duplicate would have to contain. They weren't in the rocks. Thana cleared out the useless rock specimens with a professional air.

"I'm afraid you're right, Link, about the uffts."

"How?" asked Link.

"Harl thinks about manners all the time. He's not practical, like you."

"I've never been accused of being practical before," said Link dryly.

Thana put the re-duplied knife in the materials hopper.

She added more rocks. When the chair descended she said, "What did you do with yourself before you came here, Link?"

"Oh, I went hither and yon," said Link, "and did this and that."

The chair rose and the duplier reappeared. There was again another knife. It, also, was soft iron. Thana cleared away these unsatisfactory rock samples also. She shifted the soft iron knife to the first hopper and put in more pebbles. When the duplier went down and came up again, the re-duplied knife had vanished from the materials hopper and reappeared in the third hopper where duplied products did appear. There

was no crumbling among the pebbles which might
be ores. She replaced them with still others and the
duplication cycle began again.

"Where's your home, Link?"

"Anywhere," said Link. He watched the duplier
descend and the chair-of-state come down to cover
the pit. It rose again to disclose a re-re-re-duplicated
knife. This time, too, the edge was not good. She
substituted still other pebbles and sent the duplier
down to do its duplying all over again.

"Where's anywhere?" asked Thana. She looked at
him intently.

He told her. As the duplier went through the
process of making and re-making the knife according to the provided sample, but without the alloy
material that would turn it to steel, he answered
seemingly idle questions and presently was more or
less sketching out the story of his life. He told her
about Glaeth. He told her about his two years at
the Merchant Space Academy on Malibu. He found
himself saying,

"That's where I met Imogene."

"Your girlfriend?" asked Thana with possibly exaggerated casualness.

"No," said Link. "Oh, for a while I suppose you'd
say she was. I wanted to marry her. I don't know
why. It seemed like a good idea at the time. But
she asked me businesslike questions about did I have
any property anywhere and what were my prospects,
and so on. She said we were congenial enough, but
marriage was a girl's career and one had to know all
the facts before deciding anything so important. Very
pretty girl, though," said Link.

Thana removed the assortment of stones that still again had been proved to contain no metalliferous steel-hardening alloy. She put in more. Among the ones to be tested this time there was a sample of a peach-colored rock he'd noted earlier as familiar. Link stiffened for a moment. Then he reached inside his shirt and into a pocket of his stake-belt. By feeling only, he selected a small, gritty crystal. He placed it beside the sample knife.

The dais and the chair-of-state descended. He waited for it to rise up again.

"What happened?" asked Thana. Again she was unconvincingly casual.

"Oh," said Link, "I went back to where I was lodging and counted up my assets. I'd been toying with the idea of going to Glaeth to get rich. I had enough for that and about two thousand credits over. So I bought the necessary tickets and stuff, and reserved a place on a spaceship leaving that afternoon. Then I went to a florist."

Thana said blankly,

"Why?"

"I wanted to put her on ice."

The duplier came up. An irregular lump of grayish-black rock had visibly disintegrated. It was not all gone, but a good tenth of its substance had disappeared. There were glittering scales to prove its crumbling. The peach-colored stone had dropped a fine dust, too.

"This looks promising!" said Link.

He tested the edge of the duplied knife. It was excellent, equivalent to the original. It should have been. Tungsten steel does take a good edge, and hold it, too. He handed the knife to Thana, and fumbled in the bottom of the product hopper. There was a small, very bright crystal there. He picked it up, together with the other sample crystal from his stake-belt. Very, very calmly he put two gritty crystals into the stake-belt pocket from which he'd extracted one. Thana held the duplied but this time tungsten-steel knife. She should have been enraptured. But instead she asked, almost urgently,

"Why did you go to a florist?"

"I bought two thousand credits worth of flowers," said Link. "I ordered them delivered to Imogene. They'd fill every room in her parents' home with some left over to hang out the windows. I wrote a note with them, bidding her good-bye."

Thana stared at him with a remarkable amount of interest.

"She wanted a rich husband and I hated to disappoint her," he explained. "And also, there was a chance that I might get rich on Glaeth. So I told her in my note that my multi-millionaire father had consented for me to roam the galaxy until I could find a girl who would love me for myself alone, not knowing of his millions. And I'd found her. And she was the only woman I could ever love. It was a fairly long note," Link added.

"But . . . but—"

"I said I was going away for a year to see if I could live without her. If I couldn't—even though she considered my father's millions—I'd come back and sadly ask her to marry me though my father's millions counted. If I could, I said, I'd spend the rest of my life exploring strange planets and brooding because the one woman I could love could not love me for myself, as I loved her. A very nice piece of romantic literature."

Thana said blankly, "Then what?"

Harl appeared for the second time in the doorway. He wad enraged. His hands were clenched. He scowled formidably.

"They wouldn't let my fella ride through," he said in an ominous tone. "They bit his unicorn's heels. They'd ha' pulled it down and him too! So he came back. Uffts never dared try a trick like that before! Not in this household! An' they never will again!"

"What—"

"I'm going to duply that gun you used last night, Link," said Harl ferociously, "and me and a bunch of my fellas will go out an' sting them up like you did, only plenty! When uffts say a man's got to be hung and a householder can't send a message, that ain't just no manners! That's . . . that's—"

He stopped, at a loss for a word to express behavior more reprehensible than bad manners. Link noted that on Sord Three "manners" had come to imply all that was admirable, as in other places and other times words like "honor" and "intellectual" and "piety" and "patriotic" had become synonyms for "good." And, as in those other cases, something was missing. But he said, "Thana and I already tried duplying it, Harl. The duplied one doesn't work, just as duplied knives don't hold an edge."

Harl stared at him.

"Sput! Y'sure?"

"Quite sure," said Link. "We solved the problem of the knife, but the raw material to make a duplied stun gun is rare everywhere. We haven't got it and I wouldn't know it if I saw it."

Harl said "Sput!" again, and began to pace up and down. After a minute and more he said bitterly;

"I'm not goin' to let my Household starve! So far's I know no man has ever killed an ufft in a hundred years. They act crazy, but they can't hold a spear to fight with, even if they could make 'em. So it'd be a disgrace to use a spear on them. But it'd be a disgrace to hang a man just because the uffts wanted him hung! And to let 'em search our houses any time they felt like it, just because they can't fight! Anyhow I'm not goin' to let my household go hungry because uffts say they've got to!'

He stamped his feet. He ground his teeth. He started for the doorway. Link said,

"Hold it, Harl! I've got an idea. You don't want to use spears on uffts."

"I got to!"

"No. And if you use the only stun gun on the planet, it'll make them madder than ever."

"Can I help that?"

"You don't even want them to stop trading with your Household, greenstuff for beer."

"I want," said Harl savagely, "for things to be like they was in the old days, when the old folks were polite to the uffts and the uffts to them! When humans didn't need uffts and tools were good and knives were sharp."

"And everybody had beans for breakfast," Link finished for him. "But I've got an idea, Harl. Uffts like speeches." Harl scowled at him.

"They like my speeches," added Link.

Harl's scowl did not diminish.

"I," said Link, "will go out and make a speech to them. If they won't listen, I'll high-tail it back. But if they do listen I'll gather them in a splendid public meeting with a program and orations about . . . oh, work hours and fringe benefits or something like that. I'll organize them into committees. Then I'll adjourn them to a more convenient place."

Harl said cagily, "Then what?"

"They'll have adjourned away from any place near your Household, and you and your forty or fifty unicorns can go guesting and come back with your food. And," said Link, "meanwhile the uffts will be talking. And talking is thirsty work. That will be an urge toward negotiations by which the uffts can get themselves some beer."

Harl continued to frown, but not as deeply. After a time he said heavily, "It might fix things for now. But things are bad, Link, an' they keep gettin' worse. This'd be only for right now."

"Ah!" said Link briskly. "Just what I was coming to! In your guesting, Harl, you will talk to your hosts about the good old days. You'll point out how superior they were to now. You'll propose an assembly of Householders to organize for the bringing back of the Good Old Days. That, all by itself, is a complete program for a political party of wide and popular appeal!"

"Mmmmmmh!" said Harl slowly. "It's about time somebody started that!"

"Just so," said Link. "So if Thana will fix me up a light lunch—the uffts had no food for Thistlethwaite to eat—I'll go out and try a little silver-tongued oratory. With all due modesty, I think I can sway a crowd. Of uffts."

Harl's frown was not wholly gone, yet. But he said,

"I like that idea of goin' back to the good old days!"

"If you're allowed to define them," agreed Link. "But in the meantime we'll let the uffts talk themselves thirsty so they'll have to bring in greenstuff to get beer to lubricate more talk."

Harl said, very heavily indeed, "We'll try it. You got words, Link. I'll get you a unicorn ready. That's a good idea about the good old days."

He disappeared. Thana said, "You didn't finish telling me about Imogene."

"Oh, she must be married to somebody else by now," Link told her. "I'd wonder if she wasn't. Anyhow—"

"I'll fix you a lunch," said Thana. "I think you're going to accomplish a lot on Sord Three, Link!"

He looked startled.

"Why?"

"You," said Thana, "look at things in such a practical way!"

She vanished, in her turn. Link spread out his hands in a gesture there was nobody around to see. He heard a faint, faint noise. He pricked up his ears. He went to an open door and listened. A shrill ululation came from somewhere beyond the village. It was the high-pitched voices of uffts. A rhythm established itself. The uffts were chanting,

"*Death . . . to . . . men! Death to men! Death to men!*"

Chapter 8

An hour later, Link went streaking away from the
Household, urging his unicorn to the utmost, while
Harl led shouts of anger and irritation among the
houses. Another rider came after Link. His mount
had been carefully selected, and it had no chance at
all of overtaking Link. Then came two other riders,
one shortly after another, and then a knot of nearly a
dozen, as if pursuit of Link had begun as fast as men
could get unicorns saddled for the chase. They rushed
after Link with seeming fury. But he had a faster
mount, a distinctly, prearrangedly faster animal.

But it was not the most comfortable of all animals
to ride. Unicorns jolted. They put down their large
and tender feet with lavish and ungainly motions, the
object of which seemed to be to shake their riders'
livers loose. The faster they traveled, the more lavish
the leg-motions and the more violent the jarring of
the man riding them. The drooping fleshy appendages which dangled from their foreheads flapped and
bumped as they ran.

Link's pursuers seemed to strive desperately to
overtake him. They shook fists and spears at him as
he increased his lead. He topped a hillside half a mile
from the Household, went down its farther slope, and
squealed insults from uffts' throats seemed to give
the Household posse pause. When Link was out of
sight the voices of invisible uffts hurled epithets at
his pursuers. The chase-party slackened speed and
finally halted. They seemed to confer. Uffts shouted
at them. *"Murderers!"* was a mild word. *"Assassins!"*

was more frequent. *"Shame! Shame! Shame!"* was commonplace.

The men from the Household, as if reluctantly, turned their mounts homeward, and uffts came scuttling across the uneven ground to shout, *"Cowards!"* after them, and more elaborately, *"Scared to fight! Yah! Yah! Yah!"* As the riders pressed their mounts, the uffts became more daring. Rotund small animals almost caught up with the retreating spear bearers, yapping at their unicorns' heels and shouting every insult an ufftish mind could conceive.

When the mounted men reentered the village, however, the uffts went racing and bounding to see what had happened to Link. The painted message on the *Glamorgan*'s fin had represented him as pro-ufft, while Thistlethwaite was represented as having villainous intentions toward them. And Link had made them a noble speech, presenting a problem that could be argued about indefinitely. The important thing, though, was that he had fled from the Household, with pursuers hot on his trail. If the humans of the Household disliked him enough to chase him, uffts were practically ready to make him an honorary member of their race.

He kept up his headlong flight for a full mile. Then he gradually slackened speed, as repeated glances to the rear showed no sign of his pursuers. Presently he ceased altogether to urge the unicorn he rode, and proceeded at a leisurely, bumpy walk.

He became aware that uffts trotted or galloped on parallel courses to see what he would do. At first they did not show themselves, and he only caught fugitive glimpses of one or two at a time. But there were evidently some hundreds of them, staying out of sight but keeping pace with him on either side.

He reined in and waited.

Uffts' voices murmured. There were even squabblings in low tones, as if uffts behind boulders and just behind hilltops were arguing with each other over who should go out into plain view and open a conversation. The buzzing voices became almost angry. Then Link let his unicorn move very slowly to one side while voices mumbled indignantly. *"Who's afraid of him?" "You are, that's who." "That's a lie! You're the scared one!" "... Then if you aren't scared, go out and talk to him!" "You do it! ... Huh! I dare you to go out and talk to him!" "But I double-dare you!" "I triple-dare you. ... I quadruple-dare—"*

Then Link's head appeared above a hilltop, and the uffts knew that he could see a close-packed mass of them trying to insult each other into making the first contact with him.

"My friends!" said Link in a carrying voice. "I put myself in your hands! I ask political asylum from the Householders and tyrants who are your enemies no less than the enemies of every person in favor of your being favored!"

Every ufft gazed at him. Those nearest him tended to look scared. But Link waved his arms.

"On a previous occasion," he said splendidly, "I spoke to you of the galaxy-wide admiration of your intellect, and presented to you a problem the logicians and metaphysicians of other worlds have found unsolvable, though some solution must exist. At that time I did not realize that the sociological-economic conditions of your life had driven you to revolt. I was not aware that you were actually and unthinkably expected to earn the beer so necessary to the higher functions of the intellect. I did not know that you, the most brilliant race in the galaxy, were frustrated by a caste system of which you were less than the highest grade. But I began to suspect it last night, when you made a political demonstration in the Household streets. I confirmed it this morning. And when I expressed my indignation that uffts, here—uffts, my friends!—were not gladly supported by the humans who should listen to them with reverence, when I learned of the unbelievable withholding of the subservience due you—"

Link listened interestedly to himself. A man who doesn't believe too firmly in his own importance can often overhear remarkable things if he simply starts to talk and then leans back to listen. One's mouth, allowed to say what it pleases, sometimes astonishes its owner. Of course, it sometimes gets him into trouble, too.

Link found himself waving his arms splendidly while he passed from mere flattery to exhortation, and from exhortation to the outlining of a plan of action. He didn't like to disappoint anybody, and the uffts were capable of disappointment.

A part of his mind said wryly that he was making a fool of himself when all he needed was to get the uffts to move off so Harl could get away with a pack-train of unicorns and return with some unicorn-loads of groceries. But another part of his mind went on grandly, not disappointing the uffts.

"Your revolution," he told them eloquently, "has the sympathy of every lover of liberty, of license, and of uffts! I look to see the spontaneous uprising you have already made become the pattern for a planet-wide defiance! I look to see committees formed for correspondence with uffts on all this world! A committee to coordinate the publicity which will draw all uffts to your standards! I look to see committees for the organization of revolutionary units! Every talent possessed by uffts must be thrown into the struggle! Why not a committee of poets, to phrase in deathless words the aspirations of the ufftian race? My friends, I ask you! Who favors a committee of correspondence, to inform the whole planet of your intolerable grievances! Who favors it?"

There was some cheering. Nearby uffts cheered raggedly. Those farther away cheered because those nearer cheered. Those quite beyond the reach of Link's voice cheered because there was cheering going on. But those far away ones were not following developments closely. A more-than-usually-fanatical ufft cried shrilly, "Death to all humans!"

"Splendid!" shouted Link valorously. "Now, who favors a committee to form revolutionary units for the liberation of the uffts?"

Those nearby cheered more loudly. Again, from the fringes of the gathering, there came bloodthirsty outcries.

"The ayes have it!" Link cried triumphantly. "Who's for a propaganda organization to stimulate the patriotism and the resolution of all uffts, everywhere?"

There were more cheers.

"Who volunteers for the Ufftian Revolutionary Council, to determine the policies which are to make uffts independent of all humans and raise them to their proper, inalienable position of superiority?"

Cheers. Yells. Uproar.

"My friends!" roared Link. "It is not befitting the glorious traditions of ufftdom that the Ufftian Provisional Government meet on the edge of a human Household, spied upon by humans! Let us march to some strictly ufftian area where the ufftian world capital will presently appear! Let us plan this metropolis! Let us organize our revolt! Let us march forward, shouting the slogans of ufftian freedom! Who marches?"

There was an uproar of cheering which was distinctly heard and unfavorably reacted upon in the Household from which Link had seemingly fled a short time before.

With a grandiose gesture, Link set his unicorn in motion, headed in a distinctly general direction. There was a stirring, and presently innumerable plump animals, with pinkish skin showing through the sparse hairiness, came trotting and galloping to be close to him. He leaned in his saddle and addressed those nearest him on the right.

"Will someone volunteer to lead the cadence of the march?" he asked. "We should have marching units, chanting the principles of this splendid revolt. Leaders, please!"

Voices clamored to be appointed. He appointed them all, with definitely non-specific wavings of his hand. He gave them a march cadence chant. They tried it as a group and almost instantly abandoned the group to lead other groupings. Link knew by intuition that anybody who wants to talk like the uffts, would want to lead others of his kind. It seemed that immediately there were half a dozen assemblages of uffts gathered about voluble, self-appointed leaders, giving out a rhythmic outcry,

"Brackety-ax, co-ax, co-ax! Onward, onward, uffts! Brackety-ax, co-ax, co-ax! Onward, onward, uffts!"

"That for the right wing of the Army of Liberation," he observed profoundly to those on his left. "Chant leaders? Who will lead the chants?"

Uffts by dozens vociferously demanded to be appointed. He appointed them all. He furnished them with slogans. Shortly there were bands of the pig-like creatures swarming over the countryside shrilling,

"Uffts triumphant! Uffts supreme! Uffts are now a single team!" There was another, *"Uffts have risen up to fight! Tremble, tremble at their might!"* A simpler one was still more successful, *"Uffts, uffts, on our way! Uffts, uffts, rise and slay!"*

The aboriginal population of Sord Three—the uffts—spread over an astonishing area as they scrambled up hillsides and flowed down the descending slopes. Those with satisfactory slogans to chant tended to stay more closely together, and to shout more loudly. Link's inventiveness gave out, and he appointed a Committee for Marching Recitatives to create other slogans and to pass on words of genius devised by anybody who happened to consider himself a genius.

There was much squabbling, and some remarkably bloodthirsty marching chants were devised, but the committee throve.

With a fine disregard for practicality but a completely sound estimate of the voluble mind, Link established all committees in an admirably vague state so any ufft who wanted to belong to any committee *ex officio* became a member. He tossed off committee titles with

abandon. The Committee on Logistics for the Army
of Liberation. The Joint Chiefs of Staff. The Strategy
Council of the Ufftian Army. The Committee for
Propaganda. The Committee on the Ufftian National
Constitution. The Committee of Committeemen for
the Coordination of the War Effort . . .

There were hills in the distance, and Link more
or less headed for them. The afternoon sun was hot.
The ground was only thinly covered with vegetation.
It was probably a good idea to head for an area
where herbivorous creatures like the uffts could find
something to eat. The hills looked green. And they
might be cooler.

He set the marching pace at a comfortable strolling
rate. He was leading the uffts who earlier had been
besieging Harl's household and shouting insults at its
inhabitants. He was creating the diversion needed for
Harl to take a pack-train to a neighbor's Household
and stock up with foodstuffs to endure a siege.

He found his role congenial. He liked novelty. He
liked excitement. On occasion he enjoyed tumult. The
present situation supplied all three. He was almost
regretful that it wouldn't last. He considered it certain that when the Ufftian Army of Liberation got
tired of walking, it would sit down on its haunches
as quadrupeds do, and rest, and get discouraged, and
eventually go home. Meanwhile, though, he was a
generalissimo of a strictly improvised army.

There were troops of uffts scrambling up hillsides
and down again, shrilling, *"Brackety-ax, co-ax, co-ax!
Uffts! Uffts! Uffts!"*

The original marching slogan had been modified.
Link admitted to himself that it was improved. His

Committee for Marching Recitatives had, astonishingly, turned out some others. As time passed they began to appear spontaneously in ever-forming and ever-re-forming groups of uffts. They continued to appear in new forms as the afternoon wore on. There were other signs of initiative. Uffts came galloping to his side to identify themselves as—self-appointed—commanders of the rear guard, the scouts, the Undefeatable Reserves, the Ufftian Commandos, the Rangers, the Guerillas and other military groups, and to tell him that all went well with their commands. They went away with their appointments confirmed by his acceptance of their reports. In some cases they simply went off to form the units they had just designed for themselves.

Sunset approached. The hills grew higher and steeper. The vegetation grew less sparse. Link began to be astonished by the persistence of the uffts in what he'd thought would be not much more than an hour or so of dramatic make-believe. He began, indeed, to worry a little.

There were deep shadows on the hillsides when an ufft from the self-appointed advance-guards came galloping back from the leading part of the march. He pranced splendidly in a half-circle, came alongside Link's unicorn, and said in a strictly military manner:

"General, sir, the colonel in command of the advance-guard asks if you wish to occupy the abandoned human Household in the valley to the left, sir. He suggests that for logistic reasons it may be a suitable temporary headquarters. There's a large spring, sir, with good water. What are your orders?"

"By all means occupy it," said Link. "We'll at least bivouac there for the night."

But he blinked at the now-steep hillsides around him. It was almost dark. The situation began to seem less than merely amusing. The uffts really meant this revolt business! He hadn't taken them seriously. It was not easy to do so now. They acted like children, to be sure. But children would have gotten tired of this play-acting and marching long ago. Children, indeed, would have abandoned the encirclement of Harl's Household.

It occurred to Link that the uffts had more brains than he'd credited them with. They were desperately concerned about the stun gun with which they'd been peppered the night before. If such weapons were to be available to the humans on Sord Three, the uffts would be in a very bad fix. They couldn't fight back. They had little hoofs instead of hands, and their brains were of no use to them because they lacked fingers and especially an opposable thumb.

Naturally, in the presence of human co-inhabitants of Sord Three, they had to lie to themselves to be able to endure their handicap. They pretended to despise humans. They were childishly bitter. They scornfully said that to have hands instead of hoofs was a shameful thing. But they knew, just the same, that the introduction of stun guns on Sord Three would make them utterly helpless as against humans. So with a naive desperation they were taking the only action they could imagine, under the only leadership they could consider qualified. It was not wise action. It could hardly be effective action. But Link felt obscurely ashamed of himself. He'd started it.

The hillsides to right and left became steeper and the valley in which the Army marched became deeper. Link saw his following more or less as a mass for the first time. There were some thousands of the uffts. They would have covered an acre or more in the closest possible marching order. Spread out, they were an impressive lot of creatures.

Here there was a band of a hundred or more, keeping close together and silent for the time being. There was a knot of twenty or thereabouts, chanting a slogan as they marched. He noticed that they looked weary. They also looked absurd. And they were totally unsophisticated in such practical matters as self-defense against men mounted on unicorns and carrying spears. They could be hunted down as corresponding creatures have been hunted down on ten thousand colonized worlds. The only difference between them and the wild lower animals of other planets was the uffts had brains. But brains in the absence of an opposable thumb left them ridiculous.

The swarming, now leg-weary small horde of uffts swung into a narrower valley which entered this one from the left. Far up this second valley there were human structures. Even in the gathering dusk they could be seen to be abandoned. The valley walls were almost precipitous. Rock strata of varying colors alternated in slanting streaks of stone. Link saw a stratum of extremely familiar peach-colored stone. He shrugged his shoulders.

The uffts flowed on, in small clumps and big ones, some few as individuals, many in pairs. Weariness was breaking down the undisciplined bunching of the march. They were now merely a very large number of very weary small animals, sturdily following Link's leadership because he'd made a speech, and they couldn't do much but make speeches themselves, and so could not estimate the uselessness of speechmaking.

Some of them began to hurry, now. There was a small stream, which dwindled to a thread down the valley up which Link now rode morosely. Near the deserted and crumbling structures it was larger. At its source it was a considerable spring. Link saw crowds of the uffts drinking thirstily, and moving away, and being replaced by others.

His own escort—he realized suddenly that some uffts had appointed themselves his personal escort and staff—moved on to the human structures. The roofs of the smaller buildings had collapsed. The Household or village must have been abandoned for many years. The largest structure would correspond with Harl's residence. It had been the residence of the Householder of this place. Doors had fallen. Windows gaped.

Link's escort stopped before it.

"I suppose," said Link, "that I'd better take this over as my headquarters."

"Yes, sir," said an ufft's voice. "You'll give us more orders in the morning, sir? You've plans for the War of Liberation, sir?"

"I'll make them," said Link. He was vexed.

He dismounted, and many small aches and pains reminded him that a unicorn is not the most comfortable of riding animals. He went into the abandoned Householder's residence to survey it while some little light remained.

Inside was desolation. There was furniture remaining,

but some of it had collapsed, and some was ready to fall of its own weight at any instant. There was a great hall, with an imposing chair of state like the one in Harl's great room. The flooring of the great hall was stone. Link gathered bits of dry-rotted furniture and kicked them. They fell apart. He built a fire, as much to cheer himself as for warmth.

Thana had prepared a lunch for him. He hadn't had time to consume it. It was bread and beans, but there were three plastic bottles of beer. Link ate a part of the bread-and-beans lunch. He started to drink one of the bottles of beer.

Then he looked up at the chair of state upon its dais. He shrugged, and again started to open the beer. But again he stopped.

With the flickering fire for light, he went over to the chair of state. He searched, and found a button. He pressed it. There were creaking, groaning sounds. The chair of state rose toward the ceiling. Something excessively dusty rose out of the pit beneath it. It was a duplier. Link stared at it.

"It won't work," he told himself firmly. "It can't! They abandoned this place because it stopped working!"

It would have been sufficient reason. If the art of alloying steel had been lost, and even the art of weaving, and if agriculture had been practically abandoned, certainly nobody would have remembered how a duplier worked, to repair it when it broke down.

But Link tried the device. He put a scrap of wood in the middle bin, for a sample, and another scrap of wood in the raw materials bin, and pressed the button. The duplier sank into the pit and the chair-of-state, creaking, descended to the floor. The button again. The process reversed. The duplier came back into view.

It hadn't worked. Nothing had happened.

Link went back to his tiny fire. He brooded. He liked novelty and excitement and sometimes tumult. He had none of these things about him now. He scowled at the firelight.

Presently he took a burning brand and went back to the duplier. He looked it over. It was complex. It utilized principles that he could not even guess. But there were wires threading here and there. He blew away the dust and stared at them.

One had rusted through. At another place a contact was badly rusted. Insulation was gone from a wire, which thereby must be shorted. He shifted the wires to find out how many were broken or whose contacts were loose.

He was irritated with himself, but the reasoning was sound. If nobody remembered even vaguely how electrical apparatus worked—and Harl said that there used to be lectric but it existed no longer—and if nobody bothered to understand, maybe they didn't know what a short-circuit would do! They might not even understand what a loose contact could do!

He used up four torches, fumbling with obvious defects which any ten-year-old boy on another planet would have observed. Eventually he went back to the button. He pressed it. The duplier and after it the chair of state descended. He pressed the button once more and they rose in their established sequence.

The duplier worked. A scrap of wood in the materials hopper had almost disappeared. Another scrap of wood—a duplicate of the one in the sample bin—had appeared.

Link went out and barked orders. Uffts came tiredly in the darkness. Link took off the embroidered shirt he wore.

"I want some greenstuff," he said firmly, "and I want this shirt soaked in water and brought back dripping wet."

He hunted for more furniture to build up his fire while his orders were obeyed. Presently he put his dripping shirt—uffts could hardly carry water in any other manner—with branches and weeds into the duplier. He put one of his three bottles of beer in the sample hopper. He pressed the button.

Shortly he owned four bottles of beer. The plastic containers were made out of the cellulose of the greenstuff stems. The beer was made out of the organic compounds involved and the water brought in the saturated shirt.

There was, then, a very, very great stirring in the darkness about the abandoned household. Uffts excitedly foraged for greenstuff about the buildings. Weeds grew high. There were trees. Some were small, but some were of considerable size because this human Household was abandoned. Link necessarily duplied his shirt so that more water could be brought by uffts who had no other way to carry it. The chair of state ascended and descended and rose and sank down again.

When Link lay down to sleep on a very hard floor, it was late at night. The morale of the Ufftian Army of Liberation was high. Excessively high. He'd taught some uffts how to keep the duplier in operation with thirty-two bottles of beer in the sample hopper. The duplier worked steadily.

Outside, in the darkness, uffts chanted gloriously, in splendid confidence of all the future:

"General Link, what do you think?
Brought his army here!
When he stopped, up he popped
Passing out bottles of beer!"

Link went to sleep with various uncoordinated choruses chanting it. But he wasn't easy in his mind.

In fact, he had nightmares.

Chapter 9

Link made a speech next morning. He'd hammered out, very painfully, the only possible action he could advise or command his followers to take. Essentially, it was to take no action at all. But he couldn't put it that way. It was obvious that if the culture of the human inhabitants of Sord Three had deteriorated because of the lack of contact with the galactic civilization, the status of the uffts had diminished, too. But it was also absolutely certain that if there had been contact with the rest of the galaxy, there'd have been hell to pay.

At the least, every duplier on Sord Three would have been taken forcibly away by adventurers landing with modern weapons and no scruples whatever. As a side line, such space-rovers would have come upon the uffts. They'd have kidnapped them and sold them

as intelligent freaks on a thousand worlds while one
planet after another collapsed into chaos as a result of
the dupliers. Ultimately, in fact, the citizens of Sord
Three would have starved for the lack of dupliers
while the rest of the galaxy went hungry because it
possessed them. Transported and enslaved uffts would
have been involved in the collapse of human civilization, and the galaxy at large would have gone to hell
in a handbasket.

It was still a strong probability. Link was the only
person anywhere who realized it. If it was to be prevented, he had to do the preventing. The responsibility
was overwhelming.

Therefore he made his speech.

"My friends!" he said resoundingly, from an extremely
rickety balcony in the outer wall of the householder's
crumbling residence. "My friends, it is necessary to
decide upon a policy of action for the realization of the
objectives of the Ufftian Revolution. Let me say that
when I came here to ask your help in the solution of
an abstract question, I did not realize the emergency
that existed here. I urge that the problem, my problem,
of the barber and who shaves him be put aside for
the duration of the emergency. All the resources of
the ufftian race, including its unbelievable intellect,
should be devoted to the single purpose—freedom!"

There were cheers. They were more prompt and
louder than the day before, because Link had appointed
a Committee for Emphasizing the Unanimity of Ufftian Opinion, and they cheered whenever he paused
in the course of an oration.

"You are here as an army," said Link, oratorically,
"and an army you should remain. But you are the most

intelligent race in the galaxy. Therefore it is natural for you to adopt the most intelligent strategy for the achievement of your ends. Your master strategists have undoubtedly discussed that classic of military doctrine *Power in Space* and have determined to apply the principle of the space fleet in being to the basic problem of this war, so ensuring ufftian victory."

He paused, and cheers rose confusedly in the morning sunlight.

"An army in being," announced Link profoundly, "is an undefeated army. By the fact that it is in being, it has proved that it is undefeatable. To be an army in being is to be a victorious army, because if it were not victorious it could not continue to be! Therefore the first item of Ufftian policy is to keep the army in being and therefore to keep it undefeated and victorious, an inspiration of uffts everywhere, drawing them to join it and share in its glory and its triumph!"

Cheers. The Committee for Emphasizing the Unanimity of Ufftian Opinion took its cue more promptly, and there was a high, shrill tumult of approval, much greater than before.

"Specifically," said Link with a fine precision, "the policy of the Ufftian Provisional Government is to maintain its army in being, to spread propaganda everywhere to cause uffts everywhere to join and increase that army, to cause its enemies to realize the futility of conflict, and ultimately to make a generous and equitable peace which shall realize all Ufftian national aspirations and establish the Ufftian Nation in permanent, unquestioned, and unquestionable solidity!"

Cheers now echoed and reechoed from the walls of the valley. Link held up his hand for attention.

"In pursuance of this policy," he said valiantly, "we shall immediately organize the Committee for Propaganda upon a new scale. We shall enlarge the organization of G-1 and G-2, our intelligence and counter-intelligence groups. More volunteers for this necessary work are needed. We shall need volunteers to explain the policies of the Ufftian National Constitution to the uffts who will shortly join the Ufftian Revolutionary Army. We must have volunteers for security services, for communications, for espionage, for education, and for a survey of the cultural monuments and purposes to be preserved and obeyed, and for the preparation of a history—a detailed history—of this epoch-making and unanimous uprising of all uffts for the realization of these traditional aims! And—"

It was an admirable speech. When he'd finished, his hearers were almost hoarse from their cheering. He retired into the tumble-down Householder's residence with a forlorn kind of satisfaction. He was still the leader of the revolution. The uffts believed they were going to accomplish something unique under his guidance. It was conceivable that they might. No ufft could possibly topple him from his post as leader, because all uffts knew that *they* were inexorably restricted in achievement by the fact that their hands were hoofs. They could only believe in accomplishment associated with hands. There could be uffts wrought up to sabotage or crime by a purely ufftian leader, but Link alone could be the nucleus around which a genuinely large number of uffts would gather.

There were two main reasons for it. One was his psychological advantage in that he could make speeches and had hands besides. The other was discretion. He'd asked for volunteers for innumerable committees and high-sounding boards and councils. But he hadn't even referred to the organization of combat units. The Ufftian Revolutionary Army was prepared for propaganda, espionage, education, counter-espionage, and probably social services and psychoanalysis. But Link had at no time suggested that anybody get ready to fight.

An important but subsidiary reason was the free beer issued by the Quartermaster Corps to any ufft or group of uffts who came into the great hall of state, dragging a reasonable amount of greenstuff and a sufficient number of water-soaked shirts, ready-duplied for the transport of water required in beer. Unquestionably, the free beer helped.

Its appeal showed up on the second day of the revolutionary movement. A little knot of traveling uffts, some twenty in number, were halted by security uffts as they crossed the mountains on private business of their own. They were questioned, given beer, and turned loose. Half of them did not leave. The rest went on to tell their friends and bring them back. Various of the original marchers appointed themselves recruiting officers of glamorously named organizations and went home after new members. They got them.

By the third day there was a steady trickle of volunteers for the army and especially the civil service of the provisional government. They came through mountain passes or across the rolling foothills toward the formerly human household. By the fourth day, the loss of ufft-power was noticeable in human households as much as fifty miles in every direction. Harl's household reposed in a vast tranquility. Groups of pack-animals could go and come between neighboring households without even a shouted *"Murderers!"* flung at them along the way. But all the householders were faced with the need to go guesting to get needed foodstuffs. There were no more ufft-carts coming in with greenstuff. There was no general strike, of course, but the result was the same. Uffts were gathering at the Ufft Future World Capital up a rather steep small valley, where anybody could have all the beer he wanted for the greenstuff required to make it. Link had started out with perhaps two or three thousand followers. Four days later there were twenty thousand about the former human settlement. Some of the uffts, females, no doubt, disapproved of the bivouac idea. Permanent burrows began to appear here and there.

From time to time Link performed some ritual to remind the uffts that they were a revolutionary army. On one occasion he presided over a marching-recitative competition, when small bands of uffts marched past his residence chanting vainglorious doggerel for inspirational purposes. The slogans, of course, stressed loyalty to the principles of the Provisional Government, the National Constitution, the Declaration of Freedom, the Appeal to Intellects, and so on.

On another occasion he solemnly led an organization down the valley to where a vein of very familiar peach-colored rock showed in the valley wall. He picked up a fist-sized bit of it, fallen out of the vein, and carried it back to the Household. He placed it as the first stone in a six-foot-high cairn of peach-colored rocks to mark the place where the Ufftian National Bill of Rights would presently be adopted. It hadn't been drawn up yet. Discussion of its details

required much beer, and the self-appointed committee to compose it had to spend so much time hauling the necessary greenstuff that not much time was
left for deliberation. It was already apparent to Link
that in the absence of ufft-carts, the beer dragged
to the duplier cost more time and effort per bottle
than when it could be hauled on wheels and humans
took a toll of it.

But matters in households nearby had become
serious. There were practically no uffts remaining as
hangers-on about human villages in a very large area.
A space roughly two hundred miles across was denuded
of uffts. It extended from the sea to the eastward of
Link's headquarters, well beyond the mountains in
which he commanded. In some of those households,
men had actually been forced to gather greenstuff or
go hungry. The fact caused anti-ufft feeling to run high.
Already it had occurred to Link that if he could find
another abandoned household with a duplier as readily
repairable as this first one, he could start a new center
of ufftian independence. Given dupliers and shirts or
their equivalents to carry water in, uffts could have
beer at will, or almost so. They gained no other tangible
benefit from their association with humans.

Paradoxically, it was Link's own doing that counter-
measures against the Revolution began. When Harl
had spoken so bitterly in favor of the good old days,
Link had agreed with him. He'd suggested that Harl
call an assembly to bring about their return. It was a
suggestion with infinite appeal. Everybody can think
of good old days they'd like to recall. No two people
will want to recall the same good old days, but the
theory is attractive.

Harl fumed at the desertion of the uffts who had made his household a livable place. He argued the matter with other householders forlornly traveling about trying to get food without working for it. They tended to agree more furiously as the number of uffts on their households diminished, and the conditions more nearly approached the real good old days when Sord Three was first colonized.

Link continued depressedly to be the acting head of the Ufftian Provisional Government, the Ufftian Army of Liberation, the Coordinator of the War Effort, and a considerable number of other things. He drank a bottle of beer occasionally. For other subsistence he had to depend on duplied repetitions of the lunch Thana had made for him. It was a fair lunch, but it was a horribly monotonous diet. But there was nothing he could do about it. He was followed everywhere by devoted uffts who—it was irritatingly touching—seemed honestly to believe that they were getting somewhere.

Perhaps they were. At any rate, by the fact of their absence they impressed the humans with the necessity for their presence. They made endless speeches to each other. They drank innumerable bottles of beer. And they stripped the valley of greenstuff. At the end of a week they were dragging branches two miles to get beer. In nine days the production and consumption of beer began to fall off. The work required was more than even beer was worth.

Link envisioned a change in the food provision policies of human households on Sord Three. Given agricultural machines, and seed of modern breeding, one not-too-skilled man could plough, cultivate and make ready for harvesting an enormous acreage. Uffts could weed it. Uffts could harvest it. They could enter into a real symbiotic relationship with humanity. And he was beginning to think of a way to secure the alloy materials and rare element supplies needed for the restoration of lectric and vision-casts, synthetic fibers and fabrics, and probably means of transportation superior to unicorns. He grew wistful as he pictured it to himself. Sord Three could become a paradise, and dupliers could be used for a new purpose so effectively that their original function would become forgotten. The economic system of Sord Three could gently be diverted to something really intelligent.

Link felt himself qualified to design an intelligent economic system. He'd have liked to talk to somebody about it. But the only suitable listener on Sord Three would be Thana. Making his plans, he imagined himself explaining them to her.

When disaster came, Link was absorbed in the design of a flexible new economic order which would eventually be able to stand visitors without disturbance, and the visitors would not be disturbed by what they found. Dupliers would not be recognizable as such, and so would be harmless. Designing such a system was an appalling problem, but Link attacked it valiantly—until disaster arrived.

A party of uffts brought a newcomer to the tumbledown building Link inhabited alone. The newcomer was abusive and rebellious.

"Sir," said a Security ufft in a stern voice, "here's a spy, sir. He came from Old Man Addison's Household. He was sent to spy out our military secrets."

"Yah!" snarled the spy. "You haven't got any military

secrets! There's dozens of us, and we know all about everything you do! We're a tight organization, and Old Man Addison knows every secret of every household and every ufft town, and if you hurt me he'll know who did it and get even!"

He glared defiantly about him.

"He'll know, eh?" said Link. "Maybe somebody's already telling him about your capture, eh?"

"That's right!" snapped the spy. "You don't dare hurt me!"

Link reflected. This was in a way a court-martial, except that Link was the only judge. The great hall with its chair of state was dusty and littered. The plump and angry uffts who'd brought in the prisoner made indignant noises.

"Now," said Link pleasantly, "you have a chance to be a double-spy, a very high rank in your profession. You begin by telling us everything you know about what the Householders are planning in this war."

The spy-ufft made raucous noises of derision. So Link said sternly, "We'll assemble the army. It will march past where you're held fast. Every member of the army will take one nip at you. Just one. Nobody will kill you, but somewhere in the process of receiving some tens of thousands of nips—"

The spy squealed. Link had expected it. There were not less than forty thousand uffts either in the Army of Liberation or the committees associated with it. The total might be as high as fifty thousand. The spy instantly agreed, shaking with terror, to tell everything, everything, everything.

"Take him away and question him," said Link in an official voice.

An hour later he received the report. The spy had told everything. On demand, he'd identified other spies. They'd been questioned separately, under the same threat. Their stories checked. So far as the revolt was concerned, the disaster was absolute.

Harl had begun the organization of Householders for the Restoration of the Good Old Days. There was great, grim approval and much disparity in the definitions of the good old days, but there was unanimity about present days. An ufftian army of liberation in being, equipped with a Household with a working duplier and able to supply beer with no benefit to humans, that could not be endured! Householders had mobilized their retainers. They were armed with spears. Some four or five hundred humans were gathered at Old Man Addison's household. On the morrow they would march on the Provisional Capital of the Ufftian Provisional Government. They were prepared to kill uffts with spears. They would.

That report to Link had not been completed when the Committee for Counter-Espionage clamored for his ear. Their operatives had reported substantially the same appalling facts. Members of G-1 and G-2 came galloping. The news had been brought to them. There was agitation. There was tumult. There was terror.

"My friends," said Link in stately sadness, "the cause for which we were prepared to suffer and die has had a setback. The immediate success of the Revolution is now questionable, but its final success is certain! It would not be intelligent for uffts, who are the most intelligent beings in this galaxy, to throw away their lives with anything less than certainty of its sheer necessity. But this is not true of this moment.

There is action by which the Revolution can continue. There is work to be done—organization, propaganda, planning! We shall . . . we shall go underground!"

It was the most lucid and most convincing of all possible phrases. Uffts lived in burrows. Underground. They preferred them. They meant safety, uffishness, the familiar, the normal, and the most satisfying way of life. Underground? Uffts cheered. Spontaneously!

"From this time on until the next occasion for rising," said Link splendidly, "the Provisional Government will exist in secret. The Army of Liberation will exist in the hearts of its members! And all uffts, everywhere, will remember that time marches on, life is short but war is long, in union there is strength, and the uffts will rise again! The Army will scatter. Its members will hold close the secrets of its association. And presently—"

He waved them out. Naturally, though privately, he was very much relieved. He knew that Harl, certainly, would not dream of trying to single out individual uffts for punishment for their part in the revolt. For one thing, it would be impossible. For another, if he did, the uffts would run away again. The other Households would have the same imperative reason for ignoring so far as possible the revolt of the uffts. It was even likely that they'd take some pains to keep from having much discontent among the uffts who at their own will could move from Household to Household or settle where they were best satisfied.

There was one matter in which Link was less than satisfied. He wasn't sure that Householders like Harl would be moved to reestablish agriculture to the point where food could be had without dupliers. It was

necessary for the faraway plans Link already debated.
But he wasn't sure it was going to happen. Yet.

But he had one personal reason for overwhelming
relief that he could resign as generalissimo of the
revolt. He'd been living on duplied rations, replicas
of the lunch Thana had prepared for him days ago.
In the nine days since, that lunch had gotten deplor-
ably stale. But it was worse than that. In nine days of
the same eatables, Link had gotten almost hysterically
sick of beans.

He watched a ceremonial march past of the Army
of Liberation before it dissolved into individuals and
family groups headed for their home burrows and
a vociferous denial that they'd been in the Army at
all.

But he'd reserved one unit of some two hundred
uffts, privately asked to volunteer for a last item of
military service against their oppressors, in case they
should be needed. They were members of the Ufftian
Diehard Regiment. They listened sternly and even
devotedly when he gave them their instructions. They
seemed to disperse like the rest. But—

When they were gone, he was alone in the decay-
ing Household. There was something that needed to
be done, and only he could do it. He worked nearly
all night by very indifferent torchlight. When dawn
came he cleared away the evidence of his labor. He
brought up the duplier from its pit for the last time.
Painstakingly, he re-shorted a formerly shorted wire.
Wires that had been broken he re-separated. Loose
contacts he turned into no contacts at all. The duplier
would duply no more.

And in the early morning he rode to meet the

army of householders and their retainers. In a sense,
of course, he was going to surrender. But he felt sure
that his explanation would satisfy Harl and therefore
the rest. But as he rode, his mind was not on such
matters. It dwelt hungrily upon pictures of food that
would not be beans.

He met the approaching army a dozen miles from
his former headquarters. He was mistaken about his
explanation satisfying the Householders, however.
Harl was visibly distressed both by his explanation
and its reception. Thana, riding with Harl—she was
the only girl with the armed expedition—looked at
Link inscrutably.

The human army halted to pass upon Link's behavior.
Thistlethwaite glowered at Link and loudly disclaimed
any association with him at all. He was no longer
Thistlethwaite's junior partner. He was—

They made camp, to discuss the situation in detail.
Then Thistlethwaite was astonished to be placed in
the dock as Link's fellow-criminal. The head of this
court-martial would be Old Man Addison. He was not
an amiable character, and Link took an instant dislike
to him. His air was authoritative and offensive. His
speech was very far from cordial. Link found that his
objection to Old Man Addison could be summed up
in the statement that he didn't have any manners.

But he knew what he intended the court-martial to
do, and he plainly meant to see that it did it. Against
Thistlethwaite's arguments he said acidly,

"You stuck me once. I gave you a spaceboat cargo
on your promise to come back an' pay me adequate
for some dupliers. You're back. Where's the stuff you
was to bring?"

Thistlethwaite protested despairingly.

"You' goin' to be hung," said Old Man Addison, as acidly as before. "An' I take your ship to pay me for what you cheated me out of. And any more strangers land on Sord Three get hung right off, no questions an' no foolin' around!"

The court-martial convened. Link explained lucidly that the uffts around Harl's household were already nearly in revolt, that they'd besieged Harl's Household, and that with Harl's approval he'd gone out to persuade them to go off somewhere and let pack-trains of unicorns relieve the food shortage. He pointed out that he had accomplished exactly that. He even pointed out that no human had been insulted or injured by uffts following his oratorical suggestions. He'd assumed leadership of the uffts as a favor to Harl.

Harl cast the only vote in the court-martial in favor of Link. The decision was that Link and Thistlethwaite were to be hanged the next morning. The delay was to allow other householders, hurrying to the scene, to watch the pleasant spectacle.

Link remained composed. Especially after the number of uffts usually to be seen about a gathering of humans appeared, one by one, and moved casually about the encampment. Nobody bothered them. It was the habit of humans to tolerate uffts. By midday there were at least fifty uffts moving about among the men and tents and animals. Later there were more.

Near sundown, Thana was admitted to the closely guarded place where Link and Thistlethwaite waited for morning and their doom. Thana looked at once indignant and subdued.

"I'm . . . sorry, Link," she said unhappily, "Harl's

still arguing, trying to get them to change their minds. But it doesn't look like he's going to! He's even told them that you showed me how to duply a knife so it's as good as an unduplied one! He's promised to make them all presents of shirts and beans and unduplied knives! But they listen to Old Man Addison."

"Yes," admitted Link. "He has a certain force of character. But his manners—" He shook his head. "Even Thistlethwaite doesn't approve of Old Man Addison now!"

Thana caught her breath as if trying not to cry.

"I . . . I brought you a shirt, Link. I . . . guess you didn't like that embroidered one. You took it off. This is duplied from the one you gave Harl."

"Hm," said Link. "Fine! Thanks, Thana."

She wept. He patted her shoulder.

"Is there anything . . ." she whispered, "is there anything I can do? Anything, Link!" She sobbed. "I . . . feel like it's my fault, you being in trouble. If I'd had more food stored away you wouldn't have had to lead the uffts away and . . . and—"

Link said helpfully, "If you feel that way, why . . . a couple of unicorns up the valley at midnight— If you could manage that, I'd appreciate it a lot!"

She was silent. Then she said bitterly, "You . . . you want to go back to Imogene!"

Link stared at her.

"Look, Thana, I didn't tell you the end of the story! After I got on the spaceship, and that's nearly a year ago, I looked at the receipt the florist had given me. And he'd written down Imogene's address on the back of the receipt. So he couldn't send the flowers or the note. So Imogene never heard from me again, and if I know her she's married long ago!"

She looked at him earnestly. "Honestly, Link?"

"Of course," Link said with dignity. "Have you ever known me to lie?"

"Where shall I have the unicorns?" she asked. "And how?"

"Influence," said Link. "I've got influence. Now—"

He told her a place it would not be easy to miss, perhaps a mile up the valley from the camp. She went away.

He seemed absorbed in thought for a long time after that. He didn't even pay particular attention to the uffts, which near sunset seemed to increase in number. But once an ufft winked reassuringly at him. Thistlethwaite was bitter, but Link consoled him as well as he could.

"You," he said kindly, "mistake the courtesies of business life for sentiments of deeper importance. You should reform." Thistlethwaite swore despairingly at him.

Darkness fell. Stars shone. The camp quieted. Then, at midnight, there was sudden and dithering uproar. Tents collapsed. Unicorns made dismal noises, tried to bolt, and finding their tethers bitten through by uffts, high-tailed it for the mountain slopes, with heel-nips to urge them on. Men swore, under blanketing canvas. Men tried to run after the unicorns and uffts ran between their legs and upset them. Those who tried to haul collapsed tents off their fellows suffered similarly irritating upsets. When swearing men crawled out to the open air, uffts nipped their legs and they leaped madly. There was a swarm of shouting uffts all about, ripping at any human or other heel within reach, biting through any ropes that remained intact, and bellowing contradictory orders in fairly good imitations of human voices. They turned the camp into something close to primordial chaos.

Link grunted as one of his own guards was bowled over. He grabbed at Thistlethwaite. He led the way. A small party of uffts formed around them, clearing the path. Twice, householders or their retainers seemed about to blunder into them, but each time they toppled as running uffts hit their knees from behind. Then the entire escort ran zestfully over them in what they considered the fine tradition of the Die-hard Regiment. Before disbanding his army, Link had picked them out, dramatically, for possible secret military action. This was it.

He and Thistlethwaite arrived where the unicorns should be. Around them, their escort boasted of their achievement in releasing Link. He had to warn them that these unicorns, dimly seen in the starlight, were not to be stampeded.

Then he discovered that there were three unicorns, not two. Thana flung reins to Link.

"Come on!" she said fiercely. "Maybe they'll follow!"

"I've got a rear guard," said Link, tranquilly, "and you'd better not come with us, Thana. Better turn your unicorn loose and get back to the camp."

"I won't!" said Thana. "I told Harl what I was going to do. He asked me to apologize for not coming to see us off."

"Us?" Link's mouth dropped open. Then he felt good. Remarkably good. He said warmly, "Harl has the best manners of anybody I know!"

They headed up the pass down which Link had come to surrender. The unicorns climbed. Thistlethwaite fumed and sputtered. He'd built a most extensive structure of dreams upon a supposedly firm business engagement with Old Man Addison. It was now wrecked. And Old Man Addison considered that he should be hanged. *And* the gait of riding-unicorns was excessively unpleasant. But he followed, dismally, the resolute figure of Thana, silhouetted against the stars. Link's figure was often close to it. Very close.

In an hour they were over the pass. Thana would have led the way on past the narrow valley in which the Provisional Government had functioned for nine days. But Link turned the animals into the valley bottom and took the others up to the Ufftian Provisional National Capital.

"There's something in the former Householder's home that I want to pick up," said Link. "I worked all night at it."

By the time they reached the dreary building, Link had solved the fastening of the saddlebags before him on the unicorn. They were quite large enough for his purpose. He dismounted and pointed out where a cairn of peach-colored rocks had been considerably reduced in size. He explained to Thana why it had been partly pulled down, and what he wanted to carry away. When they entered the great hall of the chair of state she was with him. He showed her what he'd used the peach-colored rocks to be raw material for.

"Pretty!" said Thana.

She helped him with his burden. They had to make two trips, filling up the saddlebags. They remounted and headed down the valley again. Thana said interestedly,

"They're beautiful! I never saw anything like that before!" They went on. And on. And on. When the hills were well behind, Link said,

"Thistlethwaite, you welded up everything, including the lifeboat blister. Where's the oxygen torch?"

Thistlethwaite sputtered a reply.

"We can't use the ship," said Link cheerfully. "With at least one hull-plate torn off and general structural weakness all over, we'll have to use the lifeboat."

Thistlethwaite mumbled. A faint, faint light glowed, far away.

"That's the Household," said Link. "Harl's Household."

"Y-yes," said Thana in a singularly small voice.

"We can take you there."

"Do you want to?"

"No!" said Link explosively. "No!"

The feeble light in the Household was a guide. Presently they came to the ufft city and the unicorns' night-vision helped them avoid both the burrows and the mounds of dirt dug out from them. They heard querulous, frightened voices around them. Link stopped.

"My friends," he said profoundly, "this is Link Denham, escaped from your oppressors. I go to function as a government in exile and to prepare for the resurgence of the Ufftian race! I will be back with the means to resume the struggle of the uffts to attain that recognition, that status, that independence of humanity which is their justified aspiration!"

There were cheers, but they were only half-hearted.

"Meanwhile," boomed Link, "follow us. In the ship there are gifts and treasures. You might call them the treasury of the Ufftian Republic. We will distribute them. You may use them in bargains with men! Follow us!"

To Thistlethwaite he said cheerfully,

"I'll pay for the cargo."

Thistlethwaite said bitterly,

"If I can't get it away, I don't want Old Man Addison to have it!"

They went across the city. They were accompanied, escorted, surrounded by a swarm of uffts. They went beyond the city to the ship. Thistlethwaite, swearing corrosively, produced the oxygen torch.

There came squealings from the distance. Men on unicorns were headed for the ship. They would be, of course, pursuers of Link and Thistlethwaite, who hadn't spent any time in a diversion like a trip to the Ufftian National Capital. Link reassumed command. He ordered the uffts to bite the heels of the riding-unicorns, to try to disperse and in any case to delay their pursuers. With a fine, brisk competence he took the oxygen torch and cleared the lifeboat blister so it could be entered and the lifeboat used. He heaved the saddlebags into the boat. He began to open the cargo compartments for the uffts. They swarmed into the ship. As a compartment door came open, they rushed in. They would be rich. They could make beautifully insulting bargains with the humans of Sord Three. They could—

There was faint, faint gray light to the east. Link cut his way into the control room to get the *Galactic Directory*. He came back.

"Where's Thana? Where's Thana?" He grew alarmed. She appeared, scared but smiling.

"I . . . wanted to be sure you'd . . . miss me."

He bundled her into the spaceboat with the directory. He shoved Thistlethwaite in after her. He opened the outer doors of the lifeboat blister and shouted to the swarming uffts below.

"I shall return! I shall return!"

There was a knot of riding-animals coming from the west. Uffts scurried and raced about them. The men on the unicorns advanced only very slowly in consequence.

Link leaped into the spaceboat. He pressed appropriate buttons and moved appropriate levers. The lifeboat seemed to topple outward. Its rockets roared furiously; it surged ahead.

It was a near thing. Lifeboats are designed to be launched in space. But the nose of this one swung skyward, and its rockets thrust steadily and violently upward, and presently their roaring changed in that subtle fashion indicating pure emptiness outside the spaceboat. Then it leaped toward the star-filled firmament.

Days later Thistlethwaite worked zestfully, with a portentous scowling, upon a new contract he proposed to Link. It was to form a new organization, the Sord Three Development Corporation. Link was to provide the entire working capital. Thistlethwaite was to have the final say in all business decisions. The details of the operation had been thrashed out in conversation, and Thistlethwaite was putting them into business phraseology, with at least one booby-trap in each two paragraphs of the contract. Link would purchase and lead up a first-class modern spaceship. He would carry back to Sord Three samples of all needed alloying materials. He would establish a duplier by the seashore to remove from flowing sea water—as raw material—the rare minerals needed to duply the large inventory of new, currently undupliable objects and instruments needed on Sord. Link, privately, had designed beer making equipment intended to be run by uffts. There would be enormous dislocations of the present economy when uffts didn't need to trade with humans for beer. Humans would start to grow vegetation. They would, in fact, start to grow crops. Their dupliers would be more valuable extracting alloying metals than duplying roots, barks, herbs, berries, blossoms and flowers.

There would be hell to pay on Sord Three when Link went back. It would provide novel experiences. Exciting ones. From time to time there would doubtless be tumult. But if no other ship landed on Sord Three for just a very few years, when another ship landed there'd be no disaster. There'd be no dupliers in action. Nobody would recognize the galaxy-wide disaster that could be brought about if certain mineral-extracting devices, working on sea water, were put to other uses. Everything would be swell!

Link pointed out a small crescent against the stars to be seen from the lifeboat's ports.

"We're going to land there?" asked Thana.

Link nodded. Thana said in a low tone,

"Link, are you going to sign that contract he's drawing up?"

"Of course not!" said Link. "But it makes him happy

to write it. Actually, he'll like the deal I'll give him better than the trick one he's contriving."

Thana said uneasily,

"When we land—"

"I'll go to see a jeweler," said Link mildly. "I'll sell him a few carynths, a quart or so. I'll start things working for our return trip. And then— Do you mind a quiet wedding?"

"N-not at all."

He nodded. They held hands as the lifeboat headed for the planet before them. There were seas, and continents, and ice-caps. There were cities. Four saddlebags full of carynths would hardly all be sold on one planet without breaking the price, but a discreet distribution by spaceship to responsible jewelers in other worlds . . .

"We can start back," Link promised, "in a month or so."

And they did. But they were delayed a few days, at that. Link had arranged for something special and they had to wait for Thana's second carynth necklace to be finished. It was said that she was the only woman in the galaxy who owned more than one.

THE FOURTH-DIMENSIONAL DEMONSTRATOR

Pete Davidson was engaged to Miss Daisy Manners of the Green Paradise floor show. He had just inherited all the properties of an uncle who had been an authority on the fourth dimension, and he was the custodian of an unusually amiable kangaroo named Arthur. But still he was not happy; it showed this morning.

Inside his uncle's laboratory, Pete scribbled on paper. He added, and ran his hands through his hair in desperation. Then he subtracted, divided and multiplied. But the results were invariably problems as incapable of solution as his deceased relative's fourth-dimensional equations. From time to time a long, horselike, hopeful face peered in at him. That was Thomas, his uncle's servant, whom Pete was afraid he had also inherited.

"Beg pardon, sir," said Thomas tentatively.

Pete leaned harassedly back in his chair.

"What is it, Thomas? What has Arthur been doing now?"

"He is browsing in the dahlias, sir. I wished to ask about lunch, sir. What shall I prepare?"

"Anything!" said Pete. "Anything at all! No. On second thought, trying to untangle Uncle Robert's affairs calls for brains. Give me something rich in phosphorus and vitamins; I need them."

"Yes, sir," said Thomas. "But the grocer, sir—"

"Again?" demanded Pete hopelessly.

"Yes, sir," said Thomas, coming into the laboratory. "I hoped, sir, that matters might be looking better."

Pete shook his head, regarding his calculations depressedly. "They aren't. Cash to pay the grocer's bill is still a dim and misty hope. It is horrible, Thomas! I remembered my uncle as simply reeking with cash, and I thought the fourth dimension was mathematics, not debauchery. But Uncle Robert must have had positive orgies with quanta and space-time continua! I shan't break even on the heir business, let alone make a profit!"

Thomas made a noise suggesting sympathy.

"I could stand it for myself alone," said Pete gloomily. "Even Arthur, in his simple, kangaroo's heart, bears up well. But Daisy! There's the rub! Daisy!"

"Daisy, sir?"

"My fiancée," said Pete. "She's in the Green Paradise floor show. She is technically Arthur's owner. I told Daisy, Thomas, that I had inherited a fortune. And she's going to be disappointed."

"Too bad, sir," said Thomas.

"That statement is one of humorous underemphasis, Thomas. Daisy is not a person to take disappointments lightly. When I explain that my uncle's fortune has flown off into the fourth dimension, Daisy is going to look absent-minded and stop listening. Did you ever try to make love to a girl who looked absent-minded?"

"No, sir," said Thomas. "But about lunch, sir—"

"We'll have to pay for it. Damn!" Pete said morbidly. "I've just forty cents in my clothes, Thomas, and Arthur at least mustn't be allowed to starve. Daisy wouldn't like it. Let's see!"

He moved away from the desk and surveyed the laboratory with a predatory air. It was not exactly a homey place. There was a skeletonlike thing of iron rods, some four feet high. Thomas had said it was a tesseract—a model of a cube existing in four dimensions instead of three.

To Pete, it looked rather like a medieval instrument of torture—something to be used in theological argument with a heretic. Pete could not imagine anybody but his uncle wanting it. There were other pieces of apparatus of all sizes, but largely dismantled. They looked like the product of someone putting vast amounts of money and patience into an effort to do something which would be unsatisfactory when accomplished.

"There's nothing here to pawn," said Pete depressedly. "Not even anything I could use for a hand organ, with Arthur substituting for the monkey!"

"There's the demonstrator, sir," said Thomas hopefully. "Your uncle finished it, sir, and it worked, and he had a stroke, sir."

"Cheerful!" said Pete. "What is this demonstrator? What's it supposed to do?"

"Why, sir, it demonstrates the fourth dimension," said Thomas. "It's your uncle's life work, sir."

"Then let's take a look at it," said Pete. "Maybe we can support ourselves demonstrating the fourth dimension in shop windows for advertising purposes. But I don't think Daisy will care for the career."

Thomas marched solemnly to a curtain just behind the desk. Pete had thought it hid a cupboard. He slid the cover back and displayed a huge contrivance which seemed to have the solitary virtue of completion. Pete could see a monstrous brass horseshoe all of seven feet high. It was apparently hollow and full of cryptic cogs and wheels. Beneath it there was a circular plate of inch-thick glass which seemed to be designed to revolve. Below that, in turn, there was a massive base to which ran certain copper tubes from a refrigerating unit out of an ice box.

Thomas turned on a switch and the unit began to purr. Pete watched.

"Your uncle talked to himself quite a bit about this, sir," said Thomas. "I gathered that it's quite a scientific triumph, sir. You see, sir, the fourth dimension is time."

"I'm glad to hear it explained so simply," said Pete.

"Yes, sir. As I understand it, sir, if one were motoring and saw a pretty girl about to step on a banana peel, sir, and if one wished to tip her off, so to speak, but didn't quite realize for—say, two minutes, until one had gone on half a mile—"

"The pretty girl would have stepped on the banana

peel and nature would have taken its course," said Pete.

"Except for this demonstrator, sir. You see, to tip off the young lady one would have to retrace the half mile and the time too, sir, or one would be too late. That is, one would have to go back not only the half mile but the two minutes. And so your uncle, sir, built this demonstrator—"

"So he could cope with such a situation when it arose," finished Pete. "I see! But I'm afraid it won't settle our financial troubles."

The refrigeration unit ceased to purr. Thomas solemnly struck a safety match.

"If I may finish the demonstration, sir," he said hopefully. "I blow out this match, and put it on the glass plate between the ends of the horseshoe. The temperature's right, so it should work."

There were self-satisfied clucking sounds from the base of the machine. They went on for seconds. The huge glass plate suddenly revolved perhaps the eighth of a revolution. A humming noise began. It stopped. Suddenly there was another burnt safety match on the glass plate. The machine began to cluck triumphantly.

"You see, sir?" said Thomas. "It's produced another burnt match. Dragged it forward out of the past, sir. There was a burnt match at that spot, until the glass plate moved a few seconds ago. Like the girl and the banana peel, sir. The machine went back to the place where the match had been, and then it went back in time to where the match was, and then it brought it forward."

The plate turned another eighth of a revolution.

The machine clucked and hummed. The humming stopped. There was a third burnt match on the glass plate. The clucking clatter began once more.

"It will keep that up indefinitely, sir," said Thomas hopefully.

"I begin," said Pete, "to see the true greatness of modern science. With only two tons of brass and steel, and at a cost of only a couple of hundred thousand dollars and a lifetime of effort, my Uncle Robert has left me a machine which will keep me supplied with burnt matches for years to come! Thomas, this machine is a scientific triumph!"

Thomas beamed.

"Splendid, sir! I'm glad you approve. And what shall I do about lunch, sir?"

The machine, having clucked and hummed appropriately, now produced a fourth burnt match and clucked more triumphantly still. It prepared to reach again into the hitherto unreachable past.

Pete looked reproachfully at the servant he had apparently inherited. He reached in his pocket and drew out his forty cents. Then the machine hummed. Pete jerked his head and stared at it.

"Speaking of science, now," he said an instant later. "I have a very commercial thought. I blush to contemplate it." He looked at the monstrous, clucking demonstrator of the fourth dimension. "Clear out of here for ten minutes, Thomas. I'm going to be busy!"

Thomas vanished. Pete turned off the demonstrator. He risked a nickel, placing it firmly on the inch-thick glass plate. The machine went on again. It clucked, hummed, ceased to hum—and there were two nickels.

Pete added a dime to the second nickel. At the end of another cycle he ran his hand rather desperately through his hair and added his entire remaining wealth—a quarter. Then, after incredulously watching what happened, he began to pyramid.

Thomas tapped decorously some ten minutes later.

"Beg pardon, sir," he said hopefully. "About lunch, sir—"

Pete turned off the demonstrator. He gulped.

"Thomas," he said in careful calm, "I shall let you write the menu for lunch. Take a basketful of this small change and go shopping. And—Thomas, have you any item of currency larger than a quarter? A fifty-cent piece would be about right. I'd like to have something really impressive to show to Daisy when she comes."

Miss Daisy Manners of the Green Paradise floor show was just the person to accept the fourth-dimensional demonstrator without question and to make full use of the results of modern scientific research. She greeted Pete abstractedly and interestedly asked just how much he'd inherited. And Pete took her to the laboratory. He unveiled the demonstrator.

"These are my jewels," said Pete impressively. "Darling, it's going to be a shock, but—have you got a quarter?"

"You've got nerve, asking me for money," said Daisy. "And if you lied about inheriting some money—"

Pete smiled tenderly upon her. He produced a quarter of his own.

"Watch, my dear! I'm doing this for you!"

He turned on the demonstrator and explained

complacently as the first cluckings came from the base. The glass plate moved, a second quarter appeared, and Pete pyramided the two while he continued to explain. In the fraction of a minute, there were four quarters. Again Pete pyramided. There were eight quarters—sixteen, thirty-two, sixty-four, one hundred twenty-eight— At this point the stack collapsed and Pete shut off the switch.

"You see, my dear? Out of the fourth dimension to you! Uncle invested it, I inherited it, and—shall I change your money for you?"

Daisy did not look at all absent-minded now. Pete gave her a neat little sheaf of bank notes.

"And from now on, darling," he said cheerfully, "whenever you want money just come in here, start the machine—and there you are! Isn't that nice?"

"I want some more money now," said Daisy. "I have to buy a trousseau."

"I hoped you'd feel that way!" said Pete enthusiastically. "Here goes! And we have a reunion while the pennies roll in."

The demonstrator began to cluck and clatter with bills instead of quarters on the plate. Once, to be sure, it suspended all operations and the refrigeration unit purred busily for a time. Then it resumed its self-satisfied delving into the immediate past.

"I haven't been making any definite plans," explained Pete, "until I talked to you. Just getting things in line. But I've looked after Arthur carefully. You know how he loves cigarettes. He eats them, and though it may be eccentric in a kangaroo, they seem to agree with him. I've used the demonstrator to lay up a huge supply of cigarettes for him—his favorite brand, too.

And I've been trying to build up a bank account. I thought it would seem strange if we bought a house on Park Avenue and just casually offered a trunkful of bank notes in payment. It might look as if we'd been running a snatch racket."

"Stupid!" said Daisy.

"What ?"

"You could be pyramiding those bills like you did the quarters," said Daisy. "Then there'd be lots more of them!"

"Darling," said Pete fondly, "does it matter how much you have when I have so much?"

"Yes," said Daisy. "You might get angry with me."

"Never!" protested Pete. Then he added reminiscently, "Before we thought of the bank note idea, Thomas and I filled up the coal bin with quarters and half dollars. They're still there."

"Gold pieces would be nice," suggested Daisy, thinking hard, "if you could get hold of some. Maybe we could."

"Ah!" said Pete. "But Thomas had a gold filling in one tooth. We took it out and ran it up to half a pound or so. Then we melted that into a little brick and put it on the demonstrator. Darling, you'd really be surprised if you looked in the woodshed."

"And there's jewelry," said Daisy. "It would be faster still!"

"If you feel in the mood for jewelry," said Pete tenderly, "just look in the vegetable bin. We'd about run out of storage space when the idea occurred to us."

"I think," said Daisy enthusiastically, "we'd better get married right away. Don't you?"

"Sure! Let's go and do it now! I'll get the car around!"

"Do, darling," said Daisy. "I'll watch the demonstrator."

Beaming, Pete kissed her ecstatically and rushed from the laboratory. He rang for Thomas, and rang again. It was not until the third ring that Thomas appeared. And Thomas was very pale. He said agitatedly:

"Beg pardon, sir, but shall I pack your bag?"

"I'm going to be— Pack my bag? What for?"

"We're going to be arrested, sir," said Thomas. He gulped. "I thought you might want it, sir. An acquaintance in the village, sir, believes we are among the lower-numbered public enemies, sir, and respects us accordingly. He telephoned me the news."

"Thomas, have you been drinking?"

"No, sir," said Thomas pallidly. "Not yet, sir. But it is a splendid suggestion, thank you, sir." Then he said desperately: "It's the money, sir—the bank notes. If you recall, we never changed but one lot of silver into notes, sir. We got a one, a five, a ten and so on, sir."

"Of course," said Pete. "That was all we needed. Why not?"

"It's the serial number, sir! All the one-dollar bills the demonstrator turned out have the same serial number—and all the fives and tens and the rest, sir. Some person with a hobby for looking for kidnap bills, sir, found he had several with the same number. The Secret Service has traced them back. They're coming for us, sir. The penalty for counterfeiting is twenty years, sir. My—my friend in the village asked if we intended to shoot it out with them, sir, because if so he'd like to watch."

Thomas wrung his hands. Pete stared at him.

"Come to think of it," he said meditatively, "they are counterfeits. It hadn't occurred to me before. We'll have to plead guilty, Thomas. And perhaps Daisy won't want to marry me if I'm going to prison. I'll go tell her the news."

Then he stared. He heard Daisy's voice, speaking very angrily. An instant later the sound grew louder. It became a continuous, shrill, soprano babble. It grew louder yet. Pete ran.

He burst into the laboratory and was stunned. The demonstrator was still running. Daisy had seen Pete piling up the bills as they were turned out, pyramiding to make the next pile larger. She had evidently essayed the same feat. But the pile was a bit unwieldy, now, and Daisy had climbed on the glass plate. She had come into the scope of the demonstrator's action.

There were three of her in the laboratory when Pete first entered. As he froze in horror, the three became four. The demonstrator clucked and hummed what was almost a hoot of triumph. Then it produced a fifth Daisy. Pete dashed frantically forward and turned off the switch just too late to prevent the appearance of a sixth copy of Miss Daisy Manners of the Green Paradise floor show. She made a splendid sister act, but Pete gazed in paralyzed horror at this plethora of his heart's desire.

Because all of Daisy was identical, with not only the same exterior and—so to speak—the same serial number, but with the same opinions and convictions.

And all six of Daisy were convinced that they, individually, owned the heap of bank notes now on the glass plate. All six of her were trying to get it. And Daisy was quarreling furiously with herself. She was telling herself what she thought of herself, in fact, and on the whole her opinion was not flattering.

Arthur, like Daisy, possessed a fortunate disposition. He was not one of those kangaroos who go around looking for things to be upset about. He browsed peacefully upon the lawn, eating up the dahlias and now and again hopping over the six-foot hedge in hopes that there might be a dog come along the lane to bark at him. Or, failing to see a dog, that somebody might have come by who would drop a cigarette butt that he might salvage.

At his first coming to this place, both pleasing events had been frequent. The average unwarned passer-by, on seeing a five-foot kangaroo soaring toward him in this part of the world, did have a tendency to throw down everything and run. Sometimes, among the things he threw down was a cigarette.

There had been a good supply of dogs, too, but they didn't seem to care to play with Arthur any more. Arthur's idea of playfulness with a strange dog—especially one that barked at him—was to grab him with both front paws and then kick the living daylights out of him.

Arthur browsed, and was somewhat bored. Because of his boredom he was likely to take a hand in almost anything that turned up. There was a riot going on in the laboratory, but Arthur did not care for family quarrels. He was interested, however, in the government officers when they arrived. There were two of them and they came in a roadster. They stopped at the gate and marched truculently up to the front door.

Arthur came hopping around from the back just as they knocked thunderously. He'd been back there digging up a few incipient cabbages of Thomas' planting, to see why they didn't grow faster. He soared at least an easy thirty feet, and propped himself on his tail to look interestedly at the visitors.

"G-good God!" said the short, squat officer. He had been smoking a cigarette. He threw it down and grabbed his gun.

That was his mistake. Arthur liked cigarettes. This one was a mere fifteen feet from him. He soared toward it.

The government man squawked, seeing Arthur in mid-air and heading straight for him. Arthur looked rather alarming, just then. The officer fired recklessly, missing Arthur. And Arthur remained calm. To him, the shots were not threats. They were merely the noises made by an automobile whose carburetor needed adjustment. He landed blandly, almost on the officer's toes—and the officer attacked him hysterically with fist and clubbed gun.

Arthur was an amiable kangaroo, but he resented the attack, actively.

The short, squat officer squawked again as Arthur grabbed him with his forepaws. His companion backed against the door, prepared to sell his life dearly. But then—and the two things happened at once—while Arthur proceeded to kick the living daylights out of the short, squat officer, Thomas resignedly opened the door behind the other and he fell backward suddenly and knocked himself cold against the doorstep.

Some fifteen minutes later the short, squat officer said gloomily: "It was a bum steer. Thanks for pulling that critter off me, and Casey's much obliged for the drinks. But we're hunting a bunch of counterfeiters that have been turning out damn good phony bills. The line led straight to you. You could have shot us. You didn't. So we got to do the work all over."

"I'm afraid," admitted Pete, "the trail would lead right back. Perhaps, as government officials, you can do something about the fourth-dimensional demonstrator. That's the guilty party. I'll show you."

He led the way to the laboratory. Arthur appeared, looking vengeful. The two officers looked apprehensive.

"Better give him a cigarette," said Pete. "He eats them. Then he'll be your friend for life."

"Hell, no!" said the short, squat man. "You keep between him and me! Maybe Casey'll want to get friendly."

"No cigarettes," said Casey apprehensively. "Would a cigar do?"

"Rather heavy, for so early in the morning," considered Pete, "but you might try."

Arthur soared. He landed within two feet of Casey. Casey thrust a cigar at him. Arthur sniffed at it and accepted it. He put one end in his mouth and bit off the tip.

"There!" said Pete cheerfully. "He likes it. Come on!"

They moved on to the laboratory. They entered—and tumult engulfed them. The demonstrator was running and Thomas—pale and despairing—supervised its action. The demonstrator was turning out currency by what was, approximately, wheelbarrow loads. As each load materialized from the fourth dimension, Thomas gathered it up and handed it to Daisy, who in theory was standing in line to receive it in equitable division. But Daisy was having a furious quarrel among herself, because some one or other of her had tried to cheat.

"These," said Pete calmly, "are my fiancée."

But the short, squat man saw loads of greenbacks appearing from nowhere. He drew out a short, squat revolver.

"You got a press turning out the stuff behind that wall, huh?" he said shrewdly. "I'll take a look!"

He thrust forward masterfully. He pushed Thomas aside and mounted the inch-thick glass plate. Pete reached, horrified, for the switch. But it was too late. The glass plate revolved one-eighth of a revolution. The demonstrator hummed gleefully; and the officer appeared in duplicate just as Pete's nerveless fingers cut off everything.

Both of the officers looked at each other in flat, incredulous stupefaction. Casey stared, and the hair rose from his head. Then Arthur put a front paw tentatively upon Casey's shoulder. Arthur had liked the cigar. The door to the laboratory had been left open. He had come in to ask for another cigar. But Casey was hopelessly unnerved. He yelled and fled, imagining Arthur in hot pursuit. He crashed into the model of a tesseract and entangled himself hopelessly.

Arthur was an amiable kangaroo, but he was sensitive. Casey's squeal of horror upset him. He leaped blindly, knocking Pete over on the switch and turning it on, and landing between the two stupefied copies of the other officer. They, sharing memories of Arthur, moved in panic just before the glass plate turned.

Arthur bounced down again at the demonstrator's hoot. The nearest copy of the short, squat man made a long, graceful leap and went flying out of the door. Pete struggled with the other, who waved his gun and demanded explanations, growing hoarse from his earnestness.

Pete attempted to explain in terms of pretty girls stepping on banana peels, but it struck the officer as irrelevant. He shouted hoarsely while another Arthur hopped down from the glass plate—while a third, and fourth, and fifth, and sixth, and seventh Arthur appeared on the scene.

He barked at Pete until screams from practically all of Daisy made him turn to see the laboratory overflowing with five-foot Arthurs, all very pleasantly astonished and anxious to make friends with himself so he could play.

Arthur was the only person who really approved the course events had taken. He had existed largely in his own society. But now his own company was numerous. From a solitary kangaroo, in fact, Arthur had become a good-sized herd. And in his happy excitement over the fact, Arthur forgot all decorum and began to play an hysterical form of disorganized leapfrog all about the laboratory.

The officer went down and became a take-off spot for the game. Daisy shrieked furiously. And Arthur—all of him—chose new points of vantage for his leaps until one of him chose the driving motor of the demonstrator. That industrious mechanism emitted bright sparks and bit him. And Arthur soared in terror through the window, followed by all the rest of himself, who still thought it part of the game.

In seconds, the laboratory was empty of Arthurs. But the demonstrator was making weird, pained noises. Casey remained entangled in the bars of the tesseract, through which he gazed with much the expression of an inmate of a padded cell. Only one of the short, squat officers remained in the building. He had no breath left. And Daisy was too angry to make a sound—all six of her. Pete alone was sanely calm.

"Well," he said philosophically, "things seem to have settled down a bit. But something's happened to the demonstrator."

"I'm sorry, sir," said Thomas pallidly, "I'm no hand at machinery."

One of Daisy said angrily to another of Daisy: "You've got a nerve! That money on the plate is mine!"

Both advanced. Three more, protesting indignantly, joined in the rush. The sixth—and it seemed to Pete that she must have been the original Daisy—hastily began to sneak what she could from the several piles accumulated by the others.

Meanwhile, the demonstrator made queer noises. And Pete despairingly investigated. He found where Arthur's leap had disarranged a handle which evidently controlled the motor speed of the demonstrator. At random, he pushed the handle. The demonstrator clucked relievedly. Then Pete realized in sick terror that five of Daisy were on the glass plate. He tried to turn it off—but it was too late.

He closed his eyes, struggling to retain calmness, but admitting despair. He had been extremely fond of one Daisy. But six Daisies had been too much. Now, looking forward to eleven and—

A harsh voice grated in his ear.

"Huh! That's where you keep the press and the queer, huh—and trick mirrors so I see double? I'm going through that trapdoor where those girls went! And if there's any funny business on the other side, somebody gets hurt!"

The extra officer stepped up on the glass plate, inexplicably empty now. The demonstrator clucked. It hummed. The plate moved—backward! The officer vanished—at once, utterly. As he had come out of the past, he returned to it, intrepidly and equally by accident. Because one of Arthur had kicked the drive lever into neutral, and Pete had inadvertently shoved it into reverse. He saw the officer vanish and he knew where the supernumerary Daisies had gone—also where all embarrassing bank notes would go. He sighed in relief.

But Casey—untangled from the tesseract—was not relieved. He tore loose from Thomas' helpful fingers and fled to the car. There he found his companion, staring at nineteen Arthurs playing leapfrog over the garage. After explanations the government men would be more upset still. Pete saw the roadster drive away, wobbling.

"I don't think they'll come back, sir," said Thomas hopefully.

"Neither do I," said Pete in a fine, high calm. He turned to the remaining Daisy, scared but still acquisitive. "Darling," he said tenderly, "all those bank notes are counterfeit, as it develops. We'll have to put them all back and struggle along with the contents of the woodshed and the vegetable bin."

Daisy tried to look absent-minded, and failed.

"I think you've got nerve!" said Daisy indignantly.

THE PIRATES OF ZAN

Chapter 1

It had not been impulsive action when Bron Hoddan had started for the planet Walden by stowing away on a police ship that had come to his native planet to hang all his relatives. He'd planned it long before. Getting to Walden had been his long-cherished dream. As it had turned out, his relatives had not been hanged. This they had avoided with their usual technique of acting aggrieved and innocent. They had given proof that they were simple people leading blameless lives. They had made their would-be executioners feel ashamed and apologetic. And, as soon as the strangers had left, Bron knew that these "simple, blameless" folk had returned to their normal way of life, which was piracy.

Bron's stow-away ride had only taken him partway to Walden. It had taken him a long time to earn the rest of his passage, since he had to travel from one solar system to another. But he had held to his idea. Walden was the most civilized planet in that part of the galaxy. On Walden Bron had intended, (a) to achieve splendid things as an electronic engineer, (b) to grow satisfyingly rich, (c) to marry a delightful girl, and (d) to end his life with the reputation of being a great man.

He had spent his first two years on Walden trying to achieve the first of his objectives.

And it was only the night before the police broke into his room, that the accomplishment of his first objective seemed imminent.

He had gone to bed and slept soundly. He was calmly sure that his ambitions were about to be realized. At practically any instant his brilliance would be discovered and he'd be well-to-do; his friend Derec would admire him, and even Nedda would probably decide to marry him right away.

Bron was happy to be on Walden; it was a fine world. Outside the capital city was the spaceport that received shipments of luxuries and raw materials from halfway across the galaxy. Its landing-grid reared skyward and tapped the planet's ionosphere for power with which to hoist ships to clear-space and pluck down others from emptiness. There was commerce and manufacturing, wealth and culture, and Walden modestly admitted that its standard of living was the highest in the Nurmi cluster. Its citizens had no reason to worry about anything but a supply of tranquilizers to enable them to stand the boredom of their lives.

Even Hoddan was satisfied, as of the moment. On his native planet there wasn't even a landing-grid. The few battered ships the inhabitants owned had to take off precariously on rockets. They came back blackened and more battered and sometimes they were accompanied by great hulls whose crews and passengers were mysteriously missing. These extra ships had to be landed on their emergency rockets, and of course couldn't take off again, but they always vanished quickly just the same. And the people of Zan, on which Hoddan had been born, always affected innocent indignation when embattled spacecraft came and furiously demanded that they be produced.

There were some people who said that all the inhabitants of Zan were space-pirates and ought to be hanged; compared with such a planet, Walden seemed a very fine place indeed. So on a certain night Bron Hoddan went confidently to bed and slept soundly until three hours after sunrise. Then the police broke in his door.

They made a tremendous crash in doing it, but they were in great haste. The noise waked Hoddan, and he blinked his eyes open. Before he could stir, four uniformed men grabbed him and dragged him out of bed. They searched him frantically for anything like a weapon. Then they stood him against a wall with two stun-pistols on him, and the main body of cops began to tear his room apart. He could not guess what they were looking for. Then his friend Derec came hesitantly to the door and looked at him remorsefully. He wrung his hands.

"I had to do it, Bron," he said agitatedly. "I couldn't help doing it!"

"What's happened?" asked Hoddan blankly. "What's this about?"

Derec said miserably:

"You killed someone, Bron. An innocent man! You didn't mean to, but you did . . . it's terrible!"

"*Me,* kill somebody! That's ridiculous!" protested Hoddan.

"They found him outside the power-house," said Derec bitterly. "Outside the Mid-Continent station that you—"

"Mid-Continent? Oh!" Hoddan was relieved. It was amazing how much he was relieved. He'd had a terrible fear for a moment that somebody might have found out he'd been born and raised on Zan. This would have ruined everything. It was almost impossible to imagine, but still it was a great relief to find out he was only suspected of a murder he hadn't committed. And he was only suspected because his first great achievement as an electronic engineer had been discovered. "They found the thing at Mid-Continent, eh? But I didn't kill anybody. And there's no harm done. The thing's been running two weeks, now. I was going to the Power Board in a couple of days." He addressed the police. "I know what's up, now," he said. "Give me some clothes and let's go get this straightened out."

A cop waved a stun-pistol at him.

"One word out of line, and it's pfft!"

"Don't talk, Bron!" said Derec in panic. "Just keep quiet! It's bad enough! Don't make it worse."

A cop handed Hoddan a garment. He put it on. He became aware that the cop was scared. So was Derec. Everybody in the room was scared except himself. Hoddan found himself incredulous. People didn't act this way on super-civilized, highest-peak-of-culture Walden.

"Who'd I kill?" he demanded. "And why?"

"You wouldn't know him, Bron," said Derec mournfully. "You didn't mean to do murder. But it's only luck that you killed only him instead of everybody."

"*Everybody!*" Hoddan stared.

"No more talk!" snapped the nearest cop. His teeth were chattering. "Keep quiet or else!"

Hoddan shut up. His clothing was inspected and then handed to him. He dressed while the cops completed the examination of his room. They were insanely thorough, though Hoddan hadn't the least idea what they might be looking for. When they began to rip up the floor and pull down the walls, the other cops led him outside.

There was a fleet of police trucks in the shaded street. They piled him in one, and four cops climbed after him, keeping stun-pistols trained on him during the maneuver. Out of the corner of his eye he saw Derec climbing into another truck. The entire fleet sped away. The whole affair had been taken with enormous seriousness by the police. Traffic was detoured from their route. When they swung up on an elevated expressway, there was no other vehicle in sight. They raced on downtown.

They rolled off the expressway, then down a cleared avenue. Hoddan recognized the Detention Building. Its gate swung wide. The truck he rode in went inside. The gate closed. The other trucks went away, rapidly. Hoddan alighted and saw that the grim, gray wall of the courtyard had a surprising number of guards mustered to sweep the open space with gunfire if anybody made a suspicious movement.

He shook his head. Nobody had mentioned Zan, so this simply didn't make sense. His conscience was wholly clear except about his native planet. This was insanity! He went curiously into the building and into the hearing-room. His guards surrendered him to courtroom guards and went away with almost hysterical haste. Nobody wanted to be near him.

Hoddan stared about. The courtroom was highly informal. The justice sat at an ordinary desk. There were comfortable chairs. The air was clean. The atmosphere was that of a conference room in which reasonable men could discuss differences of opinion in calm leisure. Only on a world like Walden would a police prisoner be dealt with in such surroundings.

Derec came in by another door, with him a man Hoddan recognized as the attorney who'd represented Nedda's father in certain past interviews. There'd been no mention of Nedda at these meetings; it had been strictly business. Nedda's father was chairman of the Power Board, a director of the Planetary Association of Manufacturers, a committeeman of the Bankers' League, and he held other important posts. Hoddan had been thrown out of his offices several times. He now scowled ungraciously at the lawyer who had ordered him thrown out. He saw Derec wringing his hands.

An agitated man in court uniform came to this side.

"I'm the citizen's representative," he said uneasily. "I'm to look after your interests. Do you want a personal lawyer?"

"Why?" asked Hoddan. He felt splendidly confident.

"The charges . . . Do you wish a psychiatric examination, claiming no responsibility?" asked the representative anxiously. "It might—it might really be best."

"I'm not crazy," said Hoddan.

The citizen's representative spoke to the justice.

"Sir, the accused waives psychiatric examination, without prejudice to a later claim of no responsibility."

Nedda's father's attorney watched with bland eyes. Hoddan said impatiently:

"Let's get started so this will make some sense! I know what I've done. Now, what monstrous crime am I charged with?"

"The charges against you," said the justice politely, "are that on the night of three, twenty-seven last, you, Bron Hoddan, entered the fenced-in grounds surrounding the Mid-Continent power receptor station. It is charged that you passed two no-admittance signs. You arrived at a door marked 'Authorized Personnel Only.' You broke the lock of that door. Inside, you smashed the power receptor. This power receptor converts broadcast power for industrial units by which two hundred thousand men are employed. You smashed the receptor, imperiling their employment." The justice paused. "Do you wish to challenge any of these charges as contrary to fact?"

The citizen's representative said hurriedly:

"You have the right to deny any of them, of course."

"Why should I?" asked Hoddan. "I did them! But what's this about my killing somebody? Why'd they tear my place apart looking for something? Who'd I kill, anyhow?"

"Don't bring that up!" pleaded the citizen's representative. "Please don't bring that up! You will be much, much better off if that is not mentioned!"

"But I didn't kill anybody!" insisted Hoddan.

"Nobody's said a word about it," said the citizen's representative, jittering. "Let's not have it in the record! The record has to be published!" He turned to the justice. "Sir, the facts are conceded as stated."

"Then," said the justice to Hoddan, "do you choose to answer these charges at this time?"

"Why not?" asked Hoddan. "Of course!"

"Proceed," said the justice.

Hoddan drew a deep breath. He didn't understand why the man's death, charged to him, was not mentioned. He didn't like the scared way everybody looked at him.

"About the burglary business," he said confidently. "What did I do in the power station before I smashed the receptor?" The justice looked at Nedda's father's attorney.

"Why," said that gentleman amiably, "speaking for the Power Board as complainant, before you smashed the standard receptor you connected a device of your own design across the power leads. It was a receptor unit of an apparently original pattern. It appears to have been a very interesting device."

"I'd offered it to the Power Board," said Hoddan, with satisfaction, "and I was thrown out. You had me thrown out! What did it do?"

"It substituted for the receptor you smashed," said the attorney. "It continued to supply some two hundred million kilowatts for the Mid-Continent industrial area. In fact, your crime was only discovered because the original receptor had to be regularly serviced. Being set to draw peak power at all times, the unused power is wasted by burning carbon. So when the attendants went to replace the supposedly burned carbon and found it unused, they discovered what you had done."

"My receptor saved carbon, then," said Hoddan triumphantly. "That means it saved money. I saved the Power Board plenty while it was connected! They wouldn't believe I could. Now they know. I did!"

The justice said:

"Irrelevant. You have the charges. In legal terms, you are charged with burglary, trespassing, breaking and entering, unlawful entry, malicious mischief, breach of the peace, sabotage, and endangering the employment of citizens. Discuss the charges, please!"

"I'm telling you!" protested Hoddan. "I offered the thing to the Power Board. They said they were satisfied with what they had and wouldn't listen. So I proved what they wouldn't listen to! That receptor saved them ten thousand credits' worth of carbon a week! It'll save half a million credits a year in every power station that uses it! If I know the Power Board, they're going right on using it while they arrest me for putting it to work!"

The courtroom, in its entirety, visibly shivered.

"Aren't they?" demanded Hoddan belligerently.

"They are not," said the justice, tight-lipped. "It has been smashed and melted down."

"Then they'll look at my patents!" insisted Hoddan. "It's stupid—"

"The patent records," said the justice with unnecessary vehemence, "have been destroyed. Your possessions have been searched for copies. Nobody will ever look at your drawings again—not if they are wise!"

"Wha-a-at?" demanded Hoddan incredulously. "Wha-a-at?"

"I will amend the record of this hearing before it is published," said the justice shakily. "I should not have made that comment. I ask permission of the citizen's representative to amend."

"Granted," said the representative before he had finished. The justice said quickly:

"The charges have been admitted by the defendant. Since the complainant does not wish punitive action taken against him—"

"He'd be silly if he did," grunted Hoddan.

"—and merely wishes security against repetition of the offense, I rule that the defendant may be released upon posting suitable bond for good behavior in the future. That is, he will be required to post bond which will be forfeited if he ever again enters a power station enclosure, passes no-trespassing signs, ignores no-admittance signs, and-or smashes apparatus belonging to the complainant."

"All right," said Hoddan indignantly. "I'll raise it somehow. If they're too stupid to save money . . . How much bond?"

"The court will take it under advisement and will notify the defendant within the customary two hours," said the justice at top speed. He swallowed. "The defendant will be kept in close confinement until the bond is posted. The hearing is ended."

He did not look at Hoddan. Courtroom guards

put stun-pistols against Hoddan's body and ushered him out.

Presently his friend Derec came to see him in the tool-steel cell in which he had been placed. Derec looked white and stricken.

"I'm in trouble because I'm your friend, Bron," he said miserably, "but I asked permission to explain things to you. After all, I caused your arrest. I urged you not to connect up your receptor without permission!"

"I know," growled Hoddan, "but there are some people so stupid you have to show them everything. I didn't realize that there are people so stupid you can't show them *anything!*"

"You showed something you didn't intend," said Derec miserably. "Bron, I—I have to tell you. When they went to charge the carbon bins at the power station, they—they found a dead man, Bron!"

Hoddan sat up.

"What's that?"

"Your machine . . . killed him. He was outside the building at the foot of a tree. Your receptor killed him through a stone wall! It broke his bones and killed him." Derec wrung his hands. "At some stage of power-drain your receptor makes death rays!"

Hoddan had had a good many shocks today. When Derec arrived, he'd been incredulously comparing the treatment he'd received and the panic about him, with the charges made against him in court. They didn't add up. This new, previously undisclosed item left him speechless. He goggled at Derec, who fairly wept.

"Don't you see?" asked Derec pleadingly. "That's why I had to tell the police it was you. We can't have death rays! The police can't let anybody go free who knows how to make them! This is a wonderful world, but there are lots of crackpots. They'll do anything! The police daren't let it even be suspected that death rays can be made! That's why you weren't charged with murder. People all over the planet would start doing research, and sooner or later would come up with what you discovered. With such a tool in the hands of the crackpots, life would be cheap, indeed! For the sake of our civilization your secret has to be suppressed—and you with it. It's terrible for you, Bron, but there's nothing else to do!"

Hoddan said dazedly:

"But I only have to put up a bond to be released!"

"The justice," said Derec tearfully, "didn't name it in court, because it would have to be published. But he's set your bond at fifty million credits. Nobody could raise that for you, Bron! And with the reason for it what it is, you'll never be able to get it reduced!"

"But anybody who looks at the plans of the receptor will know it can't make death rays!" protested Hoddan blankly.

"Nobody will look," said Derec tearfully. "Anybody who knows how to make it will have to be locked up. They checked the patent examiners. They've forgotten. Nobody dared examine the device you had working. They'd be jailed if they understood it! Nobody will ever risk learning how to make death rays—not on a world as civilized as this, with so many people anxious to kill everybody else. You have to be locked up forever, Bron. You have to!"

Hoddan said inadequately:

"Oh."

"I beg your forgiveness for having you arrested," said Derec in abysmal sorrow, "but I couldn't do anything but tell . . ."

Hoddan stared at his cell wall. Derec went away weeping. He was an admirable, honorable, not-too-bright young man who had been Hoddan's only friend.

Hoddan stared blankly at nothing. As an event, it was preposterous, and yet it was wholly natural. When in the course of human events somebody does something that puts somebody else to the trouble of adjusting the numb routine of his life, the adjustee is resentful. The richer he is and the more satisfactory he considers his life, the more resentful he is at any change, however minute. And of all the changes which offend people, changes which require them to think are most disliked. The high brass on the Power Board considered that everything was moving smoothly. There was no need to consider new devices. Hoddan's drawings and plans had simply never been bothered with, because there was no recognized need for them. And when he forced acknowledgment that his receptor worked, the unwelcome demonstration was highly offensive in itself. It was natural, it was inevitable, it should have been infallibly certain that any possible excuse for not thinking about the receptor would be seized upon. And a single dead man found near the operating demonstrator . . . Now, if one assumed that the demonstrator had killed him, why one could react emotionally, feel vast indignation, frantically command that the device and its inventor be suppressed together—and then go on living happily without doing any thinking or making any other change in anything at all.

Hoddan was appalled. Now that it had happened, he could see that it had to. The world of Walden was at the very peak of human culture. It had arrived at so splendid a plane of civilization that nobody could imagine any improvement; unless a better tranquilizer could be designed to make the boredom more endurable. Nobody can want anything he doesn't know exists, or that he can't imagine to exist. On Walden nobody wanted anything, unless it was relief from the tedium of ultra-civilized life. Hoddan's electronic device did not fill a human need, only a technical one. It had, therefore, no value that would make anybody hospitable to it.

And Hoddan would spend his life in jail for failing to recognize this fact soon enough.

He revolted immediately. *He* wanted something! He wanted out. He set about designing his escape. He put his mind to work on the problem, simply and directly. And this time he would not make the mistake of furnishing other people with what they did not want. He took the view that he must *seem*, at least, to give his captors and jailers and—as he saw it—his persecutors, what they wanted.

They would be pleased to have him dead, provided their consciences were clear. He built on that as a foundation.

Very shortly before nightfall he performed certain cryptic actions. He unraveled threads from his shirt and put them aside. There would be a vision-lens in the ceiling of his cell, and somebody would certainly notice what he did. He turned on a light. He put the threads in his mouth, set fire to his mattress, and lay down calmly upon it. The mattress was of excellent quality. It would smell very badly as it smoldered.

It did. Lying flat, he kicked convulsively for a few seconds. He looked like somebody who had taken poison. Then he waited.

It was a long time before his jailer came down the corridor, dragging a fire hose. Hoddan had been correct in assuming that he was watched. His actions had been those of a man who'd anticipated a possible need to commit suicide, and who'd had poison in a part of his shirt for convenience. The jailer did not hurry, because if the inventor of a death ray committed suicide, everybody would feel better. Hoddan had been allowed a reasonable time in which to die.

He seemed impressively dead when the jailer opened his cell door, dragged him out, removed the so-far-unscorched other furniture, and set up the fire hose to make an aerosol fog which would put out the fire. He went back to the corridor to wait for the fire to be extinguished.

Hoddan crowned him with a stool, feeling an unexpected satisfaction in the act. The jailer collapsed.

He did not carry keys. The system was for him to be let out of this corridor by a guard outside. Hoddan took the fire hose. He turned its nozzle back to make a stream instead of a mist. Water came out at four hundred pounds pressure. He smashed open the corridor door with it. He strolled through and bowled over a startled guard with the same stream. He took the guard's stun-pistol. He washed open another door leading to the courtyard. He marched out, washed down two guards who sighted him, and took the trouble to flush them across the pavement until they wedged in a drain opening. Then he thoughtfully reset the hose to fill the courtyard with fog, climbed into the driver's seat of a parked truck, started it, and smashed through the gateway to the street outside. Behind him, the courtyard filled with dense white mist.

He was free, but only temporarily. Around him lay the capital city of Walden—the highest civilization in this part of the galaxy. Trees lined its ways. Towers rose splendidly toward the skies, with thousands of less ambitious structures in between. There were open squares and parkways and malls, and it did not smell like a city at all. But he wasn't loose three minutes before the communicator in the truck squawked the all-police alarm for him.

It was to be expected. All the city would shortly be one enormous man trap, set to catch Bron Hoddan. There was only one place on the planet, in fact, where he could be safe. And ironically, he wouldn't have been safe there if he'd been officially charged with murder. But since the police had tactfully failed to mention murder, he could get at least breathing-time by taking refuge in the Interstellar Embassy.

He headed for it, bowling along splendidly. The police truck hummed on its way until the great open square before the embassy became visible. The embassy was not that of a single planet, of course. By pure necessity every human-inhabited world was independent of all others, but the Interstellar Diplomatic Service represented humanity at large upon each individual globe. Its ambassador was the only person who Hoddan could even imagine as listening to him, and that because he came from off-planet, as Hoddan did. But he mainly counted upon a breathing-space in the embassy, during which to make more plans as yet unformed and unformable. He began, though, to see some virtues in the simple, lawless, piratical world on which he had spent his childhood.

Another police truck rushed frantically toward him down a side street. Stun-pistols made little pinging noises against the body of his vehicle. He put on more speed, but the other truck overtook him. It ranged alongside, its occupants bellowing stern commands to halt. And then, just before they swerved to force him off the highway, he swung instead and they crashed thunderously. One of his own wheels collapsed. He drove on with the crumpled wheel producing an up-and-down motion that threatened to make him seasick. Then he heard yelling behind him. The cops had piled out of the truck and were in pursuit on foot.

The tall, stone wall of the embassy was visible, now, beyond the monument to the first settlers of Walden. He leaped to the ground and ran. Stun-pistol bolts, a little beyond their effective range, stung like fire. They spurred him on.

The gate of the embassy was closed. He bolted around the corner and scrambled up the conveniently rugged stones of the wall. He was well aloft before the cops spotted him. Then they fired at him industriously and the charges crackled all around him.

But he'd reached the top and had both arms over the parapet before a charge hit his legs and paralyzed them. He hung fast, swearing at his bad luck.

Then hands grasped his wrists. A white-haired man appeared on the other side of the parapet. He took a good, solid grip, and heaved. He drew Hoddan over the top of the wall and helped him down to the walkway.

"A near thing, that!" said the white-haired man pleasantly. "I was taking a walk in the garden when I heard the excitement. I got to the wall just in time." He paused, and added, "I do hope you're not just a common murderer, we can't offer asylum to such. But if you're a political offender . . ."

Hoddan began to try to rub sensation and usefulness back into his legs. Feeling came back, and was not pleasant.

"I'm the Interstellar Ambassador," said the white-haired man politely.

"My name," said Hoddan bitterly "is Bron Hoddan and I'm guilty of trying to save the Power Board millions of credits a year." Then he said more bitterly, "If you want to know, I ran away from Zan to try to be a civilized man and live a civilized life. It was a mistake. Now I'm to be permanently jailed for using my brains!"

The ambassador cocked his head thoughtfully to one side.

"Zan?" he said. "The name Hoddan fits with that somehow . . . Oh, yes! Space-piracy! They say the people of Zan capture and loot a dozen or so ships a year, only there's no way to prove it on them. And there's a man named Hoddan who's supposed to head a particularly ruffianly gang."

"My grandfather," said Hoddan defiantly. "What are you going to do about it? I'm outlawed! I've defied the planetary government! I'm disreputable by descent, and worst of all I've tried to use my brains!"

"Deplorable!" said the ambassador mildly. "I don't

mean outlawry is deplorable, you understand, or defiance of the government, or being disreputable. But trying to use one's brains is bad business! A serious offense! Are your legs all right now? Then come on down with me and I'll have you given some dinner and some fresh clothing. Offhand," he added amiably, "it would seem that using one's brains would be classed as a political offense rather than a criminal one on Walden. We'll see."

Hoddan gaped up at him.

"You mean there's a possibility that—"

"Of course!" said the ambassador in surprise. "You haven't phrased it that way, but you're actually a rebel. A revolutionist. You defy authority and tradition and governments and such things. Naturally the Interstellar Diplomatic Service is inclined to be on your side. What do you think it's for?"

Chapter 2

In something under two hours Hoddan was ushered into the ambassador's office. He'd been refreshed, his torn clothing replaced by more respectable garments, and the places where stun-pistols had stung him, soothed by ointments.

But, more important, he'd worked out and firmly adopted a new point of view.

He'd been a misfit at home on Zan. He was not contented with the humdrum and monotonous life as a member of a space-pirate community. Piracy was a matter of dangerous take-offs in cranky rocket ships, to be followed by weeks or months of tedious and uncomfortable boredom in highly unhealthy re-breathed air. No voyage ever contained more than ten seconds of satisfactory action. All fighting took place just out of the atmosphere of the embattled planet. Regardless of the result of the fight, the pirates had to get away fast when it was over, lest overwhelming forces swarm up from the nearby world. It was intolerably devoid of anything an ambitious young man would want.

Even when one had made a good prize—with the life-boats of the foreign ship darting frantically for ground—and even after one got back to Zan with the captured ship, even then there was little satisfaction to a pirate's career. Zan had not a large population. Piracy couldn't support a large number of people. Zan couldn't attempt to defend itself against even single, heavily armed ships that sometimes came in passionate resolve to avenge the disappearance of a rich freighter or a fast, new liner. So the people of Zan, to avoid being hanged, had to play innocent. They had to be convincingly simple, harmless folk who cultivated their fields and lived quiet, blameless lives. They might loot, but they couldn't use their loot where investigators could find it. They had to build their own houses and make their own furniture and grow their own food. So life on Zan was dull. Piracy was not profitable in the sense that one could live well by it. It simply wasn't a trade for anybody like Hoddan.

So he'd abandoned all that. He'd studied electronics in books looted from passenger-ship libraries. Within months after his arrival on a law-abiding planet, he was able to earn a living at electronics as an honest trade.

And that was unsatisfactory, too. Law-abiding communities were no more thrilling or rewarding than piratical ones. A payday now and then did not make up for the tedium of earning. Even when one had money there was not much to do with it. On Walden, to be sure, the level of civilization was so high that most people took to psychiatric treatments so they could stand it, and the neurotics vastly out-numbered the more normal folk. But on Walden, electronics was only a way to make a living, like piracy, and there was no more fun to be had out of being civilized.

What Hoddan craved, of course, was a sense of achievement. Technically, there were opportunities all about him. He'd developed one, and it would save millions of credits a year if it were adopted. But it did not happen to be anything that anybody wanted. He'd tried to force its use and he was in trouble. Now he saw clearly that a law-abiding world was no more satisfactory than a piratical one.

The ambassador received him with a cordial wave of the hand.

"Things move fast," he said cheerfully. "You weren't here half an hour before there was a police captain at the gate. He explained that an excessively dangerous criminal had escaped jail and been seen climbing the embassy wall. He very generously offered to bring some men in and capture you and take you away—with my permission, of course. He was shocked when I declined."

"I can understand that," said Hoddan.

"By the way," said the ambassador. "Young men like yourself . . . Ah . . . is there a girl involved in this?"

Hoddan considered.

"A girl's father," he acknowledged, "is the real complainant against me."

"Does he complain," asked the ambassador, "because you want to marry her, or because you don't?"

"Neither," Hoddan told him. "She hasn't quite decided that I'm worth defying her rich father for."

"Good!" said the ambassador. "It can't be too bad a mess while a woman is being really practical. I've checked your story. Allowing for differences of viewpoint, it agrees with the official version. I've ruled that you are a political refugee, and so entitled to sanctuary in the embassy. And that's that."

"Thank you, sir," said Hoddan.

"There's no question about the crime," observed the ambassador, "or that it is primarily political. You proposed to improve a technical process in a society which considers itself beyond improvement. If you'd succeeded, the idea of change would have spread, people now poor would have gotten rich, people now rich would have gotten poor, and you'd have done what all governments are established to prevent. So you'll never be able to walk the streets of this planet again in safety. You've scared people."

"Yes, sir," said Hoddan. "It's been an unpleasant surprise to them, to be scared."

The ambassador put the tips of his fingers together.

"Do you realize," he asked, "that the whole purpose of civilization is to take the surprises out of life, so one can be bored to death? That a culture in which nothing unexpected ever happens is in what is called its 'golden age'? That when nobody can even imagine anything happening unexpectedly, that they later fondly refer to that period as the 'good old days'?"

"I hadn't thought of it in just those words, sir."

"It is one of the most avoided facts of life," said the ambassador. "Government, in the local or planetary sense of the word, is an organization for the suppression of adventure. Taxes are, in part, the insurance premiums one pays for protection against the unpredictable. And your act has been an offense against everything that is the foundation of a stable, orderly and damnably tedious way of life—against civilization, in fact."

Hoddan frowned.

"Yet, you've granted me asylum."

"Naturally!" said the ambassador. "The Diplomatic Service works for the welfare of humanity. That doesn't mean stuffiness. A golden age in any civilization is always followed by collapse. In ancient days savages came and camped outside the walls of super-civilized towns. They were unwashed, unmannerly, and unsanitary. Super-civilized people refused even to think about them! So presently the savages stormed the city walls and another civilization went up in flames."

"But now," objected Hoddan, "there are no savages."

"They invent themselves," the ambassador told him. "My point is that the Diplomatic Service cherishes individuals and causes which battle stuffiness and complacency and golden ages and monstrous things like that. Not thieves, of course. They're degradation, like body-lice. But rebels and crackpots and revolutionaries who prevent hardening of the arteries of commerce and furnish wholesome exercise to the body politic—they're worth cherishing!"

"I think I see, sir," said Hoddan.

"I hope you do," said the ambassador. "My action on your behalf is pure diplomatic policy. To encourage the dissatisfied is to insure against the menace of universal satisfaction. Walden is in a bad way. You are the most encouraging thing that has happened here in a long time. And you're not a native."

"No-o-o," agreed Hoddan. "I come from Zan."

"Never mind." The ambassador turned to a stellar atlas. "Consider yourself a good symptom, and valued as such. If you could start a contagion, you'd be doing a service to your fellow citizens. Savages can always invent themselves. But enough . . . let us set about your affairs." He consulted the atlas. "Where would you like to go, since you must leave Walden?"

"Not too far, sir."

"The girl, eh?" The ambassador did not smile. He ran his finger down a page. "The nearest inhabited worlds are Krim and Darth. Krim is a place of lively commercial activity, where an electronics engineer should easily find employment. It is said to be progressive and there is much organized research."

"I wouldn't want to be a kept engineer, sir," said Hoddan apologetically. "I'd rather—well—putter on my own."

"Impractical, but sensible," commented the ambassador. He turned a page. "There's Darth. Its social system is practically feudal. It's technically backward. There's a landing-grid, but space-exports are skins and metal ingots and practically nothing else. There is no broadcast power. Strangers find the local customs difficult. There is no town larger than twenty thousand people, and few approach that size. Most settled places are mere villages near some feudal castle, and roads are so few and bad that wheeled transport is rare."

He leaned back and said in a detached voice:

"I had a letter from there a couple of months ago. It was rather arrogant. The writer was one Don Loris, and he explained that his dignity would not let him make a commercial offer, but an electronic engineer who put himself under his protection would not be the loser. Are you interested? No kings on Darth, just feudal chiefs."

Hoddan thought it over.

"I'll go to Darth," he decided. "It's bound to be better than Zan, and it can't be worse than Walden."

The ambassador looked impassive. An embassy servant came in and offered an indoor communicator. The ambassador put it to his ear. After a moment he said:

"Show him in." He turned to Hoddan. "You did kick up a storm! The Minister of State, no less, is here to demand your surrender. I'll counter with a formal request for an exit permit. I'll talk to you again when he leaves."

Hoddan went out. He paced up and down the other room into which he was shown. Darth wouldn't be in a golden age! He was wiser now than he'd been just this morning. He recognized that he'd made mistakes. Now he could see rather ruefully how completely improbable it was that anybody could put across a technical device merely by proving its value, without first making anybody want it. He shook his head regretfully at the blunder.

The ambassador sent for him.

"I've had a pleasant time," he told Hoddan genially. "There was a beautiful row. You've really scared people, Hoddan. You deserve well of the republic. Every government and every person needs to be thoroughly terrified occasionally. It limbers up the brain."

"Yes, sir," said Hoddan. "I've—"

"The planetary government," said the ambassador with relish, "insists that you have to be locked up with the key thrown away. It seems you know how to make death rays. I said it was nonsense, and you were a political refugee in sanctuary. The Minister of State said the Cabinet would consider removing you forcibly from the embassy if you weren't surrendered. I said that if the embassy were violated, no ship would clear for Walden from any other civilized planet. They wouldn't like losing their off-planet trade! Then he said that the government would not give you an exit permit, and that he would hold me personally responsible if you killed everybody on Walden, including himself and me. I said he insulted me by suggesting that I'd permit such shenanigans. He said the government would take an extremely grave view of my attitude, and I said they would be silly if they did. Then he went off with great dignity—but shaking with panic—to think up more nonsense."

"Evidently," said Hoddan in relief, "you believe me when I say that my gadget doesn't make death rays."

The ambassador looked slightly embarrassed.

"To be honest," he admitted, "I've no doubt that you invented it independently, but they've been using such a device for half a century in the Cetis cluster. They've had no trouble."

Hoddan winced.

"Did you tell the minister that?"

"Hardly," said the ambassador. "It would have done you no good. You're in open revolt and have performed overt acts of violence against the police. It was impolite enough for me to suggest that the local government was stupid. It would have been most undiplomatic to prove it."

Hoddan did not feel very proud, just then.

"I'm thinking that the cops—quite unofficially—might try to kidnap me from the embassy. They'll deny that they tried, especially if they manage it. But I think they'll try."

"Very likely," said the ambassador. "We'll take precautions."

"I'd like to make something—not lethal—just in case," said Hoddan. "If you can trust me not to make death rays, I'd like to make a generator of odd-shaped microwaves. They're described in textbooks. They ionize the air where they strike. That's all. They make air a high-resistance conductor. Nothing more than that."

The ambassador said:

"There was an old-fashioned way to make ozone . . ." When Hoddan nodded, a little surprised, the ambassador said, "By all means go ahead! You should be able to get parts from your room vision-receiver. I'll have some tools given you." Then he added, "Diplomacy has to understand the things that control events. Once it was social position. For a time it was weapons. Then it was commerce. Now it's technology. But I wonder how you'll use the ionization of air to protect yourself from kidnapers? Don't tell me! I'd rather try to guess."

He waved his hand in cordial dismissal and an embassy servant showed Hoddan to his quarters. Ten minutes later another staff man brought him tools. He was left alone.

He delicately disassembled the set in his room and began to put some of the parts together in a novel but wholly rational fashion. The science of electronics, like the science of mathematics, had progressed away beyond the point where all of it had practical application. One could spend a lifetime learning things that research had discovered in the past, and industry had never found a use for. On Zan, industriously reading pirated books, Hoddan hadn't known where utility stopped. He'd kept on learning long after a practical man would have stopped studying to get a paying job.

Any electronic engineer could have made the device he now assembled. It only needed to be wanted, and apparently he was the first person to want it. In this respect it was like the receptor that had gotten him into trouble. As he put the small parts together, he felt a certain loneliness. A man Hoddan's age needed to have some girl admire him from time to time. If Nedda had been sitting cross-legged before him, listening raptly while he explained, Hoddan would probably have been perfectly happy. But she wasn't. It wasn't likely she ever would be. Hoddan scowled.

Inside of an hour he'd made a hand-sized, five watt, wave-guide projector of waves of eccentric form. In the beam of that projector, air became ionized. Air became a high-resistance conductor comparable to nichrome wire, when and where the projector sent its microwaves.

He was wrapping tape about the pistol-like hand-grip when a servant brought him a scribbled note. It had been handed in at the embassy gate by a woman who fled after leaving it. It looked like Nedda's handwriting. It read like Nedda's phrasing. It appeared to have been written by somebody in a highly emotional state. But it wasn't quite—not absolutely—convincing.

He went to find the ambassador. He handed over the note. The ambassador read it and raised his eyebrows.

"Well?"

"It could be authentic," admitted Hoddan.

"In other words," said the ambassador, "you are not sure that it is a booby trap—an invitation to a date with the police?"

"I'm not sure," said Hoddan. "I think I'd better bite. If I have any illusions left after this morning, I'd better find it out. I thought Nedda liked me quite a bit."

"I make no comment," observed the ambassador. "Can I help you in any way?"

"I have to leave the embassy," said Hoddan, "and there's almost a solid line of police outside the walls. Could I borrow some old clothes, a few pillows, and a length of rope?"

Half an hour later a rope uncoiled itself at the very darkest outside corner of the embassy wall. It dangled down to the ground. This was at the rear of the embassy enclosure. The night was bright with stars, and the city's towers glittered with many lights. But here there was almost complete blackness and that silence of a city which is sometimes so companionable.

The rope remained hanging from the wall. No light reached the ground there. The tiny crescent of Walden's farthest moon cast an insufficient glow. Nothing could be seen by it.

The rope went up, as if it had been lowered merely to make sure that it was long enough for its purpose. Then it descended again. This time a figure dangled at its end. It came down, swaying a little. It reached the blackest part of the shadow at the wall's base. It stayed there.

Nothing happened. The figure rose swiftly, hauled up in rapid pullings of the rope. Then the line came down again and again a figure descended. But this figure moved. The rope swayed and oscillated. The figure came down a good halfway to the ground. It paused, and then descended with much movement to two-thirds of the way from the top.

There something seemed to alarm it. It began to rise with violent writhings of the rope. It climbed.

There was a crackling noise. A stun-pistol. The figure seemed to climb more frantically. More cracklings. They were stun-pistol charges and there were tiny sparks where they hit. The dangling figure seemed convulsed. It went limp, but it did not fall. More charges poured into it. It hung motionless halfway up the wall of the embassy.

Movements began in the darkness. Men appeared, talking in low tones and straining their eyes toward the now motionless figure. They gathered underneath it. One went off at a run, carrying a message. Someone of authority arrived, panting. There was more low-toned argument. More and still more men appeared. There were forty or fifty figures at the base of the wall.

One of those figures began to climb the rope hand over hand. He reached the motionless object. He swore in a shocked voice. He was shushed from below. He let the figure drop. It made no sound when it landed.

Then there was a rushing, as the guards about the embassy went furiously back to their proper posts to keep anybody from slipping out. The two men who remained swore bitterly over a dummy made of old clothes and pillows.

Hoddan was then some blocks away. He suffered painful doubt about the note ostensibly from Nedda. The guards about the embassy would have tried to catch him in any case, but it did seem very plausible that the note had been sent him to get him to try to climb down the wall. On the other hand, a false descent of a palpably dummy-like dummy had been plausible too. He'd drawn all the guards to one spot by his seeming doubt and by testing out their vigilance with a dummy. The only thing improbable in his behavior had been that after testing their vigilance with a dummy, he'd made use of it.

A fair distance away, he turned sedately into a narrow lane between buildings. This paralleled another lane serving the home of a girl friend of Nedda's. The note had named the garden behind that other girl's home as a rendezvous. But Hoddan was not going to that garden. He wanted to make sure. If the cops had forged the note . . .

He judged his position carefully. If he climbed this tree . . . kind of the city-planners of Walden to use trees so lavishly . . . if he climbed this tree he could look into the garden where Nedda, in theory, waited in tears. He climbed it. He sat astride a thick limb and considered further. Presently he brought out his wave projector. There was deepest darkness hereabouts. Trees and shrubbery were blacker than their surroundings. But there was reason for suspicion. Neither in the house of Nedda's girl friend, nor in the nearer house between, was there a single lighted window.

Hoddan adjusted the wave guide and pressed the stud of his instrument. He pointed it carefully into the nearer garden.

A man grunted in a surprised tone. There was a stirring. A man swore. The words seemed inappropriate to a citizen merely taking a breath of evening air.

Hoddan frowned. The note from Nedda seemed to have been a forgery. To make sure, he readjusted the wave guide to project a thin but fan-shaped beam. He aimed again. Painstakingly, he traversed the area in which men would have been posted to jump him. If Nedda were there, she would feel no effect. If police lay in wait, they would notice at once.

They did. A man howled. Two men yelled together. Somebody bellowed. Somebody squealed. Someone in charge of the flares made ready to give light for the police was so startled by a strange sensation that he jerked the cord. An immense, cold-white brilliance appeared. The garden where Nedda definitely was not present became bathed in incandescence. Light spilled over the wall of one garden into the next and disclosed a squirming mass of police in the nearer garden also. Some of them leaped wildly and ungracefully while clawing behind them. Some stood still and struggled desperately to accomplish something to their rear, while others gazed blankly at them until Hoddan swung his instrument their way, also.

A man tore off his pants and struggled over the wall to get away from something intolerable. Others imitated him. Some removed their trousers before they fled, but others tried to get them off while fleeing! The latter did not fare too well. Mostly they stumbled and other men fell over them.

Hoddan let the confusion mount past any unscrambling, and then slid down the tree and joined in the rush. With the glare in the air behind him, he only feigned to stumble over one figure after another. Once he grunted as he scorched his own fingers. But he came out of the lane with a dozen stun-pistols, mostly uncomfortably warm, as trophies of the ambush.

As they cooled off he stowed them away in his belt and pockets, strolling away down the tree-lined street. Behind him, cops realized their trouserless condition and appealed plaintively to householders to notify headquarters of their state.

Hoddan did not feel particularly disillusioned, somehow. It occurred to him, even, that this particular event was likely to help him get off of Walden. If he was to leave against the cops' will, he needed to have them at less than top efficiency. And men who have had their pants scorched off them are not apt to think too clearly. Hoddan felt a certain confidence increase in his mind. He'd worked the thing out very nicely. If ionization made air a high-resistance conductor, then an ionizing beam would make a high-resistance short between the power terminals of a stun-pistol. With the power a stun-pistol carried, that short would get hot. So would the pistol. It would get hot enough, in fact, to scorch cloth in contact with it. Which had happened.

If the effect had been produced in the soles of policemen's feet, Hoddan would have given every cop a hot-foot. But since they carried their stun-pistols in their hip-pockets . . .

The thought of Nedda diminished his satisfaction. The note could be pure forgery, or the police could have learned about it through the treachery of the servant she sent to the embassy with it. It would be worthwhile to know. He headed toward the home of her father. If she were loyal to him, it would complicate things considerably. But he felt it necessary to find out.

He neared the spot where Nedda lived. This was an especially desirable residential area. The houses were large and gracefully designed, and the gardens were especially lush. Presently he heard music ahead. He went on. He came to a place where strolling citizens had paused under the trees to listen to the melody and the sound of voices that accompanied it. The music and festivity was in Nedda's name. She was having a party, on the night of the terrible day in which he'd been framed for life imprisonment.

It was a shock. Then there was a rush of vehicles, and police trucks were disgorging cops before the door. They formed a cordon about the house, and some knocked and were admitted in haste. Then Hoddan nodded dourly to himself.

His escape from the embassy was now known. No less certainly, the failure of the trap Nedda's note had baited had been reported. The police were now turning the whole city into a trap for one Bron Hoddan. Soon they'd have cops from other cities pouring in to aid in the search. And certainly and positively they'd take every measure they could to keep him from getting back to the embassy.

It was a situation that would have appalled Hoddan only that morning. Now, though, he only shook his head sadly. He moved on. Somehow he must get back into the embassy.

It was not far from Nedda's house to a public-safety kiosk. He entered it. It was unattended, of course. It was simply an out-of-door installation where cops could be summoned, fires reported, or emergencies described by citizens independently of the regular home communicators. It had occurred to Hoddan that the planetary authorities would be greatly pleased to hear of a situation, in a place, that would seem to hint at his presence. There were all sorts of public services that would be delighted to operate impressively in their own lines. There were bureaus which would rejoice at a chance to show off their efficiency.

He used his micro-wave generator—which at short enough range would short-circuit anything—upon the apparatus in the kiosk. It was perfectly simple, if one knew how. He worked with a sort of tender thoroughness, shorting this item, shorting that, giving this frantic emergency call, stating that baseless lie. When he went out of the kiosk he walked briskly toward an appointment he had made.

And presently the murmur of the city at night had new sounds added to it. They began as a faint, confused clamor at the edges of the city. The uproar moved centralward and grew louder. There were clanging bells and sirens and beeper-horns warning all non-official vehicles to keep out of the way. On the raised-up expressway snorting metal monsters rushed with squealing excitement. On the fragrant lesser streets, smaller vehicles rushed with proportionately louder howlings. Police trucks poured out of their cubby-holes and plunged valiantly through the dark. Broadcast units signaled emergency and cut off the air to make the placid ether waves available to authority.

All the noises and all this tumult moved toward a single point. The outer parts of the city regained their former quiet. But in the mid-city area the noise of racing vehicles clamoring for the right-of-way grew louder and louder. The sound was deafening as the vehicles converged on the large open square in front of the Interstellar Embassy. From every street and avenue fire-fighting equipment poured into that square. In between and behind, hooting loudly for precedence, were the police trucks. Emergency vehicles of all the civic bureaus appeared, all of them with immense conviction of their importance.

It was a very large, open square, that space before the embassy. From its edge, the monument to the first settlers in the center looked small. But even that vast plaza filled up with trucks of every imaginable variety, from the hose towers which could throw streams of water four hundred feet straight up, to the miniature trouble-wagons of Electricity Supply. Staff cars of fire and police and sanitary services crowded each other and bumped fenders with tree-surgeon trucks prepared to move fallen trees, and with public-address trucks ready to lend stentorian tones to any voice of authority.

But there was no situation except that there was no situation. There was no fire. There was no riot. There were not even stray dogs for the pound-wagons to pursue, nor broken watermains for the water department technicians to shut off and repair. There was nothing for anybody to do but ask everybody else what the hell they were doing there, and presently to swear at each other for cluttering up the way.

The din of arriving horns and sirens had stopped, and a mutter of profanity was developing, when a last vehicle arrived. It was an ambulance, and it came purposefully out of a side avenue and swung toward a particular place as if it knew exactly what it was about. When its way was blocked, it hooted impatiently for passage. Its lights blinked violently red, demanding clearance. A giant fire-fighting unit pulled aside. The ambulance ran past and hooted at a cluster of police trucks. They made way for it. It blared at a gathering of dismounted, irritated truck personnel. It made its way through them. It moved in a straight line for the gate of the Interstellar Embassy.

A hundred yards from that gate, its horn blatted irritably at the car of the acting head of municipal police. That car obediently made way for it.

The ambulance rolled briskly up to the very gate of the embassy. There it stopped. A figure got down from the driver's seat and walked purposefully in the gate.

Thereafter nothing happened at all until a second figure rolled and toppled itself out on the ground from the seat beside the ambulance driver's. That figure kicked and writhed on the ground. A policeman went to find out what was the matter.

It was the ambulance driver. Not the one who'd driven the ambulance to the embassy gate, but the one who should have. He was bound hand and foot and not too tightly gagged. When released he swore vividly while panting that he had been captured and bound by somebody who said he was Bron Hoddan and was in a hurry to get back to the Interstellar Embassy.

There was no uproar. Those to whom Hoddan's name had meaning were struck speechless with rage. The fury of the police was even too deep for tears.

But Bron Hoddan, back in the quarters assigned him in the embassy, unloaded a dozen cooled-off stun-pistols from his pockets and sent word to the ambassador that he was back, and that the note ostensibly from Nedda had actually been a police trap.

Getting ready to retire, he reviewed his situation. In some respects it was not too bad. All but Nedda's share in trying to trap him, and having a party the same night. He stared morosely at the wall. Then he saw, very simply, that she mightn't have known even of his arrest. She lived a highly sheltered life. Her father could have had her kept in complete ignorance.

He cheered immediately. This would be his last night on Walden, if he were lucky. Already vague plans revolved in his mind. Yes . . . he'd achieve splendid things; he'd grow rich; he'd come back and marry that delightful girl, Nedda; and then end as a great man. Already, today, he'd done a number of things worth doing, and on the whole he'd done them well.

Chapter 3

When dawn broke over the capital city of Walden, the sight was appropriately glamorous. There were shining towers and the curving tree-bordered ways, above which innumerable small birds flew. The dawn, in fact, was heralded by chirpings everywhere. During the darkness there had been a deep-toned humming sound, audible all over the city. That was the landing-grid in operation out at the space-port, letting down a huge liner from Rigel, Cetis, and the Nearer Rim. Presently it would take off for Krim, Darth, and the Coalsack Stars, and if Hoddan were lucky he would be on it. At the earliest part of the day there was only tranquility over the city and the square and the Interstellar Embassy.

At the gate of the embassy enclosure, staff members piled up boxes and bales and parcels for transport to the spaceport. There were dispatches to Delil, where the Interstellar Diplomatic Service had a sector head-quarters, and there were packets of embassy-stamped invoices for Lohala and Tralee and Famagusta. There were boxes for Sind and Maja, and metal-bound cases for Kent. The early explorers of this part of the galaxy had christened the huge suns with the names of little villages and territories back on Earth.

The sound of the stacking of freight parcels was crisp and distinct in the morning hush. The dew deposited during the night had not yet dried from the pavement of the square. Damp, unhappy figures loafed nearby. They were the secret police, as yet unrelieved after a night's vigil about the embassy's rugged wall. They were sleepy, and their clothing stuck soggily to them, and none of them had anything warm to eat for many hours. They had not, either, anything to look forward to from their superiors. Hoddan was again in sanctuary inside the embassy they'd guarded so ineptly through the dark. He'd gotten out without their leave, and had made a number of their fellows quite uncomfortable. Then he had made all the police and municipal authorities ridiculous by the manner of his return. The police guards about the embassy were positively not in a cheery mood. But one of them saw an embassy servant he knew. He'd stood the man drinks, in times past, to establish a contact that might be useful. He smiled and beckoned to the man.

The embassy servant came briskly to him, rubbing his hands after having put a moderately heavy case of documents on top of the waiting pile.

"That Hoddan," said the plainclothesman, attempting hearty ruefulness, "he certainly put it over on us last night!" The servant nodded.

"Look," said the plainclothesman, "there could be something in it for you if you—hm—wanted to make a little extra money."

The servant looked regretful.

"No chance," he said. "He's leaving today."

The plainclothesman jumped.

"Today?"

"For Darth," said the embassy servant. "The ambassador's shipping him off on the spaceliner that came in last night."

The plainclothesman dithered.

"How's he going to get to the spaceport?"

"I wouldn't know," said the servant. "They've

figured out some way. I could use a little extra money, too."

He lingered, but the plainclothesman was staring at the innocent, inviolable parcels about to leave the embassy for distant parts. He took note of sizes and descriptions. No. Not yet. But if Hoddan was leaving, he had to leave the embassy. If he left the embassy . . .

The plainclothesman bolted. He made a breathless report by the portable communicator. He told what the embassy servant had said. Orders came back to him. Orders were given in all directions. Somebody was going to distinguish himself by catching Hoddan, and undercover politics worked to decide who it should be. Even the job of guarding the embassy became desirable. So fresh, alert plainclothesmen arrived. They were bright eyed men and bushy tailed, and they took over. Weary, hungry men yielded up their posts. They went home. The man who'd gotten the clue went home too, disgruntled because he wouldn't be allowed a share in the credit for Hoddan's actual capture. But he was glad of it later.

Inside the embassy, Hoddan finished his breakfast with the ambassador.

"I'm giving you," said the ambassador, "a letter to that character on Darth. I told you about him. He's some sort of nobleman and has need of an electronic engineer. On Darth they're rare to nonexistent. But his letter wasn't too specific."

"I remember," agreed Hoddan. "I'll look him up. Thanks."

"Somehow," said the ambassador, "I cherish unreasonable hopes for you, Hoddan. A psychologist would say that your group identification is low and your cyclothymia practically a minus quantity, while your ergic tension is pleasingly high. He'd mean that with reasonable good fortune you will raise more hell than most. I wish you that good fortune. And Hoddan—"

"Yes?"

"I urge you not to be vengeful," explained the ambassador, "but I do hope you won't be too forgiving of these characters who'd have jailed you for life. You've scared them badly. It's very good for them. Anything more you can do along that line will be really a kindness, even though it will positively not be appreciated. But it'll be well worth doing. I say this because I like the way you plan things. And any time I can be of service . . ."

"Thanks," said Hoddan. "Now I'd better get going for the spaceport." He'd write Nedda from Darth. "I'll get set for it."

He rose. The ambassador stood up, too.

"I like the way you plan things," he repeated appreciatively. "We'll check over that box."

They left the embassy dining room together.

It was well after sunrise when Hoddan finished his breakfast, and the bright and watchful new plainclothesmen were very much on the alert outside. By this time the sunshine had lost its early ruddy tint, and the trees about the city were vividly green, and the sky had become appropriately blue—as the skies on all human-occupied planets are. There was the beginning of traffic. Some was routine movement of goods and vehicles. But some was special.

For example, the trucks which came to carry the

embassy shipment to the spaceport. They were perfectly ordinary trucks, hired in a perfectly ordinary way by the ambassador's secretary. They came trundling across the square and into the embassy gate. The ostentatiously loafing plainclothesmen could look in and see the waiting parcels loaded on them. The first truck load was quite unsuspicious. There was no package in the lot which could have held a man even in the most impossibly cramped of positions.

But the police took no chances. Ten blocks from the embassy the cops stopped it and verified the licenses and identities of the driver and his helper. This was a moderately lengthy business. While it went on, plainclothesmen walked over the packages in the truck's body and put stethoscopes to any of more than one cubic foot capacity.

They waved the truck on. Meanwhile the second truck was loading up. And those watching saw that the last item to be loaded was a large box which hadn't been seen before. It was carried with some care, and it was marked fragile, put into place and wedged fast with other parcels.

The plainclothesmen looked at each other with anticipatory glee. One of them reported the last large box with almost lyric enthusiasm. When the second truck left the embassy with the large box, a police truck came innocently out of nowhere and just happened to be going the same way. Ten blocks away, again the truckload of embassy parcels was flagged down and its driver's license and identity was verified. A plainclothesman put a stethoscope on the questionable case. He beamed, and made a suitable signal.

The truck went on, while zestful, Machiavellian plans took effect.

Five blocks farther, an unmarked empty truck came hurtling out of a side street, sideswiped the truck from the embassy, and went careening away down the street without stopping. The trailing police truck made no attempt at pursuit. Instead, it stopped helpfully by the truck which had been hit. A wheel was hopelessly gone. So uniformed police, with conspicuously happy expressions, cleared a space around the stalled truck and stood guard over the parcels under diplomatic seal. With eager helpfulness, they sent for other transportation for the embassy's shipment.

A sneeze was heard from within the mass of guarded freight, and the policemen shook hands with each other. When substitute trucks came—there were two of them—they loaded one high with embassy parcels and sent it off to the spaceport with their blessings. There remained just one, single, large box to be put on the second vehicle. They bumped it on the ground, and a startled grunt came from within.

There was an atmosphere of innocent enjoyment all about as the police tenderly loaded this large box on a second truck. Strangely, they did not head directly for the space-port. The police carefully explained this to each other in loud voices. Then some of them were afraid the box hadn't heard, so they knocked on it. The box coughed, and it seemed hilariously amusing to the policemen that the contents of a freight parcel should cough. They expressed deep concern and—addressing the box—explained that they were taking it to the Detention Building, where they would give it some cough medicine.

The box swore at them, despairingly. They howled with childish laughter, and assured the box that after they had opened it and given it cough medicine they would close it again very carefully—leaving the diplomatic seal unbroken—and deliver it to the spaceport so it could go on its way.

The box swore again, luridly. The truck which carried it hastened. The box teetered and bumped and jounced with the swift motion of the vehicle that carried it and all the police around it. Bitter, enraged, and highly unprintable language came from within.

The police were charmed. When the Detention Building gate opened for it, and closed again behind it, there was a welcoming committee in the courtyard. It included a jailer with a bandaged head and a look of vengeful satisfaction on his face, and no less than the three guards who had been given baths by a high-pressure hose. They wore unamiable expressions.

And then, while the box swore very bitterly, somebody tenderly loosened a plank—being careful not to disturb the diplomatic seal—and pulled it away with a triumphant gesture. Then all the police could look into the box. And they did.

Then there was a dead silence, except for the voice that came from a two-way communicator set inside.

"And now," said the voice from the box, "and now we take our leave of the planet Walden and its happy police force, who wave to us as our spaceliner lifts toward the skies. The next sound you hear will be that of their lamentations at our departure."

But the next sound was a howl of fury. The police were very much disappointed to find that it hadn't been Hoddan in the box, but only one-half of a two-way communication pair. Hoddan *had* coughed, sneezed and sworn at them, but from the other instrument somewhere else. Now he signed off.

The spaceliner was not lifting off just yet. It was still solidly aground in the center of the landing-grid. Hoddan had bade farewell to his audience from the floor of the ambassador's car, which at that moment was safely within the extraterritorial circle about the spaceship. He turned off the set and got up and brushed himself off. He got out of the car. The ambassador followed him and shook his hand.

"You have a touch," said the ambassador sedately. "You seem inspired at times, Hoddan! You have a gift for infuriating constituted authority. You may go far!"

He shook hands again and watched Hoddan walk into the lift which raised him to the entrance port of the space-liner.

Twenty minutes later the forcefields of the giant landing-grid lifted the liner smoothly out to space. The vessel went out to five planetary diameters, where its Lawlor drive could take hold of relatively unstressed space. There the ship jockeyed for line, and then there was that curious, momentary disturbance of all one's sensations which was the effect of the over-drive field going on. Then everything was normal again, except that the liner was speeding for the planet Krim at something more than thirty times the speed of light.

Normalcy extended through all the galaxy so far inhabited by men. There were worlds on which there was peace, and worlds on which there was tumult. There were busy, restful young worlds, and languid, weary old ones. From the Near Rim to the farthest of occupied systems, planets circled their suns, and men lived on them, and every man took himself seriously and did not quite believe that the universe had existed before he was born or would long survive his loss.

Time passed. Comets let out vast streamers like bridal veils and swept toward and around their suns. The liner bearing Hoddan sped through the void.

In time it made a landfall on the planet Krim. He went aground and observed the spaceport city. It was new and bustling with tall buildings and traffic jams and a feverish conviction that the purpose of living was to earn more money this year than last. Its spaceport was chaotically busy. Hoddan had time for swift sight-seeing in one city only. He saw slums and gracious public buildings, and went back to the spaceport and the liner which then rose upon the landing-grid's forcefields until Krim was a great round ball below it. Then there was again a jockeying for line, and the liner winked out of sight and was again journeying at thirty times the speed of light.

Again time passed. In one of the most remote galaxies a super-nova flamed, and on a rocky, barren world a small living thing squirmed experimentally—to mankind the one event was just as important as the other.

But presently the liner from Walden via Krim appeared on Darth as the tiniest of shimmering pearly specks against the blue. To the north and east and west of the spaceport, rugged mountains rose steeply. Patches of snow showed here and there, and naked rock reared boldly in spurs and precipices. But there were trees on all the lower slopes, and there was not really a timber line.

The spaceliner increased in size, descending toward the landing-grid. The grid itself was a monstrous lattice of steel, a half-mile high and enclosing a circle not less in diameter. It filled the larger part of the level valley floor, and horned *duryas* and what Hoddan later learned were horses grazed in it. The animals paid no attention to the deep humming noise the grid made in its operation.

The ship seemed the size of a pea. Presently it was the size of an apple. Then it was the size of a basketball, and then it swelled enormously and put out spidery metal legs with large splay metal feet on which it alighted and settled gently to the ground. The humming stopped.

There were shoutings. Whips cracked. Straining, horn-tossing *duryas* heaved and dragged something, very deliberately, out from between warehouses and under the arches of the grid. There were two dozen of the *duryas*, and despite the shouts and whip cracking they moved with a stubborn slowness. It took a long time for the object with the big clumsy wheels to reach a spot below the spacecraft. Then it took longer, seemingly, for brakes to be set on each wheel, and then for the draft animals to be arranged to pull as two teams against each other.

More shoutings and whip-crackings. A long, slanting, ladder-like arm rose. It teetered, and a man with a vivid purple cloak rose with it at its very end. The ship's airlock opened and a crewman threw a rope. The purple-cloaked man caught it and made it fast. From somewhere inside the ship, the line was hauled

in. The end of the landing ramp touched the sill of
the airlock. Somebody made these fast and the purple-
cloaked man triumphantly entered the ship.

There was a pause. Men loaded carts with cargo to
be sent to other remote planets. In the airlock, Bron
Hoddan stepped to the unloading-ramp and descended
to the ground. He was the only passenger. He had
barely reached a firm footing when objects followed
him. His own shipbag and then parcels, bales, boxes,
and other such nondescript items of freight. For a
mere five minutes the flow of freight continued. Darth
was not an important center of trade.

Hoddan stared incredulously at the town outside
one side of the grid. It was only a town, and was
almost a village. Its houses had steep, gabled roofs,
of which some seemed to be tile and others thatch.
Its buildings leaned over the narrow streets, which
were unpaved. They looked like mud. And there was
not a power-driven ground-vehicle anywhere in sight,
nor anything man-made in the air.

Great carts trailed out to the unloading-belt. They
dumped bales of skins and ingots of metal, and more
bales and more ingots. Those objects rode up to the
airlock and vanished. Hoddan was ignored. He felt
that without great care he might be crowded back
into the reversed loading-belt and be carried back
into the ship.

The loading process ended. The man with the
purple cloak, who'd ridden the teetering ladder up,
reappeared and came striding grandly down to ground.
Somebody cast off, above. Ropes writhed, fell and
dangled. The ship's air-lock door closed.

There was a vast humming sound. The ship lifted

sedately. It seemed to hover momentarily over the group of *duryas* and humans in the center of the grid's enclosure. But it was hovering. It shrank. It was rising in an absolutely vertical line. It dwindled to the size of a basketball and then an apple. Then to the size of a pea. And then that pea diminished until the spaceship from Krim, Walden, Cetis, Rigel and the Nearer Rim had become the size of a dust mote and then could not be seen at all. But one knew that it was going on to Lohala and Tralee and Famagusta and the Coalsack Stars.

Hoddan shrugged and began to trudge toward the warehouses. The *durya*-drawn landing-ramp began to roll slowly in the same direction. Carts and wagons loaded the stuff discharged from the ship. Creaking, plodding, with the curved horns of the *duryas* rising and falling, the wagons overtook Hoddan and passed him. He saw his shipbag on one of the carts. It was a gift from the Interstellar Ambassador on Walden. He'd assured Hoddan that there was a fund for the assistance of political refugees, and that the bag and its contents was normal. But in addition to this, Hoddan had a number of stun-pistols, formerly equipment of the police department of Walden's capital city.

He followed his bag to a warehouse. Arrived there, he found the bag surrounded by a group of whiskered Darthian characters wearing felt pants and large sheath knives. They had opened the bag and were in the act of ferocious dispute about who should get what of its contents. Incidentally they argued over the stun-pistols, which looked like weapons but weren't because nothing happened when one pulled the trigger. Hoddan grimaced. They'd been in store on the liner during the voyage. Normally they picked up a trickle charge from broadcast power, on Walden, but there was no broadcast power on the liner, nor on Darth. They'd leaked their charges and were quite useless. The one in his pocket would be useless, too.

He grimaced again and swerved to the building where the landing-grid controls must be. He opened the door and went in. The interior was smoky and vile-smelling, but the equipment was wholly familiar. Two unshaven men in violently colored shirts languidly played cards. Only one, a redhead, paid attention to the controls of the landing-grid. He watched dials. As Hoddan pushed his way in, he threw a switch and yawned. The ship was five diameters out from Darth, and he'd released it from the landing-grid fields. He turned and saw Hoddan.

"What the hell do you want?" he demanded sharply.

"A few kilowatts," said Hoddan. The redhead's manner was not amiable.

"Get outta here!" he barked.

The transformers and snaky cables leading to relays outside—all were clear as print to Hoddan. He moved confidently toward an especially understandable panel, pulling out his stun-pistol and briskly breaking back the butt for charging. He shoved the pistol butt to contact with two terminals devised for another purpose, and the pistol slipped for an instant and a blue spark flared.

"Quit that!" roared the man. The unshaven men pushed back from their game of cards. One of them stood up, smiling unpleasantly.

The stun-pistol clicked. Hoddan withdrew it from

charging-contact, flipped the butt shut, and turned toward the three men. Two of them charged him suddenly—the redhead and the unpleasant smiler.

The stun-pistol hummed. The redhead howled. He'd been hit in the hand. His unshaven companion buckled in the middle and fell to the floor. The third man backed away in panic, automatically raising his arms in surrender.

Hoddan saw no need for further action. He nodded graciously and went out of the control building, swinging the re-charged pistol in his hand. In the warehouse, argument still raged over his possessions. He went in. Nobody looked at him. The casual appropriation of unguarded property was apparently a social norm here. The man in the purple cloak was insisting furiously that he was a Darthian gentleman and he'd have his share—or else!

"Those things," said Hoddan, "are mine. Put them back."

Faces turned to him, expressing shocked surprise. A man in dirty yellow pants stood up with a suit of Hoddan's underwear and a pair of shoes. He moved to depart with great dignity.

The stun-pistol buzzed. He leaped and howled and fled.

There was a concerted gasp of outrage. Men leaped to their feet. Large knives came out of elaborate holsters. Figures in all the colors of the rainbow—all badly soiled—roared their indignation and charged at Hoddan. They waved knives as they came.

He held down the stun-pistol trigger and traversed the rushing men. The whining buzz of the weapon was inaudible, at first, but before he released the trigger it was plainly to be heard. Then there was silence. His attackers formed a very untidy heap on the floor. They breathed stertorously. Hoddan began to retrieve his possessions. He rolled a man over, for this purpose; a pair of very blue, apprehensive eyes stared at him. Their owner had stumbled over one man and been stumbled over by others. He gazed up at Hoddan, speechless.

"Hand me that, please," said Hoddan. He pointed.

The man in the purple cloak obeyed, shaking. Hoddan completed the recovery of all his belongings. He turned. The man in the purple cloak winced and closed his eyes.

"Hm," said Hoddan. He needed information. He spoke to the man: "I have a letter of introduction to one Don Loris. Would you have any idea how I could reach him?"

The man in the purple cloak gaped at Hoddan.

"He is . . . is my chieftain," he said, aghast. "I—am Thal, his most trusted retainer." Then he practically wailed. "You must be the man I was sent to meet! He sent me to learn if you came on the ship! I should have fought by your side! This is disgrace!"

"It's disgraceful," agreed Hoddan grimly. But he, who had been born and raised in a space-pirate community, was not too critical of others. "Let it go. How do I find him?"

"I should take you!" complained Thal bitterly. "But you have killed all these men. Their friends and chieftains are honor bound to cut your throat! And you shot Merk, but he ran away, and he will be summoning his friends to come and kill you now!

This is shame!" Then he said hopefully, "Your strange weapon . . . how many men can you fight? If fifty, we may live to ride away. If more, we may even reach Don Loris' castle. How many?"

"We'll see what we see," said Hoddan dourly. "But I'd better charge these other pistols. You can come with me, or wait. I haven't killed these men. They're only stunned. They'll come around presently."

He went out of the warehouse, carrying the bag which was again loaded with uncharged stun-pistols. He went back to the grid's control-room. He pushed it open and entered for the second time. The redhead swore and rubbed at his hand. The man who'd smiled unpleasantly lay in a heap on the floor. The second unshaven man jittered visibly at sight of Hoddan.

"I'm back," said Hoddan politely, "for more kilo-watts."

He put his bag conveniently close to the terminals at which his pistols could be recharged. He snapped open a pistol butt and presented it to the electric contacts.

"Quaint customs you have here," he said conversationally. "Robbing a newcomer. Resenting his need for a few watts of power that comes free from the sky." The stun-pistol clicked. He snapped the butt shut and opened another, which he placed in contact for charging. "Making him act," he added acidly, "with manners as bad as the local ones. Going at him with knives so he has to be resentful in his turn." The second stun-pistol clicked. He closed it and began to charge a third. He said severely, "Innocent tourists—relatively innocent ones, anyhow—are not likely to be favorably impressed with Darth!" He had the charging process going swiftly now. He began to charge a fourth weapon. "It's particularly bad manners," he added sternly, "to stand there grinding your teeth at me while your friend behind the desk crawls after an old-fashioned chemical gun to shoot me with."

He snapped the fourth pistol shut and went after the man who'd dropped down behind a desk. He came upon that man, hopelessly panicked, just as his hands closed on a clumsy gun that was supposed to set off a chemical explosive to propel a metal bullet.

"Don't!" said Hoddan severely. "If I have to shoot you at this range, you'll have blisters!"

He took the weapon out of the other man's hands. He went back and finished charging the rest of the pistols.

He returned most of them to his bag, though he stuck others in his belt and pockets to the point where he looked like the fiction-tape version of a space-pirate. He moved to the door. As a last thought, he picked up the bullet-firing weapon.

"There's only one spaceship here a month," he observed politely, "so I'll be around. If you want to get in touch with me, ask Don Loris. I'm going to visit him while I look over the professional opportunities on Darth."

He went out once more. Somehow he felt more cheerful than a half-hour since, when he'd landed as the only passenger from the spaceliner. Then he'd felt ignored and lonely and friendless on a strange and primitive world. He still had no friends, but he had already acquired some enemies and therefore material for more or less worthwhile achievement.

He surveyed the sunlit scene about him from the control-room door.

Thal, the purple-cloaked man, had brought two shaggy-haired animals around to the door of the warehouse. Hoddan later learned that they were horses. He was in furious haste to mount one of them. As he climbed up, small bright metal disks cascaded from a pocket. He tried to stop the flow of money as he got feverishly into the saddle.

From the small town a mob of some fifty mounted men plunged toward the landing-grid. They wore garments of yellow and blue and magenta. They waved huge knives and made bloodthirsty noises. Thal saw them and bolted, riding one horse and towing the other by a lead rope. It happened that his line of retreat passed by where Hoddan stood.

Hoddan held up his hand. Thal reined in.

"Mount!" Thal cried hoarsely. "Mount and ride!"

Hoddan passed him the chemical gun. Thal seized it frantically.

"Hurry!" he panted. "Don Loris would have my throat cut if I deserted you! Mount and ride!"

Hoddan painstakingly fastened his bag to the saddle of his horse. He unfastened the lead rope. He'd noticed that Thal pulled in the leather reins to stop the horse. He'd seen that he kicked it furiously to urge it on. He deduced that one steered the animal by pulling on one strap or the other. He climbed clumsily to a seat.

There was a howl from the racing, mounted men. They waved their knives and yelled in zestful anticipation of murder.

Hoddan pulled on a rein. His horse turned obediently.

He kicked it. The animal broke into a run toward the rushing mob. The jolting motion amazed Hoddan. One could not shoot straight while being shaken up like this! He dragged back on the reins. The horse stopped.

"Come!" yelled Thal despairingly. "This way! Quick!"

Hoddan got out a stun-pistol. Sitting erect, frowning a little in his concentration, he began to take pot shots at the advancing men.

Three of them got close enough to be blistered when stun-pistol bolts hit them. Others toppled from their saddles at distances ranging from one hundred yards to twenty. A good dozen, however, saw what was happening in time to swerve their mounts and hightail it away. But there were eighteen luridly-tinted heaps of garments on the ground inside the landing-grid. Two or three of them squirmed and swore. Hoddan had partly missed on them. He heard the chemical weapon booming thunderously. Now that victory was won, Thal was shooting. Hoddan held up his hand for cease-fire. Thal rode up beside him, not quite believing what he'd seen.

"Wonderful!" he said shakily. "Wonderful! Don Loris will be pleased! He will give me gifts for my help to you. This is a great fight! We will be great men, after this!"

"Then let's go and brag," said Hoddan.

Thal was shocked.

"You need me," he said. "It is fortunate that Don Loris chose me to fight beside you!"

He sent his horse trotting toward the unconscious men on the ground. He alighted. Hoddan saw him happily and publicly pick the pockets of the stun-gun's victims. He came back beaming.

"We will be famous!" he said zestfully. "Two against thirty, and some ran away!" he gloated. "And it was a good haul! We share, of course, because we are companions."

"Is it the custom," asked Hoddan mildly, "to loot defenseless men?"

"But of course!" said Thal. "How else can a gentleman live, if he has no chieftain to give him presents? You defeated them, so of course you take their possessions!"

"Ah, yes," said Hoddan. "To be sure!"

He rode on. The road was a mere horse track. Presently it was less than that. He saw a frowning, battlemented stronghold away off to the left. Thal openly hoped that somebody would come from that castle and try to charge them toll for riding over their lord's land. After Hoddan had knocked them over with the stun-pistols, Thal would add to the heavy weight of coins already in his possession.

It did not look promising, in a way. But just before sunset, Hoddan saw three tiny bright lights flash across the sky from west to east. They moved in formation and at identical speeds. Hoddan knew a spaceship in orbit when he saw one. He bristled, and muttered under his breath.

"What's that?" asked Thal. "What did you say?"

"I said," said Hoddan dourly, "that I've got to do something about Walden. When they get an idea in their heads . . ."

Chapter 4

According to the fiction-tapes, the colonized worlds of the galaxy vary wildly from each other. In cold and unromantic fact, it isn't so. Space travel is too cheap and Sol-type solar systems too numerous to justify the settlement of hostile worlds. Therefore Bron Hoddan encountered no remarkable features in the landscape of Darth as he rode through the deepening night. There were grass, bushes, trees, birds, and various other commonplace living things whose ancestors had been dumped on Darth some centuries before. The ecological system had worked itself out strictly by hit-or-miss, but the result was not unusual. There was, though, the unfamiliar star-pattern. Hoddan tried to organize it in his mind. He knew where the sun had set, which would be west. He asked the latitude of the Darthian spaceport. Thal did not know it. He asked about major geographical features—seas, continents, and so on. Thal had no ideas on the subject.

Hoddan fumed. He hadn't worried about such things on Walden. Of course, on Walden he'd had one friend, Derec, and believed he had a sweetheart, Nedda. There he was lonely and schemed to acquire the admiration of others. He ignored the sky. Here on Darth he had no friends, but there were a number of local citizens now recovering from stun-pistol bolts and yearning to carve him up with large knives. He did not feel lonely, but the instinct to know where he was, was again in operation.

The ground was rocky and far from level. After two hours of riding on a small and wiry horse with no built-in springs, Hoddan hurt in a great many places. He and Thal rode in an indeterminate direction with an irregular scarp of low mountains silhouetted against the unfamiliar stars. A vagrant night wind blew. Thal had said it was a three-hour ride to Don Loris' castle. After something over two of them, he said meditatively:

"I think that if you wish to give me a present I will take it and not make a gift in return. You could give me," he added helpfully, "your share of the plunder from our victims."

"Why?" demanded Hoddan. "Why should I give you a present?"

"If I accepted it," explained Thal, "and make no gift in return, I will become your retainer. Then it will be my obligation as a Darthian gentleman to ride beside you, advise, counsel, and fight in your defense, and generally to uphold your dignity."

"How about Don Loris? Aren't you his retainer?" he asked suspiciously.

"Between the two of us," said Thal, "he's stingy. His presents are not as lavish as they could be. I can make him a return-present of part of the money we won in combat. That frees me of duty to him. Then I could accept the balance of the money from you, and become a retainer of yours."

"Oh," said Hoddan.

"You need a retainer badly," said Thal. "You do not know the customs here. For example, there is enmity between Don Loris and the young Lord Ghek. If the young Lord Ghek is as enterprising as he should be, some of his retainers should be lying in wait to cut our throats as we approach Don Loris' stronghold."

"Hm," said Hoddan grimly. But Thal seemed undisturbed. "This system of gifts and presents sounds complicated. Why doesn't Don Loris simply give you so much a year, or week, or whatnot?"

Thal made a shocked sound.

"That would be pay! A Darthian gentleman does not serve for pay! To offer it would be insult!" Then he said, "Listen!"

He reined in. Hoddan clumsily followed his example. After a moment or two Thal clucked to his horse and started off again.

"It was nothing," he said regretfully. "I hoped we were riding into an ambush."

Hoddan grunted. It could be that he was being told a tall tale. But back at the spaceport, the men who came after him waving large knives had seemed sincere enough.

"Why should we be ambushed?" he asked. "And why do you hope for it?"

"Your weapons would destroy our enemies," said Thal placidly, "and the pickings would be good." He added, "We should be ambushed because the Lady Fani refused to marry the Lord Ghek. She is Don Loris' daughter, and to refuse to marry a man is naturally a deadly insult. So he should ravage Don Loris' lands at every opportunity until he gets a chance to carry off the Lady Fani and marry her by force. That is the only way the insult can be wiped out."

"I see," said Hoddan ironically.

He didn't. The two horses topped a rise, and far in the distance there was a yellow light, with a mist above it as of illuminated smoke.

"That is Don Loris' stronghold," said Thal. He sighed. "It looks like we may not be ambushed."

They weren't. It was very dark where the horses forged ahead through brushwood. As they moved onward, the single light became two. They were great bonfires burning in iron cages some forty feet up in the air. Those cages projected from the battlements of a massive, cut-stone wall. There was no light anywhere else.

Thal rode almost under the cressets and shouted upward. A voice answered. Presently a gate clanked open and a black, cave-like opening appeared behind it. Thal rode grandly in, and Hoddan followed.

The gate clanked shut. Torches waved overhead. Hoddan found that he and Thal had ridden into a very tiny courtyard. Twenty feet above them, an inner battlemented wall offered excellent opportunities for the inhabitants of the castle to throw things down at visitors who, after admission, turned out to be undesired.

Thal shouted further identifications, including a boastful and entirely untruthful declaration that he and Hoddan, together, had slaughtered twenty men in one place and thirty in another, and left them lying in their gore.

The voices that replied sounded derisive. Somebody came down a rope and fastened the gate from the inside. With an extreme amount of creaking, an inner gate swung wide. Men came out of it and took the horses. Hoddan dismounted, and it seemed to him that he creaked as loudly as the gate. Thal swaggered, displaying coins he had picked from the pockets of the men the stun-pistols had disabled. He said splendidly to Hoddan:

"I go to announce your coming to Don Loris. These are his retainers. They will give you to drink." He added amiably, "If you were given food, it would be disgraceful to cut your throat."

He disappeared. Hoddan carried his shipbag and followed a man in a dirty pink shirt to a stone-walled room containing a table and a chair. He sat down, relieved. The man in the pink shirt brought him a flagon of wine. He disappeared again.

Hoddan drank the sour wine and brooded. He was very hungry and very tired, and it seemed to him that he had been disillusioned in a new dimension. Morbidly, he remembered a frequently given lecture from his grandfather on Zan.

"It's no use!" his grandfather used to say. "There's not a bit o' use in having brains! All they do is get you into trouble! A lucky idiot's ten times better off than a brainy man with a jinx on him! A smart man starts thinkin', and he thinks himself into a jail cell if his luck is bad, and good luck's wasted on him because it ain't reasonable and he don't believe in it when it happens! It's taken me a lifetime to keep my brains from ruinin' me! No, sir! I hope none o' my descendants inherit my brains. I pity 'em if they do!"

Hoddan had been on Darth not more than four hours. In that time he'd found himself robbed, had been the object of two spirited attempts at assassination, had ridden an excruciating number of miles on an unfamiliar animal, and now found himself in a stone dungeon and deprived of food lest feeding him obligate his host not to cut his throat. And he'd gotten into this by himself! He'd chosen it! He'd practically asked for it!

He began strongly to share his grandfather's disillusioned view of brains.

After a long time the door of the cell opened. Thal was back, chastened.

"Don Loris wants to talk to you," he said in a subdued voice. "He's not pleased."

Hoddan took another gulp of the wine. He picked up his shipbag and limped to the door. He decided painfully that he was limping on the wrong leg. He tried the other. No improvement. He really needed to limp on both.

He followed a singularly silent Thal through a long stone corridor and up stone steps until they came to a monstrous hall lit with torches. It was barbarically hung with banners, but it was not exactly a cheery place. At the far end logs burned in a great fireplace.

Don Loris sat in a carved chair beside it; wizened and white-bearded, in a fur-trimmed velvet robe, with a peevish expression on his face.

"My chieftain," said Thal submissively, "here is the engineer from Walden."

Hoddan scowled at Don Loris, whose expression of peevishness did not lighten. He did regard Hoddan with a flicker of interest, however. A stranger who unfeignedly scowls at a feudal lord with no superior and many inferiors, is anyhow a novelty.

"Thal tells me," said Don Loris fretfully, "that you and he, together, slaughtered some dozens of the retainers of my neighbors today. I consider it unfortunate. They may ask me to have the two of you hanged, and it would be impolite to refuse."

Hoddan said truculently:

"I considered it impolite for your neighbors' retainers to march toward me waving large knives."

"Yes," agreed Don Loris impatiently. "I concede that point. It is natural enough to act hastily at such times. But still . . . How many did you kill?"

"None," said Hoddan curtly. "I shot them with stun-pistols I'd just charged in the control-room of the landing-grid." Don Loris sat up straight.

"Stun-pistols?" he demanded sharply. "You used stun-pistols on Darth?"

"Naturally on Darth," said Hoddan with some tartness. "I was here! But nobody was killed. One or two may be slightly blistered. All of them had their pockets picked by Thal. I understand that is a local custom. There's nothing to worry about."

But Don Loris stared at him, aghast.

"But this is deplorable!" he protested. "Stun-pistols used here? It is the one thing I would have given strict orders to avoid! My neighbors will talk about it. Some of them may even think about it! You could have used any other weapon, but of all things why did you have to use a stun-pistol?"

"I had one," said Hoddan briefly.

"Horrible!" said Don Loris peevishly. "The worst thing you could possibly have done! I have to disown you. Unmistakably! You'll have to disappear at once. We'll blame it on Ghek's retainers."

"Disappear? Me?" Hoddan exclaimed.

"Vanish," said Don Loris. "I suppose there's no real necessity to cut your throat, but you plainly have to disappear, though it would have been much more discreet if you'd simply gotten killed."

"I was indiscreet to survive?" demanded Hoddan bristling.

"Extremely so!" snapped Don Loris. "Here I had you come all the way from Walden to help arrange a delicate matter, and before you'd traveled even the few miles to my castle—within minutes of landing on Darth—you spoiled everything! I am a reasonable man, but there are the facts! You used stun-pistols, so you have to disappear. I think it generous of me to say only until people on Darth forget that such things exist. But the two of you—oh, for a year or so—there are some fairly cozy dungeons."

Hoddan seethed suddenly. He'd tried to do something brilliant on Walden, and had been framed into jail for life. He'd defended his life and property on Darth, and nearly the same thing popped up as a prospect. Hoddan angrily suspected fate and chance of plain conspiracy against him.

But there was an interruption. A clanking of arms sounded somewhere nearby. Men with long, gruesome, glittering spears came through a doorway. They stood aside. A girl entered the great hall. More spearmen followed her. They stopped by the door. The girl came across the hall.

She was a pretty girl, but Hoddan hardly noticed the fact with so many other things on his mind.

Thal, behind him, said in a quivering voice:

"My Lady Fani, I beg you to plead with your father for his most faithful retainer!"

The girl looked in surprise at him. Her eyes fell on Hoddan. She looked interested. Hoddan, at that moment, was very nearly as disgusted and as indignant as a man could be. He did not look romantically at

her—which to the Lady Fani, daughter of that powerful lord, Don Loris, was a novelty. He did not look
at her at all. He ground his teeth.

"Don't try to wheedle me, Fani!" snapped Don
Loris. "I am a reasonable man, but I indulge you
too much—even to allowing you to refuse that young
imbecile Ghek, with no end of inconvenience as a
result. But I will not have you question my decision
about Thal and this Hoddan person!"

The girl said pleasantly:

"Of course not, father. But what have they
done?"

"The two of them," snapped Don Loris again, "fought
twenty men today and defeated all of them! Thal plundered them. Then thirty other men, mounted, tried
to avenge the first and they defeated them also! Thal
plundered eighteen. And all this was permissible, if
unlikely. But they did it with stun-pistols! Everybody
will soon be talking of it! They'll know that this Hoddan
came to Darth to see me! They'll suspect that I imported
new weapons for political purposes! They'll guess at the
prettiest scheme I've had these twenty years!"

"But did they really defeat so many?" she asked,
marveling. "That's wonderful! And Thal was undoubtedly fighting in defense of someone you'd told him to
protect, as a loyal retainer should do. Wasn't he?"

"I wish," fumed her father, "that you would not
throw in irrelevancies! I sent him to get Hoddan this
afternoon, not to massacre my neighbors' retainers—or
rather, not to not massacre them. A little bloodletting
would have done no harm, but stun-pistols—"

"He was protecting somebody he was told to protect," said Fani. "And this other man, this—"

"Hoddan, Bron Hoddan," said her father irritably. "Yes. He was protecting himself! Doubtless he thought he did me a service in doing that! But if he'd only let himself get killed quietly, the whole affair would be simplified!"

The Lady Fani said with quiet dignity:

"By the same reasoning, father, it would simplify things greatly if I let the Lord Ghek kidnap me."

"It's not the same thing at all."

"At least," said Fani, "I wouldn't have a pack of spearmen following me about like foul-breathed puppies everywhere I go!"

"It's not the same."

"And it's especially unreasonable," continued the Lady Fani with even greater dignity, "when you could put Thal and this Hoddan person on duty to guard me instead. If they can fight twenty and thirty men at once, all by themselves, it doesn't seem to me that you think much of my safety when you want to lock them up somewhere instead of using them to keep your daughter safe from that particularly horrible Ghek!"

Don Loris swore in a cracked voice. Then he said:

"To end the argument I'll think it over. Until tomorrow. Now go away!"

Fani, beaming, rose and kissed him on the forehead. He squirmed. She turned to leave, and beckoned casually for Thal and Hoddan to follow her.

"My chieftain," said Thal tremulously, "do we depart too?"

"Yes!" rasped Don Loris. "Get out of my sight!"

Thal moved with agility in the wake of the Lady

Fani. Hoddan picked up his bag and followed. This, he considered darkly, was in the nature of a reprieve only; if those three spaceships overhead did come from Walden . . . but why three?

The Lady Fani went out the door she'd entered by. Some of the spearmen went ahead, and others closed in behind her. Hoddan followed. There were stone steps leading upward. They were steep and uneven and interminable. Hoddan climbed on aching legs for what seemed ages.

Stars appeared. The leading spearmen stepped out on a flagstoned level area. When Hoddan got there he saw that they had arrived at the battlements of a high part of the castle wall. Starlight showed a rambling wall of circumvallation, with peaked roofs inside it. He could look down into a courtyard where a fire burned and several men busily did things beside it. But there were no other lights. Beyond the castle wall the ground stretched away toward a nearby range of rugged low mountains. It was vaguely splotched with different degrees of darkness, where fields and pastures and woodland copses stood.

"Here's a bench," said Fani cheerfully, "and you can sit down beside me and explain things. What's your name, again, and where did you come from?"

"I'm Bron Hoddan," said Hoddan. He found himself scowling. "I come from Zan, where everybody is a space-pirate. My grandfather heads the most notorious of the pirate gangs."

"Wonderful!" said Fani, admiringly. "I knew you couldn't be just an ordinary person and fight like my father said you did today!"

Thal cleared his throat.

"Lady Fani."

"Hush!" said Fani. "You're a nice old fuddy-duddy that father sent to the spaceport because he figured you'd be too timid to get into trouble. Hush!" To Hoddan she said, "Now, tell me all about the fighting. It must have been terrible!"

She watched him with her head on one side, expectantly.

"The fighting I did today," said Hoddan angrily, "was exactly as dangerous and as difficult as shooting fish in a bucket. A little more trouble, but not much."

Even in the starlight he could see that her expression was more admiring than before.

"I thought you'd say something like that!" she said contentedly. "Go on!"

"That's all," said Hoddan.

"Quite all?"

"I can't think of anything else," he told her. He added drearily: "I rode a horse for three hours today. I'm not used to it. I ache. Your father is thinking of putting me in a dungeon until some scheme or other of his goes through. I'm disappointed. I'm worried about three lights that went across the sky at sundown and I'm simply too tired and befuddled for normal conversation."

"Oh," said Fani.

"If I may take my leave," said Hoddan querulously, "I'll get some rest and do some thinking when I get up. I'll hope to have more entertaining things to say."

He got to his feet and picked up his bag.

Fani regarded him enigmatically. Thal squirmed.

"Thal will show you." Then Fani said deliberately, "Bron Hoddan, will you fight for me?"

Thal plucked anxiously at his arm. Hoddan said politely:

"If at all desirable, yes."

"Thank you," said Fani. "I am troubled by the Lord Ghek."

She watched him move away. Thal, moaning softly, went with him down another monstrosity of a stone stairway.

"Oh, what folly!" mourned Thal. "I tried to warn you! You would not pay attention! When the Lady Fani asked if you would fight for her, you should have said if her father permitted you that honor. But you said yes! The spearmen heard you! Now you must either fight the Lord Ghek within a night and day or be disgraced!"

"I doubt," said Hoddan tiredly, "that the obligations of Darthian gentility apply to the grandson of a pirate or an escap—to me."

"But they do apply!" said Thal, shocked. "A man who has been disgraced has no rights! Any man may plunder him, any man may kill him at will. But if he resists plundering or kills anybody else in self-defense, he is hanged!"

Hoddan stopped short in his descent of the uneven stone steps.

"That's me from now on?" he asked sardonically. "Of course the Lady Fani didn't mean to put me on such a spot!"

"You were not polite," explained Thal. "She'd persuaded her father out of putting us in a dungeon until he thought of us again. You should at least have shown good manners! You should have said that you came here across deserts and flaming oceans because of the fame of her beauty. You might have said you heard songs of her sweetness beside campfires many worlds away. She might not have believed you, but—"

"Hold it!" said Hoddan. "That's just manners? What do you say to a girl you really like?"

"Oh, then," said Thal, "you get complimentary!"

Hoddan went heavily down the rest of the steps. He was not in the least pleased. On a strange world, with strange customs, and with his weapons losing their charges every hour, he did not need any handicaps. But if he got into a worse-than-outlawed category such as Thal described . . .

At the bottom of the stairs he said, seething:

"When you've tucked me in bed, go back and ask the Lady Fani to arrange for me to have a horse and permission to go fight this Lord Ghek right after breakfast!"

He was too much enraged to think further. He let himself be led into some sort of quarters which probably answered Don Loris' description of a cozy dungeon. Thal vanished and came back with ointments for Hoddan's blisters, but no food. He explained again that if food were given to Hoddan it would make it disgraceful to cut his throat. And Hoddan swore poisonously, but stripped off his garments and smeared himself lavishly where he had lost skin. The ointment stung like fire, and he presently lay awake in a sort of dreary fury. And he was ravenous.

It seemed to him that he lay awake for aeons, but he must have dozed off because he was wakened by a yell. It was not a complete yell, only the first part of one. It stopped in a particularly unpleasant fashion, and its echoes went reverberating through the stony walls of the castle. Hoddan was out of bed with a stun-pistol in his hand in a hurry. The first yell was followed by other shouts and outcries, by the clashing of steel upon steel, and all the frenzied tumult of combat in the dark. The uproar moved. In seconds the sound of fighting came from a plainly different direction, as if the striking force were rushing through only indifferently defended corridors.

It would not pass before Hoddan's door, but he growled to himself. On a feudal world, presumably one might expect anything. But there was a situation in being, here, in which etiquette required a rejected suitor to carry off a certain scornful maiden by force. Some young lordling named Ghek had to carry off Fani or be considered a man of no spirit.

A chemical gun went off somewhere. It went off again. There was almost an instant of silence. Then an intolerable screeching of triumph, and shrieks of another sort entirely, and the excessively loud clash of arms once more.

Hoddan was now clothed. He jerked on the door to open it.

The door was locked. He raged. He flung himself against it and it barely quivered. It was barred on the outside. He swore in highly indecorous terms, and tore his bedstead apart to get a battering-ram.

The fighting reached a climax. He heard a girl scream, and without question knew that it was Lady Fani, and equally without question knew that he would fight to keep any girl from being abducted by a man she didn't want to marry. He swung the log which was the corner-post of his bed. Something cracked. He swung again.

The sound of battle changed to that of a running fight. The objective of the raiders had been reached. Having gotten what they came for—and it could only be Fani—they retreated swiftly, fighting only to cover their retreat. Hoddan swung his bed-leg with furious anger. He heard a flurry of yells and swordplay, and a fierce, desperate cry from Fani among them, and a plank in his guestroom-dungeon door gave way. He struck again. The running raiders poured past a corner some yards away. He battered and swore, and swore and battered as the tumult moved, and he suddenly heard a scurrying thunder of horses' hoofs outside the castle. There were yells of derisive triumph and the pounding, rumbling sound of horses headed away in the night.

Still raging inarticulately, Hoddan crashed his small log at the door. He was not consciously concerned about the distress Don Loris might feel over the abduction of his daughter. But there is an instinct in most men against the forcing of a girl to marriage against her will. Hoddan battered at his door. Around him the castle began to hum like a hive of bees. Women cried out or exclaimed, and men shouted furiously to one another; off-duty fighting men came belatedly, looking for somebody to fight, dragging weapons behind them and not knowing where to find enemies.

Bron Hoddan probably made as much noise as any four of them. Somebody brought a light somewhere near. It shone through the cracks in the splintered planks. He could see to aim. He smote savagely and the door came apart. It fell outward and he found himself in the corridor outside, being stared at by complete strangers.

"It's the engineer," someone explained to someone else. "I saw him when he rode in with Thal."

"I want Thal," said Hoddan coldly. "I want a dozen horses. I want men to ride them with me." He pushed his way forward. "Which way to the stables?"

But then he went back and picked up his bag of stun-pistols. His air was purposeful and his manner furious. The retainers of Don Loris were in an extremely apologetic frame of mind. The Lady Fani had been carried off into the night by a raiding-party undoubtedly led by Lord Ghek. The defenders of the castle hadn't prevented it. So there was no special reason to obey Hoddan, but there was every reason to seem to be doing something useful.

He found himself almost swept along by agitated retainers trying to look as if they were about a purposeful affair. They went down a long ramp, calling uneasily to each other. They eddied around a place where two men lay quite still on the floor. Then there were shouts of, "Thal! This way, Thal!" and Hoddan found himself in a small, stone-walled courtyard. It was filled with milling figures and many waving torches. And there was Thal, desperately pale and frightened. Behind him there was Don Loris, his eyes burning and his hands twitching, literally speechless from fury.

"Pick a dozen men, Thal!" commanded Hoddan. "Get 'em on horses! Get a horse for me, dammit! I'll show 'em how to use the stun-pistols as we ride!"

Thal panted, shaking:

"They hamstrung most of the horses!"

"Get the ones that are left!" barked Hoddan. He suddenly raged at Don Loris. "Here's another time stun-pistols get used on Darth! Object to this if you want to!"

Hoofbeats. Thal on a horse that shied and reared at the flames and confusion. Other horses, skittish and scared, with the smell of spilled blood in their nostrils, fighting the men who led them, their eyes rolling.

Thal called names as he looked about him. There was plenty of light. As he called a name, a man climbed on a horse. Some of the chosen men swaggered; some looked woefully unhappy. But with Don Loris glaring frenziedly upon them in the smoky glare, no man refused.

Hoddan climbed ungracefully upon the mount that four or five men held for him. Thal, with a fine sense of drama, seized a torch and waved it above his head. There was a vast creaking, and an unsuspected gate opened, and Thal rode out with a great clattering of hoofs and the others rode out after him.

There were lights everywhere about the castle, now. All along the battlements men had lighted the fire-baskets and lowered them partway down the walls, to disclose any attacking force which might have dishonorable intentions toward the stronghold. Others waved torches from the battlements. Streaming smoke, lighted by the flames, made weird patterns in the starlit night.

Thal swung his torch and pointed to the ground.

"They rode here!" he called to Hoddan. "They ride for Ghek's castle!"

Hoddan said angrily:

"Put out that light! Do you want to advertise how few we are and what we're doing? Here, ride close!"

Thal flung down the torch. There was confusion

and crowding on Hoddan's right-hand side. The smell of horse-flesh was strong. Thal boomed:

"The pickings should be good, eh? Why do you want me?"

"You've got to learn something," snapped Hoddan. "Here! This is a stun-pistol. It's set for single-shot firing only. You hold it so, with your fingers along this rod. You point your finger at a man and pull this trigger. The pistol will buzz briefly. You let the trigger loose and point at another man and pull the trigger again. Understand? Don't try to use it over ten yards. You're no marksman! And don't waste charges! Remember what to do?"

There on a galloping horse beside Hoddan in the darkness, Thal zestfully repeated his lesson.

"Show another man and send him to me for a pistol," Hoddan commanded curtly. "I'll be showing others."

He turned to the man who rode too close to his left. Before he had fully instructed that man, another clamored for a weapon on his right. Hoddan checked his instructions and armed him.

The band of pursuing horsemen pounded through the dark night under strangely patterned stars. Hoddan held on to his saddle and harked out instructions to teach Darthians how to shoot. He felt very queer. He began to worry. With the lights of Don Loris' castle long vanished behind, he began to realize how very small his troop of pursuers happened to he. They'd be outnumbered many times by those they sought to pursue.

Thal had said something about horses being hamstrung. There must, then, have been two attacking parties. One swarmed into the stables and drew all defending retainers there. Then the other poured over a wall or in through a bribed-open sally port, and rushed for the Lady Fani's apartments. The point was that the attackers had made sure there could be only a token pursuit. They knew they were many times stronger than any who might come after them. It would be absurd for them to flee.

Hoddan kicked his horse and got up to the front of the column of riders.

"Thal!" he snapped. "They'll be idiots if they keep on running away, now they're too far off to worry about men on foot. They'll stop and wait for us . . . most of them anyhow. We're riding into an ambush!"

"Good pickings, eh?" said Thal enthusiastically. "It would be disgrace not to fight them. The plunder—"

"Idiot!" yelped Hoddan. "These men know you. You know what I can do with stun-pistols! Tell them we're riding into ambush. They're to follow close behind us two! Tell them they're not to shoot at anybody more than five yards off and not coming at them, and if any man stops to plunder I'll kill him personally!"

Thal gaped at him.

"Not stop to plunder?"

"Ghek won't!" snapped Hoddan. "He'll take Fani on to his castle, leaving most of his men behind to massacre us! We've got to catch up to him before he shuts his castle gate in our faces!"

Thal reined aside and Hoddan pounded on at the head of the tiny troop. This was the second time in his life he'd been on a horse. He held on doggedly, riding with all the grace and spirit of a sack of cement. This adventure was not exhilarating. He was badly worried about innumerable things that could go wrong. Even if everything went right he'd still have plenty of troubles! It came into his mind, depressingly, that supposedly stirring action like this was really no more satisfying than piracy or the practice of electronics as a business. It was something one got into and had to go through with. Fani, for example, had tricked him into a fix in which he had to fight Ghek or be disgraced—and to be disgraced on Darth was equivalent to suicide.

His horse started up a gentle rise in the ground. It grew steeper. The horse slacked in its galloping. The incline grew steeper still. The horse slowed to a walk. Soon the dim outline of trees appeared overhead.

"Perfect place for an ambush," Hoddan reflected dourly. He got out a stun-pistol. He set the stud for continuous fire—something he hadn't dared trust to the others.

His horse breasted the rise. There was a yell ahead and dim figures plunged toward him.

He painstakingly made ready to swing his stun-pistol from his extreme right all the way to the extreme left. The pistol should be capable of continuous fire for four seconds. But it was operating on stored charge. He didn't dare count on more than three.

He pulled the trigger. The stun-pistol hummed; its noise was inaudible through the yells of the charging partisans of the Lord Ghek.

Chapter 5

Hoddan swore from the depths of a very considerable vocabulary.

"You" (censored), "get back on your horses or I'll blast you and leave you for Ghek's men to handle when they're able to move about again! Get back on those horses!"

The men got back on their horses.

"Now go on ahead," rasped Hoddan. "All of you! I'm going to count you!"

The dozen horsemen from Don Loris' stronghold rode reluctantly on ahead. He did count them. He rode on, shepherding them before him.

"Ghek," he told them in a blood-curdling tone, "has a bigger prize than any cash you'll plunder from one of his shot-down retainers! He's got the Lady Fani! He won't stop before he has her behind castle walls! We've got to catch up with him! Do you want to try to climb into his castle by your fingernails? You'll do it if he gets there first!"

The horses moved a little faster. Thal said with surprising humility:

"If we force our horses too much, they'll be exhausted before we can catch up."

"Figure it out," snapped Hoddan. "We have to catch up!"

He settled down to more of the acute discomfort that riding was to him. Hoddan knew that his party was slowed down by him. Presently he began to feel bitterly sure that Ghek would reach his castle before he was overtaken,

"This place he's heading for," he said discouragedly to Thal, "any chance of our rushing it?"

"Oh, no!" said Thal dolefully. "Ten men could hold it against a thousand!"

"Then can't we make better time?"

Thal said resignedly:

"Ghek probably had fresh horses waiting, so he could keep on at top speed in his flight. I doubt that we will catch him, now."

"The Lady Fani," said Hoddan bitterly, "has put me in a fix so if I don't fight him I'm ruined!"

"Disgraced," corrected Thal. He added mournfully, "It's the same thing."

Gloom descended on the whole party as it filled their leaders. Insensibly, the pace of the horses slackened still more. They had done well. But a horse that can cover fifty miles a day at its own gait, can be exhausted in ten or less, if pushed. By the time Hoddan and his men were within two miles of Ghek's castle, their mounts were extremely reluctant to move faster than a walk. At a mile, they were kept in motion only by kicks.

The route they followed was specific. There was no choice of routes here in the hills. They could only follow every twist and turn of the trail, among steep mountain flanks and minor peaks. But suddenly they came to a clear, wide valley; yellow cressets burned at its upper end, no more than a half mile distant. They showed a castle gate, open, with the last of a party of horsemen filing into it. Even as Hoddan swore, the gate closed. Faint shouts of triumph came from inside the castle walls.

"I'd have bet on this," said Hoddan miserably. "Stop

here, Thal. Pick out a couple of your more hangdog characters and fix them up with their hands apparently tied behind their backs. We take a breather for five minutes."

He would not let any man dismount. He shifted himself about on his own saddle, trying to find a comfortable way to sit. He failed. At the end of five minutes he gave orders. There were still shouts occasionally from within Ghek's castle. They had that unrhythmic frequency which suggested that they were responses to a speech. Ghek was making a fine, dramatic spectacle of his capture of an unwilling bride. He was addressing his retainers and saying that through their fine loyalty, cooperation and willingness to risk all for their chieftain, they now had the Lady Fani to be their chatelaine. He thanked them from the bottom of his heart and they were invited to the official wedding, which would take place some time tomorrow, most likely.

Before the speech was quite finished, however, Hoddan and his weary followers rode up into the patch of light cast by the cressets outside the walls. Thal bellowed to the battlements.

"Prisoners!" he roared, according to instructions from Hoddan. "We caught some prisoners in the ambush! They got fancy news! Tell Lord Ghek he'd better get their story right off! No time to waste! Urgent!"

Hoddan played the part of one prisoner, just in case anybody noticed from above that one man rode as if either entirely unskilled in riding or else injured in a fight.

He heard shoutings over the walls. He glared at his men and they drooped in their saddles. The gate creaked open and the horsemen from Don Loris' castle filed inside. They showed no elation, because Hoddan had promised to ram a spear down the throat of any man who gave away his strategy ahead of time. The gate closed behind them. Men came to take their horses. This could have revealed that the newcomers were strangers, but Ghek would have recruited new and extra retainers for the emergency of tonight. There would be many strange faces in his castle just now.

"Good fight, eh?" bellowed an ancient, long-retired retainer with a wine bottle in his hand.

"Good fight!" agreed Thal.

"Good plunder, eh?" bellowed the ancient above the heads of younger men. "Like the good old days?"

"Better!" boomed Thal.

At just this instant the young Lord Ghek's personal servant appeared.

"What's this about prisoners with fancy news?" he demanded. "What is it?"

"Don Loris!" whooped Thal. "Long live the Lady Fani!"

Hoddan carefully opened fire with the continuous-fire stud of this pistol—his third tonight—pressed down. The merrymakers in the courtyard wavered and went down in windrows. Thal opened fire with a stun-pistol. The others bellowed and began to fling bolts at every living thing they saw.

"To the Lady Fani!" rasped Hoddan, getting off his horse with as many creakings as the castle gate.

His followers now dismounted. They fired with reckless abandon. A stun-pistol, which does not kill, imposes few restraints upon its user. If you shoot somebody who doesn't need to be shot, he may not like it but he isn't permanently harmed. So the twelve who'd followed Hoddan poured in what would have been a murderous fire if they'd been shooting bullets, but was no worse than devastating as matters stood.

There were screams and flight and utterly hopeless defiances by sword-armed and spear-armed men. In instants Hoddan went limping into the castle with Thal by his side, searching for Fani and Lord Ghek. Hoddan's men went raging happily through corridors and halls. They used their stun-pistols with zest. Hoddan heard Fani scream angrily and he and Thal went swiftly to see. They came upon the young Lord Ghek trying to let Fani down out of a window on a rope. He undoubtedly intended to follow her and complete his abduction on the run. But Fani bit him, and Hoddan said vexedly:

"Look here! It seems that I'm disgraced if I don't fight you somehow—"

The young Lord Ghek rushed him, sword out, eyes blazing in a fine frenzy of despair. Hoddan brought him down with a buzz of the stun-gun.

One of Hoddan's followers came hunting for him.

"Sir," he sputtered, "we got the garrison cornered in their quarters, and we've been picking them off through the windows, and they think they're dropping dead and want to surrender. Shall we let 'em?"

"By all means," Hoddan said irritably. "And Thal, go get something heavier than a nightgown for the Lady Fani to wear, and then do what plundering is practical. But I want to be out of here in a half-hour. Understand?"

"I'll attend to the costume," said the Lady Fani vengefully. "You cut his throat while I'm getting dressed."

She nodded at the unconscious Lord Ghek on the pavement. She disappeared through a door nearby. Hoddan could guess that Ghek would have prepared something elaborate in the way of a trousseau for the bride he was to carry screaming from her home. Somehow it was the sort of thing a Darthian would do. Now Fani would enjoyably attire herself in the best of it.

"Thal," said Hoddan, "help me get this character into a closet, somewhere. He's not to be killed. I don't like him, but at this moment I don't like anybody very much, and I won't play favorites."

Thal dragged the insensible young nobleman into the next room. Hoddan locked the door and pocketed the key as Fani came into view again. She was splendidly attired, now, in brocade and jewels. Ghek had evidently hoped to placate her after marriage by things of that sort and had spent lavishly for them.

Now, throughout the castle there were many and diverse noises. Sometimes—not often—there was still the crackling hum of a stun-pistol. There were many more exuberant shoutings. They apparently had to do with loot. There were some squealings in female voices, but many more gigglings.

"I need not say," said the Lady Fani with dignity, "that I thank you very much. But I do say so."

"You're quite welcome," said Hoddan politely.

"And what are you going to do now?"

"I imagine," said Hoddan, "that we'll go down into the courtyard where our horses are. I shall sit down on something which will, I hope, remain perfectly still. And I may," he added morbidly, "I may eat an apple. I've had nothing to eat since I landed on Darth. People don't want to commit themselves to not cutting my throat. But after one half-hour we'll leave."

The Lady Fani looked sympathetic.

"But the castle's surrendered to you," she protested. "You hold it! Aren't you going to try to keep it?"

"There are a good many unpleasant characters out yonder," said Hoddan, waving his hand at the great outdoors, "who've reason to dislike me very much. They'll be anxious to express their emotions, when they feel up to it. I want to dodge them. And presently the people in this castle will realize that even stun-pistols can't keep on shooting indefinitely here. I don't want to be around when it occurs to them."

He offered his arm with a reasonably grand air and went limping with her down to the courtyard just inside the gate. Two of Don Loris' retainers staggered into view as they arrived, piling up plunder which ranged from a quarter-keg of wine to a mass of frothy stuff which must be female garments. They went away and other men arrived loaded down their own accumulations of loot. Some of the local inhabitants looked on with uneasy indignation.

Hoddan found a bench and sat down. He conspicuously displayed one of the weapons which had captured the castle. Ghek's defeated retainers looked at him darkly.

"Bring me something to eat," commanded Hoddan. "Then if you bring fresh horses for my men, and one extra for each to carry his plunder on, I'll take them away. I'll even throw in the Lord Ghek, who is now unharmed, but with his life in the balance. Otherwise—"

He moved the pistol suggestively. The normal inhabitants of Ghek's castle moved away, discussing the situation in subdued voices.

The Lady Fani sat down proudly on the bench beside him.

"You are wonderful!" she said with conviction.

"I used to cherish that illusion myself," said Hoddan.

"But nobody before in all Darthian history has ever fought twenty men, and then thirty men, and destroyed an ambush, and captured a castle, all in one day!"

"And without a meal," said Hoddan darkly, "and with a lot of blisters."

He considered. Somebody came running with bread and cheese and wine. He bit into the bread and cheese. After a moment he said, his mouth full:

"I once saw a man perform the unparalleled feat of jumping over nine barrels placed in a row. It had never been done before. But I didn't envy him. I never wanted to jump over nine barrels in a row! In the same way, I never especially wanted to fight other men or break up ambushes or capture castles. I want to do what I want to do, not what other people happen to admire."

"Then what do you want to do?" she asked admiringly.

"I'm not sure now," said Hoddan gloomily. He took a fresh bite. "But a little while ago I wanted to do some interesting and useful things in electronics, and get reasonably rich, and marry a delightful girl, and become a prominent citizen on Walden. I think I'll settle for another planet, now."

"My father will make you rich," said the girl proudly. "You saved me from being married to Ghek!"

Hoddan shook his head.

"I've got my doubts," he said. "He had a scheme to import a lot of stun-pistols and arm his retainers with them. Then he meant to rush the spaceport and have me set up a broadcast power unit that'd keep them charged all the time. Then he'd sit back and enjoy life. Holding the spaceport, nobody else could get stun-weapons, and nobody could resist his retainers who had 'em. So he'd be top man on Darth. He'd have exactly as much power as he chose to seize. I think he cherished that little idea; but now I've given advance publicity to stun-pistols. Now he hasn't a ghost of a chance of pulling it off. I'm afraid he'll be displeased with me."

"I can take care of that!" said Fani confidently. She did not question that her father would be displeased.

"Maybe you can," said Hoddan, "but though he's kept a daughter he's lost a dream. And that's bereavement! I know!"

Horses came plodding into the courtyard with Ghek's retainers driving them. They were anxious to get rid of their conquerors. Hoddan's men came trickling back, with armfuls of plunder to add to the piles they'd previously gathered. Thal took charge, commanding the exchange of saddles from tired to fresh horses and that the booty be packed on the extra mounts. It was time. Nine of the dozen looters were at work on the task when there was a tumult back in the castle. Yellings and the clash of steel. Hoddan shook his head.

He conjectured that somebody's pistol went empty and the local boys found it out.

He beckoned to a listening, tense, resentful inhabitant of the castle. He held up the key of the room in which he'd locked young Ghek.

"Now open the castle gate," he commanded, "and fetch out my last three men, and we'll leave without setting fire to anything. The Lord Ghek would like it that way. He's locked up in a room that's particularly inflammable."

The last statement was a guess, only, but Ghek's retainer looked horrified. He bellowed. There was a subtle change in the bitterly hostile atmosphere. Men came angrily to help load the spare horses. Hoddan's last three men came out of a corridor, wiping blood from various scratches and complaining plaintively that their pistols had shot empty and they'd had to defend themselves with knives.

Three minutes later the cavalcade rode out of the castle gate and away into the darkness. Hoddan had arrived here when Ghek was inside with Fani as his prisoner, when there were only a dozen men without and at least a hundred inside to defend the walls. And the castle was considered impregnable.

In a half-hour Hoddan's followers had taken the castle, rescued Fani, looted it superficially, gotten fresh horses for themselves and spare ones for their plunder, and were headed away again. In only one respect were they worse off than when they arrived. Some stun-pistols were empty.

Hoddan searched the sky and pieced together the star pattern he'd noted before.

"Hold it!" he said sharply to Thal. "We don't go

back the same way we came. The gang that ambushed us will be stirring around again, and we haven't got full stun-pistols now. We make a wide circle around those characters!"

"Why?" demanded Thal. "There are only so many passes. The only other one is three times as long. And it is disgraceful to avoid a fight."

"Thal!" snapped an icy voice from beside Hoddan. "You have an order! Obey it!"

Even in the darkness, Hoddan could see Thal jump.

"Yes, my Lady Fani," said Thal shakily. "But we go a long distance roundabout."

The direction of motion through the night now changed. The long line of horses moved in deepest darkness, lessened only by the light of many stars. Even so, in time one's eyes grew accustomed and it was a glamorous spectacle.

Presently they came to a narrow defile which opened out before them. And there, far, far away, they could see the sky as vaguely brighter. As they went on, indeed, a glory of red and golden colorings appeared at the horizon.

And out of that magnificence three bright lights suddenly darted. In strict V-formation, they flashed from the sunrise toward the west. They went overhead, more brilliant than the brightest stars, and when partway down to the horizon they suddenly winked out.

"What on Earth are they?" demanded Fani. "I never saw anything like that before!"

"They're spaceships in orbit," said Hoddan. He was as astounded as the girl, but for a different reason. "I thought they'd be landed by now!"

It changed everything. He could not see what the change amounted to, but the change was there.

"We're going to the spaceport," he told Thal curtly. "We'll recharge our stun-pistols there. I thought those ships had landed. They haven't. Now we'll see if we can keep them aloft! How far to the landing-grid?"

"You insisted," complained Thal, "that we not go back to Don Loris' castle by the way we left it. There are only so many passes through the hills. The only other one is very long. We are only four miles—"

"Then we head there right now!" snapped Hoddan. "And we step up the speed!"

He barked commands to his followers. Thal, puzzled but in dread of acid comment from Fani, bustled up and down the line of men, insisting on a faster pace. Finally even the led horses, loaded with loot, managed to get up to a respectable ambling trot. The sunrise proceeded. Dew upon the straggly grass became visible. Separate drops appeared as gems upon the grass blades, and then began gradually to vanish as the sun's disk showed itself. Then the angular metal framework of the landing-grid rose dark against the sunrise sky.

When they rode up to it, Hoddan reflected that it was the only really civilized structure on the planet. Architecturally it was surely the least pleasing. It had been built when Darth was first settled on, and when ideas of commerce and interstellar trade seemed reasonable. It was a half-mile high and built of massive metal beams. It loomed hugely overhead when the double file of shaggy horses trotted under its lower arches and across the grass-grown space within it. Hoddan headed purposefully for the control shed. There was no sign of movement anywhere. The steeply gabled roofs of the nearby town showed only the fluttering of tiny birds. No smoke rose from chimneys. Yet the slanting morning sunshine was bright.

As Hoddan actually reached the control shed, he saw a sleepy man in the act of putting a key in the door. He dismounted within feet of that man, who turned and blinked sleepily at him, and then immediately looked the reverse of cordial. It was the same man he'd stung with a stun-pistol the day before.

"I've come back," said Hoddan, "for a few more kilowatts." The red-headed man swore angrily.

"Hush!" said Hoddan gently. "The Lady Fani is with us."

The red-headed man jerked his head around and paled. Thal glowered at him. Others of Don Loris' retainers shifted their positions significantly, to make their oversized knives handier.

"We'll come in," said Hoddan. "Thal, collect the pistols and bring them inside."

Fani swung lightly to the ground and followed him in. She looked curiously at the cables and instrument hoards and switches inside. On one wall a red light pulsed, and went out, and pulsed again. The red-headed man looked at it.

"You're being called," said Hoddan. "Don't answer it."

The red-headed man scowled. Thal came in with an armful of stun-pistols in various stages of discharge. Hoddan briskly broke the butt of one of his own and presented it to the terminals he'd used the day before.

"He's not to touch anything, Thal," said Hoddan. To the red-headed man he observed, "I suspect that call's been coming in all night. Something was in orbit at sundown. You closed up shop and went home early, eh?"

"Why not?" rasped the red-headed man. "There's only one ship a month!"

"Sometimes," said Hoddan, "there are specials. But I commend your negligence. It was probably good for me."

He charged one pistol, and snapped its butt shut, and snapped open another, and charged it. There was no difficulty, of course. In minutes all the pistols he'd brought from Walden were ready for use again.

He tucked away as many as he could conveniently carry on his person. He handed the rest to Thal. He went competently to the pulsing red signal. He put headphones to his ears. He listened. His expression became extremely strange, as if he did not quite understand nor wholly believe what he heard.

"Odd," he said mildly. He considered for a moment or two. Then he rummaged around in the drawers of desks. He found wire clippers. He began to snip wires in half.

The red-headed man started forward automatically. "Take care of him, Thal," said Hoddan.

He cut the microwave receiver free of its wires and cables. He lifted it experimentally and opened part of its case to make sure the thermo battery that would power it in an emergency was there and in working order. It was.

"Put this on a horse, Thal," commanded Hoddan. "We're taking it up to Don Loris'."

The red-headed man's mouth dropped open. He said stridently:

"Hey! You can't do that!" Hoddan glared at him. The redhead then said sourly: "All right, you can. I'm not trying to stop you with all those hardcases outside!"

"You can build another in a week," said Hoddan kindly. "You must have spare parts."

Thal carried the communicator outside. Hoddan opened a cabinet, threw switches, and painstakingly cut and snipped and snipped at a tangle of wires within.

"Just your instrumentation," he explained. "You won't use the grid until you've got this fixed, too. A few days of harder work than you're used to. That's all!"

He led the way out again, and on the way explained to Fani:

"Pretty old-fashioned job, this grid. They make simpler ones nowadays. They'll be able to repair it, though, in time. Now we go back to your father's castle. He may not be pleased, but he should be mollified."

He saw Fani mount lightly into her own saddle and shook his head gloomily. He climbed clumsily into his own. They moved off to return to Don Loris' stronghold. Hoddan suffered.

They reached the castle before noon, and the sight of the Lady Fani produced enthusiasm and loud cheers. The loot displayed by the returned wayfarers increased the rejoicing. There was envy among the men who had stayed behind. There were respectfully admiring looks cast upon Hoddan. He had displayed, in furnishing opportunities for plunder, the most-admired quality a leader of feudal fighting men could show.

The Lady Fani beamed as she, Thal, and Hoddan, all very dusty and travel-stained, presented themselves to her father in the castle's great hall.

"Here's your daughter, sir," said Hoddan, and yawned. "I hope there won't be any further trouble with Ghek. We took his castle and looted it a little and brought back some extra horses. Then we went to the spaceport. I recharged my stun-pistols and put the landing-grid out of order for the time being. I brought away the communicator there." He yawned again. "There's something highly improper going on, up just beyond atmosphere. There are three ships up there in orbit, and they were trying to call the spaceport in non-regulation fashion, and it's possible that some of your neighbors would be interested. So I postponed everything until I could get some sleep. It seemed to me that when better skulduggeries are concocted, that Don Loris and his associates ought to concoct them. And if you'll excuse me—"

He moved away practically dead on his feet. If he had been accustomed to horseback riding, he wouldn't have been so exhausted. But now he yawned, and yawned, and Thal took him to a room quite different from the guestroom-dungeon to which he'd been taken the night before. He noted that the door, this time, opened inward. He braced chairs against it to make sure that nobody could open it from without. He lay down and slept heavily.

He was awakened by loud poundings. He roused himself enough to say sleepily:

"Whaddyawant?"

"The lights in the sky!" cried Fani outside the door. "The ones you say are spaceships! It's sunset again, and I just saw them. But there aren't three, anymore. Now there are nine!"

"All right," said Hoddan. He laid down his head again and thrust it into his pillow. Then he was suddenly very wide awake. He sat up with a start.

Nine spaceships? That wasn't possible! That would be a spacefleet! And there were no spacefleets! Walden would certainly have never sent more than one ship to demand his surrender to its police. The Space Patrol never needed more than one ship anywhere. Commerce wouldn't cause ships to travel in company. *Piracy?* There couldn't be a pirate fleet! There'd never be enough loot anywhere to keep it in operation. Nine spaceships at one time. All traveling in orbit around a primitive planet like Darth.

It couldn't happen! Hoddan couldn't conceive of such a thing. But a recently developed pessimism suggested that since everything else, to date, had been to his disadvantage, this was probably a catastrophe also. He groaned and lay down to sleep again.

Chapter 6

When frantic bangings on the propped-shut door awakened him next morning, he confusedly imagined that they were noises in the communicator headphones.

But suddenly he opened his eyes. Somebody banged on the door once more. A voice cried angrily:

"Bron Hoddan! Wake up or I'll go away and let whatever happens to you, happen! Wake up!"

It was the voice of the Lady Fani, at once indignant, tearful, solicitous and angry.

"Hello. I'm awake. What's up?"

"Come out of there!" cried Fani's voice, simultaneously exasperated and filled with anxiety. "Things are happening! Somebody's here from Walden! They want you!"

Hoddan could not believe it. It was too unlikely. But he opened the door and Thal came in, and Fani followed.

"Good morning," said Hoddan automatically.

Thal said mournfully:

"A *bad* morning, Bron Hoddan! A bad morning! Men from Walden came riding over the hills."

"How many?"

"Two," said Fani angrily. "A fat man in a uniform, and a young man who looks like he wants to cry. They had an escort of retainers from one of my father's neighbors. They were stopped at the gate, of course, and they sent a written message to my father, and he had them brought inside right away."

Hoddan shook his head.

"They probably said that I'm a criminal and that I should be sent back to Walden. How'd they get down? The landing-grid isn't working."

"They landed in something that used rockets," Fani said viciously. "It came down close to a castle over that way—only six or seven miles from the spaceport. They asked for you. They said you'd landed from the last liner from Walden. And because you and Thal fought so splendidly, why everybody's talking about you. So the chieftain over there accepted a present of money from them, and gave them horses as a return gift, and sent them here with a guard. Thal talked to the guards. The men from Walden have promised huge gifts of money if they help take you back to the thing that uses rockets."

"I suspect," said Hoddan, "that it would be a spaceboat. Yes. With a built-in, tool-steel cell to keep me from telling anybody how to make—" He stopped and grimaced. "They'd take me to the spaceport in a soundproof can and I'd be hauled back to Walden. Fine!"

"What are you going to do?" asked Fani anxiously.

Hoddan's ideas were not clear. But Darth was not a healthy place for him. It was extremely likely, for example, that Don Loris would feel that the very bad jolt he'd given that astute schemer's plans, by using stun-pistols at the spaceport, had been neatly canceled out by his rescue of Fani. He would regard Hoddan with a mingled gratitude and aversion that would amount to calm detachment. Don Loris could not be counted on as a really warm, personal friend.

On the other hand, the social system of Darth was not favorable to a stranger with an already lurid reputation for fighting. Another disadvantage was that his weapons would be useless unless frequently recharged; he couldn't count on always being able to do that.

As a practical matter, his best bet was probably to investigate the nine inexplicable ships overhead. They hadn't cooperated with the Waldenians. It could be inferred that no confidential relationship existed up there. It was even possible that the nine ships and the Waldenians didn't know of each other's presence. There is a lot of room in space. If both called on ship-frequency and listened on ground-frequency, they would not have picked up each other's summons to the ground.

"You've got to do something!" insisted Fani. "I saw father talking to them! He looked happy, and he never looks happy unless he's planning some skulduggery!"

"I think," said Hoddan, "that I'll have some breakfast, if I may. As soon as I fasten up my shipbag."

Thal said mournfully:

"If anything happens to you, something will happen to me too, because I helped you."

"Breakfast first," said Hoddan. "That, as I understand it, should make it disgraceful for your father to have my throat cut. But beyond that . . ." He said gloomily, "Thal, get a couple of horses outside the wall. We may need to ride somewhere. I'm very much afraid we will. But first I'd like to have some breakfast."

"But aren't you going to face them? You could shoot them!" Fani said.

Hoddan shook his head.

"It wouldn't solve anything. Anyhow a practical man like your father won't sell me out before he's sure I can't pay off better. I'll bet on a conference with me before he makes a deal."

Fani stamped her foot.

"Outrageous! Think what you saved me from!"

But she did not question the possibility, Hoddan observed.

"A practical man can always make what he wants to do look like a noble sacrifice of personal inclinations to the welfare of the community," Hoddan commented. "Now I've decided that I've got to be practical myself, and that's one of the rules. How about breakfast?"

He strapped the shipbag shut on the stun-pistols his pockets would not hold. He made a minor adjustment to the communicator. It was not ruined, but nobody else could use it without much labor finding out what he'd done. This was the sort of thing his grandfather on Zan would have advised. His grandfather's views were explicit.

"Helping one's neighbor," the old man had said frequently, "is all right as a two-way job. But maybe he's laying for you. You get a chance to fix him so he can't do you no harm and you're a lot better off and he's one hell of a better neighbor!"

This was definitely true of the men from Walden. Hoddan guessed that Derec was one of them. The other would represent the police or the planetary government. It was probably just as true of Don Loris and others.

Hoddan found himself disapproving of the way the cosmos was designed.

As he sat at breakfast, Fani looked at him with interesting anxiety; he was filled with forebodings. The future looked dark. Yet what he asked of fate and chance was so simple! He asked only a career, riches, and a delightful girl to marry and the admiration of his fellow citizens. Trivial things! But it looked like he'd have to do battle for even such minor gifts of destiny.

Fani watched him eat.

"I don't understand you," she complained. "Anybody else would be proud of what he'd done and angry with my father. Or don't you think he'll act ungratefully?"

"Of course I do!" said Hoddan.

"Then why aren't you angry?"

"I'm hungry," said Hoddan.

"And you take it for granted that I want to be properly grateful," said Fani in one breath, "and yet you haven't show the least appreciation of my getting two horses over in that patch of woodland yonder!" She pointed and Hoddan nodded. "Besides having Thal there with orders to serve you faithfully—"

She stopped short. Don Loris appeared, beaming, at the top of the steps leading from the great hall where the conferences took place. He regarded Hoddan benignly.

"This is a very bad business, my dear fellow," he said benevolently. "Has Fani told you of the people who arrived from Walden in search of you? They tell me terrible things about you!"

"Yes," said Hoddan. He prepared a roll for biting. He continued, "One of them, I think, is named Derec. He's to identify me so good money isn't wasted paying for the wrong man. The other man's a policeman, isn't he?" He reflected a moment. "If I were you, I'd start talking at a million credits. You might get half that."

He bit into the roll as Don Loris looked shocked.

"Do you think," he asked indignantly, "that I would give up the rescuer of my daughter to emissaries from a foreign planet to be locked in a dungeon for life?"

"Not in those words," conceded Hoddan. "But after all, despite your deep gratitude to me, there are such things as one's duty to humanity as a whole. And while it would cause you bitter anguish if someone dear to you represented a danger to millions of innocent women and children—still, under such circumstances you might feel it necessary to do violence to your own emotions."

Don Loris looked at him with abrupt suspicion. Hoddan waved the roll.

"Moreover," he observed, "gratitude for actions done on Darth does not entitle you to be judge of my actions on Walden. While you might and even should feel obliged to defend me in all things I have done on Darth, your obligation to me does not extend to uphold my acts on Walden."

Don Loris looked extremely uneasy.

"I may have thought something like that," he admitted. "But—"

"So that," continued Hoddan, "while your debt to me cannot and should not be overlooked, nevertheless—" Hoddan put the roll into his mouth and spoke less clearly. "—nevertheless you feel that you should give consideration to the claims of Walden to inquire into my actions while there."

He chewed, swallowed, and said gravely:

"And can I make death rays?"

Don Loris brightened. He drew a deep breath of relief. He said complainingly:

"I don't see why you're so sarcastic! Yes. That is a rather important question. You see, on Walden they don't know how to. They say you do. They're very anxious that nobody should be able to. Because, while in unscrupulous hands such an instrument of destruction would be most unfortunate . . . Ah . . . under proper control . . ."

"*Yours,*" said Hoddan.

"Say *ours,*" said Don Loris hopefully. "With my

experience of men and affairs, and my loyal and devoted retainers—"

"And cozy dungeons," said Hoddan. He wiped his mouth. "No."

Don Loris started violently.

"No, what?"

"No death rays," said Hoddan. "I can't make 'em. Nobody can. If they could be made, some star somewhere would be turning them out, or some natural phenomenon would let them loose from time to time. If there were such things as death rays, all living things would have died, or else would have adjusted to their weaker manifestations and developed immunity so they wouldn't be death rays any longer. As a matter of fact, that's probably been the case, some time in the past. So far as the gadget goes that they're talking about, it's been in use for a half-century in the Cetis cluster. Nobody's died of it yet."

Don Loris looked bitterly disappointed.

"That's the truth?" he asked unhappily. "Honestly? That's your last word on it?"

"Much," said Hoddan, "much as I hate to spoil the prospects of profitable skulduggery, that's my last word and it's true."

"But those men from Walden are very anxious!" protested Don Loris. "There was no ship available, so their government got a liner that normally wouldn't stop here to take an extra lifeboat aboard. It came out of overdrive in this solar system, let out the lifeboat, and went on its way again. Those two men are extremely anxious!"

"Ambitious, maybe," said Hoddan. "They're prepared to pay to overcome your sense of gratitude to me.

Naturally, you want all the traffic will bear. I think you can get a half-million."

Don Loris looked suspicious again.

"You don't seem worried," he said fretfully. "I don't understand you!"

"I have a secret," said Hoddan.

"What is it?"

"It will develop," said Hoddan.

Don Loris hesitated and essayed to speak, and thought better of it. He shrugged his shoulders and went slowly back to the flight of stone steps. He descended. The Lady Fani started to wring her hands. Then she said hopefully: "What's your secret?"

"That your father thinks I have one," said Hoddan. "Thanks for the breakfast. Should I walk out the gate, or—"

"It's closed," said the Lady Fani forlornly. "But I have a rope for you. You can go down over the wall."

"Thanks," said Hoddan. "It's been a pleasure to rescue you."

"Will you . . ." Fani hesitated. "I've never known anybody like you before. Will you ever come back?"

Hoddan shook his head at her.

"Once you asked me if I'd fight for you, and look what it got me into! No commitments."

He glanced along the battlements. There was a fairly large coil of rope in view. He picked up his bag and went over to it. He checked the fastening of one end and tumbled the other over the wall.

Ten minutes later he trudged up to Thal, waiting in the nearby woodland with two horses.

"The Lady Fani," he said, "has the kind of brains I like. She pulled up the rope again."

Thal did not comment. He watched morosely as Hoddan made the perpetually present shipbag fast to his saddle and then distastefully climbed aboard the horse.

"What are you going to do?" asked Thal unhappily. "I didn't make a parting-present to Don Loris, so I'll be disgraced if he finds out I helped you. And I don't know where to take you."

"Where," asked Hoddan, "did those characters from Walden come down?"

Thal told him. At the castle of a powerful feudal chieftain, on the plain, some four miles from the mountain range, and six miles this side of the spaceport.

"We ride there," said Hoddan. "Liberty is said to be sweet, but the man who said that didn't have blisters from a saddle. Let's go."

They rode away. There would be no immediate pursuit, and possibly none at all. Don Loris had left Hoddan at breakfast on the battlements. The Lady Fani would make as much confusion over his disappearance as she could. But there'd be no search for him until Don Loris had made his deal.

Hoddan was sure that Fani's father would have an enjoyable morning. He would relish the bargaining session. He'd explain in great detail how valuable had been Hoddan's service to him, in rescuing Fani from an abductor who would have been an intolerable son-in-law. He'd grow almost tearful as he described his affection for Hoddan, and how he loved his daughter. He would observe grievedly that they were asking him to betray the man who had saved for him the solace of his old age. He would mention also that the price they offered was an affront to his paternal affection and his dignity. Either they'd come up or the deal was off!

But meanwhile Hoddan and Thal rode industriously toward the place from which those emissaries had come.

All was tranquil. All was calm. Once they saw a dust cloud, and Thal turned aside to a providential wooded copse, in which they remained while a cavalcade went by. Thal explained that it was a feudal chieftain on his way to the spaceport town. It was simple discretion for them not to be observed, said Thal, because they had great reputations as fighting men. Whoever defeated them would become prominent at once. So somebody might try to pick a quarrel under one of the finer points of etiquette when it would be disgrace to use anything but standard Darthian implements for massacre. Hoddan admitted that he did not feel quarrelsome.

They rode on after a time, and in late afternoon the towers and battlements of the castle they sought appeared. The ground here was only gently rolling. They approached it with caution, following the reverse slope of hills. At last they penetrated horse-high brush to the point where they could see it clearly.

If Hoddan had been a student of early terrestrial history, he might have remarked upon the reemergence of ancient architectural forms to match the revival of primitive social systems. As it was, he noted in this feudal castle the use of bastions for flanking fire upon attackers; he recognized the value of battlements for the protection of defenders while allowing them to shoot, and the tricky positioning of sally ports. He even grasped the reason for the massive, stark, unornamented keep. But his eyes did not stay on the castle for long. He saw the spaceboat in which Derec and his more authoritative companion had arrived.

It lay on the ground a half-mile from the castle walls. It was a chubby, clumsy, flattened shape some forty feet long and nearly fifteen wide. The ground about it was scorched where it had descended upon its rocket flames. There were several horses tethered near it, and men who were plainly retainers of the nearby castle reposed in its shade.

Hoddan reined in.

"Here we part," he told Thal. "When we first met I enabled you to pick the pockets of a good many of your fellow countrymen. I never asked for my split of the take. I expect you to remember me with affection."

Thal clasped both of Hoddan's hands in his.

"If you ever return," he said with mournful warmth, "I am your friend!"

Hoddan nodded and rode out of the brushwood toward the spaceboat lifeboat that had landed the emissaries from Walden. That it landed so close to the spaceport, of course, was no accident. It was known on Walden that Hoddan had taken space-passage to Darth. He'd have landed only two days before his pursuers could reach the planet. And on a roadless, primitive world like Darth he couldn't have gotten far from the spaceport. So his pursuers would have landed close by, also. But it must have taken considerable courage. When the landing-grid failed to answer, it must have seemed likely that Hoddan's death rays had been at work.

Here and now, though, there was no uneasiness.

Hoddan rode heavily, without haste, through the slanting sunshine. He was seen from a distance and watched without apprehension by the loafing guards about the boat. He looked hot and thirsty. He was both. So the posted guard merely looked at him without too much interest when he brought his dusty mount up to the shadow the lifeboat cast, and apparently decided that there wasn't room to get into it.

He grunted a greeting and looked at them speculatively. "Those two characters from Walden," he observed, "sent me to get something from this thing, here. Don Loris told 'em I was a very honest man."

He painstakingly looked like a very honest man. After a moment there were responsive grins.

"If there's anything missing when I start back," said Hoddan, "I can't imagine how it happened! None of you would take anything. Oh, no! I bet you'll blame it on me!" He shook his head and said, "Tsk. Tsk. Tsk."

One of the guards sat up and said appreciatively: "But it's locked. Good."

"Being an honest man," said Hoddan amiably, "they told me how to unlock it."

He got off his horse. He removed the bag from his saddle. He went into the grateful shadow of the metal hull. He paused and mopped his face and then went to the boat's port. He put his hand on the turning-bar. Then he painstakingly pushed in the locking-stud with his other hand. Of course the handle turned. The port opened. The two from Walden would have thought everything safe because it was under guard. On Walden that protection would have been enough. On Darth, the spaceboat had not been looted simply because locks, there, were not made with separate vibration-checks to keep vibration from loosening them. On spaceboats such a precaution was usual.

"Give me two minutes," said Hoddan over his shoulder. "I have to get what they sent me for. After that everybody starts even."

He entered and closed the door behind him. Then he locked it. By the nature of things it is as needful to be able to lock a spaceboat from the inside as it is unnecessary to lock it from without.

He looked things over. Standard equipment everywhere. He checked everything, even to the fuel supply. There were knockings on the port. He continued to inspect. He turned on the vision screens, which provided the control-room and the rest of the boat with an unobstructed view in all directions. He was satisfied.

The knocks became bangings. Something approaching indignation could be deduced. The guards around the spaceboat felt that Hoddan was taking an unfair amount of time to pick the cream of the loot inside.

He got a glass of water. It was excellent. A second. The hangings became violent hammerings.

Hoddan seated himself leisurely in the pilot's seat and turned small knobs. He waited. He touched a button. There was a mildly thunderous bang outside, and the lifeboat reacted as if to a slight shock. The vision screens showed a cloud of dust at the spaceboat's stern, roused by a deliberate explosion in the rocket tubes. It also showed the retainers in full flight.

He waited until they were in safety and made the standard takeoff preparations. A horrific roaring started up outside. He touched controls and a

monstrous weight pushed him back in his seat. The
rocket swung, lifted, and shot skyward with greater
acceleration than before.

It went up at a lifeboat's full fall-like rate of climb,
leaving a trail of blue-white flame behind it. All the
surface of Darth seemed to contract swiftly below. The
spaceport and the town rushed toward a spot beneath
the spaceboat's tail. They shrank and shrank. He saw
other places. Mountains. Castles. He saw Don Loris'
stronghold. Higher, he saw the sea.

The sky turned purple. It went black with specks of
star shine in it. Hoddan swung to a westward course
and continued to rise, watching the star images as
they shifted on the screens. The image of the sun,
of course, was automatically diminished so that it was
not dazzling. The rockets continued to roar, though
in a minor fashion because there was no longer air
outside in which a bellow could develop.

Hoddan painstakingly made use of those rule-of-
thumb methods of astrogation which his piratical fathers
had developed and which a boy on Zan absorbed
without being aware. He wanted an orbit around
Darth. He didn't want to take time to try to compute
it. So he watched the star-images ahead and astern.
If the stars ahead rose above the planet's edge faster
than those behind sank down below it, he would he
climbing. If the stars behind sank down faster than
those ahead rose up, he would be descending. If all
the stars rose equally he'd be moving straight down.
It was not a complex method, and it worked.

Presently he relaxed. He sped swiftly toward the
sunrise line on Darth. This was the reverse of a normal
orbit, but it was the direction followed by the ships

up here. He hoped his orbit was lower than theirs. If it was, he'd overtake them from behind. If he were higher, they'd overtake him.

He turned on the spacephone. Its reception indicator was piously placed at *ground*. He shifted it to space, so that it would pick up calls going planetward, instead of listening vainly for replies from the non-operative landing-grid.

Instantly voices boomed in his ears. Many voices. An impossibly large number of voices. Many, many, many more than nine transmitters were in operation now!

"Idiot!" said a voice in quiet passion, "sheer off or you'll get in our drive-field!" A high-pitched voice said, "—and group two take second orbit position." Somebody bellowed, "But why don't they answer?" And another voice still, said formally, "Reporting group five, but four ships are staying behind with tanker, *Toya*, which is having stabilizer trouble."

Hoddan's eyes opened very wide. He turned down the sound while he tried to think. But there wasn't anything to think. He'd come aloft to scout three ships that had turned to nine, because he was in such a fix on Darth that anything strange might be changed into something useful. But this was more than nine ships—itself an impossibly large space-fleet. There was no reason why ships of space should ever travel together. There were innumerable reasons why they shouldn't. There was a limit to the number of ships that could be accommodated at any spaceport in the galaxy. There was no point, no profit, no purpose in a number of ships traveling together.

Darth's sunrise-line appeared far ahead. The lifeboat

would soon cease to be a bright light in the sky, now. The sun's image vanished from the rear screens. The boat went hurtling onward through the blackness of the planet's shadow while voices squabbled, wrangled, and formally reported.

During the period of darkness, Hoddan racked his brains for the vaguest of ideas on why so many ships should appear about an obscure and unimportant world like Darth. Presently the sunset-line appeared ahead, and far away he saw moving lights which were the hulls of the volubly communicating vessels. He stared, blankly. There were tens. Scores. He was forced to guess at the stark impossibility of more than a hundred spacecraft in view. As the boat rushed onward he had to raise the guess. It couldn't be, but . . .

He turned on the outside telescope, and the image on its screen was more incredible than the voices and the existence of the fleet itself. The scope focused first on a bulging monster. It was an antiquated freighter that had not been built for a hundred years. The second view was of a passenger-liner with the elaborate ornamentation that in past generations was considered suitable for space. There was a bulk-cargo ship, with no emergency rockets at all and the crew's quarters in long blisters built outside the gigantic tank which was the ship itself. There was a needle-like spaceyacht. More freighters, with streaks of rust on their sides where they had lain aground for tens of years.

The fleet was an anomaly, and each of its component parts was a separate freak. It was a gathering together of all the outmoded and obsolete hulks and monstrosities of space. One would have to scavenge half the galaxy to bring together so many crazy, overage derelicts that should have been in junk yards.

Then Hoddan drew an explosive deep breath. It was suddenly clear what the fleet was and what its reason must be. Why it stopped here, he could not yet guess.

Hoddan watched absorbedly. There was some emergency. It could be in the line of what an electronic engineer could handle.

Chapter 7

The spaceboat floated on upon a collision course with the arriving fleet. That would not mean, of course, actual contact with any of the strange vessels themselves. Crowded as the sunlit specks might seem from Darth's night-side shadow, they were sufficiently separated. It was more than likely that even with ten-mile intervals the ships would be considered much too crowded. But they came pouring out of emptiness to go into a swirling, plainly pre-intended orbit about the planet from which Hoddan had risen less than an hour before.

It was a gigantic traffic tangle, and Hoddan's boat drifted toward and into it. He counted a hundred ships, then . . . Long before he gave up, he'd numbered two hundred forty-seven of the oddities swarming to make a whirling band—a ring—around the planet Darth.

He was fairly sure that he knew what they were, now. But he could not possibly guess where they came from. And most mysterious of all was the question of why they'd come out of faster-than-light drive to make of themselves a celestial feature about a planet which had practically nothing to offer to anybody.

Presently the spaceboat was in the very thick of the fleet. His communicator spouted voices whose tones ranged from *basso profundo* to high tenor, and whose ideas of proper astrogation seemed to vary more widely still.

"You there!" boomed a voice with deafening volume. "You're in our clear-space! Sheer off!"

The volume of a signal in space varies as the square of the distance. This voice was thunderous. It came apparently from a nearby, potbellied ship of ancient vintage.

Hoddan's spaceboat floated on. The relative position of the two ships changed slowly. Another voice said indignantly:

"That's the same thing that missed us by less than a mile! You, there! Stop acting like a squig! Get on your own course!"

A third voice:

"What boat's that? I don't recognize it! I thought I knew all the freaks in this fleet, too!"

A fourth voice said sharply:

"That's not one of us! Look at the design! That's not us!"

Other voices broke in. There was babbling. Then a harsh voice roared:

"Quiet! I order it!" There was silence. The harsh voice said heavily, "Relay the image to me." There was a pause. The same voice said grimly: "It is not of our fleet. You, stranger! Identify yourself! Who are you and why did you slip secretly among us?"

Hoddan pushed the transmit button.

"My name is Bron Hoddan," he said. "I came up to find out why three ships, and then nine ships, went into orbit around Darth. It was somewhat alarming. Our landing-grid's disabled, anyhow, and it seemed wisest to look you over before we communicated and possibly told you something you might not believe."

The harsh voice said as grimly as before:

"You come from the planet below us? Darth? Why is your ship so small? The smallest of ours is greater."

"This is a lifeboat," said Hoddan pleasantly. "It's supposed to be carried on larger ships in case of emergency."

"If you will come to our leading ship," said the voice, "we will answer all your questions. I will have a smoke flare set off to guide you."

Hoddan said to himself:

No threats and no offers. I can guess why there are no threats. But they should offer something!

He waited. There was a sudden, huge eruption of vapor in space some two hundred miles away. Perhaps an ounce of explosion had been introduced into a rocket tube and fired. The smoke particles, naturally ionized, added their self-repulsion to the expansiveness of the explosive's gases. A cauliflower-like shape of filmy whiteness appeared and grew larger and thinner.

Hoddan drove toward the spot. He swung the boat around and killed its relative velocity. The leading ship was a sort of gigantic, shapeless, utterly preposterous ark-like thing. Hoddan could neither imagine a purpose for which it could have been used, nor a time when men would have built anything like it. Its huge sides seemed to be made exclusively of great doorways now tightly closed.

One of those doorways gaped wide. It would have admitted a good-sized modern ship. A nervous voice essayed to give Hoddan directions for getting the spaceboat inside what was plainly an enormous hold now pumped empty of air. He grunted and made the attempt. It was tricky. He sweated when he cut off his power. But he felt fairly safe. Rocket flames would burn down such a door, if necessary. He could work havoc if hostilities began.

The great door swung shut. The outside-pressure needle swung sharply and stopped at thirty centimeters of mercury pressure. There was a clanging. A smaller door evidently opened somewhere. Lights came on. Then figures appeared through a door leading to some other part of this ship.

Hoddan nodded to himself. The costume was odd. It was awkward. It was even primitive, but not in the fashion of the soiled, gaudily-colored garments of Darth. These men wore unrelieved black, with gray shirts. There was no touch of color about them. Even the younger ones wore beards. And of all unnecessary things, they wore flat-brimmed hats—in a spaceship!

Hoddan opened the door and said politely:

"Good morning. I'm Bron Hoddan. You were talking to me."

The oldest and most fiercely bearded of the men said harshly:

"I am the leader here. We are the people of Colin." He frowned when Hoddan's expression remained unchanged. "The people of Colin!" he repeated more loudly. "The people whose forefathers settled that planet, and made it a world of peace and plenty, and then foolishly welcomed strangers to their midst!"

"Too bad," said Hoddan. He knew what these people were doing, he believed, but putting a name to where they'd come from told him nothing of what they wanted of Darth.

"We made it a fair world," said the bearded man fiercely. "But it was my great-grandfather who destroyed it. He believed that we should share it. It was he who persuaded the Synod to allow strangers to settle among us, believing that they would become like us."

Hoddan nodded expectantly. These people were in some sort of trouble or they wouldn't have come out of overdrive. But they'd talked about it until it had become an emotionalized obsession that couldn't be summarized. When they encountered a stranger, they had to picture their predicament passionately and at length.

This bearded man looked at Hoddan with burning eyes. When he went on, it was with gestures as if he were making a speech. But it was a special sort of speech. The first sentence told what kind.

"They clung to their sins!" said the bearded man bitterly. "They did not adopt our ways! Our example went for naught! They brought others of their kind to Colin. After a little they laughed at us. In a little more they outnumbered us! Then they ruled that the laws of our Synod should not govern them. And they lured our young people to imitate them—frivolous, sinful, riotous folk that they were!"

Hoddan nodded again. There were elderly people

on Zan who talked like this. Not *his* grandfather! If you listened long enough they'd come to some point or other, but they had arranged their thoughts so solidly that any attempt to get quickly at their meaning would only produce confusion.

"Twenty years since," said the bearded man with an angry gesture, "we made a bargain. We held a third of all the land of the planet, but our young men were falling away from the ways of their fathers. We made a bargain with the newcomers. We would trade our lands, our cities, our farms, our highways, for ships to take us to a new world, and food for the journey and machines for the taming of the planet we would select. We sent some of our number to find a world to which we could move. Ten years back, they returned. They had found it. The planet Thetis."

Again Hoddan had no reaction. The name meant nothing.

"We began to prepare," said the old man, his eyes flashing. "Five years since, we were ready. But we had to wait three more before the bargainers were ready to complete the trade. They had to buy and collect the ships. They had to design and build the machinery we would need. They had to collect the food supplies. Two years ago we moved our animals into the ships, and loaded our food and our furnishings, and took our places. We set out. For two years we have journeyed toward Thetis."

Hoddan felt an instinctive respect for people who would undertake to move themselves, the third of the population of a planet, over a distance that meant years of voyaging. They might have tastes in costume that he did not share, and they might go in for elaborate oratory instead of matter-of-fact statement, but they had courage.

"Yes, sir," said Hoddan. "I take it this brings us up to the present."

"No," said the old man. "Six months ago we considered that we might well begin to train the operators of the machines we would use on Thetis. We uncrated machines. We found ourselves cheated!"

Hoddan found that he could make a fairly dispassionate guess of what advantage—say—Nedda's father would take of people who would not check on his good faith for two years and until they were two years' journey away.

"How badly were you cheated?" asked Hoddan.

"Of our lives!" said the angry old man. "Do you know machinery?"

"Some kinds," admitted Hoddan.

"Come," said the leader of the fleet.

With a sort of dignity that was theatrical only because he was aware of it, the leader of the people of Colin showed the way. The hold was packed tightly with cases of machinery. One huge crate had been opened and its contents fully disclosed. Others had been hacked at enough to show their contents.

The uncrated machine was a jungle plow. It was a powerful piece of equipment which would attack jungle on a thirty-foot front, knock down all vegetation up to trees of four-foot diameter, shred it, loosen and sift the soil to a three-foot depth, and leave behind it smoothed, broken, pulverized dirt mixed with ground-up vegetation ready to break down into humus. Such a machine would clear tens of acres in a day, turning jungle into farm land ready for crops.

"We ran this for five minutes," said the bearded man fiercely as Hoddan nodded. He lifted a motor hood.

The motors were burned out. Worthless insulation. Gears were splintered and smashed. Low-grade metal castings. Assembly-bolts had parted. Tractor treads were bent and cracked. It was not a machine except in shape. It was a mock-up in worthless materials which probably cost its maker the twentieth part of what an honest jungle plow would cost to build.

Hoddan felt the anger any man feels when he sees betrayal of that honor a competent machine represents. "It's not all like this!" he said incredulously.

"Some is worse," said the old man, with dignity. "There are crates which are marked to contain turbines. Their contents are ancient, worn-out brick-making machines. There are crates marked to contain generators. They are filled with corroded irrigation pipes and broken castings. We have ship-loads of crush-baled, rusted sheet-metal trimmings! We have been cheated of our lives!"

Hoddan found himself sick with honest fury. The population of one-third of a planet, packed into spaceships for two years and more, would be appropriate subjects for sympathy at the best of times. But it was only accident that had kept these people from landing on Thetis by rocket—since none of their ships would be expected ever to rise again—and from having their men go out and joyfully hack at alien jungle to make room for their machines to land—and then find out they'd brought scrap metal for some thousands of light-years to no purpose.

They'd have starved outright. In fact, they were in not much better case right now. Because there was nowhere else that they could go! There was no new colony which could absorb so many people, with only their bare hands for equipment to live by. There was no civilized, settled world which could admit so many paupers without starving its own population. There was nowhere for these people to go!

Hoddan's anger took on the feeling of guilt. He could do nothing, and something had to be done.

"Why—why did you come to Darth?" he asked. "What can you gain by orbiting here? You can't expect—"

The old man faced him.

"We are beggars," he said with bitter dignity. "We stopped here to ask for charity . . . for the old and worn-out machines the people of Darth can spare us. We will be grateful for even a single rusty plow. Because we have to go on. We can do nothing else. We will land on Thetis. And one plow can mean that a few of us will live who would otherwise die."

Hoddan ran his hands through his hair. This was not his trouble, but he could not ignore it.

"But again, why Darth?" he asked helplessly. "Why not stop at a world with riches to spare? Darth's a poor place."

"Because it is the poor who are generous," said the bearded man evenly.

Hoddan paced up and down. Presently he said jerkily:

"With all the goodwill in the world . . . Darth is poverty-stricken. It has no industries. It has no technology. It has not even roads! It is a planet of little villages and tiny towns. A ship from elsewhere stops here only once a month. Ground communications are almost non-existent. To spread the word of your need over Darth would require months. But to collect what might be given, without roads or even wheeled vehicles—it's impossible! And I have the only space-vessel on the planet, and it's not fit for a journey between suns."

The bearded man waited with a sort of implacable despair.

"But," continued Hoddan grimly, "I have an idea. I have contacts on Walden. The government of Walden does not regard charity with favor. The need for charity seems a—ah—a criticism of the Waldenian standard of living."

The bearded man said coldly:

"I can understand that. The hearts of the rich are hardened. The existence of the poor is a reproach to them."

But Hoddan began suddenly to see real possibilities. This was not a direct move toward the realization of his personal ambitions. But on the other hand, it wasn't a movement away from them. Hoddan suddenly remembered an oration he'd heard his grandfather give many, many times in the past.

Straight thinkin', the old man had said obstinately, *is a delusion. You think things out clear and simple, and you can see yourself ruined and your family starving any day! Real things ain't simple! Any time you try to figure things out so they's simple and straightforward, you're goin' against nature and you're going to get 'em mixed up! So when something happens, and you're in a straightforward, hopeless fix, why, you go along with nature! Make it as complicated as you can, and the people who want you in trouble will get hopeless confused and you can get out!*

Hoddan adverted to his grandfather's wisdom, not making it the reason for doing what he could, but accepting the fact that it might possibly apply. He saw one possibility right away. It looked fairly good. After a minute's examination it looked better. It was astonishing how plausible . . .

"Hmmmmmm," he said. "I have planned work of my own, as you may have guessed. I am here because of—ah—people on Walden. If I could make a quick trip to Walden my—hm—present position might let me help you. I cannot promise very much, but if I can borrow even the smallest of your ships for the journey my spaceboat can't make, why, I may be able to do something. Much more than can be done on Darth!"

The bearded man looked at his companions.

"He seems frank," he said, "and we can lose nothing. We have stopped our journey and are in orbit. We can wait. Our people should not go to Walden. Fleshpots—"

"I can find a crew," said Hoddan cheerfully. Inwardly he was tremendously relieved. "If you say the word, I'll go down to ground and come back with them. I'll want a very small ship!"

"It will be," said the old man. "We thank you."

"Get it inboard, here," suggested Hoddan, "so I can come inside as before, transfer my crew without spacesuits, and leave my boat in your care until I come back."

"It shall be done," said the old man firmly. He added gravely, "You must have had an excellent upbringing,

young man, to be willing to live among the poverty-
stricken people you describe, and to be willing to go
so far to help strangers like ourselves."

"Eh?" Then Hoddan said enigmatically. "What
lessons I shall apply to your affairs, I learned at the
knee of my beloved grandfather."

Of course, his grandfather was head of the most
notorious gang of pirates on the disreputable planet
Zan, but Hoddan found himself increasingly respectful of the old gentleman as he gained experience on
various worlds.

He went briskly back to his spaceboat. On the way
he made verbal arrangements for the enterprise he'd
envisioned so swiftly. It was remarkable how two sets
of troubles could provide suggestions for their joint
alleviation. He actually saw possible achievement before
him. Even in electronics!

By the time the cargo-hold was again pumped
empty and the great door opened to the vastness
of space, Hoddan had a very broad view of things.
He'd said that same day to Fani that a practical
man can always make what he wants to do look like
a sacrifice for others' welfare. He began to suspect,
now, that the welfare of others can often coincide
with one's own.

He needed some rather extensive changes in the
relationship of the cosmos to himself. Walden was
prepared to pay bribes for him. Don Loris felt it necessary to have him confined somewhere. There were a
number of Darthian gentlemen who would assuredly
like to slaughter him if he weren't kept out of their
reach in some cozy dungeon. But up to now there
had been not even a practical way to leave Darth, to

act upon Walden, or even to change his status in the eyes of Darthians.

He backed out of the big ship and consulted the charts of the lifeboat. They had been consulted before, of course, to locate the landing-grid which did not answer calls. He found its position. He began to compare the chart with what he saw from out here in orbit above Darth. He identified a small ocean, with Darth's highest mountain chain just beyond its eastern limit. He identified a river system, emptying into that sea. And here he began to get rid of his excess velocity, because the landing-grid was not very far distant.

To a scientific pilot, his maneuvering from that time on would have been a complex task. The advantage of computation over astrogation by ear, however, is largely a matter of saving fuel. A perfectly computed course for landing will get down to ground with the use of the least number of centigrams of fuel. But fuel-efficent maneuvers are rarely time-efficient ones.

Hoddan hadn't the time or the data for computation. He swung the spaceboat end for end, very judgematically used rocket power to slow himself to a suitable east-west velocity, and at the last and proper instant applied full power for deceleration and went down practically like a stone. One cannot really learn this. It has to be absorbed through the pores of one's skin. That was the way Hoddan had absorbed it, on Zan.

Within minutes, then, the stronghold of Don Loris was startled by a roaring mutter in the sky overhead. Helmeted sentries on the battlements stared upward. The mutter rose to a howl, and the howl to the volume of thunder, and the thunder to a very great noise which made loose pebbles dance and quiver.

Then there was a speck of white cloudiness in the late afternoon sky. It grew swiftly in size, and a winking blue-white light appeared in its center. That light grew brighter and the noise managed somehow to increase and presently the ruddy sunlight was diluted by light from the rockets.

Then, abruptly, the rockets cut off, and something dark plunged downward, and the rockets flamed again and a vast mass of steam arose from scorched ground. The space-boat lay in a circle of wildly smoking, carbonized Darthian soil. The return of tranquility after so much tumult was startling.

Absolutely nothing happened. Hoddan unstrapped himself from the pilot's seat, examined his surroundings thoughtfully, and turned off the vision apparatus. He went back and examined the feeding arrangements of the boat. He'd had nothing to eat since breakfast in this same time zone. The food in store was extremely easy to prepare and not especially appetizing. He ate with great deliberation, continuing to make plans which linked the necessities of the emigrants from Colin to his own plans and predicaments. He also thought very respectfully about his grandfather's opinions on many subjects, including space-piracy. Hoddan found himself much more in agreement with his grandfather than he'd believed possible.

Outside the boat, birds which had dived to ground and cowered there during the boat's descent now flew about again, their terror forgotten. Horses which had galloped wildly in their pastures, or kicked in panic in the castle stalls, returned to their oats and hay.

And there were human reactions. Don Loris had been in an excessively fretful state of mind since the conclusion of his deal with the pair from Walden. Hoddan had estimated that Don Loris ought to get a half-million credits for delivering him to Derec and the Waldenian police. But actually Don Loris had been unable to get the cop to promise more than half so much. But he'd closed the deal and sent for Hoddan—and Hoddan was gone.

Now the landing of this spaceboat roused a lively uneasiness in Don Loris. It might be new bargainers for Hoddan. It might be anything. Hoddan had said he had a secret. This might be it. Don Loris vexedly tried to contrive some useful skulduggery without the information to base it on.

Fani looked at the spaceboat with bright eyes. Thal was back at the castle. He'd told her of Hoddan riding up to the spaceboat near another chieftain's castle, entering it, and then taking to the skies in an aura of flames, smoke and thunder. Fani hoped that he might have returned. But she worried while she waited for him to do something.

Hoddan did nothing. The spaceboat gave no sign of life.

The sun set, and the sky twinkled with darting lights which flew toward the west and vanished. Twilight followed, and more lights flashed across the heavens as if pursuing the sun. Fani had learned to associate three and then nine such lights with spacecraft, but she could not dream of a fleet of hundreds. She dismissed the lights from her mind, being much more concerned with Hoddan. He would be in as bad a fix as ever if he came out of the boat.

Twilight remained, a half-light in which all things looked much more charming than they really were. And Don Loris, reduced to peevish sputtering, summoned Thal. It should be remembered that Don Loris knew nothing of the disappearance of the spaceboat from his neighbor's land. He knew nothing of Thal's journey with Hoddan. But he did remember that Hoddan had seemed unworried at breakfast and explained his calm by saying that he had a secret. The feudal chieftain was worried that this spaceboat contained Hoddan's secret.

"Thal," said Don Loris peevishly, sitting beside the great fireplace in the enormous hall. "Thal, you know this Bron Hoddan better than anybody else."

Thal breathed heavily. He turned pale.

"Where is he?" demanded Don Loris.

"I don't know," said Thal. It was true. So far as he was concerned, Hoddan had vanished into the sky.

"What does he plan to do?" demanded Don Loris.

"I don't know," said Thal helplessly.

"Where does that—that thing outside the castle come from?"

"I don't know," said Thal.

Don Loris drummed on the arm of his intricately carved chair.

"I don't like people who don't know things!" he said fretfully. "There must be somebody in that *thing*. Why don't they show themselves? What are they here for? Why did they come down, especially here? Because of Bron Hoddan?"

"I don't know," said Thal humbly.

"Then go find out!" snapped Don Loris. "Take a

reasonable guard with you. The thing must have a
door. Knock on it and ask who's inside and why they
came here. Tell them I sent you to ask."

Thal saluted. With his teeth chattering, he gathered
a half-dozen of his fellows and went tramping out the
castle gate. Some of the half-dozen had been involved
in the rescue of the Lady Fani from Ghek. They were
still in a happy mood because of the plunder they'd
brought back. It was much more than a mere retainer
could usually hope for in a year.

"What's this all about, Thal?" demanded one of
them as Thal arranged them in two lines to make a
proper military appearance, spears dressed upright
and shields on their left arms.

"Frrrrd *harch!*" barked Thal, and they swung into
motion. Thal said gloomily, "Don Loris said to find
out who landed that thing out yonder. He keeps asking about Bron Hoddan, too."

He strode in step with the others. The seven men
made an impressively soldierly group, tramping away
from the castle wall.

"What happened to him?" asked a rear-file man.
He marched on, eyes front, chest out, spear swinging
splendidly in time with his marching. "That lad has
a nose for loot! Don't take it himself, though. If he
set up in business as a chieftain, now—"

"*Hup,* two, three, four," muttered Thal. "*Hup,* two,
three—"

"Don Loris's a hard chieftain," growled the right-
hand man in the second file. "Plenty of grub and beer,
but no fighting and no loot. I didn't get to go with
you the other day, but what you brought back . . ."

"Wasn't half of what was there," mourned a front-file

man. "Wasn't half! Those pistols he issued got shot out and we had to get outta there fast! Hm . . . here's this thing, Thal. What do we do with it?"

"Hrrrmp, *halt!*" barked Thal. He stared at the motionless, seemingly lifeless, shapeless spaceboat. He'd seen one like it earlier today. That one spouted fire and went up out of sight. He was wary of this one. He grumbled. "Those pipes in the back of it, steer clear of 'em. They spit fire. No door on this side. Don Loris said knock on the door. We go around the front. Frrrrd *harch!* two, three, four, *hup*, two, three, four. Left turn here and mind those rocks. Don Loris'd give us hell if somebody fell down. Left turn again. *Hup*, two, three, four."

The seven men tramped splendidly around the front of the lifeboat. On the far side, its bulk hid even Don Loris' castle from view. The six spearmen, with Thal, came to a second halt.

"Here goes," rumbled Thal. "I tell you, boys, if she starts to spit fire, you get the hell away!"

He marched up to spaceboat's port. He knocked on it. There was no response. He knocked again.

Hoddan opened the door. He nodded cheerfully to Thal.

"Afternoon, Thal! Glad to see you. I've been hoping you'd come over this way. Who's with you?" He peered through the semi-darkness. "Some of the boys, eh? Come in!" He beckoned and said casually, "Lean your spears against the hull, there."

Thal hesitated and was lost. The others obeyed. There were clatterings as the spears came to rest against the metal hull. Six of Don Loris' retainers followed Thal admiringly into the spaceboat's interior, to gaze at it and at Bron Hoddan who so recently had given them the chance to loot a nearby castle.

"Sit down!" said Hoddan cordially. "If you want to feel what a spaceboat's really like, clasp the seat-belts around you. You'll feel exactly like you're about to make a journey out of atmosphere. That's it, lean back. You notice there are no viewports in the hull? That's because we use these vision screens to see around with."

He flicked on the screens. Thal and his companions were charmed to see the landscape outside portrayed on screens. Hoddan shifted the sensitivity point toward infrared, and details came out that would have been invisible to the naked eye.

"With the port closed," said Hoddan, "like this," the port clanged shut and grumbled for half a second as the locking-dogs went home, "we're all set for take-off. I need only get into the pilot's seat . . ." he did so, "and throw on the fuel pump." A tiny humming sounded. "And we move when I advance this throttle!"

He pressed the firing-stud. There was a soul-shaking roar. There was a terrific pressure. The seven men from Don Loris' stronghold were pressed back in their seats with an overwhelming, irresistible pressure which held them absolutely helpless. Their mouths dropped open. Appalled protests tried to come out, but were pushed back by the seemingly ever-increasing acceleration.

The screens, showing the outside, displayed a great and confused tumult of smoke and fumes and dust to rearward. They showed only stars ahead. Those stars grew brighter and brighter, as the roar of the rockets diminished to a deafening sound. Suddenly the disk of the local sun appeared, rising above the horizon to the west. The spaceboat, naturally, overtook it as it rose into an orbit headed east to west instead of the other way about.

Presently Hoddan turned off the fuel pump. He turned to look thoughtfully at the seven men. They were very pale. They all sat very still, because they could see in the vision-screens that a strange, mottled, again-sunlit surface flowed past them with an appalling velocity. They were very much afraid that they knew what it was. They did. It was the surface of the planet Darth.

"I'm glad you boys came along," said Hoddan. "We'll catch up with the fleet in a moment or two. The pirate fleet, you know! I'm very pleased with you. Not many groundlings would volunteer for space-piracy, not even with the loot there is in it."

Thal choked slightly, but no one else made a sound. No one even protested. Protests would have been no use. There were looks of anguish, but nothing else. Hoddan was the only one in the spaceboat who had the least idea of how to get it down again. His passengers had to go along for the ride, no matter where it led.

Numbly, they waited for what would befall.

Chapter 8

Hoddan did not worry about his captive-followers. Soon he saw the weird spacefleet.

The spaceboat drew up alongside the gigantic hulk of the leader's ship. The seven Darthians were still numbed by their kidnaping and the situation in which they found themselves. They looked with dull eyes at the mountainous object they approached. It had actually been designed as a fighter-carrier of space, intended to carry smaller craft. It must have been sold for scrap a couple of hundred years since, and patched up for this emigration.

Hoddan waited for the huge door to open. It did. He headed into the opening, noticing as he did so that an object two or three times the size of the spaceboat was already there. It cut down the room for maneuvering, but a thing once done is easier thereafter. Hoddan got the boat inside, and there was a very small scraping and the great door closed before the boat could drift out again.

Hoddan turned to his victim-followers once the spaceboat was still.

"This," he said in a manner which could only be described as one of smiling ferocity, "this is a pirate ship, belonging to the pirate fleet we passed through on the way here. It's manned by characters so murderous that their leaders don't dare land anywhere away from their home star-cluster, or all the galaxy would combine against them, to exterminate them or be exterminated. You've joined that fleet. You're going to get out of this boat and march over to that ship yonder. Then you're going to be space-pirates under me."

They quivered, but did not protest.

"I'll try you for one voyage," he told them. "There will be plunder. There will be pirate revels. If you serve faithfully and fight well, I'll return you to Don Loris' strong-hold with your loot after the one voyage. If you don't—" He grinned mirthlessly at them, "if you don't, out the airlock with you, to float forever between the stars. Understand?"

The last was pure savagery. They cringed. The outside-pressure meter went up to normal. Hoddan turned off the vision screens, so ending any views of the interior of the hold. He opened the port and went out. Sitting in something like continued paralysis in their seats, the seven spearmen of Darth heard his voice in conversation outside the boat. They could catch no words, but Hoddan's tone was strictly businesslike. He came back.

"All right," he said shortly. "Thal, march 'em over."

Thal gulped. He loosened his seat-belt. The enlistment of the seven in the pirate fleet was tacitly acknowledged. They were unarmed save for the conventional large knives at their belts.

"Frrrd, *harch!*" rasped Thal with a lump in his throat. "Two, three, four. *Hup,* two, three, four. *Hup* . . ."

Seven men marched dismally out of the spaceboat and down to the floor of the huge hold. Eyes front, chests out, throats dry, they marched to the larger but still small vessel that shared this hold compartment. They marched into that ship. Thal barked, "Hmmmmm *halt!*" and they stopped. They waited.

Hoddan came in very matter-of-factly only moments later. He closed the entrance port, so sealing the ship. He nodded approvingly.

"You can break ranks now," he said. "There's food and such stuff around. The ship's yours. But don't turn knobs or push buttons."

He went forward, and a door closed behind him.

He looked at the control board, and could have done with a little information himself. When the ship was built, generations ago, there'd been controls installed which would be quite useless now. When the present working instruments were installed, it had been done so hastily that the wires and relays behind them were not concealed, and it was these that gave him the clues to understand them.

The space-ark's door opened. Hoddan backed his ship out. Its rockets had surprising power. He reflected that the Lawlor drive wouldn't have been designed for this present ship, either. There'd probably been a quantity order for so many Lawlor drives, and they'd been installed on whatever needed a modern drive-system, which was every ship in the fleet. But since this was one of the smallest craft in the lot, with its low mass it should be fast.

"We'll see," he said to nobody in particular.

Out in emptiness, but naturally sharing the orbit of the ship from which it had just come, Hoddan tried it out tentatively. He got the feel of it. Then as a matter of simple, rule-of-thumb astrogation, he got from a low orbit to a five-diameter height where the Lawlor drive would hold by mere touches of rocket power. It was simply a matter of stretching the orbit to extreme eccentricity as all the ships went round the planet. After the fourth go round he was fully five diameters out at aphelion. He touched the drive button and everybody had that very peculiar distur-bance of all their senses which accompanies going into overdrive. The small craft sped through emptiness at a high multiple of the speed of light.

Hoddan's knowledge of astrogation was strictly practical. He went over his ship. From a look at it outside he'd guessed that it once had been a yacht. Various touches inside verified that idea. There were two staterooms. All the space was for living and supplies. None was for cargo. He nodded. There was a faint mustiness about it. But there'd been a time when it was some rich man's pride.

He went back to the control-room to make an estimate. From the pilot's seat one could see a speck of brightness directly ahead. Infinitesimal dots of brightness appeared swiftly brighter and then darted outward. As they darted they disappeared because their motion became too swift to follow. There were, of course, methods of measuring this phenomenon so that one could get an accurate measure of one's speed in overdrive. Hoddan had no instrument for the purpose. But he had the feel of things. This was a very fast ship indeed, at full Lawlor thrust.

Presently he went out to the central cabin. His followers had found provisions. There were novelties—hydroponic fruit, for instance—and they'd gloomily stuffed themselves. They were almost resigned, now. Memory of the loot he'd led them to at Ghek's castle inclined them to be hopeful. But they looked uneasy when he stopped where they were gathered.

"Well?" he said sharply.

Thal swallowed.

"We have been companions, Bron Hoddan," he said unhappily. "We fought together in great battles, two against fifty, and we plundered the slain."

"True enough," agreed Hoddan. If Thal wanted to edit his memories of the fighting at the spaceport, that was all right with him. "Now we're headed for something much better."

"But what?" asked Thal miserably. "Here we are high above our native world—"

"Oh, no!" said Hoddan. "You couldn't even pick out its sun, from where we are now!"

Thal gulped.

"I do not understand what you want with us," he protested. "We are not experienced in space! We are simple men . . ."

"You're pirates now," Hoddan told him with a sort of genial bloodthirstiness. "You'll do what I tell you until we fight. Then you'll fight well or die. That's all you need to know!"

He left them. When men are to be led it is rarely wise to discuss policy or tactics with them. Most men work best when they know only what is expected of them. Then they can't get confused and they do not get ideas of how to do things better.

Hoddan inspected the yacht more carefully. There were still traces of decorative features which had nothing to do with spaceworthiness. But the mere antiquity of the ship made Hoddan hunt more carefully. He found a small compartment packed solidly with supplies. A supply cabinet did not belong where it was. He hauled out stuff to make sure. It was—it had been—a machine shop in miniature. In the early days, before space-phones were long-range devices, a yacht or a ship that went beyond orbital distance was strictly on its own. If there were a breakdown it was strictly of private concern. It had to be repaired by its own, or else. So all early spacecraft carried amazingly complete equipment for repairs. Only liners had been equipped that way in recent generations, and it is almost unheard-of for their tool shops to be used.

But there was the remnant of a shop on the yacht that Hoddan was using for his errand to Walden. He'd told the emigrant leaders that he went to ask for charity. He'd just assured his followers that their journey was for piracy. Now . . .

He began to empty the cubbyhole of all the items that had been packed into it for storage. It had been very ingenious, this miniature repair shop. The lathe was built in with strength-members of the walls as part of its structure. The drill press was recessed. The welding apparatus had its coils and condensers under the floor. The briefest of examinations showed the condensers to be in bad shape, and the coils might be hopeless. But there was good material used in the old days. Hoddan began to have quite unreasonable hopes.

He went back to the control-room to meditate.

He'd had a reasonably sound plan of action for the pirating of a spaceliner, even though he had no weapons mounted on the ship nor anything more deadly than stun-pistols for his reluctant crew. But he considered it likely that he could make the same sort of landing with this yacht that he'd already done with the spaceboat. Which should be enough.

If he waited off Walden until a liner went down to the planet's great spaceport, he could try it. He would go into a close orbit around Walden which would bring him, very low, over the landing-grid within an hour or so of the liner's landing. He'd turn the yacht end for end and apply full rocket power for deceleration. The yacht would drop like a stone into the landing-grid. Everything would happen too quickly for the grid crew to think of clapping a forcefield on it, or for them to manage it if they tried. He'd be aground before they realized it.

The rest was simply fast action. Hoddan and seven Darthians, stun-pistols humming, would tumble out of the yacht and dash for the control-room of the grid. Hoddan would smash the controls. Then they'd rush the landed liner, seize it, shoot down anybody who tried to oppose them, and seal up the ship.

And then they'd take off on the liner's rockets, which were carried for emergency landing only, but could be used for a single take-off. After one such use they'd be exhausted. And with the grid's controls smashed, nobody could even try to stop them.

It wasn't a bad idea. He had a good deal of confidence in it. It was the reason for his Darthian crew. Nobody'd expect such a thing to be tried, so it almost certainly could be done. But it did have the drawback that the yacht would have to be left behind, a dead loss, when the liner was seized.

Hoddan thought it over soberly. Long before he reached Walden, of course, he could have his own crew so terrified that they'd fight like fiends for fear of what he might do to them if they didn't. But if he could keep the spaceyacht also . . .

He nodded gravely. He liked the new possibility. If it didn't work, there was the first plan in reserve. In any case he'd get a modern spaceliner and suitable cargo to present to emigrants of Colin.

There were certain electronic circuits which were akin. The Lawlor drive unit formed a forcefield, a stress in space, into which a nearby ship necessarily moved. The faster-than-light angle came from the fact that it worked like a donkey trotting after a carrot held in front of him by a stick. The ship moving into the stressed area moved the stress. The forcefields of a landing-grid were similar. A turning principle was involved, but basically a landing-grid clamped an area of stress around a spaceship, and the ship couldn't move out of it. When the landing-grid moved the stressed area up or down—why—that was it.

All this was known to everybody. But a third trick had been evolved on Zan. It was based on the fact that ball lightning could be generated by a circuit fundamentally akin to the other two. Ball lightning was an area of space so stressed that its energy content could leak out only very slowly, unless it made contact with a conductor, when all bets were off. It blew. And the Zan pirates used ball lightning to force the surrender of their victims.

Hoddan began to draw diagrams. The Lawlor drive unit had been installed long after the yacht was built. It would be modern, with no nonsense about it. With such-and-such of its electronic components cut out, and such-and-such other ones cut in, it would become a perfectly practical ball-lightning generator, capable of placing bolts wherever one wanted them. This was standard Zan practice. Hoddan's grandfather had used it for years. It had the advantage that it could be used inside a gravity field, where a Lawlor drive could not. It had the other advantage that commercial spacecraft could not mount such gadgets for defense, because the insurance companies objected to meddling with Lawlor drive installations.

Hoddan set to work with the remnants of a tool

shop on the ancient yacht and some antique coils and condensers and such. He became filled with zest. He almost forgot that he was the skipper of an elderly craft which should have been junked before he was born.

But even he grew hungry, and he realized that nobody offered him food. He went indignantly into the yacht's central saloon and found his seven crew members snoring stertorously, sprawled in stray places here and there.

He woke them with great sternness. He set them furiously to work on housekeeping—including making meals.

He went back to work. Suddenly he stopped and meditated afresh, and ceased his actual labor to draw a diagram which he regarded with great affection. He returned to his adaptation of the Lawlor drive to the production of ball lightning.

Once finished, he examined the stars. The nearby suns were totally strange in their arrangement. But the Coalsack area was a spacemark good for half a sector of the galaxy. There was a condensation in the Nearer Rim for a second bearing. And a certain calcium cloud with a star-cluster behind it which was as good as a highway sign for locating oneself.

He lined up the yacht again and went into overdrive once more. Two days later he came out, again surveyed the cosmos, again went into overdrive, again came out, once more made a hop in faster-than-light travel, and finally he was in the solar system of which Walden was the ornament and pride.

He used the telescope and contemplated Walden on its screen. The spaceyacht moved briskly toward it. His seven Darthian crewmen, aware of coming action, dolefully sharpened their two-foot knives. They did not know what else to do, but they were far from happy.

Hoddan shared their depression. Such gloomy anticipations before stirring events are proof that a man is not a fool. Hoddan's grandfather had been known to observe that when a man can imagine all kinds of troubles and risks and disasters ahead of him, he is usually right. Hoddan shared that view. But it would not do to back out now.

He examined Walden painstakingly while the yacht sped toward it. He saw an ocean come out of the twilight zone of dawn. By the charts, the capital city and the spaceport should be on that ocean's western shore. After a suitable and very long interval, the site of the capital city came around the edge of the planet.

From a bare hundred thousand miles, Hoddan stepped up magnification to its limit and looked again. Then Walden more than filled the telescope's field. He could see only a very small fraction of the planet's surface. He had to hunt before he found the capital city again. Then it was very clear. He saw the curving lines of its highways and the criss-cross pattern of its streets. Buildings as such, however, did not show. But he made out the spaceport and the shadow of the landing-grid, and in the very center of that grid there was something silvery which cast a shadow of its own. A ship. A liner.

Then the silvery thing moved visibly across other objects, and its shadow ceased to be. It was thrust surely and ever more swiftly skyward by the grid. The liner was rising to outer space.

There was a tap on the control-room door. Thal.

"Anything happening?" he asked uneasily.

"I just sighted the ship we're going to take," said Hoddan.

Thal looked unhappy. He withdrew. Hoddan plotted out the extremely roundabout course he must take to end up with the liner and the yacht traveling in the same direction and the same speed, so capture would be possible. It could not be attempted in clear space. Five diameters out, the liner could whisk into overdrive and be gone forever. On the other hand, within five diameters the yacht couldn't use its drive, either. And yet again, the liner and the yacht had to be moving away from the planet at the time of capture, with enough velocity to attain clear space on their momentum, or there'd be no point in the attack. If the yacht did not float on out past the five-diameter limit, it could be gathered in by the landing-grid and brought to ground for such measures which might seem appropriate.

Hoddan worked out the angles and the speeds. He had to dive past Walden, swing around its farther side, and come back like a boomerang so his and the liner's speed and line of motion would match up into a collision course. Then rockets . . .

He put the yacht on the line required. He threw on full power. Actually, he headed partly away from his intended victim. The little yacht plunged forward. Nothing seemed to happen. Time passed. Hoddan had nothing to do but worry. He worried.

Thal tapped on the door again.

"About time to get ready to fight?" he asked dolefully.

"Not yet," said Hoddan. "I'm running away from our victim, now."

Another half-hour. The course changed. The yacht was around behind Walden. The whole planet lay between it and its intended prey. The course of the small ship curved, now. It would pass almost close enough to clip the topmost tips of Walden's atmosphere. There was nothing for Hoddan to do but think morbid thoughts. He thought them.

The Lawlor drive began to burble. He cut it off. He sat gloomily in the control-room, occasionally glancing at the nearing expanse of rushing mottled surface presented by the now-nearby planet. Its attraction bent the path of the yacht. It was now a parabolic curve.

Presently the surface diminished a little. The yacht was increasing its distance from it. Hoddan used the telescope. He searched the space ahead with full-width field. He found the liner. It rose steadily. The grid still thrust it upward with an even, continuous acceleration. It had to be not less than forty thousand miles out before it could take to over-drive. But at that distance it would have an outward velocity which would take it on out indefinitely. At ten thousand miles, certainly, the grid-fields would let go.

They did. Hoddan could tell because the liner wobbled slightly. It was free. It was no longer held solidly. From now on it floated up on momentum.

Hoddan nibbled at his fingernails. There was nothing to be done for forty minutes more. Presently there was nothing to be done for thirty. For twenty. Ten. Five. Three. Two—

The liner was barely twenty miles away when

Hoddan fired his rockets. They made a colossal cloud of vapor in emptiness. The yacht stirred faintly, shifted deftly, lost just a suitable amount of velocity—which now was nearly straight up from the planet—and moved with precision and directness toward the liner. Hoddan stirred his controls and swung the whole small ship. He flipped a switch that cut out certain elements of the Lawlor unit and cut in those others which made the modified drive unit into a ball-lightning projector.

A flaming speck of pure incandescence sped from the yacht through emptiness. It would miss . . . No! Hoddan swerved it. It struck the liner's hull. It would momentarily paralyze every bit of electric equipment in the ship. It would definitely not go unnoticed.

"Calling liner," said Hoddan painfully into a microphone. "Calling liner! We are pirates, attacking your ship. You have ten seconds to get into your lifeboats or we will hull you!"

He settled back, again nibbling at his fingernails. He was acutely disturbed. At the end of ten seconds the distance between the two ships was perceptibly less.

He flung a second ball-lightning bolt across the diminished space. He sent it whirling round and round the liner in a tight spiral. He ended by having it touch the liner's bow. Liquid light ran over the entire hull.

"Your ten seconds are up," he said worriedly. "If you don't get out—"

But then he relaxed. A boat-blister on the liner opened. The boat did not release itself. It could not possibly take on its complement of passengers and

crew in so short a time. The opening of the blister
was a sign of surrender.

The two first ball-lightning bolts were miniatures.
Hoddan now projected a full-sized ball. It glittered
viciously in emptiness. It sped toward the liner and
hung off its side, menacingly. The yacht from Darth
moved steadily closer. Five miles. Two.

"All out," said Hoddan regretfully. "We can't wait
any longer!"

A boat darted away from the liner. A second. A third
and fourth and fifth. The last boat lingered desperately.
The yacht was less than a mile away when it broke
free and plunged frantically toward the planet it had
left a little while before. The other boats were already
streaking downward, trails of rocket fumes expanding
behind them. The crew of the landing-grid would pick
them up for safe and gentle landing.

Hoddan sighed in relief. He played delicately upon
the yacht's rocket controls. He carefully maneuvered
the very last of the novelties he had built into the
originally simple Lawlor drive unit. The two ships
came together with a distant clanking sound. It seemed
horribly loud.

Thal jerked open the door, ashen white.

"W-we hit something! Wh-when do we fight?"

"I forgot. The fighting's over," Hoddan said ruefully.
"But bring your stun-pistols. Nobody'd stay behind,
but somebody might have gotten left."

He rose, to take over the captured ship.

Chapter 9

Normally, at overdrive cruising speed, it would be a week's journey from Walden to the planet Krim. Hoddan made it in five days. There was reason. He wanted to beat the news of his piracy to Krim. He could endure suspicion, and he wouldn't mind doubt, but he did not want certainty of his nefarious behavior to interfere with the purposes of his call.

The spaceyacht, sealed tightly, floated in an orbit far out in emptiness. The big ship went down alone by landing-grid. It glittered brightly as it descended. When it touched ground and the grid's forcefields cut off, it looked very modern and very crisp and strictly businesslike. Actually, the capture of this particular liner was a bit of luck, for Hoddan. It was not one of the giant inter-cluster ships which make runs of thousands of light-years and deign to stop only at very major planets. It was a medium ship of five thousand tons, designed for service in the Horsehead Nebula region. It was brand-new and on the way from its builders to its owners when Hoddan interfered. Naturally, though, it carried cargo on its maiden voyage.

Hoddan spoke curtly to the control-room of the grid. "I'm non-sked," he explained. "New ship. I got a freak charter-party over on Walden for from here for Darth and have to get rid of my cargo. How about shifting me to delay space until I can talk to some brokers?"

The forcefields came on again and the liner moved very delicately to a position at the side of the grid's central space. There it would be out of the way.

Hoddan dressed himself carefully in garments found in the liner's skipper's cabin. He found Thal wearing an apron and an embittered expression. He ceased to wield a mop as Hoddan halted before him.

"I'm going ashore," said Hoddan crisply. "You're in charge until I get back."

"In charge of what?" demanded Thal bitterly. "Of a bunch of male housemaids! I run a mop! And me a Darthian gentleman! I thought I was being a pirate! What do I do? I scrub floors! I wash paint! I stencil cases in cargo-holds! I paint over names and put others in their places! Me, a Darthian gentleman!"

"No," said Hoddan. "A pirate. If you don't get back, you and the others can't work this ship, and presently the police of Krim will ask why. They'll recheck my careful forgeries, and you'll all be hung for piracy. So don't let anybody in. Don't talk to anybody. If you do, pfft!"

He drew his finger across his throat, and nodded, and went cheerfully out the crew's landing-door in the very base of the ship. He went across the tarmac and out between two of the gigantic steel arches of the grid. He hired a car.

"Where?" asked the driver.

"Hm," said Hoddan. "There's a firm of lawyers . . . I can't remember the names . . ."

"There's millions of 'em," said the driver.

"This is a special one," explained Hoddan. "It's so dignified they won't talk to you unless you're a great-grandson of a client. They're so ethical they won't touch a case of under a million credits. They've got about nineteen names in the firm-title and—"

"Oh!" said the driver. "That'll be— Hell! I can't

remember the name, either. But I'll take you there."

He drove out into traffic. Hoddan relaxed. Then he tensed again. He had not been in a city since he stopped briefly in this one on the way to Darth. The traffic was abominable. And he, who'd been in various pitched battles on Darth and had only lately captured a ship in space—Hoddan grew apprehensive as his cab charged into the thick of hooting, rushing, squealing vehicles. When the car came to a stop he was relieved.

"It's yonder," said the driver. "You'll find the name on the directory."

Hoddan paid and went inside the gigantic building. He looked at the directory and shrugged. He went to the downstairs guard. He explained that he was looking for a firm of lawyers whose name was not on the directory list. They were extremely conservative and of the highest possible reputation. They didn't seek clients.

"Forty-two and forty-three," said the guard, frowning. "I ain't supposed to give it out, but—floors forty-two and forty-three."

Hoddan went up. He was unknown. A receptionist looked at him with surprised aversion.

"I have a case of space-piracy," said Hoddan politely. "A member of the firm, please."

Ten minutes later he eased himself into a fluffy chair. A gray-haired man of infinite dignity said:

"Well?"

"I am," said Hoddan modestly, "a pirate. I have a ship in the spaceport with very convincing papers and a cargo of Rigellian furs, jewelry from the Cetis planets, and a rather large quantity of bulk melacynth. I want to dispose of the cargo and invest a considerable part of the proceeds in conservative stocks on Krim."

The lawyer frowned. He looked shocked. Then he said carefully:

"You made two statements. One was that you are a pirate. Taken by itself, that is not my concern. The other is that you wish to dispose of certain cargo and invest in reputable business on Krim. I assume that there is no connection between the two facts."

He paused. Hoddan said nothing. The lawyer went on, with dignity:

"Of course our firm is not in the brokerage business. However, we can represent you in your dealing with local brokers. And obviously we can advise you."

"I also wish to buy," said Hoddan, "a complete shipload of agricultural machinery, a microfilm technical library, machine tools, vision-tape technical instructors and libraries of tape for them, generators, and such things."

"Hm," said the lawyer, "I will send one of our clerks to examine your cargo so he can deal properly with the brokers. You will tell him more in detail what you wish to buy."

Hoddan stood up.

"I'll take him to the ship now."

He was mildly surprised at the smoothness with which matters proceeded. He took a young clerk to the ship. He showed him the ship's papers as edited by himself. He took him through the cargo holds. He discussed in some detail what he wished to buy.

When the clerk left, Thal came to complain again.

"Look here!" he said bitterly, "we've scrubbed this dam' ship from one end to the other! There's not a speck or a fingermark on it. And we're still scrubbing! We captured this ship! Is this pirate revels?"

Hoddan said:

"There's money coming. I'll let you boys ashore with some cash in your pockets presently."

Brokers came, escorted by the lawyer's clerk. They squabbled furiously with him. But the dignity of the firm he represented was extreme. There was no suspicion—no overt suspicion anyhow—and the furs went. The clerk painstakingly informed Hoddan that he could draw so much. More brokers came. The jewelry went. The lawyer's clerk jotted down figures and told Hoddan the net. The bulk melacynth was taken over by a group of brokers, none of whom could handle it alone.

Hoddan drew cash and sent his Darthians ashore with a thousand credits apiece. With bright and shining faces, they headed for the nearest bars.

"As soon as my ship's loaded," Hoddan told the clerk, "I'll want to get them out of jail."

The clerk nodded. He brought salesmen of agricultural machinery. Representatives of microfilm libraries. Manufacturers of generators, vision-tape instructors and allied lines. Hoddan bought, painstakingly. Delivery was promised for the next day.

"Now," said the clerk, "about the investments you wish to make with the balance?"

"I'll want a reasonable sum in cash," said Hoddan reflectively. "But—well . . . I've been told that insurance is a fine, conservative business. As I understand it, most insurance organizations are divided into divisions which are separately incorporated. There will be a life insurance division, a casualty division, and so on. Is that right? And one may invest in any of them separately?"

The clerk said impassively:

"I was given to understand, sir, that you are interested in risk insurance. Perhaps especially risk insurance covering piracy. I was given quotations on the risk insurance divisions of all Krim companies. Of course those are not very active stocks, but if there were a rumor of a pirate ship acting in this part of the galaxy, one might anticipate . . ."

"I do," said Hoddan. "Let's see . . . my cargo brought so much . . . hm . . . my purchases will come to so much. My legal fees, of course . . . I mentioned a sum in cash. Yes. This will be the balance, more or less, which you will put in the stocks you've named. But since I anticipate activity in them, I'll want to leave some special instructions."

He gave a detailed, thoughtful account of what he anticipated might be found in news reports of later dates. The clerk noted it all down, impassively. Hoddan added instructions.

"Yes, sir," said the clerk without intonation when he was through. "If you will come to the office in the morning, sir, the papers will be drawn up and matters can be concluded. Your new cargo can hardly be delivered before then, and if I may say so, sir, your crew won't be ready. I'd estimate two hours of festivity for each man; and fourteen hours for recovery."

"Thank you," said Hoddan. "I'll see you in the morning."

He sealed up the ship when the lawyer's clerk

departed. Then he felt lonely. He was the only living thing in the ship. His footsteps echoed hollowly. There was nobody to speak to. Not even anybody to threaten. He'd done a lot of threatening lately.

He went forlornly to the cabin once occupied by the liner's former skipper. His loneliness increased, he began to have self-doubts. Today's actions were the ones which bothered his conscience. He felt that they were not quite adequate. The balance left in the lawyer's hands would not be nearly enough to cover a certain deficit which in justice he felt himself bound to make up. It had been his thought to make this enterprise self-liquidating—everybody concerned making a profit, including the owners of the ship and cargo he had pirated. But he wasn't sure.

He reflected that his grandfather would not have been disturbed about such a matter. That elderly pirate would have felt wholly at ease. It was his conviction that piracy was an essential part of the working of the galaxy's economic system. Hoddan, indeed, could remember him saying:

"I tell y', piracy's what keeps the galaxy's business thriving. Everybody knows business suffers when retail trade slacks down. It backs up the movement of inventories. They get too big. That backs up orders to the factories. They lay off men. And when men are laid off they don't have money to spend, so retail trade slacks off some more, and that backs up inventories some more, and that backs up orders to factories and makes unemployment and hurts retail trade again. It's a feedback. See?" It was Hoddan's grandfather's custom, at this point, to stare shrewdly at each of his listeners in turn. "But suppose somebody pirates a ship? The owners don't lose. It's insured. They order another ship built right away. Men get hired to build it and they're paid money to spend in retail trade and that moves inventories and industry picks up. More'n that, more people insure against piracy. Insurance companies hire more clerks and bookkeepers. They get more money for retail trade and to move inventories and keep factories going and get more people hired. Y'see . . . it's piracy that keeps business in this galaxy goin'!"

Hoddan had doubts about this, but it could not be entirely wrong. He'd put a good part of the proceeds of his piracy in risk-insurance stocks, and he counted on them to make all his actions as benevolent to everybody concerned as his intentions had been, and were. But it might not be true enough. It might be less than—well—sufficiently true in a particular instance. And therefore . . .

Then he saw how things could be worked out so that there could be no doubt. He began to work out the details. He drifted off to sleep in the act of composing a letter in his head to his grandfather on the pirate planet Zan.

When morning came on Krim, catawheel trucks came bringing gigantic agricultural machines. There came generators, turbines and tanks of plastic; another bevy of trucks brought vision-tape instructors and great boxes full of tape for them. There were machine tools and cutting-tips—these last in vast quantity—and very many items that the emigrants of Colin probably would not expect, and might not even recognize. The cargo holds of the liner filled.

He went to the office of his attorneys. He read

and signed papers, in an atmosphere of great dignity and ethical purpose. The lawyer's clerk attended him to the police office, where seven dreary Darthians with over-sized hangovers tried dismally to cheer themselves by memories of how they got that way. He got them out and to the ship. The lawyer's clerk produced a rather weighty if small box with an air of extreme solemnity.

"The currency you wanted, sir."

"Thank you," said Hoddan. "That's the last of our business?"

"Yes, sir," said the clerk. He hesitated, and for the first time showed a trace of human curiosity. "Could I ask a question, sir, about piracy?"

"Why not?" asked Hoddan. "Go ahead."

"When you—ah—captured this ship, sir," said the clerk hopefully, "Did you—ah—shoot the men and keep the women?"

Hoddan sighed.

"Much," he said regretfully, "much as I hate to spoil an enlivening theory—no. These are modern days. Efficiency has invaded even the pirate business. I used my crew for floor scrubbing and cooking."

He closed the port gently and went up to the control-room to call the landing-grid operators. In minutes the captured liner, loaded down again, lifted toward the stars.

And all the journey back to Darth was as anticlimatic as that. There was no trouble finding the spaceyacht in its remote orbit. Hoddan sent out an unlocking signal, and a keyed transmitter began to send a signal on which to home. When the liner nudged alongside it, Hoddan's last contrivance operated and the yacht clung fast to the larger ship's hull. There were four days in overdrive. There were three or four pauses for position-finding. The stopover on Krim had cost some delay, but Hoddan arrived back at a positive sight of Darth's sun within a day or so. Then there was little or no time lost in getting into orbit with the junk yard spacefleet of the emigrants. Shortly thereafter he called the leader's ship with only mild worries about possible disasters that might have happened while he was away.

"Calling the leader's ship," he said crisply. "Calling the leader's ship! This is Bron Hoddan, reporting back from Walden with a ship and machinery contributed for your use!"

The harsh voice of the bearded old leader of the emigrants seemed somehow broken when he replied. He called down blessings on Hoddan, who could use them. Then there was the matter of getting the emigrants on board the new ship. They didn't know how to use the lifeboat tubes. Hoddan had to demonstrate. But shortly after, there were twenty, thirty, fifty of the folk from Colin, feverishly searching the ship and incredulously reporting what they found.

"It's impossible!" said the old man. "It's impossible!"

"I wouldn't say that," said Hoddan. "It's unlikely, but it's happened. I'm only afraid it's not enough."

"It is many times more than what we hoped," said the old man humbly. "Only—" he stopped. "We are more grateful than we can say."

Hoddan took a deep breath.

"I'd like to take my crew back home," he explained. "And come back. Perhaps I can be useful explaining things. And I'd like to ask a great favor of you—for my own work."

"But naturally," said the old man. "Of course. We will await your return."

Hoddan was relieved. There seemed to be a strange limitation to the happiness of the emigrants. They were passionately rejoiceful over the agricultural machinery. But they seemed dutifully rather than truly happy over the microfilm library. The vision-tape instructors were the objects of polite comment only. Hoddan felt a vague discomfort. There seemed to be a sort of secret desperation in the atmosphere, which they would not admit or mention. But he was coming back. Of course.

He brought the spaceboat over to the new liner. He hooked onto a lifeboat blister and his seven Darthians crawled through the lifeboat tube. Hoddan pulled away quickly before somebody thought to ask why there were no lifeboats in the places so plainly made for them.

He headed downward when the landmarks on Darth's surface told him that Don Loris' castle would shortly come over the horizon. He was just touching atmosphere when it did. The boat's tanks had been refilled, and he burned fuel recklessly to make a dramatic landing within a hundred yards of the battlements where Fani had once thoughtfully had a coil of rope ready for him.

Heads peered at the lifeboat over those same battlements now, but the gate was closed. It stayed closed. There was somehow an atmosphere of suspicion amounting to enmity. Hoddan felt unwelcome.

"All right, boys," he said resignedly. "Out with you

and to the castle. Here's your loot from the voyage."
He counted out for each of them rather more actual
cash than any of them really believed in. "And I want
you to take this box to Don Loris. It's a gift from me.
And I want to consult with him about cooperation
between the two of us in some plans I have. Ask if
I may come and talk to him."

His seven former spearmen tumbled out. They
marched gleefully to the castle gate. Hoddan saw
them make a tantalizing display of the large sums of
cash to the watchers above them. Thal held up the
box for Don Loris. It was the box the lawyer's clerk
had turned over to him, with a tidy sum in cash in it.
The sum was partly depleted now. Hoddan had paid
off his involuntary crew with it. But there was still
more in it than Don Loris would have gotten from
Walden for selling him out.

The castle gate opened, as if grudgingly. The seven
went in.

Time passed. Much time. Hoddan went over the
arguments he meant to use on Don Loris. He needed
to make up a very great sum, and it could be done
thus-and-so, but thus-and-so required occasional pirate
raids, which called for crews, and if Don Loris would
encourage his retainers . . . He could have gone to
another Darthian chieftain, of course, but he knew
what kind of scoundrel Don Loris was. He'd have to
find out about another man.

Nearly an hour elapsed before the castle gate
opened again. Two files of spearmen marched out.
There were eight men with a sergeant in command.
Hoddan did not recognize any of them. They came
to the spaceboat. The sergeant formally presented an

official message. Don Loris would admit Bron Hoddan to his presence, to hear what he had to say.

Hoddan felt excessively uncomfortable. Waiting, he'd thought about that secret despair in the emigrant fleet. He worried about it. He was concerned because Don Loris had not welcomed him with cordiality, now that he'd brought back his retainers in good working order. In a sudden gloomy premonition, he checked his stun-pistols. They needed charging. He managed it from the lifeboat unit.

He went with foreboding toward the castle with the eight spearmen surrounding him as cops had once surrounded him on Walden. He did not like to be reminded of it. He frowned to himself as he went in the castle gate, and along a long stone passage, and up stone stairs into the great hall of state. Don Loris, as once before, sat peevishly by the huge fireplace. This time he was almost inside it, with its hood and mantel actually over his head. The Lady Fani sat there with him.

Don Loris seemed to put aside his peevishness only a little to greet Hoddan.

"My dear fellow," he said complainingly, "I don't like to welcome you with reproaches, but do you know that when you absconded with that spaceboat, you made a mortal enemy for me? It's a fact! My neighbor, on whose land the boat descended, was deeply hurt. He considered it his property. He had summoned his retainers for a fight over it when I heard of his resentment and partly soothed him with apologies and presents. But he still considers that I should return it to him, whenever you appear here with it!"

"Oh," said Hoddan. "That's too bad."

Things looked ominous. The Lady Fani looked at him strangely. As if she were trying to tell him something without speaking. She looked as if she had wept lately.

"To be sure," said Don Loris fretfully, "to be sure you gave me a very pretty present just now. But my retainers tell me that you came back with a ship. A very fine ship. What became of it? The landing-grid has been repaired at last and you could have landed there. What happened to it?"

"I gave it away," said Hoddan. He saw what Fani was trying to tell him. Leading into the great hall was a corridor filled with spearmen. His tone turned sardonic. "I gave it to a poor old man."

Don Loris shook his head.

"That's not right, Hoddan! That fleet overhead, now. If they are pirates and want some of my men for crews, they should come to me! I don't take kindly to the idea of your kidnapping my men and carrying them off on piratical excursions! They must be profitable! But on the other hand, if you can afford to give me presents like this, and be so lavish with my retainers—why maybe . . ."

Hoddan grimaced.

"I came to arrange a deal on that order," he observed.

"I don't think I like it," said Don Loris peevishly. "I prefer to deal with people direct. I'll arrange about the landing-grid, and for a regular recruiting service, which I will conduct, of course. But you—you are irresponsible! I wish you well, but when you carry my men off for pirates, and make my neighbors into my enemies, and infect my daughter with strange notions and the government of a friendly planet asks me in so many words not to shelter you any longer—why, that's the end, Hoddan. So with great regret . . ."

"The regret is mine," said Hoddan. Thoughtfully, he aimed a stun-pistol at a slowly opening corridor door. He pulled the trigger. Yells followed its humming, because not everybody it hit was knocked out. Nor did it hit everybody in the corridor. Men came surging out of one door, and then two.

Then a spear went past Hoddan's face and missed him only by inches. It buried its point in the floor. A whirling knife spun past his nose. He glanced up. There were balconies all around the great hall, and men popped up from behind the railings and threw things at him. They popped down out of sight instantly. There was no rhythm involved. He could not anticipate their rising, nor shoot them through the balcony-front. And more men infiltrated the hall, getting behind heavy chairs and tables. More spears and knives flew.

"Bron!" cried the Lady Fani, throatily.

He thought she had an exit for him. He sprang to her side.

"I—I didn't want you to come," she wept.

There was a singular pause in the clangings and clashings of weapons on the floor. Then one man popped up and hurled a knife. The clang of its fall was a very lonely one. Don Loris fairly howled at him.

"Idiot! Think of the Lady Fani!"

The Lady Fani suddenly smiled tremulously.

"Wonderful!" she said. "They don't dare do anything while you're as close to me as this!"

"Do you suppose," asked Hoddan, "I could count on that?"

"I'm certain of it!" said Fani. "And I think you'd better."

"Then, excuse me," said Hoddan with great politeness. He swung her up and over his shoulder. With a stun-pistol in his free hand he headed down the hall.

"Outside," she said zestfully, "get out the side door and turn left, and nobody can jump down on your neck. Then left again to the gate."

He obeyed. Now and again he got in a pot-shot with his pistol. Don Loris had turned the castle into a very pretty trap. The Lady Fani said plaintively:

"This is terribly undignified, and I can't see where we're going. Where are we now?"

"Almost at the gate," panted Hoddan. "At it, now." He swung out of the massive entrance to Don Loris' stronghold. "I'll put you down now."

"I wouldn't," said the Lady Fani. "I think you'd better make for the spaceboat exactly as we are."

Again Hoddan obeyed, racing across the open ground. Howls of fury followed him. It was evidently the opinion of the castle that the Lady Fani was to be abducted in the place of the seven returned spearmen.

Hoddan, breathing hard, reached the spaceboat. He put Fani down and said anxiously:

"You're all right? I'm very much in your debt! I was in a spot!" Then he nodded toward the castle. "They're upset, aren't they? They must think I mean to kidnap you."

The Lady Fani beamed.

"It would be terrible if you did," she said hopefully. "I couldn't do a thing to stop you! And a successful public abduction's a legal marriage, on Darth! Wouldn't it be terrible?"

Hoddan mopped his face and patted her reassuringly on the shoulder.

"Don't worry!" he said warmly. "You just got me out of an awful fix! You're my friend! And anyhow I'm going to marry a girl on Walden, named Nedda. Goodbye, Fani! Keep clear of the rocket blast."

He went into the boat's port, turned to smile paternally back at her, and shut the port behind him. Seconds later the spaceboat took off. It left behind clouds of rocket smoke.

And, though Hoddan hadn't the faintest idea of it, he had left behind the maddest girl in several solar systems.

Chapter 10

It is the custom of all men, everywhere, to be obtuse where women are concerned: Hoddan went skyward in the spaceboat with feelings of warm gratitude toward the Lady Fani. He had not the slightest inkling that she had anything but the friendliest of feelings toward him.

As Hoddan drove on up and up, the sky became deep purple and then black velvet set with flecks of fire. He was relieved by the welcome he'd received earlier today from the emigrants, but he remained slightly puzzled by a very faint impression of desperation remaining. He felt very virtuous on the whole, however, and his plans for the future were specific. He'd already composed a letter to his grandfather, which he'd ask the emigrant fleet to deliver. He had another letter in mind, a form letter—practically a public-relations circular—which he hoped to whip into shape before the emigrants got too anxious to be on their way. He considered that he needed to earn a little more of their gratitude so he could make everything come out even; everybody being satisfied and happy but himself.

For himself he anticipated only the deep satisfaction of accomplishment. He'd wanted to do great things since he was a small boy. He'd gone to Walden in the hope of achievement. There, of course, he failed because in a free economy, industrialists consider that freedom is the privilege of being stupid without penalty. But Hoddan now believed himself in the fascinating situation of having knowledge and abilities which were needed by other people.

It was only when he'd made contact with the fleet, and was in the act of maneuvering toward a boat-blister on the liner he'd brought back, that doubts again assailed him. He had done a few things—accomplished little. He'd devised a broadcast-power receptor and a microwave projector and he'd turned a Lawlor drive into a ball-lightning projector and worked out a few little things like that. But the first had been invented before by somebody in the Cetis cluster, and the second could have been made by anybody and the third was standard practice on Zan. He still had to do something significant.

When he made fast to the liner and crawled through the tube to its hull, he was in a state of doubt which passed very well for modesty.

The bearded old man received him in the skipper's quarters, which Hoddan himself had occupied for a few days. He looked very weary. He seemed to have aged, in hours.

"We grow more astounded by the minute," he told Hoddan heavily, "by what you have brought us. Ten shiploads like this and we would be better equipped than we believed ourselves in the beginning. It looks as if some thousands of us will now be able to survive our colonization of the planet Thetis."

Hoddan gaped at him. The old man put his hand on Hoddan's shoulder.

"We are grateful," he said with a pathetic attempt at warmth. "Please do not doubt that! It is only that . . . that . . . I cannot help wishing very desperately that . . . that instead of unfamiliar tools for metal-working and machines with tapes which show pictures—I wish that even one more jungle plow had been included!"

Hoddan's jaw dropped. The people of Colin wanted planet-subduing machinery. They wanted it so badly that they did not want anything else. They could not even see that anything else had any value at all. Most of them could only look forward to starvation when the ships' supplies were exhausted, because not enough ground could be broken and cultivated early enough to grow food enough in time.

"Would it," asked the old man desperately, "would it be possible to exchange these useless machines for others that will be useful?"

"Let me talk to your mechanics, sir," said Hoddan unhappily. "Maybe something can be done."

He restrained himself from tearing his hair as he went to where the mechanics of the fleet looked over their new equipment. He'd come up to the fleet again to gloat and do great things for people who needed him and knew it. But he faced the hopelessness of people to whom his utmost effort seemed mockery because it was so far from being enough.

He gathered together the men who'd tried to keep the fleet's ships in working order during their flight. They were competent men, of course. They were resolute. But now they had given up hope. Hoddan began to lecture them. They needed machines. He hadn't brought the machines they wanted, perhaps, but he'd brought the machines to make them with. Here were automatic shapers, turret lathes, dicers. He'd brought these because they already had the raw material—the ships themselves! Even some of the junk they carried in crates was good metal, merely worn out in its present form. They could make anything they needed with what he'd brought them. For example, he'd show them how to make a lumber saw.

He showed them how to make the slender, rapier-like revolving tool with which a man stabbed a tree and cut outward with the speed of a hot knife cutting butter. And one could mount it so, and cut out planks and beams for temporary bridges and such constructions.

They watched, baffled. They gave no sign of hope. They did not want lumber saws. They wanted jungle-breaking machinery.

"I've brought you everything!" he insisted. "You've

got a civilization, compact, on this ship! You've got life instead of starvation! Look at this. I'll make a water pump to irrigate your fields!"

Before their eyes he turned out an irrigation pump on an automatic shaper. He showed them that the shaper went on, by itself, making other pumps without further instructions.

The mechanics stirred uneasily. They had watched without comprehension. Now they listened without enthusiasm. Their eyes were like those of children who watch marvels without comprehension.

He made a sledge whose runners slid on the air between themselves and whatever object would otherwise have touched them. It was practically frictionless. He made a machine to make nails. He made a power-hammer which hummed and pushed nails into any object that needed to be nailed. He made—

He stopped abruptly, and sat down with his head in his hands. The people of the fleet faced so overwhelming a catastrophe that they could not see through it. They could only experience it. As their leader would have been unable to answer questions about the fleet's predicament before he'd poured out the tale in the form it had taken in his mind, now these mechanics were unable to see ahead. They were paralyzed by the completeness of the disaster before them. They could live until the supplies of the fleet gave out. They could not grow fresh supplies without jungle-breaking machinery. They had to have jungle-breaking machinery. They could not imagine wanting anything more or less than jungle-breaking machinery.

Hoddan raised his head. The mechanics looked dully at him.

"You men do maintenance?" he asked. "You repair things when they wear out on the ship? Have you run out of some of the materials you need for repairs?"

After a long time a tired-looking man said slowly:

"On the ship I come from, we're having trouble. Our hydroponic garden keeps the air fresh, o'course. But the water-circulation pipes are gone. Rusted through. We haven't got any pipe to fix them with. We have to keep the water moving with buckets."

Hoddan got up. He looked about him. He hadn't brought hydroponic piping. And there was no raw material. He took a pair of power-snips and cut away a section of wall lining. He cut it into strips. He asked the diameter of the pipe. Before their eyes he made pipe—spirally wound around a mandrel and line-welded to solidity.

"I need some of that on my ship," said another man. The bearded man said heavily:

"We'll make some and send it to the ships that need it."

"No," said Hoddan. "We'll send the tools to make it. We can make the tools here. There must be other kinds of repairs, too. With the machines I've brought, we'll make the tools to make repairs. Picture-tape machines have reels that show exactly how to do it."

It was a new idea. The mechanics had other and immediate problems beside the over-all disaster of the fleet. Pumps that did not work. Motors that heated up. They could envision the meeting of those problems, and they could envision the obtaining of jungle plows. But they couldn't imagine anything in between. They were capable of learning how to make tools for repairs.

Hoddan taught them. In one day there were five ships being brought into better operating condition—for ultimate futility—because of what he'd brought. Two days. Three. Mechanics began to come to the liner. Those who'd learned first, pompously passed on what they knew. On the fourth day somebody began to use a vision-tape machine to get information on a fine point in welding. On the fifth day there were lines of men waiting to use them.

On the sixth day a mechanic on what had been a luxury passenger liner scores of years ago, asked to talk to Hoddan by space-phone. He'd been working feverishly at the minor repairs he'd been unable to make for so long. To get material he pulled a crate off one of the junk machines supplied the fleet. He looked it over. He believed that if this piece were made new, and that replaced with sound metal, the machine might be usable!

Hoddan had him come to the liner which was now the flagship of the fleet. Discussion began and Hoddan began to draw diagrams. They were not clear. He drew more. Abruptly, he stared at what he'd outlined. He saw something remarkable. If one applied a perfectly well-known bit of pure-science information that nobody bothered with . . . He finished the diagram and a vast, soothing satisfaction came over him.

"We've got to get out of here!" he said. "Not enough room!"

He looked about him. Insensibly, as he talked to the first man on the fleet to show imagination, other men had gathered around. They were now absorbed.

"I think," said Hoddan, "that we can make an electronic field that'll soften the cementite between the crystals of steel, without heating up anything else. If it works, we can use plastic dies! And then that useless junk you've got can be rebuilt."

They listened gravely, nodding as he talked. They did not quite understand everything, but they had the habit of believing him now.

Soon Hoddan had a cold-metal die-stamper in operation. It was very large. It drew on the big ship's drive-unit for power. One put a rough mass of steel in place between plastic dies. One turned on the power. In a tenth of a second the steel was soft as putty. Then it stiffened and was warm. But in that tenth of a second it had been shaped with precision.

It took two days to duplicate the jungle plow Hoddan had first been shown, in new, sound metal. But after the first one worked triumphantly, they made forty of each part at a time and turned out enough jungle plows for the subjugation of all Thetis' forests.

One day Hoddan waked from a cat nap with a diagram in his head. He drew it, half-asleep, and later looked and found that his unconscious mind had designed a power-supply system which made Walden's look rather primitive.

During the first six days Hoddan did not sleep to speak of, and after that he merely cat-napped when he could. But he finally agreed with the emigrants' leader—now no longer fierce, but fiercely triumphant—that he thought they could go on. And he would ask a favor. He propped his eyelids open with his fingers and wrote the letter to his grandfather that he'd composed in his mind in the liner on Krim. He managed to make one copy, unaddressed, of the public-relations letter that he'd worked out at the same time. He put it through a facsimile machine and managed to address each of fifty copies. Then he yawned uncontrollably.

He still yawned when he went to take leave of the leader of the people of Colin. That person regarded him with warm eyes.

"I think everything's all right," said Hoddan exhaustedly. "You've got a dozen machine-shops and they're multiplying themselves, and you've got some enthusiastic mechanics, now, who're drinking in the vision-tape stuff and finding out more than they guessed there ever was. And they're thinking, now and then, for themselves. I think you'll make out."

The bearded man said humbly:

"I have waited until you said all was well. Will you come with us?"

"No-o-o," said Hoddan. He yawned again. "I've got to work here. There's an obligation I have to meet."

"It must be very admirable work," said the old man wistfully. "I wish we had some young men like you among us."

"You have," said Hoddan. "They'll be giving you trouble presently."

The old man shook his head, looking at Hoddan very affectionately.

"We will deliver your letters," he said warmly. "First to Krim, and then to Walden. Then we will go on and let down your letter and gift to your grandfather on Zan. Then we will go on toward Thetis. Our mechanics will work at building machines while we are in overdrive. But also they will build new tool shops and train new mechanics, so that every so often we will need to come out of overdrive to transfer the tools and the men to new ships."

Hoddan nodded exhaustedly. This was right.

"So," said the old man contentedly, "we will simply make those transfers in orbit about the planets for which we have your letters. You will pardon us if we only let down your letters, and do not visit those planets? We have prejudices."

"Perfectly satisfactory," said Hoddan.

"The mechanics you have trained," said the old man proudly, "have made a little ship ready for you. It is not much larger than your spaceboat, but it is fit for travel between suns, which will be convenient for your work. I hope you will accept it. There is even a tiny tool shop on it!"

Hoddan would have been more touched if he hadn't known about it. But one of the men entrusted with the job had needed his advice. He knew what he was getting. It was the spaceyacht he'd used before, refurbished and fitted with everything the emigrants could provide.

He affected great surprise and expressed unfeigned appreciation. Barely an hour later he transferred to it with the spaceboat in tow. He watched the emigrant fleet swing out to emptiness and resume its valiant journey. But it was not a hopeless journey, now. In fact, the colony on Thetis ought to start out better equipped than most settled planets.

And he went to sleep. He'd nothing urgent to do, except allow a certain amount of time pass before he did anything. He was exhausted. He slept the clock round, and waked and ate sluggishly, and went back to sleep again. On the whole, the cosmos did not notice the difference. Stars flamed in emptiness, and planets rotated sedately. Comets flung out gossamer veils or retracted them, and spaceliners went about upon their lawful occasions.

When he waked again he was rested, and he reviewed all his actions and his situation. It appeared that matters promised fairly well on the emigrant fleet now gone forever. They would remember Hoddan with affection for a year or so, and dimly after that. But settling a new world would be enthralling and important work. Nobody'd think of him at all, after a certain length of time. But he had to think of an obligation he'd assumed on their account.

He considered his own affairs. He'd told Fani he was going to marry Nedda. The way things looked, that was no longer so probable. Of course, in a year or two, or a few years, he might be out from under the obligations he now considered due. In time even the Waldenian government would realize that death rays didn't exist, and a lawyer might be able to clear things for his return to Walden. But Nedda was a nice girl . . .

He frowned. That was it. She was a remarkably nice girl. But Hoddan suddenly doubted if she were a delightful one. He found himself questioning that she was exactly and perfectly what his long-cherished ambitions described. He tried to imagine spending his declining years with Nedda. He couldn't quite picture it as exciting. She did tend to be a little insipid.

Presently, gloomy and a trifle dogged about it, he brought the spaceboat around to the modernized boat-port of the yacht. He got into it, leaving the yacht in orbit. He headed down toward Darth. Now that he'd rested, he had work to do which could not be neglected. To carry out that work, he needed a crew able and willing to pass for pirates for a pirate's pay. And there were innumerable castles on Darth, with quite as many shifty noblemen, and certainly no fewer plunder-hungry Darthian gentlemen hanging around them. But Don Loris' castle had one real advantage and one which existed only in Hoddan's mind.

Don Loris' retainers knew that Hoddan had led their companions to loot. Large loot. He'd have less trouble and more enthusiastic support from Don Loris' retainers than any other. This was true.

The illusion was that the Lady Fani was his firm personal friend with no nonsense about her. This was a very great mistake.

He landed for the fourth time outside Don Loris' castle. This time he had no booty-laden men to march to the castle and act as heralds of his presence. The spaceboat's vision screens showed Don Loris' stronghold as squat, immense, dark and menacing. Banners flew from its turrets, their colors bright in the ruddy light of near-sunset. The gate remained closed. For a long time there was no sign that his landing had been noted. Then there was movement on the battlements, and a figure began to descend outside the wall. It was lowered to the ground by a long rope.

It reached the ground and shook itself. It marched toward the spaceboat through the red and nearly level rays of the dying sun. Hoddan watched with a frown on his face. This wasn't a retainer of Don Loris'. It assuredly wasn't Fani. He couldn't even make out its gender until the figure was very near.

Then he looked astonished. It was his old friend

Derec, arrived on Darth a long while since in the spaceboat Hoddan had been using ever since. Derec had been his boon companion in the days when he expected to become rich by splendid exploits in electronics. Derec was also the character who'd conscientiously told the cops on Hoddan, when they found his power-receptor sneaked into a Mid-Continent station and a stray corpse coincidentally outside.

He opened the boat-port and stood in the opening. Derec had been a guest in Don Loris' castle for a good long while, now. Hoddan wondered if he considered his quarters cozy.

"Evening, Derec," said Hoddan cordially. "You're looking well!"

"I don't feel it," said Derec dismally. "I feel like a fool in the castle yonder. And the high police official I came here with has gotten grumpy and snaps when I try to speak to him."

Hoddan said gravely:

"I'm sure the Lady Fani—"

"A tigress!" said Derec bitterly: "We don't get along."

Looking at Derec, Hoddan found himself able to understand why. Derec was the sort of friend one might make on Walden for lack of something better. He was well-meaning. He might even be capable of splendid things—even heroism. But he was horribly, terribly, appallingly civilized!

"Well! Well!" said Hoddan kindly. "And what's on your mind, Derec?"

"I came," said Derec dismally, "to plead with you again, Bron. You must surrender! There's nothing else to do! People can't have death, rays, Bron! Above all, you mustn't tell the pirates how to make them!"

Hoddan was puzzled for a moment. Then he realized that Derec's information about the fleet came from the spearmen he'd brought back, loaded down with cash. Derec hadn't noticed the absence of the flashing lights at sunset—or hadn't realized that they meant the fleet had gone away.

"Hm," said Hoddan. "Why don't you think I've already done it?"

"Because they'd have killed you," said Derec. "Don Loris pointed that out. He doesn't believe you know how to make death rays. He says it's not a secret anybody would be willing for anybody else to know. But you know the truth, Bron! You killed that poor man back on Walden. You've got to sacrifice yourself for humanity! You'll be treated kindly!"

Hoddan shook his head. It seemed somehow very startling for Derec to be harping on that same idea, after so many things had happened to Hoddan. But he didn't think Derec would actually expect him to yield to persuasion. There must be something else. Derec might even have nerved himself up to do something quite desperate.

"What did you really come here for, Derec?"

"To beg you to—"

Then, in one instant, Derec made a hysterical gesture and Hoddan's stun-pistol hummed. A small object left Derec's hand as his muscles convulsed from the stun-pistol bolt. It did not fly quite true. It fell a foot or so to one side of the boat-port instead of inside.

It exploded luridly as Derec crumpled. There was

thick, strangling smoke. Hoddan disappeared. When the thickest smoke drifted away there was nothing to be seen but Derec lying on the ground, and thinner smoke drifting out of the still-open boat-port.

Nearly half an hour later, figures came very cautiously toward the spaceboat. Thal was their leader. His expression was mournful and depressed. Other brawny retainers came uncertainly behind him. At a nod from Thal, two of them picked up Derec and carted him off toward the castle.

"I guess he got it," said Thal dismally. He peered in. He shook his head. "Wounded, maybe, and crawled off to die." He peered in again and shook his head once more. "No sign of 'im."

A spearman just behind Thal said:

"Dirty trick! I was with him to Walden, and he paid off good! A good man! Shoulda been a chieftain! Good man!"

Thal gingerly entered the spaceboat. He wrinkled his nose at the faint smell of explosive still inside. Another man came in. Another.

"Say!" one of them said in a conspiratorial voice. "We got our share of that loot from Walden. But he hadda share, too! What'd he do with it? He could've kept it in this boat here. We could take a quick look! What Don Loris don't know don't hurt him!"

"I'm going to find Hoddan first," said Thal, with dignity. "We don't have to carry him outside so's Don Loris knows we're looking for loot, but I'm going to find him first."

There were other men in the spaceboat now. A full dozen of them. Their spears were very much in the way.

The boat-door closed quietly. Don Loris' retainers stared at each other. The locking-dogs grumbled for half a second, sealing the door tightly. Don Loris' retainers began to babble protestingly.

There was a roaring outside. The spaceboat stirred. The roaring rose to thunder. The boat lurched. It flung the spear-men into a sprawling, swearing, terrified heap at the rear end of the boat's interior.

The boat went on out to space again. In the control-room Hoddan said dourly to himself:

"I'm in a rut. I've got to figure out some way to ship a pirate crew without having to kidnap them. This is getting monotonous!"

Chapter 11

There was a disturbed air which enveloped all the members of Hoddan's crew, on the way to Walden. It was not exactly reluctance, because there was self-evident enthusiasm over the idea of making a pirate voyage under him. When men went off with Hoddan, they came back rich.

But nevertheless there was an uncomfortable sort of atmosphere in the renovated yacht. They'd transshipped from the spaceboat to the yacht through lifeboat-tubes, and they were quite docile about it because none of them knew how to get back to ground. Hoddan left the spaceboat with a timing signal set for use on his return. He'd done a similar thing off Krim. He drove the little yacht well out, until Darth was only a spotted ball with visible clouds and ice-caps. Then he lined up for Walden, direct, and went into overdrive.

Within hours he noted the disturbing feel of things. His followers were not happy. They moped. They sat in corners and submerged themselves in misery. Large, massive men with drooping blond moustaches—ideal characters for the roles of pirates—had tears rolling down from their eyes at odd moments. When the ship was twelve hours on its way, the atmosphere inside it was funereal. The spearmen did not even gorge themselves on the food with which the yacht was stocked. And when a Darthian gentleman lost his appetite, something had to be wrong.

He called Thal into the control-room.

"What's the matter with the gang?" he demanded vexedly. "They look at me as if I'd broken all their hearts! Do they want to go back?"

Thal heaved a sigh, indicating depression beside which suicidal mania would be hilarity. He said pathetically:

"We cannot go back. We cannot ever return to Darth. We are lost men, doomed to wander forever among strangers, or to float as corpses between the stars."

"What happened?" demanded Hoddan. "I'm taking you on a pirate cruise where the loot should be a lot better than last time!"

Thal wept. Hoddan astonishedly regarded his whiskery countenance, contorted with grief and dampened with tears.

"It happened at the castle," said Thal miserably. "The man Derec, from Walden, had thrown a bomb at you. You seemed to be dead. But Don Loris was

not sure. He fretted, as he does. He wished to send
someone to make sure. The Lady Fani said: 'I will
make sure!' She called me to her and said, 'Thal, will
you fight for me?' And there was Don Loris suddenly
nodding beside her. So I said, 'Yes, my Lady Fani.'
Then she said: 'Thank you. I am troubled by Bron
Hoddan.' So what could I do? She said the same
thing to each of us, and each of us had to say that
he would fight for her. To each she said that she was
troubled by you. Then Don Loris sent us out to look
at your body. And now we are disgraced!"

Hoddan's mouth opened and closed and opened
again. He remembered this item of Darthian etiquette.
If a girl asked a man if he would fight for her, and
he agreed, then within a day and a night he had to
fight the man she sent him to fight, or else he was
disgraced. And disgrace on Darth meant that the
shamed man could be plundered or killed by anybody
who chose to do so—and he would be hanged by
indignant authority if he resisted. It was a great deal
worse than outlawry. It included scorn and contempt
and opprobrium. It meant dishonor and humiliation
and admitted degradation. A disgraced man was despicable in his own eyes. And Hoddan had kidnapped
these men who'd been forced to engage themselves to
fight him, and if they killed him they would obviously
die in space, and if they didn't they'd be ashamed to
stay alive. The moral tone on Darth was probably not
elevated, but etiquette was a force.

Hoddan thought it over. He looked up suddenly.

"Some of them," he said wryly, "probably figure
there's nothing to do but go through with it, eh?"

"Yes," said Thal dismally. "Then we will all die."

"Hmm," said Hoddan. "The obligation is to fight. If you fail to kill me, that's not your fault, is it? If you're conquered you're in the clear?"

"True. Too true!" Thal said miserably. "When a man is conquered he is conquered. His conqueror may plunder him, when the matter is finished, or he can spare him, then he may never fight his conqueror again."

"Draw your knife," said Hoddan. "Come at me."

Thal made a bewildered gesture. Hoddan leveled a stun-pistol and said:

"Bzzz. You're conquered. You came at me with your knife, and I shot you with my stun-pistol. It's all over. Right?"

Thal gaped at him. Then he beamed. He expanded. He gloated. He frisked. He practically wagged a non-existent tail in his exuberance. He'd been shown an out when he could see none.

"Send in the others one by one," said Hoddan. "I'll take care of them. But Thal, why did the Lady Fani want me killed?"

Thal had no idea, but he did not care. Hoddan did care. He was bewildered and inclined to be indignant. A noble friendship like theirs—

A spearman came in and saluted. Hoddan went through a symbolic duel, which was plainly the way the thing would have happened in reality. Others came in and went through the same process. Two of them did not quite grasp that it was a ritual, and he had to shoot them in the knife-arm. Then he hunted in the ship's supplies for ointment for the blisters that would appear from stun-pistol bolts at such short range. As he bandaged the places, he again tried to find out

why the Lady Fani had tried to get him carved up.
Nobody could enlighten him.

But the atmosphere improved remarkably. Since
each theoretic fight had taken place in private, nobody
was obliged to admit a compromise with etiquette.
Hoddan's followers ceased to brood. They developed
huge appetites. Those who had been aground on
Krim told zestfully of the monstrous hangovers they'd
acquired there. It appeared that Hoddan was revered
for the size of the benders he enabled his followers
to hang on.

But there remained the fact that the Lady Fani
had tried to get him massacred. He puzzled over it.
The little yacht sped through space toward Walden.
He tried to think how he'd offended Fani. He could
think of nothing. He set to work on a new electronic
set-up which would make still another modification
of the Lawlor space-drive possible. In the others,
groups of electronic components were cut out and
others substituted in rather tricky fashion from the
control board. This was trickiest of all. It required
the homemade vacuum tube to burn steadily when in
use. But it was a very simple idea. Lawlor drive and
landing-grid forcefields were formed by not dissimilar
generators, and ball-lightning force-fields were in the
same general family of phenomena. Suppose one made
the field generator that had to be on a ship if it were
to drive at all capable of all those allied, associated,
similar forcefields? If a ship could make the fields that
landing-grids did, it should be useful to pirates.

Hoddan's present errand was neither pure nor
simple piracy, but piracy it would be. The more he
considered the obligation he'd taken on himself when

he helped the emigrants, the more he doubted that he could lift it without long struggle. He was preparing to carry on that struggle for a long time. He'd more or less resigned himself to the postponement of his personal desires—Nedda for example.

But time passed, and he finished his electronic job. He came out of overdrive and made his observations and corrected his course. Finally, there came a moment when the fiery ball which was Walden's sun shone brightly in the vision-plates. It writhed and spun in the vast silence of emptiness.

Hoddan drove to a point still above the five-diameter limit of Walden. He interestedly switched on the control which made his drive-unit manufacture landing-grip type forcefields. He groped for Walden, and felt the peculiar rigidity of the ship when the field took hold somewhere underground. He made an adjustment, and felt the ship respond. Instead of pulling a ship to ground, in the set-up he'd made, the new fields pulled the ground toward the ship. When he reversed the adjustment, instead of pushing the ship away to empty space, the new field pushed the planet.

There was no practical difference, of course. The effect was simply that the spaceyacht now carried its own landing-grid. It could descend anywhere and ascend from any where without using rockets. Moreover, it could hover without using power.

Hoddan was pleased. He took the yacht down to a bare four-hundred-mile altitude. He stopped it there. It was highly satisfactory. He made quite certain that everything worked as it should. Then he made a call on the space communicator.

"Calling ground," said Hoddan. "Calling ground. Pirate ship calling ground!"

He waited for an answer. Now he'd see the results of his efforts and planning. He was apprehensive, of course. There was much responsibility on his shoulders. There was the liner he'd captured and looted and given to the emigrants. There were his followers on the yacht, now enthusiastically sharpening their two-foot knives in expectation of loot. He owed these people something. For an instant he thought of the Lady Fani and wondered how he could make reparation to her for whatever had hurt her feelings.

A whining, bitterly unhappy voice came to him.

"Pirate ship!" said the voice plaintively, "we received the fleet's warning. Please state where you intend to descend. We will take measures to prevent disorder. Repeat, please state where you intend to descend and we will take measures to prevent disorder."

Hoddan drew a sharp breath of relief. He named a spot—a high-income, residential small city, some forty miles from the planetary capital. He set his controls for a very gradual descent. He went out to where his followers made grisly zinging noises where they honed their knives.

"We'll land," said Hoddan sternly, "in about three-quarters of an hour. You will go ashore and loot in parties of not less than three! Thal, you will be ship-guard and receive the plunder and make sure that nobody from Walden gets on board. You will not waste time committing atrocities on the population!"

He went back to the control-room. He turned to general communication bands and listened to the broadcasts down below.

"Special Emergency Bulletin!" boomed a voice. "Pirates are landing in the city of Ensfield, forty miles from Walden City. The population is instructed to evacuate immediately, leaving all action to the police. Repeat! The population will evacuate Ensfield, leaving all action to the police. Take nothing with you. Take nothing with you. Leave at once."

Hoddan nodded approvingly. The voice boomed again:

"Special Emergency Bulletin! Pirates are landing. Evacuate. Take nothing with you. Leave at once."

He turned to another channel. An excited voice barked:

"Seems to be only the one pirate ship, which has been located hovering in an unknown manner over Ensfield. We are rushing cameramen to the spot and will try to give on-the-spot, as-it-happens coverage of the landing of pirates on Walden, their looting of the city of Ensfield, and the traffic jams inevitable in the departure of the citizens before the pirate ship touches ground. For background information on this the most exciting event in planetary history, I take you to our editorial rooms." Another voice took over instantly. "It will be remembered that some days since the gigantic pirate fleet then overhead sent down a communication to the planetary government, warning that single ships would appear to loot and giving notice that any resistance—"

Hoddan felt a contented, heart-warming glow. The emigrant fleet had most faithfully carried out its leader's promise to let down a letter from space while in orbit around Walden. The emigrants, of course, did not know the contents of the letter. Blithely, cheerfully, and dutifully, they gave the appearance of monstrous piratical strength. They had awed Walden thoroughly. And then they'd gone on, faithfully leaving similar letters and similar impressions on Krim, Lohala, Tralee, Famagusta, and all throughout the Coalsack stars until the stock of addressed missives ran out. They would perform this kindly act out of gratitude to Hoddan.

And every planet they visited would be left with the impression that the fleet overhead was that of bloodthirsty space-marauders who would presently send single ships to collect loot, which must be yielded without resistance. Such looting expeditions were to be looked for regularly and must be submitted to under penalty of unthinkable retribution from the monster fleet of space.

Now, as the yacht descended on Walden, it represented that mythical but impressive piratical empire. He listened with genuine pleasure to the broadcasts. When low enough, he even picked up the pictures of highways thronged with fugitives from the to-be-looted town. He saw Waldenian police directing the traffic of flight. He saw other traffic heading toward the city. Walden was the most highly civilized planet in the Nurmi Cluster, and its citizens had had no worries at all except about the tranquilizers to enable them to stand it. When something genuinely exciting turned up, they wanted to be there to see it.

The yacht descended below the clouds. Hoddan turned on an emergency flare to make a landing by. Sitting in the control-room he saw his own ship as the broadcast-cameras picked it up and relayed it to millions of homes. He was impressed. It was a glaring eye of fierce light, descending deliberately with a dark and mysterious spacecraft behind it. He heard the chattered, on-the-spot news accounts of the happening. He saw the people who had not left Ensfield joined by avid visitors. He saw all of them held back by police, who frantically shepherded them away from the area in which the pirates should begin their horrid work.

Hoddan even watched pleasurably from his control-room as the cameras daringly showed the actual touch-down of the ship: the dramatic slow opening of its port: the appearance of authentic pirates in the opening, armed to the teeth, bristling ferociously, glaring about them at the silent, deserted streets of the city left to their mercy.

It was a splendid broadcast. Hoddan would liked to have stayed and watched all of it. But he had work to do. He had to supervise the pirate raid.

It was, as it turned out, simple enough. Looting parties of three pirates each, moved skulking about, seeking plunder. Quaking cameramen dared to ask them, in shaking voices, to pose for the news cameras. It was a request no Darthian gentleman, even in an act of piracy, could possibly refuse. They posed, making pictures of malignant ruffianism.

Commentators, adding informed comment to delectably thrilling pictures, observed crisply that this did not mean that Darth as an entity had turned pirate, but only that some of her citizens had joined the pirate fleet.

The camera crews then asked apologetically if they would permit themselves to be broadcast in the act of looting. Growling savagely for their public, and occasionally adding even a fiendish "Ha!" they obliged. The cameramen helped pick out good places to loot for the sake of good pictures. The pirates cooperated in a fine, dramatic style. Millions watching vision sets all over the planet shivered in delicious horror as the pirates went about their nefarious enterprise.

Presently the press of onlookers could not be held back by police. They surrounded the pirates. Some, greatly daring, asked for autographs. Girls watched them with round, frightened, fascinated eyes. Younger men found it vastly thrilling to carry burdens of loot back to the pirate ship for them. Thal complained hoarsely that the ship was getting overloaded. Hoddan ordered greater discrimination, but his pirates by this time were in the position of directors rather than looters themselves. Romantic Waldenian admirers smashed windows and brought them treasure, for the reward of a scowling acceptance.

Hoddan had to call it off. The pirate ship was loaded. It was then the center of an agitated, excited, enthusiastic crowd. He called back his men. One party of three did not return. He took two others and fought his way through the mob. He found the trio backed against a wall while hysterical, adoring girls struggled to sieze scraps of their garments for mementos of real, live pirates looting a Waldenian town!

But Hoddan got them back to the ship. He fought a way clear for them to get into the ship. Cheers rose from the onlookers. He got the landing-port shut only by the help of police who kept pirate fans from having their fingers caught in its closing.

Then the piratical spaceyacht rose swiftly toward the stars.

An hour later there was barely any diminution of the excitement inside the ship. Darthian gentlemen all, Hoddan's followers still gazed and gloated over the plunder tucked everywhere. It crowded the living-quarters. It threatened to interfere with the astrogation of the ship. Hoddan came out of the control-room and was annoyed.

"Break it up!" he snapped. "Pack that stuff away somewhere! What the hell do you think this is?"

Thal gazed at him dully, not quite able to tear his mind and thoughts from this marvelous mass of plunder. Then intelligence came into his eyes. He grinned suddenly. He slapped his thigh.

"Boys!" he gurgled. "He don't know what we got for him!"

One man looked up. Two. They beamed. They got to their feet, dripping jewelry and stray objects of virtue. Thal went ponderously to one stateroom. At the door he turned, expansively.

"She came to the port," he said exuberantly, "and said we were wearin' clothes like they wore on Darth. Did we come from there? I said we did. Then she said did we know somebody named Bron Hoddan on Darth? And I said we did and if she'd step inside the ship she'd meet you. And here she is!"

He unfastened the stateroom door, which had been barred from without. He opened it. He looked in, and grabbed, and pulled at something. Hoddan went sick with apprehension. He groaned as the something inside the stateroom sobbed and yielded.

Thal brought Nedda out into the saloon of the yacht. Her nose and eyes were red from terrified weeping. She gazed about her in purest despairing horror. She did not see Hoddan for a moment. Her eyes were filled with the brawny, piratical figures who were Darthian gentlemen and who grinned at her in what she took for evil gloating.

She wailed.

Hoddan swallowed, with much difficulty, and said quickly: "It's all right, Nedda. It was a mistake. Nothing will happen to you. You're quite safe with me!"

And she was.

Chapter 12

Hoddan stopped off at Krim, by landing-grid, to consult his lawyers. He felt a certain amount of hope of good results from his raid on Walden, but he was desperate about Nedda. Once she was confident of her safety under his protection, she took over the operation of the spaceship. She displayed an overwhelming saccharinity that was appalling. She was sweetness and light among criminals who respectfully did not harm her, and she sweetened and lightened the atmosphere of the spaceyacht until Hoddan's followers were close to mutiny.

"It ain't that I mind her being a nice girl," one of his moustachioed Darthians explained almost tearfully to Hoddan, "but she wants to make a nice girl out of me, too!"

Hoddan, himself, cringed from her society. He would gladly have put her ashore on Krim with ample funds to return to Walden. But she was prettily and reproachfully helpless. If he did put her ashore, she would confide her kidnaping and the lovely behavior of the pirates until nobody could believe in them any more. This would be fatal.

He went to his lawyers, brooding. The news astounded him. The emigrant fleet had appeared over Krim on the way to Walden. Before it appeared, Hoddan's affairs had been prosperous enough. Right after his previous visit, news had come of the daring piratical raid which captured a ship off Walden. This was the liner Hoddan'd brought in to Krim. All merchants and ship owners immediately insured all vessels and goods in space-transit at much higher valuations. The risk insurance stocks bought on Hoddan's account had multiplied in value. Obeying his instructions, his lawyers had sold them out and held a pleasing fortune in trust for Hoddan.

Then came the fleet over Krim, with its letter threatening planetary destruction if resistance was offered to single ships which would land and loot later on. It seemed that all commerce was at the mercy of space-marauders. Risk insurance companies had undertaken to indemnify the owners of ships and freight in emptiness. Now that an unprecedented pirate fleet ranged and doubtless ravaged the skyways, the insurance companies ought to go bankrupt. Owners of stock in them dumped it at any price to get rid of it. In accordance with Hoddan's instructions, though, his lawyers had faithfully, if distastefully bought it up. To use up the funds available, they had to buy up not only all the stock of all the risk insurance companies of Krim, but all stock in all off-planet companies owned by investors on Krim.

Then time passed, and ships in space arrived unmo-
lested in port. Cargoes were delivered intact. Insurers
observed that the risk insurance companies had not
collapsed and could still pay off if necessary. They
continued their insurance. Risk companies appeared
financially sound once more. They had more business
than ever, and no more claims than usual. Suddenly
their stocks went up, or rather, what people were
willing to pay for them went up, because Hoddan
had forbidden the sale of any stock after the pirate
fleet appeared.

Now he asked hopefully if he could reimburse the
owners of the ship he'd captured off Walden. He
could. Could he pay them even the profit they'd have
made between the loss of their ship and the arrival
of a replacement? He could. Could he pay off the
shippers of Rigellian furs and jewelry from the Cetic
stars, and the owners of the bulk melacynth that had
brought so good a price on Krim? He could. In fact,
he had. The insurance companies he now owned lock,
stock, and barrel had already paid the claims on the
ship and its cargo, and it would be rather officious
to add to that reimbursement.

Hoddan was abruptly appalled. He insisted on a bonus
being paid, regardless, which his lawyers had some
trouble finding a legal fiction to fit. Then he brooded
over his position. He wasn't a businessman. He hadn't
expected to make out so well. He'd thought to have to
labor for years, perhaps, to make good the injury he'd
done the ship owners and merchants in order to help the
emigrants from Colin. But it was all done, and here he
was with a fortune and the frame-work of a burgeoning
financial empire. He didn't like it.

Gloomily, he explained matters to his attorneys. They pointed out that he had a duty, an obligation, from the nature of his unexpected success. If he let things go, now, the currently thriving business of risk insurance would return to its former unimportance. His companies—they were his, now—had taken on extra help. More bookkeepers and accountants worked for him this week than last. More mail clerks, secretaries, janitors and scrubwomen. Even more vice-presidents! He would administer a serious blow to the economy of Krim if he caused a slackening of employment by letting his companies go to pot. A slackening of employment would cause a drop in retail trade, an increase in inventories, a depression in industry.

Hoddan thought gloomily of his grandfather. He'd written to the old gentleman and the emigrant fleet would have delivered the letter. He couldn't disappoint his grandfather!

He morbidly accepted his attorney's advice, and they arranged immediately to take over the forty-first as well as the forty-second and -third floors of the building their offices were in. Commerce would march on.

And Hoddan headed for Darth. He had to return his crew, and there was something else. Several something elses. He arrived in that solar system and put his yacht in a search orbit, listening for the signal the spaceboat should give for him to come on. He found it. He maneuvered to come alongside, and there was blinding light everywhere. Alarms rang. Lights went out. Instruments registered impossibilities, the rockets fired crazily, and the whole ship reeled. Then a voice roared out of the communicator:

*"Stand and deliver! Surrender and y'll be allowed
to go to ground. But if y'even hesitate I'll hull ye and
heave ye out to space without a spacesuit!"*

Hoddan winced. Stray sparks had flown about
everywhere inside the spaceyacht. A ball-lightning bolt,
even of only warning size, makes things uncomfortable
when it strikes. Hoddan's fingers tingled as if they'd
been asleep. He threw on the transmitter switch and
said with annoyance in his voice:

"Hello, grandfather. This is Bron. Have you been
waiting for me long?"

He heard his grandfather swear disgustedly. A few
minutes later, a badly battered, blackened, scuffed
old spacecraft came rolling up on rocket impulse
and stopped with a billowing of rocket fumes. Hoddan threw a switch and used the landing-grid field
he'd used on Walden in another fashion. The ships
came together with fine precision, lifeboat tube to
lifeboat tube. He heard his grandfather swear in
amazement.

"That's a little trick I worked out, grandfather,"
said Hoddan into the transmitter. "Come aboard.
I'll pass it on." His grandfather presently appeared,
scowling and suspicious. His eyes shrewdly examined
everything, including the loot tucked in every available
space. He snorted.

"All honestly come by," said Hoddan morbidly. "It
seems I've got a license to steal. I'm not sure what
to do with it."

His grandfather stared at a placard on the wall.
It said archly: *Remember! A Lady is Present!* Nedda
had put it up.

"Hmph!" said his grandfather. "What's a woman

doing on a pirate ship? That's what your letter talked about!"

"They get on," said Hoddan, wincing, "like mice. You've had mice on a ship, haven't you? Come in the control-room and I'll explain."

He did explain, up to the point where his arrangements to pay back for a ship and cargo turned into a runaway success, and now he was responsible for the employment of innumerable bookkeepers and clerks in the insurance companies he'd come to own. There was also the fact that as the emigrant fleet went on, about fifty more planets would require the attention of pirate ships from time to time, or there would be disillusionment and injury to the economic system.

"Organization," said his grandfather, "does wonders for a tender conscience like you've got. What else?"

Hoddan explained the matter of his Darthian crew and how Don Loris might consider them disgraced because they hadn't cut his throat. Hoddan had to take care of the matter. And there was Nedda . . . Fani came into the story somehow, too. Hoddan's grandfather grunted, at the end.

"We'll go down and talk to this Don Loris," he said pugnaciously. "I've dealt with his kind before. While we're down, your cousin Oliver'll take a look at this new grid-field job. We'll put it on my ship. Hm . . . how about the time down below? Never land long after daybreak. Early in the morning, people ain't at their best."

Hoddan looked at Darth, rotating deliberately below him.

"It's not too late, sir," he said. "Will you follow me down?"

His grandfather nodded briskly, took another comprehensive look at the loot from Walden, and crawled back through the tube to his own ship.

So it was not too long after dawn, in that time zone, when a sentry on the battlements of Don Loris' castle felt a shadow over his head. He jumped a foot and stared upward. Then his hair stood up on end and almost threw his steel helmet off. He stared, unable to move a muscle.

There was a ship above him. It was not a large ship, but he could not judge of such matters. It was not supported by rockets. It should have been falling horribly to smash him under its weight. It wasn't. Instead, it floated down with a very fine precision, like a ship being landed by grid, and settled delicately to the ground some fifty yards from the base of the castle wall.

Immediately thereafter there was a muttering roar. It grew to a howl: a bellow: it became thunder. It increased from that to a noise so stupendous that it ceased altogether to be heard, and was only felt as a deep-toned battering at one's chest. When it ended there was a second ship resting in the middle of a very large scorched place close by the first.

A landing-ramp dropped down from the battered craft. It neatly spanned the scorched and still-smoking patch of soil. A port opened. Men came out, following a jaunty small figure with bushy gray whiskers. They dragged an enigmatic object behind them.

Hoddan came out of the yacht. His grandfather said waspishly:

"This the castle?"

He waved at the massive pile of cut gray stone, with walls twenty feet thick and sixty high.

"Yes, sir," said Hoddan.

"Hm," snorted his grandfather. "Looks flimsy to me!" He waved his hand again. "You remember your cousins."

Familiar, matter-of-fact nods came from the men of the battered ship. Hoddan hadn't seen any of them for years, but they were his kin. They wore commonplace, workaday garments, but carried weapons slung negligently over their shoulders. They dragged the cryptic object behind them without particular formation or apparent discipline, but somehow they looked capable.

Hoddan and his grandfather strolled to the castle gate, their companions a little to their rear. They came to the gate. Nothing happened. Nobody challenged. There was the feel of peevish refusal to associate with persons who landed in spaceships.

"Shall we hail?" asked Hoddan.

"Nah!" snorted his grandfather. "I know his kind! Make him make the advances." He waved to his descendants. "Open it up."

Somebody casually pulled back a cover and reached in and threw switches.

"Found a power broadcast unit," grunted Hoddan's grandfather, "on a ship we took. Hooked it to the ship's space-drive. When y'can't use the space-drive, you still got power. Your cousin Oliver whipped this thing up."

The enigmatic object made a spiteful noise. The castle gate shuddered and fell halfway from its hinges. The thing made a second noise. Stones splintered and began to collapse. Hoddan admired. Three more unpleasing but not violently loud sounds. Half the wall on either side of the gate was rubble, collapsing partly inside and partly outside the castle's proper boundary.

Figures began to wave hysterically from the battlements. Hoddan's grandfather yawned slightly.

"I always like to talk to people," he observed, "when they're worryin' about what I'm likely to do to them, instead of what maybe they can do to me."

Figures appeared on the ground-level. They'd come out of a sally-port to one side. They were even extravagantly cordial when Hoddan's grandfather admitted that it might be convenient to talk over his business inside the castle, where there would be an easy chair to sit in.

Presently they sat beside the fireplace in the great hall. Don Loris, jittering, shivered next to Hoddan's grandfather. The Lady Fani appeared, icy cold and defiant. She walked with frigid dignity to a place beside her father. Hoddan's grandfather regarded her with a wicked, estimating gaze.

"Not bad!" he said brightly. "Not bad at all!" Then he turned to Hoddan. "Those retainers coming?"

"On the way," said Hoddan. He was not happy. The Lady Fani had passed her eyes over him exactly as if he did not exist.

There was a murmuring noise. A dozen spearmen came marching into the great hall. They carried loot. It dripped on the floor and they blandly ignored such things as stray golden coins rolling off away from them. Stay-at-home inhabitants of the castle gazed at them in joyous wonderment.

Nedda came with them. The Lady Fani made a very slight, almost imperceptible movement. Hoddan said desperately:

"Fani, I know you hate me, though I can't guess why. But here's a thing that had to be taken care of! We made a raid on Walden—that's where the loot came from—and my men kidnapped this girl. Her name is Nedda. Nedda's in an awful fix, Fani! She's alone and friendless, and somebody just has to take care of her! Her father'll come for her eventually, no doubt, but somebody's got to take care of her in the meantime, I can't do it." Hoddan felt hysterical at the bare idea. "I can't!"

The Lady Fani looked at Nedda. And Nedda wore the brave look of a girl so determinedly sweet that nobody could possibly bear it.

"I'm very sorry," said Nedda bravely, "that I've been the cause of poor Bron's turning pirate and getting into such dreadful trouble. I cry over it every night before I go to sleep. He treated me as if I were his sister, and the other men were so gentle and respectful that I—I think it will break my heart when they are punished. When I think of them being formally and coldly executed . . ."

"On Darth," said the Lady Fani practically, "we're not very formal about such things. Just cutting somebody's throat is usually enough—but he treated you like a sister, did he? Thal?"

Thal swallowed. He'd been beaming a moment before, with his arms full of silver plate, jewelry, laces, and other bits of booty from the town of Ensfield. But now he said desperately:

"Yes, Lady Fani. But not the way I've treated my sister. My sisters, Lady Fani, bit me when they were little, slapped me when they were bigger, and scorned me when I grew up. I'm fond of 'em! But if one of my sisters'd ever lectured me because I wasn't refined, and shook a finger at me because I wasn't gentlemanly—Lady Fani, I'd've strangled her!"

There was a certain gleam in the Lady Fani's eye as she said warmly to Hoddan:

"Of course I'll take care of the poor thing! I'll let her sleep with my maids and I'm sure one of them can spare clothes for her to wear, and I'll take care of her until a spaceliner comes along and she can be shipped back to her family. And you can come to see her whenever you please, to make sure she's all right!"

Hoddan's eyes tended to grow wild. His grandfather cleared his throat loudly. Hoddan said doggedly:

"You, Fani, asked each of my men if they'd fight for you. They said yes. You sent them to cut my throat. They didn't. But they're not disgraced! I want that clear! They're good men! They're not disgraced for failing to assassinate me!"

"Of course they aren't," conceded the Lady Fani sweetly. "Whoever heard of such a thing?"

Hoddan wiped his forehead. Don Loris opened his mouth fretfully. Hoddan's grandfather forestalled him.

"You've heard about that big pirate fleet that's been floating around these parts? Eh? It's my grandson's. I run a squadron of it for him. Wonderful boy, my grandson! Bloodthirsty crews on those ships, but they love that boy!"

"Very—" Don Loris caught his breath, "very interesting."

"He likes your men," confided Hoddan's grandfather. "Used them twice. Says they make nice, well-behaved pirates. He's going to give them stun-pistols and cannon like the one that smashed your gate. Only men on Darth with guns like that! Sieze the spaceport and put in power broadcast, and make sure nobody else gets stun-weapons. Run the country. Your men'll love it. Love that boy, too! Follow him anywhere. Loot."

Don Loris quivered. It was horribly plausible. He'd had the scheme of the only stun-weapon-armed force on Darth, himself. He knew his men tended to revere Hoddan because of the plunder. Don Loris was in a very, very uncomfortable situation. Bored men from the battered spacecraft stood about his great hall. They were unimpressed. He knew that they, at least, were casually sure that they could bring his castle down about his ears in minutes if they chose.

"But if my men . . ." Don Loris quavered, "what about me?"

"Minor problem," said Hoddan's grandfather blandly. "The usual thing would be pfft! Cut your throat." He rose. "Decide that later, no doubt. Yes, Bron?"

"I've brought back my men," growled Hoddan, "and Nedda's taken care of. We're through here."

He headed abruptly for the great hall's farthest door. His grandfather followed him briskly, and the negligent, matter-of-fact, armed men who were mostly Hoddan's first and second cousins came after him. Outside the castle, Hoddan said angrily:

"Why did you tell such a preposterous story, grandfather?"

"It's not preposterous," said his grandfather. "Sounds like fun, to me! You're tired now, Bron. Lots of responsibilities and such. Take a rest. You and your cousin Oliver get together and fix those new gadgets on my ship. I'll take the other boys for a run over to this spaceport town. The boys need a run ashore, and there might be some loot. Your grandmother's fond of homespun. I'll try to pick some up for her."

Hoddan shrugged. His grandfather was a law unto himself. Hoddan saw his cousins bringing horses from the castle stables, and a very casual group went riding away as if on a pleasurable excursion. As a matter of fact, it was. Thal guided them.

For the rest of that morning and part of the afternoon Hoddan and his cousin Oliver worked at the battered ship's Lawlor drive. Hoddan was pleased with his cousin's respect for his device. He unfeignedly admired the cannon his cousin had designed. Presently they reminisced about their childhood. It was pleasant to renew family ties like this.

The riders came back about sunset. There were extra horses, with loads. There were cheerful shoutings. His grandfather came into Hoddan's ship.

"Brought back some company," he said. "Spaceliner landed while we were there. Friend of yours on it. Congenial fellow, Bron. Thinks well of you, too!"

A large figure followed his grandfather in. A large figure with snow-white hair. The amiable and relaxed Interstellar Ambassador to Walden.

"Hard-gaited horses, Hoddan," he said wryly. "I want a chair and a drink. I traveled a good many light-years to see you, and it wasn't necessary after all. I've been talking to your grandfather."

"Glad to see you, sir," said Hoddan reservedly.

His cousin Oliver brought glasses, and the ambassador buried his nose in his and said in satisfaction:

"A-a-ah! That's good! Capable man, your grandfather.

I watched him loot that town. Beautiful professional job! He got some homespun sheets for your grandmother. But about you . . ."

Hoddan sat down. His grandfather puffed and was silent. His cousins effaced themselves. The ambassador waved a hand.

"I started here," he observed, "because it looked to me like you were running wild. That spacefleet, now . . . I know something of your ability. I thought you'd contrived some way to fake it. I knew there couldn't be such a fleet. Not really! That was a sound job you did with the emigrants, by the way. Most praiseworthy! And the point was that if you ran hogwild with a faked fleet, sooner or later the Space Patrol would have to cut you down to size. And you were doing too much good work to be stopped!"

Hoddan blinked.

"Satisfaction," said the ambassador, "is well enough. But satiety is death. Walden was dying on its feet. Nobody could imagine a greater satisfaction than curling up with a good tranquilizer. You've ended that! I left Walden the day after your Ensfield raid. Young men were already trying to grow moustaches. The textile mills were making colored felt for garments. Jewelers were turning out stun-gun pins for ornaments, Darthian knives for brooches, and the song writers had eight new tunes on the air about pirate lovers, pirate queens, and dark ships that roam the lanes of night. Three new vision-play series were to start that same night with space-piracy as their theme, and one of them claimed to be based on your life. Better make them pay for that, Hoddan! In short, Walden had rediscovered the pleasure to be had by taking pains to make a fool of oneself. People who watched that raid on vision screens had thrills they'd never swap for tranquilizers! And the ones who actually mixed in with the pirate raiders— You deserve well of the republic, Hoddan!"

Hoddan said, "Hmm," because there was nothing else to be said.

"Now, your grandfather and I have canvassed the situation thoroughly. This good work must be continued. Diplomatic Service has been worried all along the line. Now we've something to work up. Your grandfather will expand his facilities and snatch ships, land and loot, and keep piracy flying. Your job is to carry on the insurance business. The ships that will be snatched will be your ships, of course. No interference with legitimate commerce. The raids will be paid for by the interplanetary piracy risk insurance companies—you. In time you'll probably have to get writers to do scripts for them, but not right away. You'll continue to get rich, but there's no harm in that so long as you reintroduce romance and adventure to a galaxy headed for decline. Savages will not invent themselves if there are plenty of heroic characters—of your making!—to slap them down!"

"I like working on electronic gadgets," Hoddan said painfully. "My cousin Oliver and I have some things we want to work out together."

His grandfather snorted. One of the cousins came in from outside the yacht. Thal followed him, glowing. He'd reported the looting of the spaceport town, and Don Loris had gone into a tantrum of despair because nobody seemed able to make headway against these strangers. Now he'd turned about and issued a belated invitation to Hoddan and his grandfather and their guest the Interstellar Ambassador—of whom he'd learned from Thal—to dinner at the castle. They could bring their own guards.

Hoddan would have refused, but the ambassador and his grandfather were insistent. Ultimately he found himself seated drearily at a long table in a stone-walled room lighted by very smoky torches. Don Loris, jittering, displayed a sort of professional conversational charm. He was making an urgent effort to overcome the bad effect of past actions by conversational brilliance. The Lady Fani sat quietly. She looked most often at her place. The talk of the oldsters became profound. They talked administration. They talked practical politics. They talked economics.

The Lady Fani looked very bored as the talk went on after the meal was over. Don Loris said brightly to her:

"My dear, we must be tedious! Young Hoddan looks uninterested, too. Why don't you two walk on the battlements and talk about such things as persons your age find interesting?"

Hoddan rose, gloomily. The Lady Fani, with a sigh of polite resignation, rose to accompany him. The ambassador said suddenly:

"Hoddan! I forgot to tell you! They found out what killed that man outside the power station!" When Hoddan showed no comprehension, the ambassador explained. "The man your friend Derec thought was killed by death rays. It developed that he'd gotten a terrific load on—drunk, you know—and climbed a tree to escape the pink, purple, and green *duryas* he thought were chasing him to gore him. He climbed too high, a branch broke, and he fell and was killed. I'll take it up with the court when I get back to Walden. No reason to lock you up any more, you know. You might even sell the Power Board on using your receptor, now!"

"Thanks," said Hoddan politely. He added. "Don Loris has that Derec and a cop from Walden here now. Tell them about it and let them go home."

He accompanied the Lady Fani to the battlements. The stars were very bright. They strolled.

"What was that the ambassador told you?" she asked.

He explained without zest. He added morbidly that it didn't matter. He could go back to Walden now, and if the ambassador was right he could even accomplish things in electronics there. But he wasn't interested. It was odd that he'd once thought such things would make him happy.

"I thought," said the Lady Fani, in gentle melancholy, "that I would be happier with you dead. You had made me very angry. But I found it was not so."

Hoddan fumbled for her meaning. It wasn't quite an apology for trying to get him killed. But at least it was a disclaimer of future intentions in that direction.

"And speaking of happiness," she added in a different tone, "this Nedda . . ." Bron shuddered, and she said, "I talked to her. Then I sent for Ghek. We're on perfectly good terms again, you know. I introduced him to Nedda. She was vanilla ice-cream with meringue and maple syrup on it. He loved it! She gazed at him with pretty sadness and told him how terrible it was of him to kidnap me. He said humbly that he'd never had her ennobling influence nor dreamed that she existed. And she loved that! They go together like strawberries and cream! I had to leave, or stop being a lady. I think I made a match."

Then she said quietly:

"But seriously, you ought to be perfectly happy. You've everything you ever said you wanted, except a delightful girl to marry."

Hoddan squirmed.

"We're old friends," said Fani kindly, "and you did me a great favor once. I'll return it. I'll round up some really delightful girls for you to look over."

"I'm leaving," said Hoddan, alarmed.

"The only thing is, I don't know what type you like. Nedda isn't it."

Hoddan shuddered.

"Nor I," said Fani. "What type would you say I was?"

"Delightful," said Hoddan hoarsely.

The Lady Fani stopped and looked up at him. She said approvingly:

"I hoped that word would occur to you one day. What does a man usually do when he discovers a girl is delightful?"

Hoddan thought it over. He started. He put his arms around her with singularly little skill. He kissed her, at first as if amazed at himself, and then with enthusiasm.

There were scraping sounds on the stone nearby. Footsteps. Don Loris appeared, gazing uncertainly about.

"Fani!" he said plaintively. "Hoddan? Our guests are going to the spaceships. I want to speak privately to Hoddan."

"Yes?" said Hoddan.

"I've been thinking," said Don Loris fretfully. "I've made some mistakes, my dear boy, and I've given you excellent reason to dislike me, but at bottom I've always thought a great deal of you. And there seems to be only one way in which I can properly express how much I admire you. How would you like to marry my daughter?"

Hoddan looked down at Fani. She did not try to move away.

"What do you think of the idea, Fani?" he asked. "How about marrying me tomorrow morning?"

"Of course not!" said Fani indignantly. "I wouldn't think of such a thing! I couldn't possibly get married before tomorrow afternoon!"